THE HISTORY OF OPHELIA

THE HISTORY OF OPHELIA

Sarah Fielding

edited by Peter Sabor

broadview editions

National Library of Canada Cataloguing in Publication

Fielding, Sarah, 1710–1768
    The history of Ophelia / Sarah Fielding ; edited by Peter Sabor.

(Broadview editions)
Includes bibliographical references.
ISBN 1-55111-120-9

    I. Sabor, Peter. II. Title. III. Series.

PR3459.F3O62 2004   823'.5   C2004-900716-5

Broadview Press Ltd. is an independent, international publishing house, incorporated in 1985. Broadview believes in shared ownership, both with its employees and with the general public; since the year 2000 Broadview shares have traded publicly on the Toronto Venture Exchange under the symbol BDP.

We welcome comments and suggestions regarding any aspect of our publications – please feel free to contact us at the addresses below or at broadview@broadviewpress.com.

North America
Post Office Box 1243, Peterborough, Ontario, Canada K9J 7H5
3576 California Road, Orchard Park, NY, USA 14127
Tel: (705) 743-8990; Fax: (705) 743-8353;
e-mail: customerservice@broadviewpress.com

UK, Ireland, and continental Europe
NBN Plymbridge, Estover Road, Plymouth PL6 7PY UK
Tel: 44 (0) 1752 202301   Fax: 44 (0) 1752 202331
Fax Order Line: 44 (0) 1752 202333
Customer Service: cservs@nbnplymbridge.com Orders: orders@nbnplymbridge.com

Australia and New Zealand
UNIREPS, University of New South Wales
Sydney, NSW, 2052
Tel: 61 2 9664 0999; Fax: 61 2 9664 5420
email: info.press@unsw.edu.au

www.broadviewpress.com

Broadview Press gratefully acknowledges the support of the Ministry of Canadian Heritage through the Book Publishing Industry Development program.

This book is printed on acid-free paper containing 30% post-consumer fibre.

Series Editor: Professor L.W. Conolly

Advisory editor for this volume: Colleen Franklin

Typesetting and assembly: True to Type Inc., Mississauga, Canada.

PRINTED IN CANADA

Certified Eco-Logo
30% Post.

Contents

Acknowledgements

For their help with various aspects of this edition, I am grateful to J.F. Burrows, John Dussinger, A.C. Elias, Jr., Jacqueline Lewis, Alison Morgan, David Oakleaf, Emmi Sabor, Jane Spencer, James Woolley, and my former research assistant, Joanna Fraser Steer. Linda Bree and Thomas Keymer provided many astute comments on the introduction and commentary, and saved me from various errors. I am also grateful to the graduate students, including Anna Atkinson and Nancy Paul, in a course on Henry and Sarah Fielding that I taught at Queen's University, and especially to Aaron Santesso for his suggestions concerning annotations. For arranging for photographs to be made from McMaster University's copy of the *Novelist's Magazine* edition of *Ophelia*, I thank Elaine Riehm. At Broadview Press I have enjoyed the support of Don LePan, the editorial expertise and assistance of Leonard Conolly and Julia Gaunce, and the copyediting skills of Colleen Franklin. For financial support for my research, I am indebted to Laval University, McGill University, and the Social Sciences and Humanities Research Council of Canada. My debt to Marie is unpayable, and grows larger with every year.

Introduction

Sarah Fielding's authorial career extended for twenty years: from 1742, when she was thirty-one, to 1762, when she was in failing health and had six more years to live. Her first two appearances in print were probably anonymous contributions to works by her famous brother Henry: a letter from Leonora to Horatio in *Joseph Andrews* (1742) and the fictional autobiography of Anne Boleyn in *A Journey from This World to the Next* (1743).[1] Her first novel, *The Adventures of David Simple*, was published anonymously in 1744, with a preface referring to the "Distress in her Circumstances" that her publications were an attempt to alleviate. A second edition, with a much longer preface by Henry replacing her own, appeared only ten weeks later. In this preface, Henry commends Sarah as a psychological novelist, with a remarkable ability to explore the motivation of her characters; her work displays "a vast Penetration into human Nature, a deep and profound Discernment of all the Mazes, Windings and Labyrinths, which perplex the Heart of Man."[2] Samuel Richardson, who printed three of her novels and who gave her professional advice on various aspects of her writing, also praised her exceptional "knowledge of

---

1 An authorial note added by Henry Fielding to the second edition of *Joseph Andrews* (II.iv) states that Leonora's letter was "written by a young Lady on reading the former" (a letter from Horatio to Leonora). A teasing note by Henry in *A Journey from This World to the Next* declares that Anne Boleyn's story "is in the Original writ in a Woman's Hand; And tho' the Observations in it are, I think, as excellent as any in the whole Volume, there seems to be a Difference in Style between this and the preceeding Chapters; and as it is the Character of a Woman which is related, I am inclined to fancy it was really written by one of that Sex" (I.xxv). Sarah's putative authorship of these items is discussed by Bertrand A. Goldgar, Introduction to Henry Fielding, *Miscellanies* II, ed. Hugh Amory (Oxford: Clarendon, 1993) xxxiv–xxxv. J.F. Burrows and A. J. Hassall contend that both pieces were collaborations between Henry and Sarah ("*Anna Boleyn* and the Authenticity of Fielding's Feminine Narratives," *Eighteenth-Century Studies* 21 (1988): 427–53).

2 *The Adventures of David Simple* and *Volume the Last*, ed. Peter Sabor (Lexington: UP of Kentucky, 1998) 345.

the human heart,"[1] while Mary Scott, in a poetic celebration of "Female Geniuses" in *The Female Advocate* (1774), alluded to Henry Fielding's prefatory remarks in a graceful couplet:

'Twas FIELDING'S talent, with ingenuous Art,
To trace the secret mazes of the Heart.[2]

Fielding capitalized on the popularity of her first novel, publishing both an epistolary sequel, *Familiar Letters Between the Principal Characters in David Simple* (1747), and a conclusion to the original, *David Simple, Volume the Last* (1753). She also published the first full-length children's novel in English, *The Governess: or, Little Female Academy* (1749), and, in the same year, the first treatise on Richardson's *Clarissa, Remarks on Clarissa, Addressed to the Author*. A year later this pamphlet was followed by another, *A Comparison between the Horace of Corneille and the Roman Father of Mr. Whitehead* (1750), newly attributed to Fielding,[3] and it is possible that her authorship of other such works of criticism in the early 1750s will still come to light. In 1754, in collaboration with Jane Collier, she published *The Cry: A New Dramatic Fable*, an ambitious, innovative work combining elements of novel, essay, and drama. After an unsuccessful attempt to interest David Garrick, manager of the Drury Lane Theatre, in a play that she hoped to have produced during the 1754-55 theatre season,[4] Fielding moved from London to

---

1 Richardson to Fielding, 7 December 1756, *The Correspondence of Henry and Sarah Fielding*, ed. Martin C. Battestin and Clive T. Probyn (Oxford: Clarendon, 1993) 132. Richardson also took the opportunity here to disparage his rival Henry Fielding, whose knowledge of the heart was "but as the knowledge of the outside of a clock-work machine."

2 *The Female Advocate*, ed. Gae Holladay (Los Angeles: Augustan Reprint Society, no. 224, 1983) ll. 257-8 and p. v. In a note to these lines, Scott lists most of Fielding's publications but not her last two novels, *The History of the Countess of Dellwyn* and *The History of Ophelia*.

3 See the letter from John Upton to James Harris, mid-March 1750, identifying Fielding as the author of this treatise on William Whitehead's play *The Roman Father*, in Donald Burrows and Rosemary Dunhill, *Music and Theatre in Handel's World: The Family Papers of James Harris 1732-1780* (Oxford: Oxford UP, 2002) 267.

4 See *Correspondence of Henry Fielding and Sarah Fielding* ,126-7. Battestin and Probyn make a persuasive case for Fielding as the recipient of a letter from Garrick of May or June 1754, and thus as the author of the play that Garrick discusses.

Bath, where she would spend the remainder of her life in a constant struggle against poverty.

In Bath, Fielding completed four more works, of which the first was a fictional biography, *The Lives of Cleopatra and Octavia*. Printed by Richardson, it was issued to 440 subscribers in May 1757. They paid half a guinea for the book, a high price for two slender volumes, but it was handsomely printed in quarto, on royal paper, with large type, and subscribers had the satisfaction of seeing their names printed in a list at the beginning of the novel. Some had ordered multiple copies: several bought ten, the Countess of Barrymore bought sixteen, and one subscriber, Thomas Towers, headed the field with a remarkable twenty. A year after publication, however, payments from stragglers were still trickling in. One of those subscribing for ten copies sent his five guineas to Fielding via Richardson's daughter, Mary Ditcher, in April 1758. In a letter to Richardson, Fielding thanked him for his "continual acts of friendship," such as helping to collect payments from latecomers: "it is indeed very acceptable to me, thanks is all I can say."[1] At the same time, Richardson was preparing a "Corrected" second edition of the *Lives*, published in July 1758. This edition, printed in duodecimo on cheaper paper, with smaller type, was not sold by subscription and cost only three shillings. It was, as its modern editor, Christopher Johnson, observes, "intended to reach a larger, less affluent audience than the first edition."[2]

Given the precarious state of Fielding's finances, the small sums of money that were still coming in from subscribers to the first edition of the *Lives*, supplemented by further earnings from the second edition, must have been welcome. Since 1754, she had been living alone as a gentlewoman in severely reduced circumstances; her three sisters had all died within a year in 1750-51, her brother Henry in 1754, and her closest friend Jane Collier, with whom she

---

1 Fielding to Richardson, 12 April 1758, private collection (Nichols Archive Database PC1/14/26 [NAD 1527]). This letter, unknown to the editors of *Correspondence of Henry and Sarah Fielding*, will be published for the first time in *The Cambridge Edition of the Correspondence of Samuel Richardson*, general eds. Thomas Keymer and Peter Sabor (Cambridge: Cambridge UP, in progress).

2 Christopher Johnson, ed., *The Lives of Cleopatra and Octavia* (Lewisburg: Bucknell UP, 1994) 20. Johnson also suggests that the revisions to the text of the second edition might well have been undertaken by Richardson, rather than by Fielding herself.

had co-authored *The Cry*, a year later in 1755. And despite her poor health, described in several letters to Richardson, Fielding strove to support herself through her writings. She received some financial support from the philanthropist Ralph Allen, from her half-brother John Fielding, and from the bluestockings Elizabeth Montagu, Montagu's sister Sarah Scott, and Scott's companion Lady Barbara Montagu, but not enough to live on; earning money from writing, though arduous, was more rewarding. Fielding's friends and acquaintances, in fact, were quick to assume that any anonymously published fiction of the 1750s was hers. Lady Mary Wortley Montagu attributed Charlotte Lennox's *The Female Quixote* (1752), Jane Collier's *The Art of Ingeniously Tormenting* (1753), and *Memoirs of Sir Charles Goodville and his Family* (1753, authorship unknown) to her, while declaring "[I] heartily pity her, constrain'd by her Circumstances to seek her bread by a method I do not doubt she despises."[1] Also tentatively assigned to Fielding, by both Catherine Talbot and Elizabeth Montagu, was *Histories of Some of the Penitents in the Magdalen-House*, a work sponsored by Lady Barbara Montagu and published anonymously in November 1759, but the fact that its printer, Samuel Richardson, never discovered its authorship argues strongly against the attribution.[2]

Among Fielding's literary projects in the late 1750s were two collaborative ventures with the philosopher James Harris, who had been on friendly terms with her brother. One of these, begun in 1758, was a memoir of Henry Fielding. In July 1758, Harris sent

---

1   Montagu to Lady Bute, 23 July 1754, *Lady Mary Wortley Montagu: Selected Letters*, ed. Isobel Grundy (Harmondsworth: Penguin, 1997) 403. In another letter to Lady Bute, 1 March 1752, Montagu seems to ascribe three more anonymously published novels to Fielding: *The Lady's Drawing Room* (1744), *Leonora* (1745), and *The History of Cornelia* (1750, by Sarah Scott); see *Selected Letters*, 368 and n. 12.

2   Talbot to Elizabeth Carter, 27 November 1759; Montagu to Carter, n.d., *A Series of Letters Between Mrs. Elizabeth Carter and Miss Catherine Talbot, 1741-1770*, ed. Montagu Pennington (London, 1808) I. 448; *The Letters of Mrs. Elizabeth Montagu*, ed. Matthew Montagu (London, 1809-13) IV. 216-7. Fielding would, I believe, have revealed her authorship to Richardson, but his unpublished correspondence with Lady Barbara Montagu shows that he remained out of the secret. A counter-argument is made by Joyce Grossman, who in "'Sympathetic Visibility', Social Reform and the English Woman Writer: *The Histories of Some of the Penitents in the Magdalen-House*," *Women's Writing* 7 (2000): 247-66, attributes the work to Fielding.

her a manuscript entitled "An Essay on the Life and Genius of Henry Fielding," designed to be prefixed to a new edition of Henry's works. Sarah was supposed to supplement it with notes of her own, some already written and approved by Harris. The edition, she hoped, would be published by Andrew Millar "early in the Winter,"[1] but Millar had other plans. Some years later, in 1762, Millar's edition was published, but with a Life of Fielding by Arthur Murphy. Millar invited Sarah to write a Life supplementing that by Murphy, but she declined; in this case her strong antipathy to Murphy's portrait of her brother outweighed her financial exigencies.[2]

A more fruitful collaboration with Harris, also begun in 1758, was Fielding's translation of Xenophon's *Memoirs of Socrates*. She first mentions the work, which was already in progress, in a letter to Harris of 6 September 1758, five months after the publication of Elizabeth Carter's pioneering translation of Epictetus. Carter's work, published by subscription, had been astonishingly successful, attracting over one thousand subscribers and receiving enthusiastic reviews. Fielding, who had been tutored in Latin and Greek by Arthur Collier and was one of the only women in England with sufficient Greek to emulate Carter, thus had a positive example for entering the highly masculine world of classical scholarship. In a series of letters from 1758 to 1761 she discussed her progress on the translation with Harris and received extensive advice on difficult passages, duly acknowledged when the work appeared in January 1762. Like Carter's translation, Fielding's was published by subscription. A promotional campaign led by Sarah Scott and Elizabeth Montagu attracted 611 subscribers, paying six shillings each for a total of 707 copies: an impressive list, but considerably smaller than that prefixed to Carter's work. In her dedication of *The Lives of Cleopatra and Octavia* to the Countess of Pomfret, Fielding had, for the first time in her life, signed her name, as "S. Fielding," to one of her publications. In her translation of Xenophon, however, she went further, signing her name in full as "Sarah Fielding," and on the title page, where she typically appeared only as the anonymous "author of *David Simple*."

---

1 Fielding to Harris, 1 July 1758, *Correspondence of Henry and Sarah Fielding*, 137. For Harris's memoir of Henry Fielding, see Clive Probyn, *The Sociable Humanist: The Life and Works of James Harris 1709-1780* (Oxford: Clarendon, 1991) 303-13. Sarah's notes on Harris's memoir have not survived.

2 Fielding to Harris, 4 March and 15 March 1762, *Correspondence of Henry and Sarah Fielding*, 172-75.

Fielding's translation of Xenophon, judging from her letters to Harris, is the work by which she wished to be remembered, but during the four years of its composition she had to find other ways of earning an income. The obvious solution was novel-writing. In a letter to Harris of September 1758, Fielding refers to her desire to finish writing "some Stuff that I am now about" so that she could focus her attention on the translation. The "Stuff" was her penultimate novel, *The History of the Countess of Dellwyn*, which would be published by Andrew Millar in March 1759. In the same letter, she asks Harris's permission to make use, "in what I am now about," of a parody of *Othello* that he had composed; the parody appears, with slight alterations, in the published text of *The Countess of Dellwyn*.[1] By December 1758, she had almost completed the new work. In a letter to Richardson, its printer, she complains of having had to add more than one hundred manuscript pages in just four weeks, in order to satisfy "the Great Mouth of the Press," and adds: "if it is necessary I must write a small Preface but I had rather not for I am quite weary."[2] The "small Preface," when published, ran to forty pages, and is of much greater interest than Fielding's protestations might suggest. It concludes with a "manuscript Essay" that she claims to have discovered "in the Study of an old Gentleman,"[3] suggesting that books provide guides to their owners' characters: volumes fall open at especially well-thumbed pages, and thus betray their readers' particular tastes and concerns. Frances Burney, who might well have been familiar with Fielding's preface, had a similar interest in the power of books to reveal their owners' reading habits. Finding a copy of her novel *Cecilia* (1782) in the collection of the Earl of Mount-Edgecumbe, she was amused to see that the book opened just where she had predicted: "the chapter, An Opera Rehearsal, was so well read, the leaves always flew apart to display it."[4]

Fielding's surviving letters to Harris and Richardson provide much useful information on the sale as well as the composition of

---

1 Fielding to Harris, 6 September 1758, *Correspondence of Henry and Sarah Fielding*, 139-41 and n. 6.
2 Fielding to Richardson, 14 December 1758, *Correspondence of Henry and Sarah Fielding*, 149.
3 *The History of the Countess of Dellwyn* (New York: Garland, 1974) I. xxxiv.
4 Burney, Journal for 24 August 1789, *Diary and Letters of Madame d'Arblay*, ed. Charlotte Barrett, rev. Austin Dobson (London: Macmillan, 1905) IV. 321.

The History of Countess of Dellwyn. Her contract with Millar, she writes to Richardson, specified a payment of sixty guineas for a first edition of one thousand copies, "and forty Guineas more if it comes to a second Edition" (144). In an attempt to promote the novel, Millar arranged for a lengthy excerpt, "The Adventures of Mrs. Bilson," to appear in a daily newspaper, the *London Chronicle*, which printed it in two instalments in April 1759. This excerpt was reprinted a month later in the *Newcastle General Magazine*.[1] The serialization was accompanied by advertisements for Millar's books, but the promotional campaign was in this case unsuccessful. Although a Dublin edition appeared in 1759 and a German translation in 1761, no second edition of *The Countess of Dellwyn* was called for, so that Fielding failed to earn the additional forty guineas she had anticipated.

Much less is known about the composition of *The History of Ophelia*, Fielding's final novel, published in March 1760, only a year after *The History of the Countess of Dellwyn*, and like *Dellwyn* costing six shillings. It was published by Robert Baldwin rather then by Andrew Millar, her usual publisher; there are no records of the payment she received, and she does not mention the novel in any of her surviving letters. It is the only one of Fielding's novels to use, on the title page, the phrase "Published by the Author of *David Simple*," rather than merely "by the author of *David Simple*," and in doing so it raises teasing questions: is Fielding the author or merely the editor, and in what sense has she "Published" the book? One possibility is that the phrase refers to the form of payment to the author. In her previous novels, Fielding had either sold the copyright to the publisher or, in two cases (*Familiar Letters Between the Principal Characters in David Simple* and *The Lives of Cleopatra and Octavia*), published by subscription. With *Ophelia* she might have followed a different course: publishing for herself. This entailed taking responsibility for the cost of paper, printing, and advertising, but keeping most of the profits on the sale.[2]

Ophelia is likewise the only one of Fielding's novels containing a preface denying her own authorship: she is, she declares, "obliged to Fortune, for the Papers I now offer to the Publick," having found

---

1   See Robert D. Mayo, *The English Novel in the Magazines 1740-1815* (Evanston: Northwestern UP, 1962) 246.

2   See Jan Fergus and Janice Farrar Thaddeus, "Women, Publishers, and Money, 1790-1820," *Studies in Eighteenth-Century Culture* 17 (1987): 191–207.

this "Work of Fancy" in an "old Buroe." The denial, a device used frequently by eighteenth-century novelists, enables her to commend her own work without fear of appearing immodest: "it is pity Adventures so new and entertaining, should be buried in Oblivion, especially, when they, and the Reflections scattered throughout the Book, are as well calculated for Instruction as Amusement" (37). By disclaiming responsibility for *Ophelia*, Fielding adroitly removes the need to defer to her readers; no apologies of the kind found in her other prefaces are called for, since she purports only to be transcribing the work of another.

In an essay in preparation, however, J.F. Burrows and A.J. Hassall take Fielding's preface at its word, suggesting that the basis for *Ophelia* was a manuscript by Henry Fielding, revised and expanded by Sarah after her brother's death.[1] *Ophelia*, Burrows writes, began as a short novel by Henry, in which he "took a step beyond his earlier experiments in first person feminine narrative and allowed a virtuous heroine to tell her own story." Using computer-assisted analyses of the text, Burrows contends, in his part of the essay, that most of Volume I of *Ophelia*, with the exception of Ophelia's account of Lord Dorchester's jealousy of Sir Charles Lisdale (chapters 21-25), is by Henry Fielding. In volume II, according to Burrows, authorship is more equally divided, with Sarah contributing chapters 34-39, and the end of chapter 48 to the conclusion. Altogether, however, Henry wrote almost two-thirds of the novel by Burrows's calculations. In supporting the argument, Hassall suggests that the "old Buroe" might be a coded reference to Henry Fielding's manuscript and that Sarah "may indeed have been re-using a family joke— Henry having pretended to find *A Journey from this World to the Next*—which included *Anna Boleyn*, her first appearance in print—wrapped around pens he bought in a stationer's shop." Sarah's having Henry's manuscript to hand, he continues, explains how she could publish the novel so soon after *The Countess of Dellwyn*. Hassall also believes that the odd misnumbering of two chapters in Volume II, in which chapters 35-36 are numbered 6-7, supports the thesis: the error "is a legacy of two different manuscripts with different chapter numberings incompletely standardized by the printer." The numbers six and seven would thus refer to a shorter manuscript in Sarah's hand, which had begun with five

---

1   J.F. Burrows and A.J. Hassall, "Henry and Sarah Fielding: The Authorship of *The History of Ophelia* (1760)," in preparation.

chapters in Volume I. The argument is ingenious, but there are other ways to account for the various puzzles. Fielding could have been working on the manuscript intermittently for many years, as she had previously done with *The Lives of Cleopatra and Octavia*, published in 1757 but begun in 1748 or earlier.[1] The misnumbering of two chapters could stem from the existence of separately numbered manuscripts, but both could, of course, be by Sarah, composed at different times. And if Sarah had used her brother's work, she would probably not have written, in her Advertisement, "I have not been able, by any Enquiry, to find out the Author, or the Lady to whom it was addressed" (37). When Sarah is known to have solicited contributions to her work from Henry, as she did in both *The Adventures of David Simple* and *Familiar Letters Between the Principal Characters in David Simple*, she makes no secret of having done so.

II

Ophelia is in some ways a simpler work than its predecessors, with fewer literary allusions, for example, than *The History of the Countess of Dellwyn*, a far lighter tone than either *Dellwyn* or *David Simple, Volume the Last*, and a much more straightforward narrative structure than *The Cry*. It is narrated by the heroine to an unnamed female correspondent, "your Ladyship," in the form of a single protracted letter. This structure resembles that of John Cleland's notorious erotic novel, *Memoirs of a Woman of Pleasure* (1748-9), a work that it is tempting to imagine Fielding reading, perhaps in a copy bought by her brother when it first appeared eleven years before *Ophelia*.[2] Cle-

---

1 In June 1748, Fielding issued 600 subscribers' receipts for the novel. There might also be an earlier allusion to it in a letter from Richardson to Edward Young of 2 May 1745; see *The Correspondence of Edward Young*, ed. Henry Pettit (Oxford: Clarendon, 1971) 198.

2 The 1755 auction catalogue of Fielding's library does not list a copy of Cleland's novel. As Frederick G. Ribble and Anne G. Ribble note, however, "the collection of English prose fiction listed in the auction catalogue is quite sparse" (*Fielding's Library: An Annotated Catalogue* [Charlottesville: Bibliographical Society of the University of Virginia, 1996], xviii): the catalogue lacks all of Sarah Fielding's novels and most of Henry's own publications. In a review of *Fielding's Library*, Thomas Keymer sees this as evidence of "the family's retention of further items" (*Review of English Studies* 49 [1998]: 364). No record of Sarah Fielding's own library, regrettably, is known.

land's novel contains two extended letters by the heroine, also to an unnamed female correspondent, one in each volume. In both cases, the epistolary framework allows the author to imitate Richardson's celebrated "writing to the moment" technique while also maintaining authorial control, since the letters are written after the events they describe. Ophelia, like Fanny Hill, can stand back from the action, inspecting motivation and explaining behaviour, but she can also lose her sense of perspective when immersed in the action she is reporting.

Ophelia is remarkable for an innovative comic sequence (chapters 32-36) in which the heroine is imprisoned in a quasi-Gothic castle, four years before the publication of the first Gothic novel, Horace Walpole's *The Castle of Otranto* (1764). Linda Bree, noting the power of "Ophelia's first vision of the castle, whose crumbling contours are rendered even more awesome by the dim light of a late afternoon," commends Fielding's "sensitivity to, and subversion of, fictional trends."[1] Having created her Gothic vision, Fielding at once undermines it; Ophelia experiences no terror during her sequestration, in the manner of a proper Gothic heroine, but rather disdain and disgust at such features of the castle as a garden "so over-run with Frogs and Toads, that it was impossible to walk there without having Multitudes of them for Companions" (173).

But if *Ophelia* looks forward to the Gothic novel, it also looks back to Richardson's fiction and, in particular, to *Clarissa* (1747-48).[2] Just as Fielding's castle is a comic version of the Gothic ruin, inspiring not fear but derision, so her hero, Lord Dorchester, is a response to Lovelace, Clarissa's abductor and rapist. In Fielding's rewriting of the *Clarissa* story, the heroine is also abducted, but then protected rather than molested. Like Lovelace, Dorchester is a libertine bent on seducing his prey, but he eventually condemns his own libertinism. In her pamphlet *Remarks on Clarissa* (1749), an astute analysis of the novel in which a lively cast of characters is created to dispute various points about the novel, Fielding gives a brief foretaste of her own novel to be. A Miss Gibson, who in a

---

1 Linda Bree, *Sarah Fielding* (New York: Macmillan, 1996) 141.
2 Nancy Paul writes that "it is suggestive to view *Ophelia* as a kind of 'writing back'" to *Clarissa*, in which "the heroine triumphantly retains her chastity and reforms her rogue admirer Dorchester into a lover worthy of marriage." She also rightly notes the "undercurrent of melancholy" in Fielding's novel ("Is Sex Necessary? Criminal Conversation and Complicity in Sarah Fielding's *Ophelia*," *Lumen* 16 (1997): 114).

letter to her friend Bellario has the last word in the treatise, writes:

> Tho' *Clarissa* unfortunately met with *Lovelace*, yet I can imagine her with a Lover whose honest Heart, assimulating with hers, would have given her leave, as she herself wishes, to have shewn the Frankness of her Disposition, and to have openly avowed her Love.[1]

Ten years later, Fielding created just such a lover, whose heart eventually proves to be honest, enabling the heroine to avow her love in exchange. As Isobel Grundy writes of another response to *Clarissa*, *Simple Facts* (1793), "both Richardson's abduction plot and his forced-marriage plot are thoroughly, though sympathetically and respectfully, rewritten and answered."[2]

Another striking feature of *Ophelia* is its setting. Sarah Fielding was born in Dorset into the ancient English family of the Fieldings, headed by the Earls of Denbigh and Desmond, which liked to trace its descent from the Hapsburgs. Her father, Edmund Fielding, was a soldier who rose to the rank of colonel; her mother, Sarah Gould, was the daughter of a wealthy Somerset lawyer. While her brother Henry was being educated at Eton, Sarah and her sisters attended Mary Rookes's boarding school in Salisbury. After spending much of her adult life in London, she lived in Bath, unmarried, until her death. She is not known ever to have crossed the channel, or even to have crossed the Severn into Wales. Her heroine, Ophelia Lenox, in contrast, is a thoroughly unEnglish figure. Born in London to Scottish parents, the granddaughter of a nobleman, she is orphaned as a baby and soon taken by her youthful aunt to an unnamed British colony in the Caribbean: possibly Jamaica, which features prominently in *David Simple, Volume the Last*. Ophelia's aunt travels abroad as the wife of a soldier who, she discovers, is already married to another woman. On discovering his duplicity, the aunt determines to avoid all mankind and sets sail from the colony, accompanied by the two-year-old Ophelia. They land in the west of

---

1 See Appendix E below, 299.
2 Isobel Grundy, "'A novel in a series of letters by a lady': Richardson and some Richardsonian Novels," in *Samuel Richardson: Tercentenary Essays*, ed. Margaret Anne Doody and Peter Sabor (Cambridge: Cambridge UP, 1989) 232. The author of *Simple Facts* is an obscure Mrs. Mathews (not Eliza Kirkham Mathews).

England, and from there, "in search of a Retreat far from the Sight of human Kind" (43), the aunt brings Ophelia to Wales. Governed by "romantic Despair," the aunt comes across a remote cottage, which Fielding describes in detail. A small building, "situated on the Side of a Hill, commanding a beautiful, though a wild and mountainous Prospect", it is over twenty miles away from any other dwelling and thus ideally suited to the aunt's desire for solitude. Its present inhabitants, two young women and their father, regard it in a very different light. The women, eager for human society, have been trying to persuade their father to sell the cottage for over a year; an offer from Ophelia's aunt rapidly persuades him to part with it. Fielding tells us nothing more about these cottage-dwellers, who disappear at once from the narrative: they could, like Ophelia's aunt, have come to Wales from England, or they could be natives of Wales and thus almost the only Welsh characters in the novel.

Ophelia spends her childhood and adolescence in Wales, but always alone with her aunt in their cottage. Fielding devotes merely a paragraph to Ophelia's formative years. The cottage has a garden, grove, and pasture-land; Ophelia and her aunt raise goats and poultry and are entirely self-sufficient. Their life is one of pastoral bliss; delighting in the beauties of nature, they seem to lack nothing, and are free from ordinary stresses and cares. Stretching the boundaries of realism beyond their limits, Fielding asks us to accept that in fifteen years of rural seclusion, from the age of two to seventeen, Ophelia meets only one human being: "an old Man who had been at our House, on Occasions necessary to our rural Life" (45). Malcolm Kelsall terms her an "eighteenth-century Miranda raised, not on a desert island, but in deserted Wales."[1] She is taught nothing of the "Manners and Customs" of England (44), and her reading matter is confined to books of divinity and history. We see nothing at all of Welsh society, clothing, diet, or anything specific to the country. Nonetheless, Ophelia is deeply marked by her sequestration in Wales, and although most of the novel is set in England, she enters society as a quasi-primitive figure, bewildered by the regulations governing English social life.

Ophelia's idyllic life in Wales is disrupted by the sudden arrival of Lord Dorchester, a wandering Englishman to whose good looks

---

1 Malcolm Kelsall, ed., *The Adventures of David Simple* (Oxford: Oxford World's Classics, 1994) xii.

and fine clothing she responds with a Miranda-like enthusiasm. Dorchester has been visiting a friend who lives on the borders of Wales. Delighted by the "wild and natural Beauties" (46) of the country, he has travelled further into the interior for two days, until arrested by the wild and natural beauty of Ophelia. During his brief stay in the cottage, he pleads in vain with the aunt to restore Ophelia to human society. He has, however, succeeded in making an impression on Ophelia's heart. To her surprise, she admits, "my former Amusements became less pleasing to me; I found less Attention to what I read, less Joy in the vernal Beauties which before delighted me" (50).

What Dorchester cannot possess through persuasion he takes by force, returning to the cottage and abducting Ophelia on horseback. At the nearest road, half a day's journey away, Dorchester's carriage is waiting, and Ophelia's account reveals her striking ignorance of even the most familiar objects in England:

> there stood a small Hut, as I thought, with two Horses fastened to it; into this, they put me; I had observed, that the Outside was fine and gay; very different from the little Hovels I had seen: The Inside likewise was neat and pretty, but seemed better calculated for Beauty than Convenience; for there was but just Room for us to sit. I did not envy the Owner his gaudy Habitation, which I imagined must be very uncomfortable to live in; when to my great Amazement I felt it move very swiftly. (53–54)

Unfamiliar with the ways of polite society after spending most of her life in the depths of a Welsh valley, Fielding's heroine, now separated from her aunt, is singularly ill-equipped for her travels with an English lord. Her "coming out," normally a ritual passage into adulthood, is for her quite literally an emergence from the fastness of Wales into a bafflingly arcane social system.

Not surprisingly, the transition is traumatic and has the immediate effect of inducing a "high Fever": shortly after her abduction from the cottage Ophelia's health has been shattered and she longs for death. Although she eventually recovers, Ophelia fears that the "natural Strength" of her "Spirits and Nerves" (55) will be forever diminished in her new milieu. The contrast here established between the healthy state of nature in Wales and the sickly state of society in England is reiterated throughout the novel. On arriving for the first time at an inn, Ophelia remarks that "the Size and Colour of the Master and Mistress of the House, made me tremble for the Slenderness of my Waist, and Fairness of my Skin, in a Country which seemed so great an Enemy to the Shape and Complexion"; English innkeepers are notable, she believes, for their "extraordinary Bulk and Redness of Face." She does, however, admire her host's kindness in providing her with food and accommodation; Dorchester has to explain to her that his "Hospitality was a mere Trade" (56-57).

Ophelia's Welshness allows her to see English society afresh in a manner comparable to that of Oliver Goldsmith's Chinese visitor to London, Lien Chi Altangi, in *The Citizen of the World*. Goldsmith's first two "Chinese letters" were published in January 1760, a few months before *Ophelia*. But unlike Altangi, Ophelia has not come from one civilization to another: she is a Welsh noble savage, not a sophisticated Chinese traveller. Altangi experiences the bewilderment of those in an alien culture, but at least he has his own culture as a point of comparison. Ophelia, in contrast, is constantly encountering objects and customs that have no counterpart in her Welsh valley. Some of these novelties delight while others offend her, but all are astonishingly new. A decade later, in his epistolary novel, *The Expedition of Humphry Clinker* (1771), Tobias Smollett also made the Welsh origin of his letter-writers crucial to their accounts of the fashionable resorts of England and Scotland: here too we see little of life in rural Wales, but much of life in urban England and Scotland as seen by the Welsh.

The freshness of Ophelia's vision also has a counterpart in the responses of the Lilliputians and Brobdingnagians, in Swift's *Gulliver's Travels* (1726), to the very English Gulliver, who is constantly obliged to explain to his incredulous hosts what has always seemed to him a perfectly orderly and well-regulated state of affairs. Other "innocent eye" fictions preceding *Ophelia* include the *Letters Writ by a Turkish Spy* (1684), Montesquieu's *Lettres persanes* (1721), and Lord Lyttelton's imitation of Montesquieu, *Letters from a Persian in England* (1735). In all of these works, however, the traveller is a man. A more useful model for Fielding might have been Zilia, the heroine of Françoise de Graffigny's *Lettres d'une Péruvienne* (1747), at once translated as *Letters Written by a Peruvian Princess* (1748) and a highly popular work in England, with several subsequent editions. Like Ophelia, Zilia is abducted from her home and brought to a great city, Paris, and like Ophelia she experiences mixed feelings towards her captor turned suitor, Déterville (see Appendix F below).

Ophelia can also be compared to Arabella, the heroine of Charlotte Lennox's *The Female Quixote* (1752), one of the novels that Lady Mary Wortley Montagu had wrongly attributed to Sarah Fielding and that the reviewer of *Ophelia* in *The Critical Review*, perhaps prompted by Ophelia's surname Lenox, regarded as a probable influence.[1] Arabella is brought up by her widowed father who, like Ophelia's aunt, is embittered and determined to avoid contact with humankind: he retreats with Arabella to a castle in a remote part of England, several miles from any town. But when she emerges from the castle, Arabella does not become, like Ophelia, an innocent-eye observer, making original observations on a society unknown to her; instead, her immersion in French romances makes her a blinkered female counterpart to Cervantes' Don Quixote. Arabella interprets all she encounters as the stuff of romance; she does not provide fresh interpretations but comically artificial ones.

On arriving at Lord Dorchester's country house, Ophelia is so struck by the magnificent building, the elegant furnishings and the elaborate paintings that she cannot control her response: "My Raptures were not silent, my Admiration broke forth into Exclamations. I ran from one Room to another, desirous of seeing more, though not weary of what I had seen" (58). The estate, with its garden, park, ha ha, terrace, parterre, and cascade is equally enchanting, as are the fashionable ornaments and clothing that Dorchester gives Ophelia to wear. Such items help alleviate Ophelia's distress at what she terms "my enforced separation from my Aunt, and my former Habitation, dragged into a new World" (60). But this new world can repel her too. She puts on a hooped petticoat, in deference to the prevailing fashion, but "immediately threw away the stiff Stays which seemed to me invented in perverse Opposition to Nature, and one of the Proofs with which I thought this Country abounded, that Man in his Folly had declared open War with her" (61-62). Ophelia is willing to alter and control her natural appearance in deference to English society, but not beyond a certain point: stays seem to her designed merely to subjugate the female figure, and she rejects such oppression outright.

Ophelia's abductor, Lord Dorchester, is a remarkably devout and respectful suitor, who takes pains to protect her reputation by presenting her as his ward. He is also determined to conceal her upbringing in Wales from public knowledge. Before taking her to

---

1 See Appendix A below, 280.

London he advises her to be "silent as to [her] Birth and former Way of Life, as well as to the Means by which [she] was taken from it" (80). If her ignorance of fashionable society becomes known, he contends, she will become an object of scorn, derided as a "fair Savage" by those who call "natural Reason and Sense, because little known to them, ridiculous Ignorance" (81). Despite the admiration for Wales he had professed during his brief travels there, Dorchester's attitude towards its inhabitants seems little different from that he here purports to condemn. Ophelia herself, despite her striking naivety, comes close to resenting the term "savage," allowing Dorchester to incur "the Anger so justly due to the People he described." But these people, the Welsh, remain unseen. Although Dorchester has promised to return Ophelia to Wales, should she still desire to do so, after she has spent a year in England, he later tells her "you would but ill relish the rustick Solitude of your former Cottage" (122) and determines to establish her in the London social world. Ophelia, ignorant even of the location of her cottage, can attain it only in her dreams. In a striking passage that exemplifies the fascination with the workings of the mind found in all of her novels, Fielding has Ophelia recount a dream that restored her to the Welsh cottage and to her aunt's embraces, while Lord Dorchester, "shewing by his smiles the Pleasure he received from our Transports; and declaring himself rewarded by the Satisfaction we enjoyed for the Journey he had taken to restore me to her, begged leave to remain a constant Spectator of our mutual Affection." The dream thus creates a curious *ménage à trois*: Ophelia in the arms of her aunt, with Dorchester neither as lover nor husband but merely a "constant Spectator" (99).

On a later occasion, Ophelia again envisages herself in Wales with Dorchester by her side. When he is about to fight a duel, having challenged a man who had insulted her, she regrets that Dorchester had not grown up with her in Wales, far from the perils of London: "I only grieved that he was not born there with me; that he had not likewise been placed in a Solitude where Death was under God's immediate Direction" (223-24). So wedded is Ophelia to her vision of sanctuary in Wales, that she forgets that she is not in fact Welsh by birth: she was born in London, the city she fears, while Dorchester's birthplace was probably his country seat.

Only midway through the second volume does Ophelia at last understand that Dorchester, always a model of sexual propriety, is intent on making her his mistress. Her desire to return to Wales and forget the English, "a vicious Race" (238), is thereby increased, yet the difficulties of finding a cottage that she could not locate on a map seem insurmountable. Confronting Dorchester, who discovers the house in London where she has concealed herself, she declares roundly:

> I have lost all my Confidence in you, and detest the rest of your Nation. I will go where I shall be secluded from Mankind, where Virtue makes every Action open and intelligible; there I am capable of living happily, without learning the Arts that here hide every real Thought. (257)

Ironically, however, it is not Ophelia who returns to Wales at last, but her now penitent suitor, Dorchester. In the final chapter of the novel, Dorchester makes his third appearance at the cottage. After assuring her aunt that Ophelia is well and unsullied, he implores the aunt's aid in persuading her niece to accept his hand in marriage. The aunt agrees, with considerable misgivings, and returns to London with Dorchester; her blessing permits the wedding to take place.

In his bachelor days Lord Dorchester had divided his year between the winter season in London and summer at his country estate, with occasional forays to spa resorts such as Bath and Tunbridge Wells. After his marriage to Ophelia, however, a major change in his social calendar takes place: the couple will now spend three months of every year with her aunt at the cottage in Wales, "which, in the Opinion of us all, was the Time when we enjoyed the most perfect Happiness, as we were there free from Interruptions." It would be tempting to deduce from this that Fielding has grafted the primitive values of her Welsh pastoral retreat onto the ways of sophisticated English society. It is, however, notable that Dorchester has settled a "very handsome Income" on the aunt, as well as ordering what seem to be extensive additions to the cottage (276).

On his first visit to Wales, Dorchester delights, or pretends to delight, in the simplicity of Ophelia's retreat, declaring that "the Whiteness of our Wooden Bowls and Platters scarcely were excelled by the Linen they were upon, [and] were in his Opinion far preferable to Silver or China" (47). Now that the aunt has, for the first time in her life, a substantial income, as well as a renovated house to furnish, the wooden bowls and platters are likely to be supplemented with silver and chinaware. At Lord Dorchester's English country house, extensive landscaping projects have ingeniously made a highly ordered estate resemble the most pleasing aspects of nature in its unadorned state: "the Variety of Grounds," as Ophelia observes, "gives it an Air of Wildness, which greatly charms in the Midst of a Country so diligently cultivated, that one expects to see there more of the Beauties of Art, than of Nature" (59). Ophelia's aunt, in contrast, has devoted her energies to making her cottage more like a miniature country house: she was "continually ornamenting it during the whole Time she stayed there, taking Pleasure in beautifying it, though no one was likely to behold either her or her Habitation" (44). By the end of the novel, the cottage is less remote, more luxurious, and less distinctive than it had been in Ophelia's childhood: it has become a desirable country dwelling, the second residence of an English aristocrat and his wife. Rather than celticizing her England, Fielding has anglicized her Wales.

It is instructive to compare the fate of Ophelia's cottage with that of two other Welsh residences mentioned in the novel. In an inset story, Captain Traverse, an impoverished decommissioned army officer, recounts his many misfortunes to Ophelia and Lord Dorchester. In order to economize, Traverse and his family have left London and "removed to the Borders of *Wales*, where we hired a small House" (150). Later, in another inset story, Sir Charles Lisdale tells Ophelia that he too had rented an isolated Welsh cottage, as an appropriately lonely place to get over his unrequited passion for her: in the Welsh borders, he tells her, "I found a little Cottage situated to my Wish, for every Thing around it appeared as desolate as my Mind" (265). Sir Charles meets the Traverse family at church, and is soon attracted to their beautiful young daughter, Fanny. When Traverse, now the fortunate protégé of Lord Dorchester, moves his family from Wales closer to London, Sir Charles also gives up his cottage to join his beloved Fanny. For Traverse and Sir Charles, Wales has filled a purely functional purpose in providing cheap or isolated accommodation; as soon as their need for Wales is removed, through new-found wealth for Traverse and a new romantic interest for Sir Charles, the country is written out of their lives.

In the late 1750s, when Fielding was writing *Ophelia*, very few novels featuring a Welsh setting had yet been published. The earliest listed by Moira Dearnley in her survey of "fictions of Wales"[1] is

---

1   Moira Dearnley, *Distant Fields: Eighteenth-Century Fictions of Wales* (Cardiff: U of Wales P, 2001).

Penelope Aubin's *The Life of Madam de Beaumont, a French Lady* (1721): a heroine who, the subtitle tells us, "lived in a Cave in *Wales* above fourteen Years undiscovered," and who marries a virtuous Welshman, Mr. Lluelling. Aubin's collected novels were published in a posthumous edition of 1739, with an anonymous preface probably by Richardson.[1] Fielding might well have read this collection, which appeared shortly before she began writing her own novels in the 1740s. Fielding might also have been familiar with a novel not mentioned by Dearnley, William Toldervy's *The History of Two Orphans*, published only four years before *Ophelia* in 1756. In volumes two and three of Toldervy's four-volume novel, as Thomas Keymer observes, a group of travellers undertake a tour of the Welsh marches, together with their servant, Humphry Copper: an intriguing anticipation, in name at least, of Smollett's Humphry Clinker.[2] Toldervy, a Shropshire-born Londoner, subsequently published the unfinished *England and Wales Described* (1762): itself perhaps impelled in part by a desire to create a version of Wales less remote from geographical and social reality than that of *Ophelia*.[3]

Ophelia preceded the later wave of novels set in Wales, including Sophia Lee's *Pembroke* (1799), by some thirty years. In an essay on the use of Wales in eighteenth-century women's fiction, Jane Aaron accounts for the popularity of novels with a Welsh context at the end of the century, a time when Wales was rapidly gaining appeal as a fashionable tourist resort.[4] The earliest novel cited by Aaron, Anna Maria Bennett's *Anna: or, Memoirs of a Welch Heiress*, appeared in 1785; her other examples, most of them by English authors, such as Susannah Gunning's *Delves: A Welch Tale* (1796), her daughter Elizabeth Gunning's *The Orphans of Snowdon* (1797), and Emily

---

1   See Wolfgang Zach, "Mrs. Aubin and Richardson's Earliest Literary Manifesto (1739)," *English Studies* 62 (1981): 271-85.
2   Thomas Keymer, "William Toldervy and the Origins of Smart's *A Translation of the Psalms of David,*" *Review of English Studies* 54 (2003): 56. Keymer also notes that Toldervy's travellers later "encounter 'a certain personage named *Clinker*' (4: 124)."
3   In his Preface, Toldervy refers to "those who, in their Chambers, have described Hills, Rocks, Woods, Caves, Meads, Rivers, and gently purling Rills in *England*, which never had Existence" (I. iv). Regrettably, Toldervy did not publish a projected second volume; volume one contains no more of Wales than the border counties.
4   Jane Aaron, "Seduction and Betrayal: Wales in Women's Fiction, 1785-1810," *Women's Writing* 1 (1994): 65-76.

Clark's *Ianthé, or the Flower of Caernarvon* (1798), were published in the late 1790s. It is in novels such as these that Wales has an interest in its own right; in Sarah Fielding's much earlier *Ophelia* it serves instead as a vantage point from which English society can be examined.[1] The contrast between Wales and England allows Fielding to explore issues of nature versus nurture, of friendship versus courtship, and of morals versus manners. Wales itself, however, is of no more intrinsic importance in *Ophelia* than Turkey in the *Turkish Spy*, Peru in *Lettres d'une Péruvienne*, or China in the *Citizen of the World*.

III

In April 1760, a month after the novel's publication, Catherine Talbot wrote to her friend Elizabeth Carter that "we are deep in and amused with Ophelia."[2] Her pleasure was not shared by the reviewers for the two principal English literary magazines, whose remarks on *Ophelia* are printed in Appendix A below. Both *The Monthly Review* and *The Critical Review* had reviewed Fielding's previous novel, *The History of the Countess of Dellwyn*, a year earlier with some enthusiasm. The *Monthly Review*, referring to the "known talents of the ingenious author of *David Simple*," declared that "not only the execution of the whole, but many parts of the history have particularly pleased us, in the perusal." *The Critical Review* compared *Dellwyn* unfavourably with Henry Fielding's *Tom Jones*, but contended that its "defects, however, are compensated by an easy familiar stile, an agreeable uninterrupted vivacity, and a pleasing insight into scenes of domestic tranquillity or distress."[3] For *Ophelia*, in contrast, *The Monthly Review* had only disdain, stating acerbically that "for any great instruction or amusement a Reader of taste and discernment will meet with in the perusal, the manuscript might as well have remained in the buroe," while *The Critical Review* damns with faint praise: *Ophelia* possesses "that del-

---

1 As Nancy Paul contends, Fielding's Wales "is a place for rest, retreat, and recuperation—not for permanent occupation. Further, it is the location of (Ophelia's) childhood and thus signifies transition" ("Is Sex Necessary?" 127, n. 5).

2 Talbot to Carter, 26 April 1760, *Letters Between Mrs. Carter and Miss Talbot*, I. 462.

3 *The Monthly Review* 20 (April 1759): 380; *The Critical Review* 7 (April 1759): 378.

icacy peculiar to female writers" and "affords as much entertainment, and harmless recreation, as most productions of this kind." A one-line notice in Smollett's *British Magazine* is equally condescending: it too finds the novel "delicate," but no more than "tolerably entertaining." Fielding's old friend and supporter, Samuel Richardson, was similarly dismissive. In an unpublished letter to Lady Bradshaigh of 20 June 1760 (Forster Collection, Victoria and Albert Museum, XI, f. 269) he writes:

> Ophelia—was sent me—I did *open this Book*; but read it not. Two of my Girls, to whom I committed it for their Opinion of it, made no such a Report of it, as excited my Curiosity, tho' the Editor was Sally Fielding.

Lady Bradshaigh herself at least read the novel, but her responses were mixed. In a letter to Richardson of 8 June 1760 (Forster Collection, XI, f. 267) she writes:

> Ophelia—uncommon, full of very odd, I am affraid some of them, unnatural circumstances, a most Romantic opening. But the reform'd Hero, pleas'd me. Every thing done in a hurry, a fatigued, & wearied writer appears thro the whole.

Other eighteenth-century readers of *Ophelia*, however, found the novel more appealing. James Hoey, after publishing an unauthorized Dublin edition in 1760 within a few months of the original publication, reissued it three years later. In his second edition, unusually, he went to the trouble of commissioning a new episode by an unknown writer (see Appendix B below), allowing him to promote this printing as "the second edition, with additions" on the title-page. Another sign of the novel's popularity was its appearance in James Harrison's *Novelist's Magazine* in 1785 (see Appendix C below): together with *The Adventures of David Simple*, *Ophelia* was one of two novels by Fielding that the magazine chose to reprint. Two years later, in 1787, another London edition was published: the novel had thus gone through a total of five printings in England and Ireland.

Ophelia also achieved surprising success in translation. German editions appeared in 1763-64, 1767, and 1772, and a French edition of 1763 was translated by Octavie Belot, also the translator of Elizabeth Montagu's contributions to Lord Lyttelton's *Dialogues of the Dead*, that had first been published in May 1760, only two months after *Ophelia.*[1] Another French edition of *Ophelia* appeared at the very end of the century, 1799, listed as "an septième" on the title-page, the seventh year of the Revolutionary calendar that began in 1792. The title of this translation, "*Ophelia, ou L'entrée d'une orpheline dans le monde,*" alludes to that of Burney's *Evelina* (1778), first published as *Evelina, or a Young Lady's Entrance Into the World;* by the end of the century, Burney's novel was better known in France than Fielding's. The edition contains two illustrations, designed by P.J. Chaillou (or Challiou), a little-known book-illustrator active in Paris from 1796 to 1800, and engraved by Edme Bovinet. Their first illustration depicts the same scene chosen for the *Novelist's Magazine,* Lord Dorchester encountering Ophelia and her aunt for the first time, but with some intriguing variations. Chaillou, in keeping with the spirit of the age, shows the aristocrat on one knee, pleading with the simply-dressed country dwellers; Courbould's Dorchester in the *Novelist's Magazine,* in contrast, remains upright. Chaillou also removes Lord Dorchester's servant from the composition, further reducing the distance between the English lord and the rustic Welshwomen. The second Chaillou-Bovinet illustration shows Ophelia, in the final chapter, "wavering between Reason and Love" (274) while Lord Dorchester successfully presses his suit, with her aunt and Mr. South looking on in agitation.

Although *Ophelia* was seldom mentioned by eighteenth-century writers, Frances Burney and Jane Austen both drew on it in their fiction. Some of the links between *Ophelia* and Burney's first novel, *Evelina,* were first discussed by Clementina Black in her essay of 1888 (see Appendix D below): in particular Ophelia's ignorance of dancing etiquette, which leads to a duel in Fielding's novel and much unpleasantness and embarrassment in Burney's. Another scene taken up by Burney but not mentioned by Black is a delightful comic episode at the opera-house, in which Ophelia applies smelling-salts to a pretentious woman gasping at the music "in a most languishing Condition" (117). In *Evelina,* when Madame Duval expresses her delight as she listens to Handel's "Coronation Anthem," Captain Mirvan likewise applies smelling-salts to her nostrils. Ophelia's well-intentioned action throws her companion "into a violent Fit of Sneezing"; Captain Mirvan's malicious treat-

---

1   See *The Yale Edition of Horace Walpole's Correspondence,* ed. W.S. Lewis (New Haven: Yale UP, 1937-83) VII. 204 and n. 2. The Index to the *Yale Edition* lists several other works translated from English to French by Belot.

ment of Madame Duval causes her such distress "that the pain and surprise made her scream aloud" (I.ix).[1]

Austen began writing the comic short fiction that she later transcribed into three notebooks in 1787, the year in which the last of the three London editions of *Ophelia* was published. In an account of Austen's amused interest in the early Welsh novel, Moira Dearnley notes the parallels between Ophelia and the heroine of "Love and Freindship" (1790), Laura, who like her predecessor "is swept off her feet by the arrival of a 'beauteous and amiable' young Englishman who finds his way to her 'rustic Cot' after being hopelessly lost.... The young people fall in love at first sight, are united on the spot and a few days after their marriage leave for the Aunt's in Middlesex."[2] The aunt—not the heroine's, in Austen's story, but her husband's—is cheerfully receptive to the marriage although ignorant of her nephew's existence, having "never even had the slightest idea of there being such a person in the World."[3] Such manipulation of her source material is typical of the youthful Austen, who wrote this story in her early teens. Another of her early writings that seems to glance at *Ophelia* is a two-page fragment, "A Tale," in which the hero, Wilhelminus, takes possession of a Welsh cottage still more remote and inaccessible than that depicted by Fielding:

> After travelling for three days and six Nights without Stopping, they arrived at the Forest and following a track which led by it's side down a steep Hill over which ten Rivulets meandered, they reached the Cottage in half an hour.[4]

Wilhelminus's beloved, Marina, with whom he will presumably share the cottage, takes her name from the character in Shakespeare's *Pericles*—perhaps in imitation of Fielding's heroine, who takes her unusual name from the Ophelia of Shakespeare's *Hamlet*.

After its appearance in 1787, no further English editions of *Ophelia* were published for almost two hundred years.[5] Throughout

---

1 These scenes from *Evelina* are printed in Appendix G below.
2 Dearnley, *Distant Fields*, xiv.
3 Austen, *Catharine and Other Writings*, ed. Margaret Anne Doody and Douglas Murray (Oxford: Oxford World's Classics, 1993) 80.
4 Austen, *Catharine*, 171.
5 In 1974, Garland Press issued a facsimile reprint of the first London edition of *Ophelia*, together with reprints of *The Adventures of David Simple, The Lives of Cleopatra and Octavia*, and *The History of the Countess of Dellwyn*.

the nineteenth and for much of the twentieth century, with Clementina Black's 1888 essay (Appendix D below) as almost the single exception, *Ophelia* was all but forgotten. Georg Plügge, author of a Leipzig doctoral dissertation on Sarah Fielding published in 1898, devotes only a paragraph to the novel and had obviously not read it. As well as giving its date as 1758 rather than 1760, he claims that in addition to finding her heroine's name in *Hamlet*, Fielding retells the story of Shakespeare's Ophelia: as though Polonius's daughter had grown up not in Denmark but in Wales, and had fallen in love not with a Danish prince but with an English lord.[1] Since the publication of Martin Battestin and Clive Probyn's scholarly edition of the Fieldings' correspondence (1993) and Linda Bree's incisive monograph (1996), interest in Fielding has increased dramatically, to the extent that three paperback editions of *The Adventures of David Simple* and *Volume the Last* are currently in print. Her place in bluestocking circles and her role in the development of sensibility and sentimentalism have been the subject of much discussion. Recent articles and book-chapters on *Ophelia* by Nancy Paul (1997), Gillian Skinner (1999), Moira Dearnley (2001), and J.F. Burrows and A.J. Hassall (in preparation) show that readers are now coming to terms with her final novel, as well as her earlier publications. In the mid-eighteenth century, Sarah Fielding was the second most popular English woman novelist, behind only Eliza Haywood.[2] And just as Haywood, in the first decade of the twenty-first century, has become a canonical author, more intensively studied than almost all of her contemporaries, male or female, Sarah Fielding's writings seem set to become widely read and vigorously debated once again.

---

1 Georg Plügge, *Miss Sarah Fielding als Romanschriftstellerin* (Leipzig: Universität Leipzig, 1898) 11. Remarkably, despite the appearance of many American doctoral dissertations on Fielding, beginning with Herman Oscar Werner's still useful "The Life and Works of Sarah Fielding" (Harvard University, 1937), Plügge's would remain the only published monograph for almost a hundred years until the publication of Linda Bree's *Sarah Fielding* (1996).

2 See James Raven, *British Fiction 1750-1770: A Chronological Check-List of Prose Fiction Printed in Britain and Ireland* (Newark: U of Delaware P, 1987) 14.

Sarah Fielding: A Brief Chronology

1710   SF born at East Stour, Dorset (8 November), fourth of seven children of Colonel Edmund Fielding and Sarah Gould Fielding. Eldest child is Henry Fielding (1707-54).

1718   Death of mother (14 April). Fielding children cared for in Dorset by their maternal aunt and grandmother, Lady Gould, while father lives in London.

1719   Edmund Fielding returns to East Stour with second wife, Anne Rapha (d. 1727), a Roman Catholic widow with two daughters.

1720-33 Together with her sisters, lives with grandmother in Salisbury, where she attends Mary Rookes's boarding school. Meets two future literary collaborators, James Harris (1709-80) and Jane Collier (1715-55), and Jane's brother Arthur Collier (1707-77), who will later tutor her in Latin and Greek.

1722   Lady Gould successfully sues for custody of her grandchildren (10 February).

1729   Father's third marriage (January), to Eleanor Hill, a Salisbury widow (d. 1739).

1733   Lady Gould dies (7 June). SF and her sisters probably return to East Stour.

1739   East Stour estate sold (14 May); proceeds divided among the six surviving children.

1741   Father's fourth marriage (9 March), to Elizabeth Sparrye (d. 1770). He dies intestate and impoverished (18 June).

1742   Letter from Leonora to Horatio, probably by SF, in Henry Fielding's *The Adventure of Joseph Andrews.*

1743   Fictional autobiography of Anna Boleyn, probably by SF, the final chapter of Henry Fielding's *A Journey from This World to the Next.*

1744   *The Adventures of David Simple*, 2 vols., published (May); second edition, with Preface by Henry Fielding replacing SF's Advertisement (July). After the death of Henry Fielding's wife (November) SF probably goes to London to live with him. SF begins friendship with Samuel Richardson in c. 1744-45.

1747   *Familiar Letters Between the Principal Characters in David Simple*, 2 vols., published by subscription (507 subscribers) with preface and five letters by Henry Fielding and two letters by James Harris (April). SF leaves Henry Fielding's household after his second marriage (27 November); probably lives with her sisters in Westminster.

1749 *The Governess; or, Little Female Academy* published, printed by Samuel Richardson (January). *Remarks on Clarissa, Addressed to the Author* also published in January.

1750 Probably author of the pamphlet *A Comparison between the Horace of Corneille and the Roman Father of Mr. Whitehead* (March).

1750-51 Death of SF's three sisters, Catharine (July 1750), Ursula (December 1750), Beatrice (January 1751). SF goes to live with Jane Collier, also in Westminster.

1753 *The Adventures of David Simple, Volume the Last*, with preface probably by Jane Collier, published (February).

1754 *The Cry: A New Dramatic Fable* (3 vols.), with Jane Collier, published (March). SF sends David Garrick the incomplete draft of a play, never published or performed. Henry Fielding embarks for Lisbon (June), where he dies (October). SF moves to Bath in ill health.

1755 Jane Collier dies. SF lives in Bathwick, close to Bath.

1757 *The Lives of Cleopatra and Octavia*, 2 vols., published by subscription (440 subscribers, May).

1758 SF collaborates with James Harris on an unpublished memoir, "An Essay on the Life and Genius of Henry Fielding," for a forthcoming edition of his works.

1759 *The History of the Countess of Dellwyn*, 2 vols., published (March).

1760 *The History of Ophelia*, 2 vols., published (March). SF buys a small cottage at Walcot, near Bath (September).

1762 Translation, *Xenophon's Memoirs of Socrates. With the Defence of Socrates*, 2 vols., published by subscription (611 subscribers), with notes and other contributions by James Harris (January).

1764 SF's benefactor Ralph Allen dies, leaving SF a legacy of £100.

1765 Lady Barbara Montagu dies, leaving SF an annuity of £10.

1766 In failing health, SF moves into lodgings in Bath, probably with her friend Sarah Scott.

1767 Elizabeth Montagu settles an annuity on SF of £10. Montagu and Scott make plans for SF to join a female community at Hitcham, Buckinghamshire, but SF too ill to move.

1768 SF dies at 57 (9 April); buried in St. Mary's Church, Charlcombe (14 April). Monument to her in Bath Abbey erected by her friend John Hoadly, poet and dramatist.

A Note on the Text

This edition has been prepared from the British Library copy of the first edition of *The History of Ophelia* (1760), microfilmed for *The Eighteenth Century* (Research Publications, Reel 5527, no. 1). A passage inserted in the Dublin edition of 1763, microfilmed for *The Eighteenth Century* (Research Publications, Reel 5344, no. 1), is reprinted in Appendix B.

This edition retains the spelling, punctuation, capitalization, and italicization of the first edition, the only one for which Fielding was responsible. The following changes have been made throughout: the long "s" is replaced with the modern "s"; running quotation marks have been removed; and missing punctuation, such as opening and closing quotation marks, or periods at the ends of sentences, has been supplied. Obvious printing errors, of which there are many in the first edition, such as "mnst" for "must" or "aud" for "and," have been silently corrected. In other cases, where the correct reading is uncertain, later editions have been consulted and explanatory notes supplied.

THE

HISTORY

OF

OPHELIA.

PUBLISHED BY

The Author of DAVID SIMPLE.

In TWO VOLUMES.

VOL. I.

ADVERTISEMENT[1]

I am obliged to Fortune, for the Papers I now offer to the Publick. I little imagined, when I bought an old Buroe, that I was purchasing a Work of Fancy; for such I must suspect this little Work to be, though it contains many Incidents that bear so much the Appearance of Reality, that they might claim some Share of our Belief. I have not been able, by any Enquiry, to find out the Author, or the Lady to whom it was addressed, but I hope I shall not give Offence to either of them by the Publication; for if the Story is fictitious, in all Probability, it must have been designed for the Press, as it is unlikely any one should put their Invention on so laborious a Task, merely for their own Amusement; and if the Story is real, it is pity Adventures so new and entertaining, should be buried in Oblivion, especially, when they, and the Reflections scattered throughout the Book, are as well calculated for Instruction as Amusement.

The Author of DAVID SIMPLE.[2]

---

1 A brief prefatory statement.
2 Exploiting the popularity of her first novel while retaining her anonymity, Fielding uses this phrase to signify authorship of each of her novels after *The Adventures of David Simple* (1744).

INTRODUCTION

Your Ladyship had little Compassion either on yourself or me, when you desired me to write you an exact Account of every Circumstance of my Life, and even of my Thoughts, or you did not consider the long Detail into which this lead me; a Detail tedious for you to read, and difficult for me to write. You expressly desire to know the Impressions I received from the first View of Customs so unlike what I had ever seen, at a Time when they are become so familiar to me, that I almost forget many of them were ever otherwise. But your Commands can meet with nothing but an implicit Obedience from me; and when I mention the Difficulties which may occur in the Execution, it is not with a Design of disputing them, but to excuse my ill Performance of the Task.

You say I must first account for the Ignorance in which I was educated. This is obliging me to trouble your Ladyship with more Adventures than my own; and is scarcely in order, since it makes me begin with the Relation of Circumstances, with which I was not acquainted till a considerable Time after my History of myself will end.

OPHELIA.

CHAPTER I

My Father, whose Name was *Lenox*, was the Son of a *Scotch* Nobleman; his future Fortune depended on his rise in the Army, wherein he was only a Captain, when he Married his Colonel's Daughter:[1] The Colonel was then in the last Stage of a Consumption, of which he expired in less than two Months after his Daughter's Marriage; besides her, he left another Daughter, and they equally shared four thousand Pounds,[2] which was his whole Fortune. My Father died in the third Year of his Marriage, leaving his Wife with Child of me: Her Grief for the Loss of her Husband was so great, her Friends feared it would prove fatal both to her and myself; but a little before the usual Time, I entered the World alive, contrary to their expectations; but my Mother expired before the End of her Month.[3]

My Father's Family were too far off *London*, the Place of my Birth, to think of so poor an Orphan as myself; for my Mother's Fortune was considerably impaired, and of her Side I had no near Relation but my Aunt, to whose Care I naturally fell, and her Humanity readily undertook the Office. My Aunt was about twenty-two Years old; and was just then deserted by an Officer with whom every preliminary of Marriage was agreed, when her Father's Death put a Stop to it, tho' he had a better Fortune than is common to Gentlemen of his Profession; it then appeared that her Charms had less Influenced her Lover than the Hopes of obtaining Preferment by her Father's Interest, for in a feigned obedience to a pretended Command from an Uncle, he broke off the Match.

---

1 A captain ranks below a major, and further below a colonel, in the military hierarchy. Sarah's father Edmund Fielding rose through the army officers' ranks to become a lieutenant general in 1739, two years before his death.

2 Two thousand pounds, the share of Ophelia's mother, would produce an annual income of £100, based on the then standard interest of 5%. This would be worth the equivalent of some £10,000 today: enough to provide bare necessities but not to live as a gentlewoman. As Linda Bree notes, Fielding's friend Sarah Scott, in *A Description of Millenium Hall* (1762), also suggests that a fortune of £2000 is inadequate, "the expensive turn of the world now being such, that no gentlewoman can live genteelly on the interest of that sum" '*The Adventures of David Simple*, ed. Linda Bree (Harmondsworth: Penguin, 2002) 459'.

3 A woman was expected to rest for a month after giving birth, and would be attended by a "monthly nurse" during this period.

As my Aunt had consented to Marry in compliance to her Father's Inclination more than with her own, her Indifference afforded her sufficient Consolation; her Lover's Behaviour filled her with Contempt, and Independance gave her Pleasure; but this was not long uninterrupted; she had Beauty to excite Love, and tho' her Understanding was uncommonly good, it could not render her insensible to the Charms of a young Nobleman, who became enamoured of her. A Woman's Heart is never in so perilous a Situation, as when Vanity joins with a Lover's Persuasions in attacking it. My Aunt at last grew so great a Slave to her Passion, that she consented to a private Marriage, which her Lover earnestly intreated as the only Means of reconciling his impatient Fondness with the Fear of his Father's Anger.

Soon after their Marriage, her Husband, who was in the Army, was stationed with his Regiment in one of the *American* Islands;[1] this gave my Aunt rather Pleasure than Concern; while she had his Company, she could not regret what she left behind; and as he promised to own her as his Wife when he had got so far out of the Observation of his Father, her only Uneasiness was removed, for notwithstanding she flattered herself, that when her Marriage should be made Public, she should recover her blasted Reputation, yet, tho' blinded with Love to the utmost Excess of Infatuation, she was mortified at the Wounds which present Secrecy made in her Character; I was the Partner of her Voyage, and we arrived safe at our destined Port.

In this Place we lived till I was two Years old; my Aunt happy, that the sole Endeavour of her Life, which was to please her Husband, succeeded so well; for tho' his Passion was visibly abated, yet still he was Easy, good Humoured, and Affectionate; but one fatal Day deprived her of this Felicity. After receiving a Packet from *England*, she perceived him thoughtful and uneasy; fearing some Misfortune had befallen him, she pressed to know the Occasion, but the more earnestly she Urged it, the more gloomy he appeared. Two or three Days passed in this Manner, which were most afflicting to her, who only lived in his Smiles. The Secrecy he observed, made her apprehend that the News particularly concerned herself, and judging of

---

1 One of the British colonies in the West Indies. In *David Simple, Volume the Last* (1753), Valentine and Cynthia move to Jamaica in the hope of making their fortune as planters. Fielding had a family connection in the West Indies: her paternal uncle John Fielding, who was Secretary to the Duke of Portland, Governor of Jamaica, died there in 1725.

his Heart by her own, imagined his great Pain was, how to impart it to her, and to support her under it; sensible that while he was well, nothing could make her wretched; her Desire of relieving his Uneasiness was greater than her Fear of any impending Evil which her Imagination could represent; and finding some Invention was necessary, to come at the Knowledge of what he would not Discover, she contrived to get at the Letters he had last received from *England*, happy in the Thoughts of putting an End to his Concern, by shewing him how well she could support any Misfortune while blessed with his tender Regard.

In this Temper of Mind she opened the only Letter he had not communicated to her; already prepared to acquaint him with the Effects of a Curiosity, which if ever it can be, was so in this Case, laudable; and to shew her Affection by her Courage and Composure; but, what was her Surprize, when she read the following Words.

"Do not imagine I am going to reproach the Man whose Perfidiousness I must ever despise; that Office I leave to your own Conscience, which must long, without my awakening it, have performed this Duty, tho' its Admonitions have had no effect on him who can break through all Ties, divine and human. I am above complaining of Injuries I can avenge, and only write to inform you that I will acquaint your Father with our Marriage, and your subsequent Behaviour, unless you, immediately, on the Receipt of this, declare it to him, and do me the Justice for which I patiently waited, till your Neglect of me, and Attachment to the Strumpet who now shares your Bed, changed all my Love into Rage and Resentment. Think not to intimidate me with the Effects of your Father's Anger, his Pride cannot inflict any Thing so cruel as your faithless Ingratitude has made me suffer. My Character will be cleared, and my Injuries revenged, which are the Wishes nearest the Heart of your much injured Wife."

Your Ladyship will easily believe that no Distress could exceed what my Aunt felt at the perusal of this fatal Letter. It was long before her Grief and Astonishment would suffer her to go through the Whole; frequently was she obliged to leave off, and give vent to Passions which for some Time rendered her unable to proceed, when every Line seemed armed with fresh Daggers to pierce her Soul. My Uncle did not come Home the whole Day, and she employed the Time of his Absence, after the first Burst of her Grief was abated, in obtaining a Command over herself, and a Composure of Behaviour, which might conceal her knowledge of his Treachery, till she could get into her Hands the Answer to this Letter, from whence she should more certainly judge of the Truth of the Affair. She was not long obliged to put this cruel Force upon herself; a Ship was to sail for *England* in two Days, and the Dispatches designed to go by it, were to be sent the Day before: My Aunt had laid her Plan, and it succeeded; but the Gratification of her Curiosity was to be always painful to her. With far different Sentiments from those with which she opened the former Letter, she now broke the Seal of her Husband's, though yet a Ray of Hope shone upon her afflicted Mind, and told her that possibly he might not be so guilty as the other had painted him; but this small and flattering Consolation was soon extinguished by reading the Contents, which were as follow.

"Can so much Cruelty and Beauty dwell together? and can the unavoidable Consequences of an afflicting Absence extinguish the remains of Love in that once fond Breast? my own Ruin I would Smile at, if it gave you Pleasure, did not yours depend upon it: Will you blast all my Endeavours towards raising you to a splendid Fortune, by an untimely Discovery? I shall soon leave this Place; stay then my Angel but till my return to *England*, and I will acknowledge you as the Choice of my Heart, and my Intreaties, united with the Force of your Charms, shall make a haughty Father confess you were made to adorn the Rank, which Avarice might wish to refuse you. That my Sincerity in one great Point may prove the Confidence you may venture to have in my Word; I frankly confess, I have a Woman here, but she is only the Amusement of my idle Moments, while all my serious Hours are spent in lamenting your Absence, and studying your Advancement. I cannot defend the inconstancy of my Actions, but my Heart has never wavered; let Youth, and this forced Separation from you, plead in my Favour, and incline you to forgive the Man who henceforward will live only for you, and be ever your most tenderly affectionate Husband."

CHAPTER II

My Aunt now convinced of her Misfortune, and spurred on by Resentment, carried the two Letters to the Governor,[1] and threw herself into his Protection. As soon as her Husband became acquainted with all that had past, he endeavoured to persuade her that his Letter was framed to pacify a desperate Woman, for whom

---

1 A governor-general, who served as the representative of the British monarch in the West Indies.

he never had but a childish Fondness, which ended with all his other boyish Fancies, but that to gain his present Purpose, he was reduced to profess to her the Sentiments he only retained for my Aunt; he assured her, that at his return to *England* he would have their Marriage ratified, and prove the other Woman's Claim was not legal; of the Falshood of this, his Letter was a sufficient Testimony; my Aunt, though she had at first suffered the Imputation, could not bear the reality of Vice; she absolutely refused to return to a House where Virtue would no longer permit her to inhabit: She demanded her Fortune and mine, which had been put into his Hands; but only five Hundred Pounds remained unspent; that, by the Governor's Authority and Influence he was obliged to pay her.

With this little Sum, my Aunt determined to fly all human Kind; deprived of the Object of her Affections, her Peace, and Reputation, what charms could the World have for her? She would relinquish all at once, and left the Country, with no Companion but myself, in search of a Retreat far from the Sight of human Kind. We landed in the West;[1] my Aunt's romantic Despair led her into *Wales*, where she found a small Cottage situated on the Side of a Hill, commanding a beautiful, though a wild and mountainous Prospect; at the Foot of the Hill was a delightful Valley, to which, from our Cottage, we were led by a fine Grove of Trees; on the side of the Grove ran a clear Brook, with several small Cascades intermixed, descending into the Valley, where it flowed in beautiful Meanders, till it lost itself in a little Wood. This Place was too well suited to a love-sick Despair not to excite my Aunt's Envy. She went to it, and found it inhabited by an old Man, and two young Women, his Daughters; she offered him whatever Price he would require, if he could be tempted to sell it. His Daughters preferring the human Species to the vegetable Creation, had, for above a Year, been endeavouring to prevail on the old Man to leave a Cottage, which was situated above twenty Miles distant from any other House; their Success continued doubtful, when my Aunt's Offer added Weight to their Persuasions. That one Sound of a little more than the Value, will tempt an old Man to sell every remaining Blessing. Avarice in the Use[2] of Life absorbs all other Passions; it is no Wonder, therefore, if so strong a Motive, united with the earnest Endeavours of the two Girls, procured my Aunt the Suc-

---

1 I.e., the West of England, at a port such as Bristol.
2 Altered by hand to "eve" of life in the British Library copy of the Dublin edition of *Ophelia* (1763), but "Use" is also possible.

cess she wished. The greatest Part of our little Pittance was laid out in the Purchase of this Cottage, a Garden belonging to it, the adjacent Grove, all the Pasture Land, with the Goats it fed, and some Poultry. My Aunt, besides necessaries for herself and me, carried several Books, Materials for Writing, and for various Kinds of Work.[1] The Impatience of the old Man's Daughters conquered the tediousness of Age, and my Aunt got into full Possession of her little Purchase, without more Delay than was necessary for her to learn to milk her Goats, and the other Parts of rural Business, so new to her. When the former Inhabitants left the Place, and my Aunt saw nothing about her but the Animals to whom she was to give her Care and Attendance, and from whom she was to receive the grateful Return of Support and Sustenance, except myself, then as ignorant of Evil, and almost as Dumb as they; she began to enjoy a greater Composure of Spirits; Despair was softened into Melancholy, and Air, Exercise, and all-healing Time, by Degrees alleviated her Sorrows, and at length raised her to Content and Tranquility. My Aunt's first Amusement was the adorning her Cottage; it was her last, likewise, for she was continually ornamenting it during the whole Time she stayed there, taking Pleasure in beautifying it, though no one was likely to behold either her or her Habitation. The Care of my Education soon shared her Leisure, and in Time became her principal Employment. But desirous not to lessen my Innocence and Simplicity while she dispelled my Ignorance, she gave me no account of the Manners and Customs of a People with whom she hoped I should never have any Intercourse. The Books she had brought into *Wales* were chiefly Books of Divinity, and such Histories as served to enlarge and instruct the Mind of the Reader, without informing him of the existence of Vices, which a pure Imagination, untaught by Observation and Experience, cannot represent to itself.[2] My Aunt so artfully diversified my Employments, that fond as I was of Reading, I had not perused all her little Library when I left this solitude, where I could for ever have contentedly remained. My Aunt's tender Affection, and reasonable Indulgence, filled my Heart and satisfied my Desires. We made our Nights very short, and yet our Days were never too long. The vernal Beauties of the finer Seasons charmed our Eyes, the tuneful Choir of Birds enchanted our Ears,

---

1 Needlework.
2 A six-page insertion in the Dublin edition of *Ophelia* (1763) follows here; see Appendix B below.

and both united to raise our Contemplations to their Creator; we were grateful for general Blessings, not less esteemed by us for being common to all Mankind, we wanted no partial Favours; we saw much to admire, much to rejoice in, and nothing to envy.

CHAPTER III

In this happy Tranquility I lived with my Aunt, till one Evening that we were just returned from walking by our little Brook, and admiring the Reflexion of the Moon, then at the full, and which shining on the Water, a new Heaven in its fair Bosom shew'd. Before we entered the House we were greatly astonished to hear a human Voice, a Sound so strange to us, that we could not sufficiently recover our Surprize to return an Answer to the Call; nor was our Wonder abated at seeing ourselves accosted by a young Gentleman whose Cloaths outshone the gentle Lustre of the Moon, at least to Eyes so unaccustomed as mine to any but the plainest Dress. At first, Surprize had fixed me to the Ground, but as I began to recover from the sudden Impression, the first Effect of my abated Fear was to fly from this strange Phantom, for such it appeared to me. I was directing my trembling Steps to the House, when the Stranger, with Accents of the greatest Earnestness and Distress, cried out, stay! beauteous Angel, stay! Whether the Harmony of his Voice, or the Sweetness of the flattering Appellation was most powerful I know not, but my Feet slackened their Pace, and looking round, I saw him bending towards me in the most suppliant Posture, with Gestures, which I thought almost prophane to address to a Mortal Being, yet was the Humility not displeasing. The Moon shone full upon him, and was bright enough to shew me a Face, which, notwithstanding female Vanity, the only innate Principle for which I contend, seemed to me far more beautiful than my own; a transcendency that before I could not conceive, having had no Opportunity of comparing myself with any Thing but my Aunt's faded Charms, worn with Age, and blasted by Misfortunes. Nor was my admiration confined to the Stranger's Countenance; in his Person appeared that elegant Proportion, that Delicacy, blended with Dignity, of which the Mind can judge without Rule or Comparison. It is not surprizing that, as I had never seen any of my own Species but my Aunt, and a few Times an old Man who had been at our House, on Occasions necessary to our rural Life, I should be struck with Beauty which I have not seen equalled since I lived in the midst of Mankind, and which had no bad Foil in the harsh Grotesque

Features of a *Swiss* Attendant,[1] who at that Time accompanied him. My Aunt, with a Politeness, ill agreeing with our rural Appearance, addressed the Stranger,[2] who informed us, that "having made a Visit to an Acquaintance on the Borders of *Wales*, the Face of the Country had so charmed him, by its wild and natural Beauties, that he had been tempted to spend a little Time in viewing more of it; accordingly he left his Friend's House two Days before, and travelled where his Fancy led him, without having been under any Difficulty for necessary Accommodations till then. Fine Woods and winding Rivers, had attracted him to some Distance from the Road, and he had pursued the way those Beauties led him, without having seen even an inhabited Hut since Morning; but had not till then given up the Expectation; when finding that in an extensive Prospect his Eye could discover no House but ours, he was induced to apply to our Hospitality for a little Refreshment, not imagining that by doing so, he should behold Charms that not only surpassed all the rural Beauties which had captivated his Fancy, but the most admirable Part of the Creation; such as must for ever make him forget that *Wales* or even the World, contained any other Treasure."

Flattery was so new to me, that I did not understand myself to be the Treasure he meant, though his Eyes, which spoke Nature's Language, an universal Dialect wherein even the Savage can want no Instruction, told his Admiration in terms more intelligible to simple Nature's Scholar; but my Aunt's Care informed me of the full Extent of his Expressions; no uncommon Effect of Prudery, which often discovers more than the most consummate Assurance. With a look of Indignation; "fye, Sir, said she, can you expect Hospitality from us, when you, with more than savage Cruelty endeavour to pervert with pernicious Flattery, a Mind hitherto Educated in Purity and Truth?"

This Rebuke, and the Stranger's Defence of himself, which greatly increased the Crime laid to his Charge; for it was only begging Pardon for the sudden Effect made on his Senses by the most striking Beauty he had ever beheld, left me no longer in Doubt for the

---

1   Swiss servants, with their reputation for reliability, signified the high social standing of their employers. The "grotesque features" of this attendant resemble those of Mr B.'s Swiss servant Colbrand in Richardson's *Pamela* (1740), whose alarming appearance the heroine describes in detail; see *Pamela*, ed. Thomas Keymer and Alice Wakely (Oxford: Oxford World's Classics, 2001) 166-7.

2   This scene is the first of three illustrated by Richard Corbould for the *Novelist's Magazine* edition (1785); see Appendix C below.

Application of his Compliment: But I could not find in myself any Sparks of my Aunt's Resentment; her's however, was pacified by the Gentleman's Assurances of restraining his Sentiments within the Bounds of Silence; and after many Intreaties, in which I at last joined, surprized to find Moroseness and want of Benevolence in a Temper which I before thought all Gentleness, Love, and Compassion, she was prevailed upon to admit the Stranger into our Cottage.

If he was so susceptible of Wonder, or surprized at the Sight of a pretty Woman, it is not extraordinary that he should be very sincerely Astonished at entering a little Hovel, and finding in it neat Rooms, furnished with the greatest Elegance, and so much in Character that even the Embroidery of the Chairs, Curtains, Bed, &c. was in a rural Taste; and every part of the House ornamented with things for which we had been indebted purely to Nature, and so peculiarly disposed as to excel all the Efforts of Art; nor had the outside of the House, the Garden, and the rest of our little Territory been neglected. The Stranger, to whom, I think, I must, to avoid circumlocution, already give his Title, and call him Lord *Dorchester*, though I knew it not at that Time, was amazed beyond Description, on entering the House. He began by an Exclamation which made my Aunt smile, and I found she did not think Compliments so dangerous when applied to herself, as when her darling Neice was the Subject of them. But I must do her the Justice to own that the more Places I have seen which the Art of Man has been exhausted to adorn, the more I am convinced that, on this Subject, no Expressions could exceed what her Ingenuity justly deserved. Sallads, Milk, and Eggs, were all our House afforded; these we set before our Guest with a Cleanliness and Simplicity, the Novelty of which delighted him, and with Truth he declared that the Whiteness of our Wooden Bowls and Platters scarcely were excelled by the Linen they were upon, were in his Opinion far preferable to Silver or China. The same Compliment he made to the freshness and sweetness of our Fare, of which, though he might well be supposed Hungry, we could not for a long Time get him to Taste, his Attention was so entirely engrossed by all the Wonders as he expressed it, around him. He asked us some Questions concerning our way of Life; I was so struck with the Novelty of the Adventure, and so abashed with the Presence of a Stranger, and his continual gazing at me, that I was quite dumb, but my Aunt freely answered him; and as our Actions were too Innocent to require Concealment, he received full Satisfaction. He made my Aunt some Compliments on her good Sense and Reason, declared the Admiration her way of Life had excited in him;

and, added with a Smile, that if she would excuse him, he must just observe that she had abated his Astonishment, at finding such a heavenly Form in that Place, since he now understood her Neice to be no more than one might expect; for, from angelic Food, an angelic Life, angelic Innocence, and the wise and virtuous Instructions of a Parent of more than human Understanding and Conduct, how could less Excellence be expected. He found that the uniting my Aunt in his Compliment would not excuse it; she knit her Brow, and awed him with Silence on that Subject; but his Eyes became so much more eloquent for the Restraint laid on his Tongue, that my Confusion was inexpressible.

His Curiosity was so happily tempered with Politeness, that though he at last enquired, how a Person, whose Qualifications shewed her to have been bred where every improvement of Taste and Understanding was to be acquired, first came fixed in such a Solitude, so little Impertinence appeared in the Request, that my Aunt, though she concealed the Circumstances, gave him such a general Account, as served at least to quiet his Curiosity. The greatest Part of the Night was spent in Conversation; but, at length, my Aunt, in Compassion for the Fatigue her Guest had undergone, offered him our Bed, the only one our Cottage contained; but he insisted on our keeping it, and assuring us he could sufficiently repose himself on a Couch that stood in the Room where we then were; we left him to his rest.

CHAPTER IV

After a short Sleep, rising to our Morning's Employments, we found Lord *Dorchester* up before us, and employed in examining our Library.

My Aunt expressed her Concern at not having had sufficient Conveniencies to afford his Lordship the necessary Refreshment the Night required; he assured her, "That was not the Reason of her finding him waking, but that his Spirits were so agitated with Surprize and Pleasure, arising from so extraordinary an Adventure, as he esteemed the finding two Persons, whom his Imagination continually represented as the Divinities presiding over that charming Country, that he had not been able to compose himself to Rest:" Adding that, "at the Dawn of Day, he arose to admire new Wonders, which he must call so valuable a Collection of Books, whose Merit made up for the smallness of their Number, but more still the Extracts from, and the Observations upon them, which he imagined were done by me, from some little Corrections in another fine Hand, which seemed to have been the Model of that wherein those Transcripts and Observations were written." The Confusion this gave me, severely punished my Negligence, in not having removed my miserable Performances into another Room. He soon made us understand by some polite Compliments, that he had examined into all the Papers, among which were many short Essays on Subjects my Aunt had given me as Exercises for my understanding, and several Things of that sort which had served as a profitable Employment, or as an Amusement for our leisure Hours.

His Lordship desired we would permit him to accompany us in the Business which called for our Attendance at that Time. He went with us to our Goats, our Poultry, and through all our Domestick Cares. We then shewed him our Garden, Grove, &c. The Elegance and Order with which they were disposed, charmed him as much as the Ingenuity that adorned them. The Seats, the Bowers,[1] the rustick Ornaments at the Outside of the House, excited his Admiration. At our Return, he begged Leave to stay with us till the next Day, that he might have Time "to come a little to his Senses, for that he could scarcely believe all he had seen was any thing but Enchantment."

My Aunt had preserved so much of her Resentment against the Sex, and was so greatly alarmed at every Hour I spent with one so amiable, that he could obtain no other Permission than what he might gather from her Silence. He put his own Construction upon it, and then acted accordingly. My Bashfulness wearing off by Degrees, during the Course of that Day, I got Courage to join in the Conversation, and, must confess, I never thought the Gift of Speech, peculiarly bestowed on Man, so great a Blessing. My Aunt, notwithstanding all her Prejudices, I could see was pleased with our Guest; his Justness of Thought, his Elegance of Expression, and the Liveliness of his Imagination, afforded us the highest Entertainment. I have since been told, that my Aunt would not suffer him to stay, but on Condition, that he should say nothing which might tend to lessen my ignorant Simplicity, having taken an Opportunity upon my leaving the Room of acquainting him with her Reasons for bringing me up in a happy Ignorance of Evil, which she hoped would never be dispelled. He then represented to her, the Impossi-

---

1   The bowers here would be formed from the natural overgrowth of foliage; bowers at country estates, in contrast, were carefully arranged by landscape gardeners.

bility of my "continuing my whole Life in that Solitude, unless, contrary to the Course of Nature, I should die before her; urged the Cruelty of secluding me from the Pleasures I might enjoy, and from the universal Adoration to which my Person," he was pleased to say, "intitled me, and to strengthen his Arguments, offered my Aunt any Assistance of Fortune, if Want of it had been her Inducement for flying from Mankind." She replied, "that was a Generosity for which such Simplicity as mine, might thank him, but a Person as well acquainted with the World as herself, would doubt what Gratitude it deserved, but must refuse it without Hesitation." Of this Conversation I could not then have the least Suspicion, and so well did he obey the Instructions he had received, that I got no Knowledge, though much Amusement, by his Stay with us. At Night he again took up with his Couch; and if the Dejection which appeared in his Countenance the next Day might be believed, he had not enjoyed more Rest on it, than the Night before; but finding it improper to intrude himself any longer upon us, about Noon he took his Leave, which he often attempted before he could execute; and, at last, he could not do it without the greatest Appearance of Force on his Inclinations. At parting, he laid aside his Fear of my Aunt's Anger, and took so tender a Farewell of me, mixing such very high Flattery, with his affectionate Expressions, as then rendered me incapable of returning any Answer; and now prevents my repeating them. While he regretted being obliged to bid me eternally adieu, a few Tears stole down his Face, and melted me so much, that I was almost ready to accompany them with some of mine. He looked back till Distance deprived us of each other's Sight: I grew pensive; and I remember my Aunt seemed disturbed at it. She endeavoured to amuse my Thoughts, but they were entirely engrossed by the Stranger: Whatever Subject she began, the Conversation was immediately turned to him. I own my former Amusements became less pleasing to me; I found less Attention to what I read, less Joy in the vernal Beauties which before delighted me, and innocently told my Aunt the Change I felt; who with a Melancholy, though a gentle forgiving Air, said, "she perceived her Company was not so sufficient to my Happiness, as mine was to hers."

This kind Reproach had the designed Effect, it first rendered me silent on the Subject, and making me think myself ungrateful in not returning an equal Affection, I took my Heart so severely to task, that I conquered, or thought I had conquered, this sudden Attachment, and was restored to my Tranquility, enjoying all the charms of our Solitude, in less than two Months after Lord *Dorchester*'s Departure.

This Victory was useless, for my Destiny had decreed that I should not abide there much longer.

CHAPTER V

On the Evening of a very hot Day I accompanied my Aunt to a Seat we had placed under the spreading Shade of a venerable Oak. The freshness of the Air made us unwilling to leave it, and with no other Light than what the twinkling Stars afforded us, we sat singing of Hymns, inspired by true Gratitude for the Blessings we enjoyed; when suddenly we were surprized with the Sound of the trampling of Horses; my Aunt immediately shrieked out, caught my Hand, and we were running with our utmost Speed to our Cottage, when I felt some one seize me, but it was too dark to distinguish the Face of the Person. My poor Aunt kept fast hold of me; begged, intreated, and used every Argument to prevail on him to let me go; we both kneeled to him, she beseeching his Compassion, I joining in the suppliant Posture; but more frighted with the Terror in which I saw her, than with any Danger I could apprehend, had not power to speak; and was greatly surprized to hear her Address him as our late Guest, reproaching him with Cruelty, Ingratitude, and the greatest Breach of Hospitality in thus returning the Reception we had given him. I could not imagine how she could suspect him of an Action that deserved such Imputations; I thought it impossible he should be guilty of any bad Thing, or that he who seemed to have conceived a greater Affection for me, than I could account for, in so short a Time, should wish to do me so irreparable an Injury as seperating me from my beloved and tender Aunt, which I now found was the Intention of the Person who held me. She has since said that she perceived Lord *Dorchester's* Passion for me to be so violent, that from the Time of his Departure she had been apprehensive of some ill Effects from it, and had never got a Dread off her Spirits; this made her immediately attribute the present Attempt to him. But how could I, ignorant of the Force of an unruly Passion, suspect it! My Aunt's Resistance and mine no longer availed than till another Person came up, who forced her to let me go, and, notwithstanding the Exclamations of Fear and Distress which we both uttered, one of them took me in his Arms, and setting me before him on Horseback, rode away as fast as the Intricacy of the Way would permit him.

At first my Terror rendered me almost senseless; I was frighted without knowing what I feared. I had indeed read of Murders, but then Ambition had been the Inducement: What had I to tempt any one to rob me of my Life? Such Wickedness could not be perpetrated without Temptation or Resentment. My Life had injured no one, nor could my Death be of any Benefit to them; therefore I could not apprehend being murdered; but my Ignorance of the Nature of the Dangers which threatened me, gave no Ease to my Mind. A Pannic is stronger than a reasonable Fear, and such mine was. After a Time, Grief succeeded to terror, and then I found some relief from Tears. The Misfortune of being separated from my beloved Aunt, of losing the Pleasures of her sweet Indulgence and tender Affection, was more than my Heart had Fortitude to support; and how was my Affliction imbittered, when I reflected on what she would suffer, deprived of her only Companion, the Object of her Love and Care; and anxious for the Fate of all that was dear to her on Earth! I wept her Sorrow, I wept my own unhappy Fate, in an excess so suitable to the Occasion, that when Day-light dispelled a little of the Terrors of my Situation, I was scarcely able to receive any advantage from it, being almost blinded with my Tears. And it was more from the Sound of a Voice once so pleasing to me, than from any Distinction my Eyes could make, that I perceived I was accosted by Lord *Dorchester*, who addressed me with every Expression of Kindness and Humility. The harsh Notes of a croaking Raven could not have been so grating to my Ears, as the Voice I before thought so harmonious.

I could not but greatly have resented the Injury done me, had it been by a perfect Stranger; but my Anger was much encreased, when I found the Injurer was one who had worn the Mask of a peculiar Regard. Hypocrisy was a Crime of which I had never heard; this was my first acquaintance with Deceit; and Hatred sprung up with it.

I was angry with myself for having ever conceived a favourable Impression of such a Wretch; and although this was, I believe, the first Passion I had ever been in, it had none of the Weakness of a new Emotion. A Person bred up in the continual Exercise of her Rage could not have expressed herself more strongly than I did to his Lordship, who endeavoured to soothe and pacify me, and he so far succeeded, that I lost all Utterance, from the Violence of my Tears: He seemed to feel my Sorrow, and wept with me. I then hoped Compassion had melted him, and seized the favourable Moment (as I thought it) to prevail on him to restore me to my afflicted Aunt: It appeared to me impossible that an Heart where Pity had ever dwelt, could refuse my Request; the ardent Desire of obtaining it, the Excess of my Sorrow and Despair, made me eloquent; I beseeched, as a Favour, what without the highest Cruelty and Injustice could not be denied me, and all the Resentment of an injured Person was lost in the Humility of the afflicted Suppliant.

I painted my Wretchedness in such strong Colours, that I at last became dumb with Horror at the melancholy Prospect; but yet, so little did it avail that I could not obtain one flattering Hope of being carried back. I could perceive he was extremely agitated, which made me continue my Intreaties, as long as I was able; but when I stopped, I learnt the little Success they had, by his crying out, "oh! my fairest, my lovely *Ophelia*! cease to distress the fondest Heart that ever was contained in a human Breast, by asking what it must refuse you: With what Joy could I comply with any Request that did not deprive me of you! Ask my Fortune, my Life, any thing but yourself, and it shall be yours: Could I have supported Life without you, I would have forborn this Violence. Your Happiness shall be all my Care, believe me my dearest Angel; though your presence is more necessary to my Existence than the Light of the Sun; yet would I restore you to your Aunt, was I not sure that in a little Time you would confess yourself happier with me, than in the dull Solitude from whence I have brought you, to introduce you into a Variety of lively and inchanting Pleasures."

"I know not your Pleasures, nor your Customs," I answered, "in my little Cottage were all my Desires gratified; and can I think that Man wishes me happy, who tears me from every Joy on Earth. My dear Aunt's tender Goodness and faithful Friendship, is a Blessing nothing can equal. You would persuade me that you have some Affection for me; are the greatest Injuries Proofs of Love? Does your Affection lead you to afflict the Object of it? When you restore me to my Cottage, I will believe I am not hateful to you; this is the only Way you can convince me. If my Heart was capable of feeling Hatred, I could not wish to torment the Object of it; nay, even you, whom I detest, I would sooner defend from Pain than inflict it, had I the Power over you which you have unjustly assumed over me: Can you be so different then, as to wish me Miserable, who never offended you? Who would not if I could."

My Tears would not suffer me to proceed, nor could Lord *Dorchester's* kindest Assurances, and most ardent Vows afford me the least Consolation. After travelling half the Day in this uneasy manner, we came to a beaten Road, where there stood a small Hut, as I thought, with two Horses fastened to it; into this, they put me; I had observed, that the Outside was fine and gay; very different from the little Hovels I had seen: The Inside likewise was neat and pretty, but seemed better calculated for Beauty than Convenience; for there was but just Room for us to sit. I did not envy the Owner his gaudy Habitation, which I imagined must be very uncomfortable to live in; when to my great Amazement I felt it move very swiftly. My Fright would have proved very dangerous to me, had not Lord *Dorchester's* Care prevented the Effects of it; for the Excess of my Surprize and Fear, made me attempt to get out at the Window; but his Lordship held me fast, till he reasoned me into Composure on that Account, explaining the Structure and Design of such Vehicles,[1] as well as their Safety. Though my Body had suffered too much from the Agitation of my Mind, to feel Ease from any thing at that Time, yet, I soon after grew perfectly well reconciled to this most agreeable Invention of the Luxurious: I did not immediately proceed far in it; for at Night, my Lord found me so much disordered, that he declared, he would remain at the Cottage, where, for Want of better Accommodation, we were obliged to stop, till I should be more able to prosecute my Journey.

CHAPTER VI

The Day after our Arrival at the Cottage, instead of being refreshed, I appeared in a high Fever, which in a few Days increased to so great a Degree, as made me expect from the quiet Hand of Death, a Release from all my Troubles. I was too unhappy to be afflicted at this Expectation. Grief for what I had lost, and Fear for what might ensue, fortified my Mind. Can the Wretched behold the Grave with Terror? that eternal Sleep from which no worldly Troubles can awaken them? that secure Asylum from the Injuries of Man, and the Frailty of their own Nature! In this pleasing Light, I then beheld it. Lord *Dorchester* was differently affected, he seemed to suffer from Anxiety, more than I did from Sickness. He was scarcely out of my Chamber, and attended me with a watchful Care, a tender Attention, which appeared far above the honest good-natured Humanity of the poor Cottager's Wife. If I was worse than common, it was more visible in his Countenance, than in mine. One would have thought his Existence depended on my Life. The least Amendment in me, raised him from a Despair, which again returned when the favourable Symptoms vanished. Conscious, that the Seat of my Distemper[2] was

---

1 Lord Dorchester's carriage is a chariot; see p. 82 below.
2 "Deranged or disordered condition of the body or mind (formerly regarded as due to disordered state of the humours); ill health, illness, disease" (*OED*).

in my Mind, he endeavoured to calm my Spirits, by promising, that, "if after a Year's Stay, in *England*, I still preferred my little Solitude, he would restore me to the Aunt, whose Loss I lamented." I thought myself so certain of a speedy Release from a World with which my first Affliction had disgusted me, as is common in the petulant Impatience of Youth yet unbroken by the Reverses of Fortune, that I believed this Consolation came too late, and relieved from my Fears, by my Expectation of an approaching End, I grew more easy, and had Leisure to attend to the apparent Signs of Lord *Dorchester*'s tender Anxiety. Tho' I could not comprehend how a strong Affection should grow in so short a Time, nor how such cruel Effects could be produced by Love, yet I began to feel some Compassion for his Affliction; I saw him suffer so much, that I almost forgot he had been the Occasion of my Distress. Even my Resentment was weakened by Sickness. My most turbulent Passions seemed buried in the Grave before me. His Sorrow, his passionate Lamentations, his tender Agonies and bitter Remorse, melted a Heart softened by the general Decay of Nature, and believing my own Pains near their End, I pitied his, which appeared then more acute, and likely to be more lasting. Every Look, every Word, and Action expressed his Love in such legible Characters, that I sometimes was ready to believe his Professions, though I thought his Affection must be of a strange contradictory Nature. But if all his Care and Tenderness only proceeded from a Return to Humanity, of which his first Action declared him at that Time void, I could not help owning to myself I never before saw that Virtue appear so very amiable. A Fortnight passed before my Fever began to abate, and it left me so very weak and low, that I thought myself nearest Death, when I really was out of all Danger of dying. Above a Month more, was spent in restoring me to sufficient Health and Spirits, to proceed on my Journey by gentle Stages.[1] The natural Strength of my Spirits and Nerves, which had then never felt any of the Disorders, that, in a Degree, afflict almost every Constitution in this Country, and by which, even mine has suffered since, returning, I bid adieu to my native Simplicity of Life. These natural Spirits, with the Turn of Thoughts my sickness had given, as I have already mentioned, which had rendered me liable to receive tender Impressions from my Lord's affectionate Attentions, together with his Promise of suffering me to return to my Cottage

---

1 Stopping places on main routes, where horses could be fed and travellers could take refreshment and lodgings.

in a stated Time, for I could not doubt but I should chuse to do so, greatly abated my Affliction, and I became capable of conversing with tolerable Ease, though my Heart was still oppressed with Sorrow.

The Evening of the Day we left the Cottage was come, before we saw any House of more noble Structure than that which had last harboured us. The first we drove by, appeared to me a most stupendous Building, though I have since learnt it was but a moderate sized House; and before Night, we stopped, at what I thought a sumptuous Palace. The Hospitality of the Inhabitants charmed me; they received us at their Door, and Pleasure sat on their Countenances; all their Words expressed a Desire of accommodating us agreeably; I could even have found Fault with the Impetuosity of their good Will, had not the Motive to which I attributed it excused, I might almost say endeared, the Inconveniences it occasioned. The Size and Colour of the Master and Mistress of the House, made me tremble for the Slenderness of my Waist, and Fairness of my Skin, in a Country which seemed so great an Enemy to the Shape and Complexion; but before the End of my Journey, my Vanity was pacified, but observing, that this extraordinary Bulk and Redness of Face, was almost peculiar to Persons in their Way of Life.

I admired no part of our Host's obliging Behaviour more than their leaving us as soon as we were seated. I felt myself too fatigued to make all the Returns my Gratitude suggested, and I imagined they left me to seek some Repose from Silence. Supper was soon after brought in, and the Master of the House followed, inquiring if we were served as we chose. I got up and brought him a Chair, making Room for him to sit down, and was shocked to see Lord *Dorchester* endeavouring to hide a Smile, but giving the old Gentleman no Encouragement to make Use of the Seat I had placed for him, who, with a Humility which hurt me, insisted on waiting behind my Chair. This made me extremely uneasy, and I was astonished that my Lord would suffer it.

When our Host and Supper were both withdrawn, I could not forbear expressing my Approbation of his indefatigable Hospitality, in sacrificing the Ease and Quiet of his Life to the Convenience of others, for I found we were not the only Guests; and touched a little on the outward Civility I thought due to him, whose kind Reception entitled him to our Esteem and Gratitude. I began to find my Apprehensions a little relieved by seeing there was so much Benevolence to be found in a People among whom I had been so forcibly introduced. Lord *Dorchester* soon put an End to this pleasing

Imagination, by telling me, that "the Reception I admired, was the Effect of their Covetousness, not their Generosity, and that their Hospitality was a mere Trade, by which they gained a Subsistence; and practised by none in this Country from other Motives." I at first exclaimed against the general Brutality, but recollecting that, my first, and hitherto only, Misfortune in Life, had been brought upon me, by our not acting with the same Churlishness, I told my Lord, "I was less surprized since I heard this, that he had not learnt how to make a proper Return to a Virtue so unknown to him, as Hospitality; and which I supposed, had been banished the Kingdom, from some such ill Consequences arising from it, as I had experienced."

Fatigue and the Relief my Spirits began to feel from the Dissipation of my Mind, by all the Novelty which surrounded me, made me inclinable to rest pretty early. Lord *Dorchester* studious to oblige me, and endeavouring to prevent my uttering a wish by his great Readiness to comply with it, before I had Time to express it, but by my Eyes, took Leave of me, saying, that "though he could converse with, and look on me for ever; yet he had rather put a Force on his Inclinations, than lay any Restraint on mine." And after asking my Permission, kissed my Hand with more Pleasure than I imagined it could bestow. Because he was pleased I was ashamed, I know no other Reason for my Blushes, for it before appeared to me, too insignificant to raise any. He then bid me a good Night, and left me to take some Rest, as I shall your Ladyship, bidding you Adieu for a little Time.

CHAPTER VII

Though the Relation of a Journey is often more tedious than the Journey itself, yet I will suppose your Ladyship's mental Fatigue to have been of no longer Duration than my bodily Weariness, and that after a short Rest, you are ready to proceed with me on my Journey. My Aunt had accustomed me to great Simplicity of Dress, I suppose, foreseeing the Inconvenience she should find, in supplying us with that Train of Variety used by People who live in the World. I had never worn any Thing round my Waist, but thin Waistcoats, nor any Cap in the Day-Time;[1] my Hair was extremely long, and curled

---

1 As feminine attire, waistcoats were worn as undergarments, in place of stays, or for warmth; fashionable women would always wear caps indoors.

naturally, for I knew no Art, and fell in Ringlets about my Neck, reaching behind below the Middle of my Waist, and in some Places incroaching on my Forehead,[1] enough to set off my Complexion by the Contrast, without hiding the Shape of it. This Peculiarity of Dress, your Ladyship may easily imagine, fixed the Observation of all who saw me; I soon became sensible of the Occasion of the excessive gazing so very painful to me, though accompanied by Expressions of Admiration, even to Exclamations of Astonishment; so fond are People of Novelty, to which, no doubt, I owed the greatest Part of the Compliments paid me. I begged Lord *Dorchester* to procure me a proper Head-dress, with which he unwillingly complied; so that before the End of my Journey, I made a decent and common Appearance.

Though I was amused by the Novelty of the Objects which passed before me in so quick a Succession, and by Lord *Dorchester's* lively and entertaining Conversation, yet I was not sorry when he told me, that our Journey was at an End; and that the House to which we drove, through a long and very wide Avenue of venerable Oaks, was his own; and the Place where our Travelling was to cease. The Magnificence of the Building first struck my Eye, but when I entered it, the Elegance of the Furniture pleased me still more. The Carving and the Pictures charmed me; the Country represented in these, appeared more enchanting than Nature itself, as the Painter's Imagination assembles Beauties, in Reality never found together.[2] My Raptures were not silent, my Admiration broke forth into Exclamations. I ran from one Room to another, desirous of seeing more, though not weary of what I had seen. Lord *Dorchester*, with Difficulty, prevailed with me to go with him into the Garden, before the Sun ceased to gild the Prospect. I was unwilling to leave a House which presented such various Beauties to my Eyes, but I could not regret it, when he led me to a Terras,[3] beneath which runs a rapid river of a considerable Breadth. On one Side it commands a very extensive and beautiful Prospect, on the other is the River, the Banks beyond which are very high, and covered with a

---

1 Ophelia's long, natural ringlets contrast with the shorter artificial curls worn at the back of the head (not over the forehead) by fashionable women.

2 Alluding to Plato's famous charge against painters and poets in *The Republic*, X.

3 I.e. terrace: a raised, level place in front of the house, designed for walking and admiring the view.

hanging Wood, ornamented with some fine Buildings, most judiciously placed.

From the End of this Terras, we entered into a Wood cut into various Walks, all terminated with fine Views, or some agreeable Objects, and many of them opening in different Parts, to let in either Prospects of the Country, or Views of the River, which runs through Part of the Wood with great Rapidity, falling down a Rock of a considerable Height at the End of one of the Walks. A little beyond this Cascade, it is hid from Sight for some Distance, and when it again appears, its Form is much altered, for it is deep, and yet so clear, that one plainly discovers every pebble at the Bottom, its Surface as smooth as Glass. In this Wood, likewise, are many Buildings most advantageously placed.[1]

The Garden is divided from the Park, only by a *Ha ha*,[2] unaccustomed to which Deception, I thought there was no Separation, till on the Brink of it. The Eagerness of an inraptured Fancy, charmed with all the Beauties around me, made me long to pass these Boundaries, but the Evening was so far advanced, I was obliged to defer this Gratification till the next Day, and only to admire, at a Distance, the Mixture of fine Lawns and venerable Groves, verdant Vallies and wooded Hills. The Extent of it is considerable, and the Variety of Grounds gives it an Air of Wildness, which greatly charms in the Midst of a Country so diligently cultivated, that one expects to see there more of the Beauties of Art, than of Nature.

When Night obliged me to return to the House, Lord *Dorchester* conducted me to an Apartment designed for me. The Bedchamber elegantly furnished; but the Dressing-Room most surprized me, it contained so many Things that were new to me, that I could scarcely guess their Use. The Ornaments and the Toilette[3] engaged my Affections for some Time, though had I been more accustomed to such Things, I should have been still more sensible of the Richness and Elegance of them. Every Thing in the Room had its Share of my Admiration, but after the momentary Wonder was passed, all

---

1 Such buildings, forming a part of country-house gardens, were designed for picturesque effect, rather than utility; Ophelia astutely notes their "advantageous" locations.

2 A ditch that forms a boundary, keeping animals away from the house without obstructing the view of the fields and woods. The word might derive from the cry of surprise of one discovering the obstacle; Ophelia thus reacts in the manner intended.

3 The articles on the dressing-table.

these nice Efforts of the Arts of the Ingenious, fell far short of my Estimation of the Beauties I beheld from the Windows, under which were Parterres[1] of the finest Flowers, mixed with the most fragrant Shrubs, and beyond them the River, the Wood, and the Park. When every Thing else had passed my Examination, Lord *Dorchester* opened some Drawers, and shewed me, that they were filled with Linen, Clothes and Trinkets, such as are customary in this Country. Having never had a Notion of any Thing in Dress beyond Neatness and Cleanliness, in the homeliest Garb, I could not help being struck at the Resplendency of all the Ornaments I beheld. The Fineness of the Linen I thought curious, but the Laces astonished me; they appeared to me of a Delicacy beyond human Workmanship. Had I been at Liberty to have indulged my Vanity, I should that Moment have tried the Effect of Things which I imagined must prove so ornamental. But my Lord's Presence awed me, and being told Supper was on Table, I was obliged to accompany him to another Room, where we spent the Remainder of the Evening, till the Hour of Repose parted us.

CHAPTER VIII

I that Night experienced, what People who live in Grandeur often find, that Pomp will not give Tranquility, which alone dispenses quiet Rest. The Agitation of my Mind allowed me very little Sleep. I had too much Matter for Reflection from Lord *Dorchester's* respectful and affectionate Behaviour, which I could by no Means think my Due, from my enforced Separation from my Aunt, and my former Habitation, dragged into a new World, wholly ignorant of the Reasons of my being so, or the Consequences of it, and from the pleasure I had conceived at the Sight of every Thing now offered to my Enjoyment; which my Lord even assured me, was my Property, affirming, all I beheld was my own. A Gift I could not suppose real, as the little I saw of the *English* in my Journey, gave me no Reason to believe them so generous and disinterested, as to make such Presents. In reflecting on these Subjects, I passed my Night, and had some Moments of Pleasure mixed with my Grief, but they bore little Proportion with each other; my Sorrow seemed deeply rooted, though its Violence was abated, while the contrary Sensation appeared only

---

1 Flower gardens in the area adjoining the house, laid out in an elaborate decorative manner.

a sudden Flutter, which played round my Head, but came not near my Heart, and would not admit of Reflection: However, I found it so comfortable a Resource, that I endeavoured to encourage it, and, prompted by Curiosity, at Break of Day, I arose to examine more minutely the Things which had so charmed me the Night before. If I believed any one was ever formed without Vanity I might be fearful of exposing myself by confessing mine; but I may hope to meet with Indulgence from one of my own Sex, who will candidly imagine herself in my Place; by her my Youth may be received as some Excuse, and if I am convicted of having had more than a common Share, may I not also claim some Title to unusual Sincerity in giving Room for the Accusation, and hope that Virtue may obtain a Pardon for my Frailty? I searched every Drawer, and after admiring the Things they contained, felt a Desire to try the Effect of this Profusion of Ornaments. The Night-Gowns, and common Undresses[1] were grown familiar to me, during my long Journey, therefore I laid them aside as not exciting my Curiosity, and selected the most resplendent Part of my Apparel and Trinkets.

For my first Trial, I chose a white Lutestring Gown and Petticoat, flounced with Pink and Silver Gauze, each Flounce edged with a Pink and Silver Fringe.[2] I wove Flowers and Jewels in with my Hair, letting the Ringlets fall down my Back, which I had lately confined under a Cap. I put a small Garland of the Flowers and Jewels round my Head, and a larger across my Waist and Neck, passing it over my Shoulder on one Side, and fixing it to the Bottom of my Waist on the other. I omitted nothing which I thought could adorn my Face and Person, and put on every Ornament that I could contrive to place becomingly. Finding my Gown too long without a Hoop,[3] I put on the smallest as a necessary Distortion, not as a pretty Part of Dress, but immediately threw away the stiff Stays[4] which seemed to me invented in perverse Opposition to Nature, and one of the

---

1 Morning gowns, which could be worn both indoors and out, and informal dress.
2 A gown made of lutestring, a glossy silk fabric. Petticoats were not undergarments, but a prominent feature of women's clothing. A flounce was a wide ornamental strip of material, sewn to the gown by its upper edge so that its lower edge could hang free.
3 Hoops, worn to increase the size of women's dresses, reached a remarkable size in the 1740s and 1750s, declining in the 1760s.
4 A corset, stiffened with material such as whalebone, to shape and support women's bodies.

Proofs with which I thought this Country abounded, that Man in his Folly had declared open War with her, and by pretending to improve, had so spoiled her Work, that scarcely any Traces of the Divine Artificer remained.

Thus equipped, the Employment of some Hours, I was so engaged in admiring my sweet Person, in the looking-Glass, doing honour to every Beauty I could discover, and making myself full amends for the Trouble I had taken, by the Satisfaction with which I beheld the Effects of it, that I did not perceive Lord *Dorchester*, who passed by my Window, and seeing me, your Ladyship will easily imagine, was tempted to take a nearer view of so diverting a Figure. He came into my Room without my perceiving him: When he entered the Chamber, he was beginning to excuse his coming in so abruptly; but on my turning round, surprized to hear his Voice, and ashamed at being thus caught in the ridiculous Indulgence of my Vanity; he was struck silent, perhaps, more from wonder at my Folly, than, as he pretended, "from Admiration at seeing me so much surpass myself, thus attired; having before, he said, thought me beyond the possibility of Improvement." I was sensible of the Flattery couched in this Speech, for with all my partiality to myself, I could not believe I had Beauty to surprize, though I fancied I had enough to please. He lavished every Expression that could shew me how much he was delighted with my Person. My Complexion, my Eyes, my Hair, every Feature, received new Praises; my Air and Shape, were not passed over in silence. He kissed my Hands a thousand Times, and would not part with them out of his. Surely no Eyes ever expressed such a mixture of Tenderness and Admiration; every look increased my Confusion: His Behaviour put me more out of Countenance, than the Reflection of having been found so foolishly employed.

I believe it was near two Hours before I could prevail on Lord *Dorchester* to cease his Flattery, or to take his Eyes off me; till at last I was reduced to tell him, that I should be glad to be left to undress, for that I was very hungry, and wanted my Breakfast, but could not appear before his Servants, thus apparelled.

He started at my saying this, and cried out, "how happy are you *Ophelia*, in that insensibility of heart, which suffers you to think of such Trifles! but how miserable does it make me!" I, who thought Breakfast a serious consideration, was surprized to find him so hurt at my mentioning it; and told him, that I could not comprehend how it should either excite Envy or Distress: But as he begged I would not undress till after Breakfast, on which Consideration, he would, himself bring it into my dressing Room, to humour my Desire of not being seen; I complied, glad to reconcile a difference of Inclination to which so serious an Air had been given.

My Lord immediately kept his Word, but during the whole Time, his Thoughts and Eyes were so fixed on me, that he did not well know what he did. He scalded his Fingers, spilt his Tea, let fall his Bread and Butter; and in short made such a Confusion, that I could not forbear laughing, though I had endeavoured it to the utmost of my Power: He at first blushed and sighed, but at last joined with me, and complemented me, in ridiculing himself.

It was almost Dinner Time[1] before I could prevail on my Lord to leave me, to put on Cloaths more proper for common wear, which at last he did, I dare say not a little pleased at finding that what he must have designed for captivating a childish Fancy, and corrupting by glaring Follies a Mind bred in Simplicity and Reason, had succeeded so well.

The remainder of this Day, and the next, were spent in seeing Lord *Dorchester*'s Park, the Extent of it, and the Variety it contained, made it a full Employ for that Time.

Two Days more passed in seeing some neighbouring Places, which were fine enough to merit Attention, though by no means equal in Beauty or Magnificence to my Lord's. In this time I had some Opportunities of observing Instances of his Humanity and Good nature, which contributed more towards abating my Fears, than his continual Endeavours to amuse me, to obtain my Pardon, and merit my Affection.

I could not believe that he had torn me from calm Happiness, for the Chance of making me happier, as he pretended; what he had done was a Mystery hitherto to me inexplicable; but I hoped the Man who could be humane and kind to others, would not be cruel to one who had the greatest Tye on his Generosity, that of being within his Power, unfriended and defenceless: Encouraged by this Hope I became able to converse with Ease, and ceased Reproaches, which might exasperate; but I had, by melancholy Experience, found were unavailing.

---

1   The chief meal of the day, dinner was eaten at about two p.m. In Richardson's *Pamela*, Mr. B. specifies two as his preferred dinner time, deploring the fashionable tendency to move the meal to later in the afternoon (369-70).

CHAPTER IX

The second Sunday after our arrival at this House, Lord *Dorchester* proposed my accompanying him to Church, to which I readily consented; though I had been taught to look on all Space as the Temple of the great Creator: Yet my Aunt had informed me that in populous Places there were Edifices erected for public Worship. When the Service was ended we walked over it; the Building is pretty, but then appeared to me too much calculated to please the Eye, and to fix the Thoughts on the Arts of Men's Hands, to be a proper Place for divine Worship; where the suppliant Soul should be intirely filled with adoration of the supreme Being to which it is dedicated. The little Fabrics the Church contained, by the Beauty of the Marble, and of the Carving, pleased me greatly, as Objects, but not as Ornaments for such a Place, till my Lord told me their solemn Purpose, informing me that they were erected to the Memory of his Ancestors.

This made me more particularly observe them, and I was soon deeply engaged in reading the Characters which I found engraven on them; this Perusal filled me with Admiration; such exalted Virtue as by these Testimonies I understood had descended through several Generations was a pleasing Subject for Contemplation. The little time I had been in the inhabited Part of this Kingdom had taught me that such Merit was not universal. My Heart was filled with a Respect approaching to Adoration, at thinking I trod on Ground sanctified by being the Repository of the sacred Remains of such God-like Men. I could not forbear addressing their departed Souls with a Zeal and Reverence little short of Worship; and praying for the Influence of their great Examples, towards enabling me to imitate their Virtues.

Lord *Dorchester* cruelly broke in upon so pleasing a Rapture, telling me, that I gave too easy Faith to the Words of Man; "though these are my Ancestors," said he, "I must confess few of them had any of the Qualities here ascribed to them. I might have suffered you, my dear *Ophelia*, to have continued in your Mistake, as it would perhaps, have given you more favourable Thoughts of the Descendant from such Worthies, had I not found myself envious of the great Share of your Esteem, which by these false Characters they had gained. Envy makes me tell you, that Epitaphs are formed on ideal Characters: The Writer collects together all the Virtues, Graces, and Accomplishments, that are scattered among Mankind; and when these are all blended together with all the Elegance he is Master of, he applies them to any one who, at his Death, wants that Memorial of his

Goodness, which his Life has not testified. To him whose Actions have raised no Character, a Tomb is erected to bear on it, that which an Epitaph can give him. Resemblance is never thought of; if the Deceased has not one of the Qualities described, it serves the Purpose just as well."

I was indeed inclined to suspect my Lord of Envy; I could scarcely believe what he said; but when he convinced me of the Truth of this Account, I sincerely resented the Pollution of these innocent Ashes, in being made Subjects of such Falshoods; and pitied the pure Marble, for having its fair outside defiled by such foul Lies. But what made this Practice appear still more ridiculous to me, was Lord *Dorchester*'s adding, that this was now so commonly known, that no one gave the least Faith to these Monumental Inscriptions; that it should have lost its Use, and yet be continued, increased my Wonder. My Lord likewise told me that many People left Directions concerning their Monuments. It is not strange if this appeared ridiculous to me then, since use has not yet taught me to see it in any other Light, nor made me cease to wonder that it should share the dying Thoughts of People, who, I should imagine, must all have something to leave behind more worthy their Care; and something to expect more deserving their Attention, than their own miserable Carcases.

I was not without Self-Love, but had no Notion that it could extend to the Dust into which we were to moulder, and make us desirous to fix our Claim to every particular particle.

Though I had not, till Lord *Dorchester* broke in upon my solitude, ever received a grain of Flattery; yet mere Nature and Constitution had given me a little Vanity, without the Benefit of Comparison, unable to soothe my Fancy with excelling Multitudes, since I had never beheld them, yet in a Degree I was vain: Nature alone suffices to make us so; but this kind of posthumous Vanity, was far above my simple Conception; and I complimented myself on my Humility, in being only reasonably fond of a living Form of delicate and curious Composition, absolutely indifferent to any poor Remains after delicacy of Complexion, symmetry of Features and elegant proportion of Body shall be confounded together in one little Heap of Dust.

Lord *Dorchester*, to save his Ancestors from my partial Censure; led me into the Church-Yard, where he shewed me that the Folly was universal, and that the Poor were as tenacious of the little Spot to which, after Death, they are consigned, as those who assert their Title to it, by nobler Structures. I confess, I was shocked at this distinction of Ranks; and to find that here the Rich and the Poor do *not* lie down together;[1] this Custom seemed to me to destroy the Equality of the Grave, which ends greater Contentions than those of Precedency.

Upon reading the Epitaphs of the meaner Sort, I found their Vanity was often confined within the narrow Bounds of having lived and died; they were little more than Certificates of their former Existence, proud to assert their having been of the human Species, for many of their wooden Monuments, more perishable than themselves, bear no other Inscription than the Date of their Birth and Death.

Though I was greatly disgusted with these proofs of the Folly of Mankind, yet at this Time the Living were more disagreeable to me than the Dead. I liked better to be an Observer, than the Subject of Observation: Though in my Dress I had conformed to the Customs of the Place, to the utmost of my Power, yet there certainly was a Strangeness in my Look or Air that drew all Eyes upon me, and which for many Years did not wear off, while I remained in the Country: I attributed it to the Curiosity natural to People who see few Strangers, but after I left it, I found that by living in a more populous Place I only had more Eyes upon me. Curious Observation fettering the Freedom of Action, I lived under constant and painful Restraint. My Lord endeavoured to make me easy by Flattery, attributing it to Reasons which might please my Vanity; but though I did due Honour to my Person, yet I could not give him Credit; and though I might now the more excusably believe it, that I have seen the Observation lessen as my Complexion has decayed; and that fewer Eyes have been upon me, since the Lustre of mine have been abated by Age; yet am I convinced that the only Superiority I had over many, who while I was present passed unregarded, was in the Air of a Stranger to every Fashion which she strove to follow; this gave the Charm of novelty to a Face and Person which could boast no other Excellence above a Thousand others which were less observed.

---

1 The allusion here might be to a poem in *Pamela*, probably by Richardson himself, in which the heroine cites some anonymous verses on "the *Rich*" and "the lab'ring *Poor*":

> ... *both alike* the *Will divine* pursue:
> And, at the last, are levell'd, *King* and *Slave*,
> Without Distinction, in the Silent Grave. (259)

There is also an echo of the Biblical prophecy in Isaiah 11.6:

> The wolf also shall dwell with the lamb, and the leopard shall lie down with the kid; and the calf and the young lion and the fatling together.

I would not have your Ladyship imagine that I am aiming to be thought humble; I am very ready to allow myself all the Beauty I am conscious I possessed, but Fashion, or Chance, often exalts us above our real Charms. If Truth did not oblige me to make this Confession, I should not venture to say it, for fear of being believed; for our Sex are as vain of having been, as of being handsome; and though they, while young, live in just terror of the Words, *She was*; yet when that fatal Period comes, their Vanity retires into it as into a Fortress; and secure in this strong Hold, from which nothing can expell it, it makes little Excursions, and supports itself with the Booty it obtains. One of our own Sex has told us with full as much Truth as Poetry, that,

"Women kind's peculiar Joys,
From past, or present Beauties rise."[1]

How often does a Woman's partial Report emulate in Falshood, the lying Epitaphs which shocked my innocent Simplicity! After the Small-Pox,[2] which frequently is the Grave of Beauty, how many women have I heard boast the Charms they never possessed! And soften the Mortification of Seams and Scars, by praising the former clearness and smoothness of their Complexions!

But this subject has led me from the Order which should be kept in a Narration; I have wandered from the Time to which I had brought my Story, and must correct my Irregularity by returning to it.

CHAPTER X

Lord *Dorchester's* desire of giving me every Pleasure in his power, led him to make me a Present of a Sum of Money: I would have excused

---

1 Anne Finch, Countess of Winchilsea, "A Pastoral Dialogue between Two Shepherdesses" (1709) ll. 79-80:
  That woman-kind's peculiar joys
  From past, or present, beauties rise.
2 Smallpox, commonplace until inoculation became widespread later in the century, left disfiguring scars. Four of Sarah's siblings (including Henry) were inoculated; Sarah had probably had smallpox naturally as a child, and may thus have borne smallpox marks herself. See Isobel Grundy, "Inoculation in Salisbury," *Scriblerian* 26 (1993): 63-5; and "Medical Advance and Female Fame: Inoculation and Its After-Effects," *Lumen* 13 (1994): 13-42.

myself from the acceptance of it, as it appeared to me entirely useless: Every thing I could want was provided for me; I wished therefore to refuse an unnecessary Burden; but he insisted, and I was obliged to acquiesce.

As I had learnt that Money was a very necessary Thing to those who were not so amply supplied with all it could purchase as I was: I thought it a Pity it should be so ill employed, and determined to distribute the Sum, to me so useless, among Persons who were in real Want of it. Accordingly, one Morning, when business had called my Lord a few Miles from Home, I walked out, in search of People who might be made happier by those Riches, which were to me intirely useless. I entered the first Cottage I saw, and bluntly asked the Inhabitants if they wanted[1] Money; they answered in the Affirmative, with an Eagerness which persuaded me they were in extreme Indigence. I now began to feel the Value of the Treasure before despised, since it could give such true Heart felt Joy as I received, from being able to relieve Wretches, of whose former Distress I judged by their present Extacies. When I gave some Guineas[2] to the Mother, she appeared quite frantic with Delight; though my Raptures were silent, yet I could not but think my Sensations were as strong. I, for some Time, indulged myself in the Contemplation of her Joy, but as my Ignorance of the Customs of this Country, so new to me, made me curious, I at last put a force on my delighted Imaginations, and enquired into the Use she would make of the Money I had given her.

Nothing but a full Knowledge of my ignorant Simplicity, can give your Ladyship a Notion of my Surprize, when I received for Answer, "That she would buy herself and Children handsome Cloaths, keep as good a House at the next Wake[3] as any Woman in the Parish, and never again work for a neighbouring Farmer's Wife, who was of meaner Birth than herself." I was shocked to find that I had been contributing to the increase of Vanity and Laziness, which must have been great before, or the good Woman could not have been so much overjoyed at obtaining the Power of gratifying it. I had no way to silence the Reproaches of my Conscience but by false Reasonings, arguing that when such unreasonable Desires are too deeply rooted to be conquered, they deserve our Compassion; and that the Money

---

1 I.e., needed
2 Handsome gold coins, worth twenty-one shillings (£1.05).
3 The next annual festival or fair of her parish, when she plans to hold a lavish reception at her home.

was better employed in relieving Wants, though they were but imaginary, than in being locked up in my Buroe.

A great Proof of my Ignorance of Mankind, was my Endeavour to reason this Woman out of her Vanity; Reason is too precious a Blessing to be in the Gift of Mortals; I could instill none into her Mind, and was at last forced to give up my Attempt, finding my Arguments had much less Influence on her, than the Desire of exciting the Admiration of her Neighbours. The Disappointment I met with in this Instance did not discourage me from continuing my Course: Such Vanity of Mind appeared to me a Monster in Nature; I could not believe the World afforded such another; therefore fearless of meeting the like ill Success again, I entered the next poor Cottage. I found the Man to whom it belonged, sitting in the Chimney Corner, with all the Marks of Sickness and Decay in his Countenance; his Wife industriously employed, and seven Children, the Eldest helping her, the younger Part playing about him. I looked some Time with Pleasure on this little Family, for Children were still a kind of Wonder to me, who had never seen any till I was torn from my Solitude; our own Infancy, by the gradual Increase of Years, making little Impression on us: I then put the same Question to these Cottagers as to the last I visited, but with less Impetuosity was answered by the sick Man, that "indeed they were very poor, and must have starved, had not his Wife been one of the best Women in the World. For he had been by Sickness disabled from working, above two Months, without Money to purchase a Cure." "Purchase a Cure," I replied, with some surprise, "is there any one who is possessed of the Power of curing Diseases, would require to be paid for it?"

"Alas!" said the Man, "nothing is to be had without Money, our Doctor must have his Fee or we can have no Cure." An Accusation of such Inhumanity made me exclaim with tears in my Eyes against this second Monster, which I thought I had discovered. I ask'd the Man, "Why, in such Necessity, he had not applied to Lord *Dorchester.*" His Answer was, "that my Lord's Steward was his Enemy,[1] and therefore he had no Hopes of receiving Relief from him, as he was ashamed to speak to my Lord himself."

I observed to him that, "Every one must be well recieved by

1   Henry Fielding's *Joseph Andrews* (1742) contains a memorable portrait (I.x and III.xii-xiii) of a rapacious steward, Peter Pounce, modelled on Peter Walter, who owned property close to the Fielding estate at East Stour.

my Lord, who gave him an Opportunity of exercising his Bounty and Humanity; that it could not be in the Power of any of his Dependents to prevent him from conferring Favours on the deserving, and relieving the distressed: But that had an Application to his Steward been necessary, whatever Offence he might have taken, his Anger must have vanished at the Sight of so much Wretchedness."

The Man shook his Head, and said, "Ah! Madam, you are very, very young, and I am afraid too good for this World, God grant you may not soon have Reason to change your Opinion of it."

I did not then understand the Force of these Words. I have since learned, that they must have proceeded from Surprize at my ignorant Belief in the Virtue of Mankind. When I had given Money to these People, I enquired into the Use they would make of it, of which they gave me so rational an Account that I doubled the Sum with the greatest Delight imaginable; happy in the Amends this made me for the Disappointment I found in the unworthiness of the last Person to whom I had given some Part of my Burden.

This Success encouraged me to continue my Round.

The next Cottage I went into pleased me by its Neatness. I saw only one Inhabitant in it; she was a very pretty Girl, extremely clean, tho' as coarsely dressed as possible; she was busy in her Dairy, and nothing about her wore such Signs of Poverty, as in the other Houses I had been in; however, desirous to see whether the Love of Money was universal, I asked her whether she wanted any.

The Girl, in answer, said she could not properly be said to want, since her Father and she, by Industry and hard Labour were supplied with the Necessaries of Life, but that she confessed she wished for Money, perhaps as much as the most Necessitous.

This appeared to me a Symptom of a depraved Appetite, but I enquired her Reason. To which she replied, that, "All questions were not to be answered." My Curiosity was perhaps more prevalent than my compassion, when I told her, "that if I thought the Motive of her Wishes a good one I might gratify them."

"If you will buy the Secret I am sure you deserve it," replied the Girl; and then very honestly informed me, tho' not without Blushes, "that a young Man in the Neighbourhood had loved her from a Child, and been equally beloved by her. That they were to have been married by the Consent of both their Parents, when, a few Days before the appointed Time, his Father died, and left Debts behind him, to the Value of twenty Pounds; an immense Sum to a poor

Labourer.[1] On this Account her Father withdrew his Consent till such time as the Whole should be paid. This was such a Spur to her Lover's Industry, that he worked far beyond his Strength, in order to raise the Money; and yet it was so much to save, out of a Labourer's small Profits, that notwithstanding his Endeavours, it must be some Years before the Debt could be paid off. She concluded by telling me that had she Money, she would shorten the Time of her Separation; during which, his Affection for her might cool, and the more reasonably as he might look on the immoderate Fatigue which oppressed his Mind, and overcame his Health, as the Consequences of his Love for her, and it was grievous to her to have that appear in his Eyes as the Source of any Evils."

A few gentle Tears trickled down the poor Girl's Cheeks, while she imparted her Apprehension, which moved my Compassion, as well as my Reason, to a Desire of relieving her. I instantly gave her the Sum she wanted, and was over-paid by the Delicacy and Vivacity of her Gratitude, from which I might not immediately have been freed, had not her Lover passed by the Window, bending under a heavy Load of Corn; this Sight attracted her with all the speed her Legs could use, and, winged with Love, she was with him before I had moved three Steps from the Spot where she had left me. I stayed a little to see the various Emotions expressed in their Countenances; she more delighted to tell, than he could be to hear; as the Fatigues he had undergone had more afflicted her than him, to whom they were sweetened by the Reward promised to their Success.

When their mutual Congratulations were over, I saw the young Man was accompanying his Mistress, as I imagined, to add his grateful Acknowledgments to hers, and that they might not have their more pleasing Conversation broke in upon, by a Return they thought necessary, I slipt out at another Door, and wandered on with the same agreeable Attention.

I had not gone far, when my Compassion was excited by the Sight of a Hut whose outward Appearance bore every sign of Poverty, and when I entered I found the Inside perfectly corresponded with it. It was one general Scene of wretchedness; the Inhabitants were almost naked, and seemed expiring with Hunger.

I was so much shocked at this Sight, that I could not speak to them till a few Tears had rendered my Compassion less painful.

---

1 For a labourer, twenty pounds would be the equivalent of some six months' wages, and thus an "immense sum."

During my silence they begged Relief, with all the Clamour of extreme Necessity; but could not be more desirous to receive, than I was to give, which I did liberally, emptying my Purse into the Lap of the Mother of the Family, whom I thought the properest Treasurer for the Whole.

Without staying to make any Acknowledgments, or leaving me Time to put my usual Question, the Woman ran up Stairs; upon this a young Girl, who seemed on the Verge of the Grave, burst into Tears, and was accompanied in them by all the rest, except an old Man, who sat by, and appeared insensible of all that passed.

I asked the wretched meagre Race, "what occasioned this sudden flow of Grief, when I had hoped I had administred present Relief to their Necessities?"

The sickly Girl answered, that, "to relieve them was beyond the Power of any Being, but him, who could change the Heart. My Mother's Avarice," added she, "will defeat the kind Intention of your Bounty; she is not the real Parent of any of us. My Father was esteemed rich for one in his Station, which tempted the Woman who has just been the Object of your generous Pity, to marry him, and thereby to reduce us all, who were the Children of a former Wife, to the greatest Misfortunes that can arise from extreme indigence.[1] She is so very covetous, that she will not afford Cloathing either for herself or us, or give us any wholesome Food; the little sustenance we obtain, just suffices to keep us enough alive to feel the Misery of continual Famine. My poor Father's Understanding was impaired by a stroke of the Palsy,[2] in a Year after she married him, happily losing thereby the quick Sense of his Misfortunes. Before I was brought into so very bad a state of Health, I used my utmost Endeavours to prevail on her to let me go to Service; but the Expence of Cloathing me as was necessary, if I left Home, appeared so formidable to her that she would never come into it."

I pitied this wretched Family more than ever, and when the Woman came down again, I tried all the Arguments I could devise, to prevail upon her to suffer me to have the laying out of part of the Money I had given her; but this Attempt so exasperated her, that she loaded me with Abuse, and I went away the Object of her Rage and

---

1 Through her father's three marriages after the death of her mother in 1718, Sarah Fielding acquired three stepmothers. In *David Simple* (1744), Fielding creates a devastating portrait of a cruel stepmother in the person of Livia.
2 Paralysis.

Fury, instead of her Gratitude; but was fully resolved to prevail with Lord *Dorchester* to administer Relief in a more judicious Manner to the Rest of this miserable Family.

CHAPTER XI

I had now disburthened myself of the Riches I had felt an Incumbrance, though they were a less Evil to me than to many others, since they would have lain by me neglected and unthought of, instead of betraying me into Vice and Folly, as is too often the Consequence. But, greatly pleased with having delivered up a Property of which my Indifference to it rendered me unworthy, I returned towards Home, strangely perplexed with the unaccountable Dispositions I had beheld in this short Progress. This Subject deeply engaged my Thoughts, when they were called from it by the melancholy Entreaties of a Woman who begged of me. She was sitting on the Grass, with two little Children by her, whom she was crying over.

I was now grieved that my Purse was empty and reproached myself for my too lavish Bounty. Though I was barren of the Means of Relief, yet I could not forbear listening to the poor Woman's Story, moved by an Appearance superior to such a Degree of Poverty. Her Tale was affecting; an Air of Sincerity in her Sorrow would have convinced me of her Truth, had I then been taught Incredulity, by the Observation of Deceit; but, at that Time, I should have believed a more improbable Story, as nothing could have appeared so incredible to me, as that a Person should utter a Falshood. I found the poor Woman was reduced by Misfortunes from easy Circumstances, and that she, her Babes, and her sick Husband, were really starving. As her Distress was so great, I desired her to accompany me Home, where I hoped to be supplied with the Means of relieving her, and Assistance in carrying her Children. A Burthen too great for her enfeebled Body.

Lord *Dorchester*, who was returned before me, being told which Way I was gone, came out to seek me, and met me in the Park with one of the poor Woman's Babes in my Arms, attended by her and the other.

I did not leave him Time to enquire how I became thus accompanied; for, as soon as he approached me, I told him, "I had been among Beggars, till I had learned to beg." Adding, that, "after I had so much Money, it was shameful to ask for more; but that I had spent all he had given me, in buying Experience, in making my own Mind wiser, and that of some others easier."

I then gave him an Account of all I had done, excusing my Errors, by my Ignorance of the Perverseness of the Tempers of his poor Neighbours, by which I had been taught, that "Charity does not consist alone in giving Money; for that those who bestow not Time and Care sufficient to discover the Merit and Necessities of the Objects of their Bounty, must often feed Vanity, Idleness, or Avarice, and render themselves unable to relieve real Distress."

Lord *Dorchester*, with a Look of sincere Affection, told me, "Nothing could make him so happy, as my affording him any Opportunity of giving me Pleasure. His Fortune could in no Way, be so conducive to his Happiness; and he thought I had laid out my Money to the best Purpose that ever any one did, since so much Experience, was never, he believed, so cheaply purchased."

He gave me a considerable Sum more, with a Chearfulness which shewed the Sincerity of his Word.

This Supply afforded me the Power of doing every Thing requisite for the poor Woman's Relief, and of enabling her to avoid the like Distress for the future. But though Money gave me, in this Way, great Enjoyment, yet I could not be quite pleased with the Invention of Coin. I looked upon it, as the Means of Unhappiness, and, therefore, could not forgive it, though it purchased me the satisfaction of relieving some of the Evils it occasioned. It appeared to me equally a Spur to Avarice, and an Incitement to Luxury. The ready Exchange of it for all Commodities, is, to the Vain and Voluptuous, as great a Temptation to Lavishness in Expence, as the Easiness of laying it up is to the Miser, to indulge the avaricious Desire of accumulating. People, whose Desires are inspired by Reason alone, can soon say, "I have enough of every Thing." But Vanity, Avarice, and Luxury, have no Bounds; they who are under their Influence, suffer almost, as much Pain from their ungratified Follies, as the Poor can feel from Indigence. I soon perceived that Luxury was universal, even the poorer People enjoyed such a Share of it, as surprized me, when I compared it with the plain Simplicity in which I had been bred.

I could not reconcile myself to Manners so unlike my own; I was not soon acquainted with many of their Vices, they were so unintelligible to me that I only accused them of Folly: But yet I saw they were void of the Simplicity I found in my own Heart. My Lord's Conduct shewed him possessed with many Virtues: But still I accused him of Inconsistency, for I could by no Means reconcile his Cruelty to me, with his Benevolence to every other Person. Though I grew too partial to him, to continue inconsolable for being separated from my beloved Aunt, yet still, often to myself, and sometimes to him, I called that Treatment cruel, and bewailed it with many Tears; especially when I reflected on what she must have suffered from the Time of my Departure; for I confess, I grieved more for her than for myself: My Lord's Conversation had Charms that afforded me great Consolation; but she could have none. I could not doubt his Affection for me; every Look, every Word, expressed it too visibly to leave any Room for Uncertainty. His Eyes were filled with Admiration and Tenderness, he could scarcely endure Absence for an Hour, all Joy would forsake his Countenance, the moment he lost Sight of me. But the Instant I appeared again, his Eyes shot Raptures, and welcomed me before his Tongue could utter a Word. It did not seem to me unnatural, that a Person who loved another so entirely as I was convinced Lord *Dorchester* did me, should be desirous of spending his Life in her Society. Not that I could excuse so forcible a Method of procuring it, nor quite understand how so strong an Affection as rendered my company necessary to his Happiness, could be conceived in that short Time. But I myself had found such an Attachment grow in so small a Space, as made it not appear to me absolutely impossible; and in no other Way, could I form any Sort of Excuse for Lord *Dorchester's* Violence, though my Heart longed to do it; for he had then got a stronger Interest in it, than I at that Time imagined. I could not suspect him of any ill Design against my Innocence; of all such Views I was totally ignorant, I knew not what they meant. The Shadow of such Schemes had never been represented to my Imagination, whose simple Purity received no Light from his Behaviour; which was so modest and respectful, that equal Innocence seemed to rule his Thoughts. Since I learnt how his Mind was corrupted by the Depravity of Custom, I have often wondered at his Command over himself; but, perhaps, he was fortunate in having none to observe him, but one so blinded by Ignorance, that she could not easily suspect him of ill. I thought his Love more tender and more ardent, than what my Aunt and I had felt for each other; this I attributed to a warmer Temper in Youth, and to the Probability that a Friendship for one of equal Age, might be stronger than where there was a Disparity in Years, as the Similitude of Taste and Disposition must naturally be greater.

A Woman sensible of the Dangers attending her Situation, might, perhaps, have taken Alarm frequently, when I saw no Cause for Fear; thus far my Ignorance was convenient to his Design, who wished to engage my Heart entirely, before I could suspect him. For this Reason an elderly Woman was appointed for my Servant; a Woman of

Sense, and more improved Education than any one ought to be, who could assist in so bad a Purpose; for she must have known the Motive of all the Instructions given her, to which she so closely adhered, that I never received the least Hint from her, that there ever was known any criminal Intercourse between Man and Woman. Equal Care was taken that no Book should fall into my Hands, that might lessen my Ignorance in this particular. My Aunt's History was kept as much a Secret by my Lord, as by herself, or that might have shewn how much our Sex had to fear from the other. To prevent my Eyes from being accidentally opened, if I went much about in the Neighbourhood, my Lord took Care, on one Pretence or other, after the little Excursion I have mentioned, that I should never go out without him, or my Servant, who, he desired might attend me, when he was obliged to be absent. By such Means was I kept in an Ignorance, that now appears to me, on Reflection, almost incredible; perhaps it will seem still more so to your Ladyship, for none can comprehend the Dulness of Apprehension in the Ignorant, who never knew that Ignorance.

CHAPTER XII

During the Remainder of the Summer, I indulged my natural Taste for rural Beauties; taught to admire Nature in all her Works, I could want no better Entertainment than what the fine Situation of Lord *Dorchester's* House and Park afforded me; especially when this was heightened and refined by his Conversation. He continued to instruct my Reason, and please my Vanity, at the same Time. Child as I was, he treated my Understanding with Deference, and appeared to me most happy when he conversed with me. He spent almost all his Time with me, endeavouring to open my Mind. When we walked out, or sat together, under the refreshing Shades the Park afforded us, he would turn the Conversation to the Objects around us, would lead my Thoughts from the lesser to the greater, from the vegetable Creation to the animal Œconomy, and sometimes rise to still sublimer Subjects. A Task for which nothing but great Affection for me, cou'd render tolerable to one of an Understanding so far superior. I could not but be delighted, when I observed how gracefully he would, by letting down his own Understanding, endeavour to raise mine, more to a Level with it, and that with an Air of Tenderness and Pleasure, not of Condescension, which by a seeming Humility, affronts our Pride.

I was sometimes inclined to fancy, that he was not so sensible of my Inferiority, as I was myself; if I made as poor a Figure in his Opinion, as in my own, I thought he could not look on me as a Companion worthy of him, and was afraid of mentioning my own Consciousness, lest I should open his Eyes to my Folly. None admire Knowledge so much as the Ignorant. My Aunt was no Philosopher; my Lord seemed inclined to make me one; and when I blushed at my Ignorance, would tell me, that, "in removing it, he meant not to represent what he taught as necessary to be known, only to open a Field to my Thoughts, which should be productive of constant Amusement, take from Solitude all Languor and Weariness; and by sharing my Mind in gayer Scenes, secure me from the Dangers attending a total Dissipation;" adding, that, "the Pleasure he received from observing the Quickness of my Apprehensions, and the Clearness of my Ideas, was no small Inducement to him to continue, as a Delight to himself, what he designed at first only as an Entertainment to me." Every Thing that bears the Face of Wonder, pleases a youthful Mind. I was charmed with all the Novelty which he represented to me, I was almost introduced into a new World, Nature wore a different Face to me; my whole Mind was engaged in contemplating her Works; and it was no small Proof of my Complaisance,[1] that I suffered the acquiring the *French* Tongue to divide my Thoughts; but Lord *Dorchester* desired it, and to please him, I applied to it with as much Earnestness, as if it had been the highest Gratification to myself. He encouraged me by Flattery on the quick Progress I made, and, by his Conversation, would enliven the dull Study of Grammar, and teach me the Language in great Measure by Discourse.

My Lord's Endeavours to amuse, were not wholly apply'd to my Understanding: My Heart was to have its Share of Pleasure. He made me the Distributer of his Favours; if he gave Relief to the poor, it went through my Hands; he enabled me to remove the Distresses to which I had been a Witness, and indulged me in my Desire of searching after Wretchedness, in order to redress it; requiring me never to go unaccompanied by my Servant, when he could not attend me; a Care which I then esteemed an additional Obligation. I was more officiously obeyed in the House than he was; his Servants seemed to have learnt from their Master to watch every Look that might signify my Inclination, which they would not give Time to rise to a Wish. They found this the

---

1 The act of making oneself agreeable.

serene[1] Road to their Lord's Favour, to which I was certainly indebted for all their Assiduity. Had real Regard for me inspired any one of them, he would have shewn it, more especially by warning me against the base Views, which they who are acquainted with the Manners of Mankind, must know their Lord entertained.

In this Manner my Time passed, till the Beginning of Winter; I was constantly employed, but never weary, for every Employment was made an Amusement; and I had nothing to prevent my being really happy, but the Loss of my Aunt's Company and the melancholy Reflections which would arise whenever I thought of her solitary State, and the Grief she must feel on Account of her Uncertainty concerning me. These would intrude themselves on my liveliest Hours; If I enjoyed any Entertainment, the Remembrance of her would check my Pleasure and reproach me for having given Way to any one while she was in Affliction. Could I have banished these Reflections, I should have been extremely happy. The Change of Season had not robbed me of all my Pleasures, it only varied them. The Ease of my Mind never depended on the gay Scenes of Nature, nor can my Chearfulness be clouded by heavy Skies, overshadowing the Sun. Every Thing that is agreeable is not necessary, the Decay of all vernal Beauties so little affected me, that I was shocked when my Lord told me, we must soon remove to *London*. I felt a Sort of Dread at the Thoughts of a Change of Place; the cruel State of my Mind during the only Journey I had ever taken, had made me associate very painful Ideas with that of travelling.

My Lord endeavoured to persuade me that I should prefer *London* to my country Habitation during the Winter: He told me of the Variety of Diversions, and Crowd of Company, which there, in constant succession, invite to Amusements.

This appeared to me no bad Opportunity of renewing a Suit, from which I had for some Time desisted; and, accordingly, I told him, that since that Place afforded such various Entertainments, he could not find the loss of so poor a Companion as myself; it would, therefore, be the noblest Proof of his Affection to comply with my ardent Wishes of being restored to my Aunt, whereby he would bind me in eternal Gratitude to his generous Humanity.

Despair of Success had made me so long silent on this Subject,

---

1 Altered by hand to "certain" in the British Library copy of the Dublin edition of *Ophelia*, but "serene" is also possible.

that I believe my Lord was the more shocked at hearing me renew my Request: I never saw greater Distress in a Countenance than was then impressed on his; he made me no immediate Answer, till seeming a little to recover himself, with a melancholy Air, which improved the Beauty of his Face, then bedewed with Tears, he pressed my Hand in his, and putting the other round my Waist, "can my lovely *Ophelia*" said he, "wish to leave me? Can you be insensible to the Misfortune it would be to me to lose that Society from which I can scarcely bear an Hour's Absence? Ask any Thing, but yourself, and judge of my Love, by the Pleasure with which I shall grant it: But Life has no Charms for me but in giving me the Power of conversing with you, and to relinquish one is giving up the other."

I was so moved with the Effect of what I had already said, that I could no longer urge my Suit; I could not even wish to go while he seemed averse to it, but told him, "It was not just to be offended with me for a Desire to return to one, with whom I had been so long united in Affection, consequently ought to love better than he could me, in so short a Time." "Cease my dearest Life," interrupted he, "cease to excuse yourself by an Apology more cruel than the Request. Compare not the cold, the dull Affection of an Aunt to that you have inspired me with; her Heart is incapable of such strong Sensations. In Pity to the Tortures your Indifference gives me, conceal it; allow me a Possibility of flattering myself again, that you make me some Return of Affection for all I feel for you; do not throw me any more back to the Pains of cruelest Disappointment, as you have now done, by the renewal of a Desire, to which I had hoped your Heart had ceased to prompt you. Surely I am the most miserable of Men, to be able to impart and teach you every Thing but that on which my Happiness most depends. Can your Mind only receive Impressions? Is the Heart of my *Ophelia* insensible to no Distress but mine? Will she who endeavours to relieve all other Wretchedness, increase that which she alone can Cure."

Tears accompanied his Words, and his Head sunk on my Shoulder: I could not forbear mingling a few with his; I grieved for having afflicted him, and wiping his Eyes with my Handkerchief, endeavoured to repair what I had done, with the strongest Assurances of my Affection, which indeed I never felt so powerfully as at that Moment; and, with a warmth which my Heart inspired, assured him, "that Gratitude to my Aunt for her care of, and Goodness to my helpless Infancy, and Pity for what she must have suffered on my Account, were the only Sentiments that could make me prefer her Society to his."

My unwillingness to give him Pain, made me ever after silent on this Subject: I thought such tender Affection deserved my Gratitude; and should have looked upon the urging this Request as a greater Breach of that Duty towards him, than my desisting from an unavailing Attempt was of my Want of Duty to my Aunt.

But neither the relinquishing that Hope, nor the kindest Expressions I could use, had power to raise my Lord's Spirits; his Dejection lasted some Days, during which he told me, "all I did now was out of Compassion, what I said before, was the Dictates of my Inclination, and while that Thought lasted, it was not in the power of Words to give him Consolation." However, these melancholy Impressions, which spread their Infection over my Heart, wore off before the Time of our Departure.

My Lord's Spirits were not raised by the Necessity of changing his Abode; he sighed after the Season of Leisure which left him to the free Enjoyment of my Company whereas his Winter Occupations[1] must frequently divide us. This was a mortifying Reflexion for me, who, both by Inclination and Custom was now taught to think his continual Conversation absolutely necessary to my Ease of Mind, while I was detained from my Solitude. But he would endeavour to persuade me that I should be better pleased in *London*; that Novelty and Gaiety would more than recompence me for his enforced Absence; and with this Notion he would increase his Dejection, though I often told him this seemed rather the Fear of Hate than Love, since his uneasiness arose from the Apprehension of my being pleased. He raved at my insensibility in Terms that I could not well comprehend, and made me find that Ignorance was dangerous when people are easily offended, for without Design I had several Times displeased him.

CHAPTER XIII

The Day before we left the Place Lord *Dorchester* told me, that "It would be advisable for me to be silent as to my Birth and former Way of Life, as well as to the Means by which I was taken from it; for the Oddness of the Event, would make People curious to see me, and so attentive in observing me, as would greatly Pain my natural

---

1 The London season for the fashionable ran from January until the beginning of summer in June. Lord Dorchester's winter "occupations" are primarily taking part in social activities; his "season of leisure," summer and autumn, would be spent at his country seat.

Bashfulness; and that if they perceived my Ignorance of the Customs of the World it would subject me to Ridicule." He therefore advised me "to give Way only to silent Wonder, if any thing surprized me, except when he only was present; for to him my Simplicity and natural Remarks must always be most delightful; but that to others it would be unnecessary to give any further Account of myself, than that I was under his Care."

Either my Pride or my Reason was hurt by the Concealment my Lord proposed; I believe the Former. Though untaught, Reason might have made me condemn those who could ridicule unavoidable Ignorance; yet only Pride could make me so warm in my Censure. I told my Lord, that, "The Openness of my Disposition made me ill qualified for any Concealment; that it would be scarcely possible for me to hide my Ignorance intirely; and when any Signs of it broke forth, it might make me appear ridiculous to such as knew not my Education; whereas those who did, could not be surprized at the necessary Effects of it. That were it a Misfortune or a Fault, it should rather excite Pity than Mirth. To triumph over the Weakness of others," I added, "is cruel, but when their Inferiority proceeds merely from the Want of Advantage and Opportunities of Improvement; 'tis no less foolish than inhuman, to be proud of a Superiority so obtained. To practice Virtue, is to live up to the Dictates of pure and divine Wisdom; to know our duty, the End and the Design of our Creation, and make it our Rule of Action; to adorn with pure and warm Devotion the Author of our Being: To be not only humane and benevolent to our fellow Creatures, but mindful even to what we esteem the lowest Work of God, is Wisdom and Knowledge, beyond what your Arts can teach; for by what I have already seen, in leading Men after vain Pursuits, they make them neglect the most important Duties."

My Lord answered, "that what I said was more agreeable to Reason than Custom. That the Multitude were foolish and inconsiderate, and would both blame and praise without just Cause. Such Opinions indeed, a rational Person might think below their Regard; but Experience would teach them, that Fools like other Reptiles could teize us with their Noise, notwithstanding our just Sense of their Insignificance."

He then represented to me, "How disagreeable I should find it, to have all Eyes upon me wherever I appeared; every one if I spoke, listening to hear what the fair Savage would say, and calling natural Reason and Sense, because little known to them, ridiculous Ignorance."

If he had not mollified the Term of Savage, he might have incurred the Anger so justly due to the People he described, but he gilded it with Love and Flattery, and the Vexation I had received at my first Appearance, from being gazed at, was so fresh in my Remembrance, that it prevailed upon me to consent to the Silence he required, concerning my past Life.

This was not the only Thing for which he was to prepare me; he now informed me, that we should not live in the same House. This shocked me, I knew not why; I could not restrain a starting Tear, I felt a Proof of abated Love; but Pride checked my uttering the Accusation, whilst Resentment under the Appearance of Surprize and Curiosity, enquired the Reason of it. My Lord told me, that, "his House was not large enough to receive me, with Convenience to myself; beside, that the great Numbers of People he was obliged to see upon Business, would be very troublesome to me." The Delicacy of these Reasons, which I did not doubt were real, made me speak plainer than Resentment had done; I assured him, that, "nothing could be so vexatious to me, as being absent from him, and that were we in different Houses, I must lose a great Deal of his Company, which I might otherwise enjoy, especially as Business would engage him so much at Home. For were I under the same Roof, the shortest Intervals would allow me the Sight of him."

Though he was transported with my Reason for begging not to be separated from him, yet he plausibly evaded all I could say, and brought me to acquiesce, though not to approve.

CHAPTER XIV

The next Day we bid Adieu to the delightful Place, where every Thing had seemed dedicated to my Inclination, and began our Journey to *London*. The first Day passed agreeably; the second was very favourable for Travelling and we set out early. But stopping on the Road to Breakfast, my Lord left me, and went to make a Visit in the Neighbourhood, where I was to call upon him after our necessary Refreshment.

Being told the Chariot[1] was ready, I went down Stairs, and finding it at the Door, got in, ordering the Servant of the House to tell my Lord's Servants to follow, not seeing them in the Readiness I expected.

---

1 A light, four-wheeled carriage, with a single back seat for two passengers.

As I had no Doubt but my Lord's Servant knew better where to call upon him than I did, I made no Attempt towards giving Directions, which could have been but very imperfect. Indeed, I had scarcely Time to seat myself, he drove on with such Rapidity. I was not inclined to complain of the Haste, for no Pace could seem too fast for me, that was to carry me to the Companion, whose Absence, short as it was, I found Time to regret. But after proceeding with unabated Speed for half an Hour, I began to wonder at the Distance which my Lord had called trifling; for we had gone some Miles, and yet were not arrived at his Friend's House. I grew alarmed, and could not help fearing that the Coachman had not received sufficient Instructions; I called to him, and exerted my Voice to its highest Key to make him hear, but all in vain; the Road was extremely stoney, and the Noise the Chariot made so great, that my weak Voice was drowned by it. I then recollected that I had never known it rattle so before; this might be the Effect of the Stoneyness of the Road; but yet I wondered, I should not have found it, in some Degree, in smoother Ways. The Lining and Inside appeared so much the same, I could not suspect I was in a different Equipage,[1] till the Coachman looking half way round, I thought, though I had but an imperfect Glance of his Face, that it was not my Lord's Servant. I then looked out at the Painting on the Outside of the Doors,[2] and was immediately sensible, that I was not in my Lord's Vehicle.

I now grew strangely alarmed, though I knew not what to think, and called to the Man to stop, as loud as I possibly could, but with as little Success as before; for my Voice had not received equal Strength with my Impatience; and after having screamed myself hoarse, was reduced to wait in Silence for a lucky Opportunity, to do what my Efforts could not; imagining something must soon stop our extraordinary Speed. In this Hope, however, I was disappointed, for it continued some Hours longer, which, fretted and fatigued as I was, appeared to me an Age. At last, the Chariot drove up to a House, and stopped at the Door; but I was by that Time, so confounded and hurried, that I was in a Kind of Stupefaction, and scarcely knew how to ask the Questions I wanted to have answered.

A fat old Woman hobbled out of the House to meet us, and opened the Chariot Door. My Consternation was too great to allow of much Connection in my Ideas, I cried out, on her taking hold of

---

1 A carriage.

2 An aristocrat such as Lord Dorchester would have his family's coat of arms painted on the doors of his carriage.

me, for her Appearance was disgustful, Who are you? Where's my Lord? What Place is this? not waiting for Answers to the respective Questions till all were uttered.

"Do not be in such a Hurry, sweet young Lady," interrupted the fat Gentlewoman, "you are with Friends, my pretty Dear; his Lordship's Honour will be here by and by. You know he must not come in broad Day-light; but fear not, as soon as it is dark, he will fly to your Arms, like any Sparrow to his Mate; and Pretty Ones they are in Faith. Ay, ay, he has an Hawk's Eye for Beauty, like to like, Beauty to Beauty, it should be so. All the Women long for him, and happy the she, that he vouchsafes to take Notice of."

If the first Sight of this Woman disgusted me, her Manner and Discourse were still more odious. As she attempted to lead me into the House, I insensibly resisted; I had no Reason to refuse it, but Confusion and Dislike directed my Actions, and I should scarcely have known how strongly they operated, had not the old Gentlewoman continued, "Why do you stare so, sweet Madam? though I am a Stranger, I will be as true and trusty to you, as ever a Woman you could meet with. You seem hugely timersome[1] truly, but I warrant we shall see you more couragiouser by and by."

Conquering Resistance which was unintended, I suffered myself to be led into the House, where she continued talking in the same fulsome Manner, till no longer able to endure her, I desired to be left alone, a Favour she would not grant, without a little Prelude to her Compliance. "A pretty Dear," cryed she, " she wants to think a little, well, well, think as much as you please till Evening. You tender ones love to pay it off with thinking: Well, Thoughts are free, as they say, or the Lord have Mercy upon us." Had not her Words flowed even more freely than her Thoughts could rise, I should have liked her Company better, and found less Occasion to cry out for Mercy, though she seemed to think Freedom of Thought so dangerous. The old Woman, indeed, was not mistaken in supposing I wanted to think, for I really had Occasion for a little Time to compose my Mind, in order to get some Light into this strange Event; but little could Reflection give me: I was more than ever at a Loss to guess at Lord *Dorchester's* Meaning in all this, and Thinking more increased my Perplexity. I repented that my Dislike to the Woman's Conversation had made me forbear trying if she could give me any Information as to my Lord's Intention, which was not impossible, as she

---

1 I.e., timorous, fearful.

seemed so well apprized of the Time he was to come there. My Repentance was in no Danger of being long, as a sincere Amendment may reasonably comfort the repentant Person, for in about an Hour she returned, and gave me an Opportunity of repairing my Neglect, though not so immediately as at her first Appearance I hoped to do; for till I had stood her Discharge of Nonsense; I had no Chance of being heard. Before I could make an Attempt to speak, she began.

"What still wishing, and wishing the Sun to make Haste to Bed? Yes, yes, to be sure, the Moon gives a more prettier Light to such a sweet Pair as you are. Well! a handsomer Couple one would not wish to see in a Summer's Day; you are perfect Beauty, Sweeting, and a more comelier Gentleman never trod this Earth. But, my pretty Jewel, one cannot live upon sheer Love; you will love the better for a little good Eating and Drinking. Do not think you shall be starved in this House; here it comes."

Accordingly, the Cloth was laid and the Table spread, in less Time than she had spent in her Preface to it; and she so notably bestirred herself in this Part of her Business, that I could not make her listen to the Questions I put concerning the Reasons of my Lord's so suddenly altering the Intentions with which he left me. I hoped for more Attention, when that Part of her Employ was over, but found her Thoughts had still a stronger Attraction; for when the Table was covered, her whole Faculties were ingrossed in doing Honour to her Entertainment, on which she made such Depredations, that I no longer wondered at her Bulk. I had little Inclination to eat, therefore repeated my Questions, but got no Answer, except, "she knew nothing of that. The first she had heard of the Affair was, that my Lord would be there as that Night, and that she might expect me in the Morning; as for any farther Design, she was ignorant of it." Finding I could learn little from her, I intreated her Absence, as soon as she had finished her Meal, and determined to wait my Lord's Arrival with what Patience I could. From him I hoped to learn the Occasion of this strange Whim, for as such I could but esteem it; and repined at my Fate, that had subjected me to be the Sport of any one's Caprice; for it had really a very disagreeable Effect on my Spirits. However, as I grew more composed, I began to persuade myself, that a Man whose Love had been so very sincere, could not mean to distress me; he could not be much to blame, Chance must certainly be partly in Fault; with these Reflections administring what Consolation I could to my Mind, I waited the Close of Day, and when that arrived, I durst not call for artificial Light, lest my fat Landlady should accompany the Candles; and she did not bring them voluntarily, I suppose, from a Notion, that I was asleep; for I got away, by expressing a Weariness, which was real, though a Desire of Sleep was not the Consequence of it.

CHAPTER XV

After I had been about an Hour in the Dark, I heard an Equipage drive into the Yard. My Heart now felt a Flutter it had never known before; this being the first Time of any long Separation from my Lord, I was, till now, ignorant of the Pain or Pleasure of Expectation. I knew not how very dear his Company was to me, till taught by being a whole Day without it. I immediately thought I penetrated his Design in this whimsical Adventure; imagining that he certainly had contrived it as a Punishment for my Desire of leaving him; and to prevent my re-urging that Request, by making me better acquainted with my own Heart, which could never be able to bear his Absence.

My Impatience would have carried me to meet him, had not the Want of Light made me unable to find my Way; however, I was pleased to discover by the Haste with which he ran up Stairs, that he was not less impatient to see me. The Door flew open, while his hobbling Guide puffed after him, with a Pace so unequal to his, that when he entered the Room, the Glimmering of her distant Light served only to give us a very imperfect View of each other. I scarcely could discern him before I found myself in his Arms. The Rapidity with which he flew to me, and the Eagerness of his Embrace, astonished and startled me: I never had seen any Degree of such Familiarity in him. I was not sensible of any Impropriety in the Expressions of Affection; but without knowing a Reason for it, I was disturbed with this Address. I could not think such Violence the necessary Consequence of Love; I was as much rejoiced, I imagined, as he could be, and yet such Behaviour did not appear natural to me. Suddenly we heard a Scream, accompanied by some Oaths in a hoarser Tone, which served as Base to the shrill Treble of the affrighted old Gentlewoman and terrified me to a great Degree. We presently heard their Steps upon the Stairs, and a Man crying out "Where is this Disgrace to my Family? restore her to me, or this Sword shall force her from you!" "never;" answered the Gentleman with me, in a Voice quite different from my Lord's, "never shall she be torn from these Arms; with my Life will I defend her." And caught fast hold of me, who was endeavouring to run as far from these horrid Threats, as I could. Had not Fear overpowered my Senses, I might have perceived there must be some Mistake in this Affair; but Fright and Ignorance made me incapable of drawing any rational Conclusions, and I had little Chance of recovering myself, as the old Woman entered trembling, with a Candle, followed by a middle-aged Gentleman, who had his drawn Sword in Hand, and Fury in his Eyes. A Lady, about the same Age, came last, though not behindhand in Anger, if one might judge by her Countenance or Words, both very expressive; but not the Shrillness of her Voice, or Sharpness of her Tongue, a Woman's only Weapons, could have terrified me so much as that same Instrument of Steel. Its Appearance was so aweful in the Eyes of the Gentleman I had supposed Lord *Dorchester*, that he let me go, that he might the better oppose his Assailant in the same Manner; and the first Use I made of my Liberty, was to fly to a Closet[1] at the other End of the Room, wherein I bolted myself with the utmost Expedition; for which I might not so conveniently have found Time, had not the Lady pushed her fat Guide, with a Violence which her Legs, oppressed by their Burden, could not support.

Down fell the mighty Load of Flesh upon the Ground, and the Lady not expecting to overthrow such a Mountain, had exerted her Strength too far, and by the old Woman's giving Way, was so drawn off her Bias,[2] that she fell over her.

Though I continued to tremble more than did Honour my Courage, yet I made Use of the Privilege the Glass Door to the Closet afforded me, observing through it, the Skirmish from which I was so happily delivered. The Clamours grew intolerable; the old Gentleman treated the young one with Fury; the younger returned it with Scorn; Names quite new to me were given and returned; each called aloud for Vengeance, but neither hastened to take it. Their Swords shone bright indeed, but appeared safe as in their Scabbards; as they were not quite resplendent enough to dazzle the Eyes, they seemed perfectly innocent.

More vigorously did our softer Sex exert itself; the Lady administred Fuel to her own Anger by reviling the Stumbling-block[3] that had ignominiously brought her to the Ground; she called her Bawd, ennobling every Sentence with that Name, which was so unknown to me, that I imagined it a synonimous Term for a fat Woman; she

---

1 A small room for privacy and retirement.
2 Course; the direction in which she was moving.
3 Here used in the sense of a physical, rather than a moral, obstacle or difficulty.

accused her of ruining her Daughter; and having worked herself up to a proper Spirit, fell to beating her most unmercifully.

The Victim of her Rage roared all the Time as if she expected every Blow would end the Life she had nourished with so much Pleasure and Care. At last, finding that Defence not sufficient to deliver her from an Enemy, whose Ears had been too much accustomed to her own, "troublous uproar,"[1] to be capable of being wounded by Clamour, she tried her Strength, and struggled with such Success, that she extricated her Arms from under her Antagonist, and returned the Blows. The Battle now grew very hot; fierce were the Attacks and vigorous the Defence. Tongues, instead of Drums animated the Combatants; for they did not suspend the Exercise of Speech, tho' their Hands sufficiently proclaimed their Animosity to Persons of any tolerable Apprehension; but they assaulted each others Ears with as much Violence as their Caps. Abuse flew as thick as Blows; and it was not long before they were both uncoiffed. The Loss of one Cap exposed to view a fine Head of grey Hair, tho' then cruelly dishevelled, that seemed to denote more Maturity of Reason and Coolness of Brain than was agreeable to what had passed. The other seized these hoary Honours; the Reverence they should have inspired being totally extinguished by Envy, which gave redoubled Rage to the Enemy. The same Accident happening to herself, having unfortunately exposed a Hairless Head, for Time had been more cruel to her; however, a few Grasps made such violent Depredations, that, as *Shakespear* says, *She made these Odds all even;*[2] for getting the better of the Partiality of Time, she reduced her Adversary to the same bald State as herself.

While the Women shewed an implacable Desire for revenge, the wiser Men still contented themselves with only declaring their Thirst for Vengeance. Their Resolutions seem'd all for Blood and Murder; every Word threatned Maiming, Scarifications, Wounds or Death; but they were too great Philosophers not to govern their Actions, though their unruly Tongues could not be controuled. They brandished their Swords, but each was careful to avoid giving any Scratch that might exasperate his Antagonist. In short, they stormed so exactly in the same Key that neither found himself so inferior to the other as to be reduced to call in a sharper Assistant. Nor could

---

1 Edmund Spenser, *The Faerie Queene* (1596) III.x.16.1: "Thus whilest all things in troublous uprore were."
2 Vincentio, in Shakespeare's *Measure for Measure*, III.i.41:
   "[...] yet death we fear / That makes these odds all even."

either prevail on himself to attempt the Destruction each swore to effect, till the old Gentleman recollecting he might gain the *Honour* of a *Murder*, without Danger of a mortal Resistance, *prudently* changed the Object of his Threats, and calling to me under the *flattering* Denomination of his shameless Daughter, swore he would break down the Door if I did not open it instantly; as solemnly assuring me, that when he could get me within his Reach he would pierce my disobedient Heart. This, no doubt, was a most *alluring* Invitation; he would have had an excellent Chance of bringing me out of my Sanctuary by such a Declaration, had I not grown sensible that I owed my Danger to a Mistake, and therefore the surest Way of avoiding the one, was to rectify the other. Tho' as soon as I became convinced of the Error which occasioned this Bustle, I began to find some Entertainment in the Fray, yet my Spirits were in too discomposed a Situation to be much pleased. I resolved to shew myself to quiet the Tempest, but knew not how to perform it safely; should that old Man remain as obstinate in his Error as the young one, he might deprive me of all Sense before I could restore him to his Senses; in Age, Anger will sometimes be quicker than the Sight. I therefore was resolved not to surrender at Discretion, but purposed to capitulate before I ventured out of my Fortress. I called out to them, that, "They were all mistaken in me, that I was united to none of them either by Blood or Affection; and if the Gentleman who supposed himself my Father would but give his Eyes Leisure to convince him of his Error, I would come forth to them."

The Promise I asked was given me, and I opened my Door, but I had not gone two Steps into the Room before the old Man, whose Eyes were grown dim by Age, and his Reason obscured by Passion, ran at me with his Sword drawn; I was flying back, into my Asylum, from whence I should not easily have been again tempted forth, had not the young Gentleman rescued me from the sudden End with which my Existence was threatened, by catching hold of the outragious Father. Upon the Promise of not letting him go till better Light had cleared up the Mistake, I consented to venture to approach the Candle, which immediately shewed them all, that they were in an Error, and gave Rise to a new kind of Uproar, one exclaiming for his *Harriet*, the other crying out for his Daughter; and all appeared so mortified to find a Stranger in her Place, that I began to apprehend a bad Reception, especially as I could give but very indifferent Answers to their various Questions. We were not long at a Loss to comprehend that all this Confusion was occasioned by the Servant at the Inn having informed me of the Readiness of this young

Nobleman's Equipage, instead of the Lady so furiously contested, and by my Heedlessness, which had prevented me from discovering the Blunder. The View of the Company was now to deceive each other, all declared the Impossibility of going in search of the Lady I had personated, in so dark and so stormy a Night, especially as the Road was intricate and hard to find. But as it appeared this was a Feint; for the old Gentleman, I suppose, considering that it would be difficult for him to steal a March[1] as he was lodged in the Enemy's Quarters, thought it better to relinquish his Hopes, in order to disappoint the other. Accordingly he told him, "He was convinced he only designed to bubble[2] him, in lulling him into Security, by agreeing with him in this Point and then setting forth after the Fugitive when he imagined his easy Dupe was fast asleep."

He acknowledged, "He had entertained the same Intention himself, but recollecting how difficult it would be to execute it, he was resolved to make it equally so to both, and would not go into Bed the whole Night, nor suffer his Horses to be unharnessed, nor his Servants to enter the House, unless his Lordship would consent that their Servants should be so lodged together, that they could not be ignorant of each other's Motions." Besides which he required, that the Keys of the House Doors, should be deposited in my Hands, and that I should not deliver them up till they met next Morning at Daybreak; promising "then to carry me to the Town from whence I had, by Mistake, been brought."

The ill Grace with which the young Nobleman agreed to a Proposal, that it was to no Purpose to reject, was a sufficient Proof that the old Gentleman had not mistaken his Views. A Supper was now served up, which I supposed was intended for a more amicable Entertainment. Every one eat as their several Disappointments would permit them, but none so little as my self. The Fatigue and great Agitation of Spirits which I had that Day endured, affected me very much; and the Uneasiness I imagin'd Lord *Dorchester* would be under, on my Account, with my Uncertainty of finding him at the Town where I was to be carried the next Day, was an additional Weight to my Spirits. However, Melancholy or ill Humour made us appear much upon an Equality, not a Word was uttered by one of the Company; the dumb Shew of Civility was scarcely kept up; and as

---

1 To gain an unexpected advantage over an opponent; in this case by leaving while the other is asleep.
2 Cheat, deceive.

soon as Supper was ended, the elderly Pair desired to have the Condition immediately complied with, and then to be shewn to their Chamber.

The young Lord would have deferred the Delivery of the Keys, on Pretence of the Earliness of the Hour, but Prudence or Positiveness, Qualities to be expected in old Age, rejected all his Evasions, in a Manner that shewed his Folly in presuming to form Expectations on the easy Credulity of one, who had arrived at the Age of Suspicion.

At last, yielding to Necessity, he delivered the Keys into my Hands, at the same Time intreating me to allow him an Hour of my Company; assuring me in a Whisper, that, "Could he obtain that Favour, he should esteem the Accident to which he should owe it as a very fortunate One." Adding, that, " A Glance of my Charms must efface the Impression which any other might have made on a Heart that had never felt their superior Excellence."

This bombast Compliment was unanswerable to my grovelling Genius,[1] so I attempted not to reply, and found no Inclination to grant his Request; for the Familiarity of Behaviour which confounded and surprized me, when I took him for Lord *Dorchester*, appeared odious to me, since I knew him to be another.

My Room was close to that wherein the Gentleman and Lady lay; as soon as I got into it, I bolted my Door, the better to secure the Trust reposed in me, fearing lest any Attempt might be made by the young Lord on the Keys in my Custody. Tho' I was not acquainted with the Merits of the Cause, yet I found myself inclined to the Side of the Parents; they had a natural Right over their Daughter; and might justly have demanded more Duty from her, than, according to the Appearances of the Affair, they seemed to me to have received. They had, among the Articles of Agreement, stipulated for my lying near them, which secured me from Molestation. Fatigue got the better of Vexation, and gave me, perhaps, a quieter Night than any of the Family.

CHAPTER XVI

Had not a Habit of early rising taught me to wake at Break of Day; the Noise in this House of Confusion would have

---

1 Natural ability; understanding.

—Broke the Bands of Sleep asunder,
And rous'd me, like a rattling Peal of Thunder.[1]

The Eagerness to depart raised them all at once, the Servants were hastened, they themselves hurried, and every Thing was ordered with so much Noise and Bustle that all were confounded; and their Intention was retarded by their Eagerness to put it in Execution.

I, by proceeding without any extraordinary Haste, was dressed and ready before any of the Company; and my Spirits being elevated by my approaching Departure from a House I had so little Reason to like, I found some Entertainment in observing how much they hindered each other by their general Hurry. At last, however, we got into the respective Vehicles, the young Lord, alone, in his, I with the old Gentleman and Lady. The former had pressed me to accept of a Place in his Equipage: But though neither of them seemed to promise a very amiable Society, yet the others appeared as if they would be the least troublesome.

To be alone in the Midst of Crowds has been the Counterpart of that Boast of abstracted Philosophy, so often, tho' so seldom, with Reason, pretended to, of never being less alone, than when alone; but my Companions might, without Vanity, have claimed all the Honour that can arise from that sublime Neglect of every Thing around us; for had each been the only Being on Earth, there could not have existed less Society. An absolute Silence was preserved during the whole Road, and such is the Force of Example, that though nothing could be more foreign to my Nature, yet I followed it implicitly, and was as dumb as my Companions. In this unsociable Way we travelled till the best Part of the Day was spent; for not having proceeded with the Expedition[2] I had done the Day before, I found it a long Journey, and somewhat the more so for growing very hungry; for none of the Company would stop on the Road. It was too much to mortify at once two such natural Appetites as Hunger, and the Love of Talking; but I could meet with no Redress. I did, indeed, break Silence just to signify my Opinion of the Necessity there was for a little Refreshment both for us and the Horses; but the only Consequence of it was a surly Sentence from the old Lady, by Way of Answer, who, in a grumbling Tone, said, "Those were lucky who

---

1 John Dryden, *Alexander's Feast* (1697) ll. 125-6:
   Break his Bands of Sleep asunder,
   And rouze him, like a rattling Peal of Thunder.
2 Speed.

were so much at their Ease as to think of such Things; for her Part, her Daughter had given her Dinner and Supper too; and if I had not been careless and foolish I might now have been where I should be." Thus rebuffed, I resumed the Silence which was never after broken by any of the Company, except by the Cough of the old Gentleman, who was somewhat ptysical.[1]

When we arrived at the Inn from which I had been so strangely carried, the first Person I saw was Lord *Dorchester*, who I afterwards understood, and then hoped, was watching at the Door. He rather lifted than handed me out of the Coach, receiving me with an Embrace, which I frankly returned, overjoyed at being once more restored to him.

My Lord led me into the Inn, and with Looks of inexpressible Delight repeated his Congratulations on my Arrival. He told me, that having waited at his Friend's House, long after the Time he expected me to call on him, he grew uneasy lest some Accident had befallen me, and came back to the Inn to learn the Occasion of my Delay. He did not long remain in Ignorance. He found a very handsome young Woman in the Inn Yard, almost frantick; all the People gathered about her, while she, insensible of the Ridicule to which she exposed herself, lamented her ill Fortune, and uttered all the Exclamations of Despair. Though the young Lady's Features were altered by Fear and Anguish, yet my Lord recollected that he had been acquainted with her in *London*, where she was educated by an Aunt with whom she lived, till her Father, who, though a Man of Fortune, was vulgar in Manners, and low in Understanding, gave her his Servant for her Mother-in-Law.[2]

The Scene was changed; he was now reduced to a more abject Servitude than his Bride was in before. This Woman insisted on her Daughter-in-Law's returning Home. Thinking her, while at a Distance, more out of her Power than was agreeable to her Love for her new acquired Dominion. Lord *Dorchester* had heard of this melancholy Change in the young Lady's Way of Life, and had pitied her, but was now alarmed by the Apprehensions of some much greater Distress. He enquired the Cause of her distracted Behaviour, and received for Answer, "that it was owing to another young Lady's having by Mistake gone in the Chariot, designed for her;" by which

---

1 Consumptive, asthmatic; corrected to "phthisical" in the 1763 Dublin edition and the 1785 *Novelist's Magazine* edition, and to "phthysical" in the 1787 London edition.
2 I.e., stepmother.

Means she was left without a Guide to the Place where she was to go; but the Occasion of her being so very much distressed about it they could not tell, nor what she meant by continually exclaiming, that "she was undone, should she be discovered, and was the most miserable Wretch upon Earth."

My Lord asked who it was that had gone in the Conveyance she so much regretted, when one of his Servants perceiving him in the Crowd, came up, and answered his Question, by telling him, "it must be Miss *Ophelia Lenox*, for she was no where to be found, and one of the Servants of the Inn had confessed, that supposing it her Equipage, he had informed her it was ready." Another belonging to the House soon confirmed this, by declaring, he saw me get into it, and had received Orders from me to bid the Servants follow directly.

My Lord was polite enough to tell me, that he was now a fit Companion for the disappointed Lady, being almost as mad as she was; till his Mind received some Consolation, by considering that the Mistake could not last long, and that he might get such Information from her, as would enable him to overtake me. Upon this, he prevailed with her, to go into a Room, where he could more conveniently enquire into the Affair, and she might with more Decency indulge her Grief.

The young Lady frankly declared to him, that from the Time she left *London*, she had received the most cruel Treatment from her Mother in Law; who not contented with the Sufferings she could herself inflict, had frequently exasperated her Father so much against her, that she had led a wretched Life. The Beginning of that Summer Lord ———came into their Neighbourhood on a Visit; he soon distinguished her by his Addresses, and, in the Opportunities repeated Visits gave him, had prevailed with her to fly from all the Miseries inflicted on her, and commit herself to his Protection. The Manner of her Flight was performed according to the Plan they had agreed on; when in the Middle of the Execution, I frustrated their Scheme, by my unlucky Mistake.

Lord *Dorchester* told me, that, out of a just Sense of the Duties a Child owes to her Parent, he endeavoured to persuade her against so great a Breach of her's, advising her to go to her Aunt; and assuring her of his most earnest Endeavours to prevail with her Father to consent to her living there.

His Care was not unavailing, the young Lady consented; and he hired her a Chariot, sending one of his Servants to escort her to *London*. All the Satisfaction he received was, from having reclaimed her from Disobedience, for she was so ignorant of what was to become of her after she got into Lord —————'s Equipage (his Servant being her Guide) that she could not give the least Account where I might be found.——However, after my Lord saw her set out towards *London*, he and his Servants went forth on a fruitless Search, till Night and Dispair of Success brought them back to the Inn, with an Intent of making a more exact Search the following Day.

Accordingly, they pursued their Purpose the next Morning as soon as Day appeared, but having been equally unsuccessful as the Night before, he returned to the Inn, still in Hopes I might be again brought thither. Reduced to this Expectation as his only Resource, he was walking every Way within Sight of the Inn, in the extremest Impatience, when his Attention was awakened by the Sound of two Vehicles from a cross Road. Probability was now unnecessary; the smallest Possibility is sufficient to flatter our Expectations in any Thing we ardently desire; my Lord's Hopes were raised, and were not disappointed; for it was our Equipages which had given Rise to them.

CHAPTER XVII

After I had performed my Part in giving an Account of all the Consequences of my Error, and made some severe Reflections on my Inadvertence; Lord *Dorchester* finding that the young Lady's Father and Mother were in the Inn, left me, in order to perform the Promise he had given, of trying the Force of his Eloquence, on a Mind too insensible to afford him any Certainty of Success.

Above two Hours passed in this Conference, at the End of which he returned to me, and informed, that he had not only prevailed on the Gentleman to forgive his Daughter's intentional Disobedience, in Consideration of her sincere Repentance, and to give her Leave to remain with her Aunt; but had even obtained the Permission, under his Hand,[1] with a Settlement on his Daughter, while she continued there; to put it out of his Wife's Power to make him recall his Promise.

I have related this Affair, as it was then told me; but I shall now give your Ladyship an exact Account of some Circumstances, which were concealed from me, till Secrecy was of no longer Use. What appeared plain enough to my undoubting Ignorance, would seem

---

1 In a document bearing his signature, and thus legally binding.

obscure to those, whose Knowledge of the World leads them to see a Deficiency in Particulars.

This Nobleman had not been long in the Neighbourhood of this Family, before he began to make his Addresses to the young Fugitive, and pretending to be unmarried, he feigned honourable Views, inventing Reasons for concealing it from her Father. He at last prevailed with her, to make her Escape from her Parents, and fly to him; promising to sanctify so rash a Step, by an immediate Marriage.

These Particulars she related to Lord *Dorchester*, who acquainted her with the Deceit put upon her Credulity; informing her, that the young Nobleman was already married to a Woman of Rank equal to himself; but was too well-known in the World, for a debauched dissolute Man.

After such a Discovery, it was not difficult to convince her, that his Views were far different from what he pretended, and that Marriage had been only made the Lure, to draw her into his Power. As Love had not extinguished her Sense of Virtue, little Consideration was requisite to determine her to fly a Man unworthy her Confidence or Esteem. But she durst not return Home, therefore could easier resolve what Course to avoid, than what to take. In such Grief of Mind, she was incapable of thinking to any Purpose; but Lord *Dorchester*'s Humanity led him to think for her, and, as I have said, he prevailed with her to go to her Aunt, from whose Goodness he encouraged her to hope a Pardon, for an Action rather rash than criminal, to which she had been driven by the ill Treatment of her Mother-in-Law, as much as she had been enticed by the Man whom she loved too well to suspect.

As I had no Notion a man could be guilty of so bad an Action, I simply believed the Story, as my Lord related it, who, chusing rather to take Advantage of my Ignorance, than to place his Hopes in corrupting the Innocence of my Mind, thought proper to conceal Circumstances, which must lead me into Reflections, that could not fail to alarm me on Account of my own Situation.

I had been so harrassed by the Events of that and the preceding Day, that my Lord would not attempt to proceed any farther till the next Morning; by which Time he hoped, I might be a little refreshed.

The Remainder of our Journey was performed with Safety and Quiet, nothing uncommon happening to us the rest of the Time. We arrived in *London* towards the Close of the Evening, and I was obliged to borrowed Light for the gay Appearance of the Multitude of Shops with which it is filled, and, by being much illuminated,[1] they received double Lustre. As all was new, all was remarkable to me, and at every Thing we drove by "I wondered with the foolish Face of Praise."[2] What then passed in my Mind, has convinced me, that Want of Experience makes us as meer Children at sixteen, as at six Years old. Every Gewgaw[3] charmed me; every tawdry Shop amazed me. I spoke only in Exclamations; every Look stared Astonishment. The Vivacity of my Sentiments made my Folly the more conspicuous; but it was, at last curbed, by observing, how much my Lord was diverted with my Behaviour. I wished him all possible Entertainment on any other Subject; but my Pride would not suffer me to continue the Object of his Mirth. With much Difficulty, I endeavoured to conceal my Emotions by Silence; but I found that my Eyes spoke them as strongly as my Words; and my Lord shewed me, to how little Purpose, a Person will pretend to act the Hypocrite, "whose Thoughts are legible in the Eyes."[4] He not only saw what my Silence would have concealed, but the Reason why I wished to do it; and, to gratify my Pride, said all that could serve to convince me, that, "Ignorance was no Reproach to those who had not the Means of Learning; all we received from Nature was Reason, this would give us a Sense of Virtue, and every valuable Sentiment; but as to the manual Operations of Art, it would be Stupidity not to be struck at the first Sight of them." By such Arguments he made me no longer appear so little in my own Eyes; I was again restored to my Speech, and forgave him the Entertainment he took in it.

My Eyes were so well amused, that I was sorry when we stopped at the House which my Lord told me was my own. The Rooms, after the spacious Mansion I had left, appeared small, but were elegant and pretty. And as I had regretted the loss of the Country Scenes I had left behind, my Lord informed me, that as far as was in his

---

1 The main shopping streets, such as Oxford Street, provided a high
   degree of lighting, by means of oil lamps, often praised by foreign visitors to London.
2 Pope, *An Epistle to Dr. Arbuthnot* (1734) ll. 210–11:
   While Wits and Templars ev'ry sentence raise,
   And wonder with a foolish face of praise.
3 A gaudy trifle.
4 Matthew Roydon, "An Elegy, or Friend's Passion, for his Astrophil"
   (1593) xviii:
   I trow that countenance cannot lie
   Whose thoughts are legible in the eye.

Power, he had supplied the want of them, having chosen a House so situated, that the back Rooms looked into St. *James's* Park.[1]

My Lord spent the Evening with me, acquainting me with the Number of my Family, which consisted only of one Maid, besides her I brought out of the Country, and one Footman.[2]

As we entered the House I observed a kind of Box, much ornamented, which attracted my Notice, and excited my Curiosity after the Use of it; this I was informed was a Sedan Chair,[3] which, that nothing might be wanting to my Convenience, had been bespoke before I came to Town. My Lord told me it was to be my Equipage, and shewed me Cloaths for the Chairmen, in the same Livery as my Footman; which differed from his Lordship's; and being left in it to his own Fancy, was the neatest and genteelest Livery I have ever seen.

When Lord *Dorchester* departed, being a good deal Fatigued with the length of our Journey, I went directly to Bed, nor could all the Novelty which had amused my Mind keep me awake. But sweet as my Slumbers were, I could not long enjoy them: Sudden Noises in the Streets awaked me in a Terror: I imagined that a dead Silence was the constant Attendant on Night; and having sat in a Room that looked into the Park, till I went to bed, I had not been undeceived in this Particular. A moderate Noise perhaps would have passed unheard by me, so soundly I slept; but some People engaged in a Quarrel, were so clamourous under my Chamber Windows, as must have roused even *Somnus*[4] himself. My Fright was so great, that I found myself at the Window, before I was sensible I had left my Bed; the Noise naturally drew me thither, in order to discover the Occasion of it: The crowd I beheld increased my Fears to a Height that rendered me motionless; but I was soon relieved by seeing them move down the Street, till they were lost both to my Sight and Hearing.

---

1 One of London's Royal parks, St James's had had a reputation for licentiousness since the Restoration, as Rochester's notorious poem, "A Ramble in St James's Park," suggests. The "Country Scenes" that Lord Dorchester might see from his London house are very different from those envisaged by Ophelia.

2 An elaborately uniformed servant, who would act as an attendant or escort of his employer.

3 Sedan chairs, carried by two chairmen, provided a convenient form of transport within London. They would be carried from the hall of the owner's home to the hall of the house being visited.

4 The Roman god of Sleep.

When the Danger was past, which I imagined had threatened me, I endeavoured to compose my Spirits and return to my Bed; but Rest was no longer to be found there. The Hour was come for the return of all my gay Neighbours to their Houses, which was proclaimed with a Noise that could not fail of disturbing the sober Part of the Neighbourhood. The Peculiarity of a Footman's Rap startled me very much; I at first fancied some strange disasterous Distress must be the Occasion of so great a Noise, but on more exact Observation, and hearing exactly the same sort of Knocking at different Doors, I began to discover an Art in it ill suited to any such Cause. Having no Notion of any other End in Knocking at a Door, that to make one's self heard, I could not suppose these Flourishes were used for so plain and simple an Intent; and at last convinced myself, that it must be one of the Pleasures of a People whom I thought capricious enough to be capable of any Thing that was ridiculous. This led me to some very severe Reflections on the Hearts of those who could indulge themselves in so foolish an Amusement, at a Time of Night when they must give great Disturbance to Persons who kept regular Hours, and might prove very hurtful to the Sick. I then had recourse to all my Learning; and with the Ignorance of many censorious Politicians, despised the Legislature which admitted such teizing Follies; and by drawing Comparisons between this neglect of Order, and the Accounts I had read of the Governments of some other Kingdoms, found, in the Disturbance of my Rest, good Reason to quarrel with our Constitution: Many of those who enveigh most strongly against it perhaps cannot assign a better. But as Politics, though enlivened by Anger and Censure, will, without Opposition become languid and dull; my wise and severe Reflections grew composing, and I again fell into a sweet Slumber. Sleep now seemed inclined to treat me like a Stranger, not with the careless dull Manner of an old Acquaintance, letting me be lost in Insensibility; but sparing no Endeavours for my Entertainment, represented to me the Cottage which had so long sheltered my Youth, gave me to my beloved Aunt's Embraces, whose Joy was beyond utterance, and to be equalled only by my own; Lord *Dorchester* shewing by his smiles the Pleasure he received from our Transports: and declaring himself rewarded by the Satisfaction we enjoyed for the Journey he had taken to restore me to her, begged leave to remain a constant Spectator of our mutual Affection. In this pleasing Deception was I entranced, only to be more afflicted by this unquiet Town; for all the sweet Delusion was at once put to flight by a Rap at my Door with a Club, as if designing to break it open, accompanied with a hollow Voice, which though loud was unintelligible to me.

I believe I was the more frighted for the Quiet I had in Imagination enjoyed; all I had hitherto felt was little to my present Terror. I ran to my Maid's Room, which was next to mine, and by catching hold of her, waked her. The Fear impressed on my Countenance, communicated itself to her Mind; she was little able to inspire me with any Courage, till I made her understand the Cause of my Fear, by desiring her to listen to the dreadful Voice which had alarmed me, but was now gone past my House, and accompanying the forceable Attacks the Club was making on other Doors. It was with Difficulty that Respect, assisted with a little Pevishness at being so unnecessarily disturbed; restrained her from laughing at my Fears. But with all the civil Gravity she could assume, she informed me of the Nature of the Grievance, and made me listen to the Words which had appeared unintelligible to me, till I understood enough to be convinced that they concerned only the Hour of the Night, and the Weather. I had not been inclined to believe this on her Word, suspecting she meant only to deceive me into a quiet State of Mind; and thought her Invention very poor, if it could furnish her with nothing better than so ridiculous a pretence, as that People should pay Money to be told the Hour and the State of the Weather, which, if they were asleep could not be of any Consequence to them, and if they were awake they might learn with less Clamour. My Ears, and some better Reasons she gave me for the Institution of Watchmen,[1] at last convinced me, and I left her to finish her Night's Rest, but not to mend mine, for the Repetition of the past Noises, and the Variety of new ones which succeeded them, soon overcame my Hopes of Sleep, and I quitted all Endeavours after it with my Bed, spending the rest of the Night in Reading and Meditation.

CHAPTER XVIII

I had long been well acquainted with the first Dawnings of Day, but was now, for the first Time, deprived of the Sight of the rising Sun, when Clouds did not conceal it from human Eyes. It was an Object that always delighted me; nor had I been accustomed to behold the Morning Light with heavy Eye-lids, and fatigued Spirits, which want

---

1 London streets were patrolled at night by the Watch: elderly men who would cry out the hour when the clock struck, proclaim the state of the weather, awake those who had asked to be summoned, etc.

of Sleep now made me experience; but as the Desire of looking on a more agreeable Scene than a narrow Street, had led me into the Dining-Room, from whence I had the View of the Park; weariness of Body and Mind tempted me to lie down on a Sopha, which made part of the Furniture of the Room, and here my Situation being much quieter, I enjoyed a little Rest, which sufficiently refreshed me.

The Sight of a great Town cannot but amuse a Girl, bred in Solitude: The Concourse of People in the Streets was a strange Appearance; all the World seemed abroad. I fancied the People were at once seized with an inability of sitting still. But tho' all I saw excited my Wonder, yet it did not sufficiently engage my Attention, to prevent my growing impatient for Lord *Dorchester's* Company. I had long been accustomed to see him every Hour; to pass a whole Day absent from him was Misery. I watched at the Window in painful Expectation of his arrival, till Evening robbed me of the Power of distinguishing Objects. In this uneasy State of Mind I sometimes feared some Accident had befallen him, or that he was sick; at others, I apprehended a still greater Evil, that the want of Desire, not the want of Power to visit me, occasioned his long Absence. This Thought brought me a relief from Tears, that enabled me to combat the Evils my Imagination had raised; but before seven o'Clock I had a better Consolation; for at last Lord *Dorchester's* Coach stopped at my Door.

My Spirits were so much sunk with the Pains of Impatience, that I could not receive him with that Joy in my Countenance, which the Pleasure he shewed in seeing me deserved. He flew up Stairs with such rapidity, that there was not a Moment's Space between the stopping of his Coach at the Door, and his entering the Dining Room.

He approached me with inexpressible Tenderness, complaining of the tediousness of every Minute of his Absence, and of the cruel Circumstances which had deprived him of a Possibility of coming to me till then.

Having Insolence enough to be piqued at not seeing him earlier in the Day; I replied, "That it must be almost impossible to many People, to deprive themselves of Amusements and good Company, without they had a stronger Inducement than a charitable Desire of relieving the Solitude, and inlivening the Mind of one who could return them no Entertainment to recompence them for the Sacrifice they made to their Humanity; and as I preferred his Happiness to my own, I was glad he had not endeavoured at so difficult a Task."

My Eyes, I believe, expressed some Resentment, but they were not free from gathering Tears, which shewed my Grief was at least equal to my Anger. He, in return, reproached me for my Inhumanity in giving him such a Reception. "Was the Pleasure" he said, "which he had been longing for all Day, turned into the Mortification of finding me offended with him; for the most cruel Disappointment he had ever experienced?" He protested, that, "he had never so ardently wished for my Company; and was incapable of receiving Pleasure from any Thing else." He then related the vexatious Circumstances by which he had been prevented from coming sooner, gave me such strong Assurances of his Affection by Words, and so much stronger still, in the silent Language of his Eyes, that I could not resist such Testimony: The most obstinate Incredulity could not stand before the Tenderness so visible in his expressive Countenance.

The perverse Temper in which Lord *Dorchester* had found me, served the more to recommend the good Humour that succeeded it; for want of a little Interruption it had begun to appear an habitual Easiness; and that, though always convenient, must cease to be meritorious, when it is discovered to be involuntary. Besides, my Pevishness shewed him as well as myself, how necessary his Company was to my Happiness; a Circumstance that could not but be agreeable to him, and could not be painful to me, while every Wish was gratified by his Presence, and the Charms of his Conversation left no room for Reflection.

We both complained of having been so long separated, and the Joy we shewed in each other's Company, proved that neither had exaggerated in the Description of what each had suffered for want of it. Conscious of no Motive that required Concealment, and ignorant of the Customs of the World; I saw no Reason for expatiating less upon my Uneasiness on that Subject than on any other. I knew not that the World would have allowed me to have grieved for the Loss of a Parrot, to have been wretched at missing a Masquerade,[1] miserable at being deprived of the Sight of a new Opera, or distressed to the last Degree at being disappointed of the principal Part of the Company at an approaching Drum;[2] but would never have

---

1 Masked balls, governed by elaborate codes of conduct, highly fashionable in the eighteenth century.
2 Memorably defined by Henry Fielding in *Tom Jones* as "an Assembly of well dressed Persons of both Sexes, most of whom play at Cards, and the rest do nothing at all; while the Mistress of the House performs the Part of the Landlady at an Inn, and [...] prides herself in the Number of her Guests" (XVII.vi). *OED* cites Eliza Haywood's *The Spectator* (1744-46) for the earliest use of the word.

forgiven me for declaring my Regret for the Loss of the most agreeable Companion that Society could afford me, if that Companion happened not to be of my own Sex. I, by no means apprehended that to declare I was pleased with the Conversation, and touched with the Affection of one tenderly attached to me, was an Offence to Decency, if the Person did not wear the same sort of Dress as myself. What my Heart innocently felt, I thought my Tongue might unreproachably utter; and accordingly, in the fullness of my Heart, spoke as frankly as my Lord, and with all the eloquent Warmth of Truth, describing the painful Sensations, and melancholy Reflections to which his Absence had given rise, as well as the Satisfaction in their being at an End, which recompenced me for all the past Sufferings. Blessings, by long Possession grow so familiar, that we, at last become insensible of their Worth, though they influence our whole Lives, and constitute our Felicity. We scarcely reflect on the Use of the Sun, unless some withering Plantation, that has been deprived of his kindly Rays, reminds us how necessary he is to all existence.

We knew not how to part again, since when once asunder, it was in the Power of perverse Circumstances to keep us so; and much of the Night was spent before Lord *Dorchester* could prevail on himself to leave me.

CHAPTER XIX

I had not been many Days in *London* before Lord *Dorchester* desired I would suffer him to introduce me to Lady *Palestine*,[1] a Relation of his, whose House was the Rendezvous of all the polite People in town, and where he assured me I should be well entertained.

The Vivacity of my Temper made me incline to Novelty and Amusement, therefore I readily acquiesced: A Day was fixed, and I was dressed with the utmost Elegance, and at no inconsiderable Expence. As Fashion, not Fancy, was to be my Guide, I left the Care of adorning my Person to my Maid, who exhausted her Art; and I dare say I should have beheld the Effects of her Labours with some Complacency, had I not been apprehensive of being gazed at for the uncommonness of my Education; an Impertinence by which I had sufficiently suffered on my first Arrival at Lord *Dorchester*'s; and indeed, in my Road to it, these Fears made me more disposed to find

---

1 Lady Palestine's name is surprising; *OED* gives the earliest use of "Palestine" as 1834.

Faults than Beauties in my Person. But my Vanity taking Alarm at this sudden Fit of Humility, brought Lord *Dorchester* to its Aid, who so strengthened its Party, that I promised, with pretty good Courage, to follow him to Lady *Palestine's*, where he was to go before, in order to be in readiness to introduce me.

Nothing had so much contributed to make me easy, as his Lordship's Assurances that no one but Lady *Palestine* knew any Thing of me, nor would ever learn from her, more than that I was a young Woman to whom he was Guardian, and therefore I had no Reason to apprehend any Observation, but what my Person excited; and he assured me that my Dress and Air were so conformable to those of the rest of the World; that there was no Room to suspect I had ever been secluded from it.

My Lord did not explain to me what was generally understood by the Word Guardian; but mentioning it as a common Thing, had I conceived any Doubts about the Propriety of my Situation, he would thereby have removed them; but I was far from imagining that being under the Care of a Gentleman, however young and agreeable he might be, was any Indecorum. I did not suspect any one of inclining to a Vice, of whose Existence I was totally Ignorant; and if I had been in that Particular better informed, I should have thought nothing so great a Security as being under a Man's peculiar Care and Protection. Some knowledge of the World was necessary to make me believe any one could wish to injure another, long Experience only convinced me that a Man could think of injuring one, whom he was bound by every tye of real Honour and Humanity to defend; nor could less have taught me that Men who act with the strictest Integrity to their own Sex, should imagine themselves less obliged to do so by ours, when they acknowledge that Nature by giving us greater gentleness of Mind, and more delicacy of Body, makes us dependant on them; which Custom has through Policy not only confirmed but increased.

But it is Time to end Reflections, which will be thought the Dregs of my recluse Education, and despised as vulgar and puritanical by the free and *polite* World, who are above such low Restraints as I may be willing to recommend; I shall therefore proceed with my Story.

With some Palpitation of Heart, I went to Lady *Palestine*; I knew she was to have Company, and the Expectation of seeing, perhaps, a Dozen of People together, discomposed that aukward Bashfulness which was the Consequence of the Solitude I had lived in; but the Flutter of my Spirits was turned into a real Terror on the Servants throwing open the Door of the first Room, which exposed to my View such a Concourse of People as I had never seen, nor assembled together in Imagination. I turned my Back upon them, and Fear being given as the best Defence to the weaker Part of the Creation, was determined to run down Stairs as fast as I could; but Lord *Dorchester*, who waited just by the Door, tho' in my Fright I had overlooked him, caught hold of my Hand, and then endeavoured to stop me by giving me Courage to encounter the Eyes of so large a Company; he lavished upon me that best Cordial to drooping Vanity, Flattery, and undertook to persuade me to endure to be looked at, by assuring me, that, "I must be the Object of the Admiration of every one who beheld me; and that if I found myself more gazed at than the rest of the Company, I might be certain it was from being more admired." This Argument has reconciled many Women to universal Observation; but with one educated as I had been, Bashfulness must be Proof against it; however, he urged one Motive that inspired me with Courage to follow him up the Room, which was shewing me how much I should oblige him by doing so. To give him Pleasure I could have performed more dangerous Adventures, tho' the passing thro' such Multitudes appeared very tremendous.

When Lady *Palestine* saw me, she came towards us, and received me in the most obliging Manner; spoke in the highest Strain in Praise of my Person, and thanked my Lord for giving her the Pleasure of my Acquaintance. This Flow of Politeness I received aukwardly enough; I was at that Time, by Confusion, rendered as incapable, as I was unqualified by Nature, for returning such Compliments; Expressions of Good-will, that I knew were dictated by Truth, my Heart could acknowledge, and therefore my Tongue could repay; but her Ladyship soared above my humble Conceptions.

As the Largeness of the Assembly made the Sphere of Lady *Palestine's* Care and Attention very extensive, she could not devote any great Portion of her Time to one Person; therefore I had sufficient Leisure to indulge my Curiosity by observing the Company; for tho' my Lord did not go to any great Distance from me, yet he was so engaged in Conversation with all the People around him, that he did not interrupt my Observations. There was something so affectionate in the Address of most of the Company to each other, that I was happy to find the People among whom Fortune had thrown me were so inclined to Friendship. I conceived a very favourable Impression of the whole Society, but was particularly pleased with one Lady, for her lively and affectionate Expressions of Joy at meeting with another;

and found myself so attracted by the amiable Disposition, I thought I discovered in her, that when she left that dear Friend, I could not forbear following her to the next: But how was I surprized to hear her, after practising the same Address, complain of the Penance she had undergone, in being obliged to suffer, for a whole Quarter of an Hour, the Conversation of the Lady she had left with all the Tokens of Regret! A secret Horror at such Falshood took Place of my beginning Attachment, and I flew from her as from a wild Beast; I believe too with a like Terror in my Countenance; for Lord *Dorchester*, whose Eyes were always upon me, enquired the Cause. The Manner in which I related it, shewed how much it affected me, and I was amazed to see him smile at it. I could not forbear asking him, "Why he chose to associate me with so vile a Set of People; for surely they would scruple no Crimes, who could unnecessarily be guilty of such flagrant Falshoods." Nor was I better contented when he told me, these were Expressions used by every one, but believed by no body, meer Words of Course. This made no Difference in my Opinion, but by giving me Reason to add the Charge of Absurdity in thus directing the only End of Speech to the Crime of Insincerity; it seemed to me a Method of ranking ourselves with the dumb Part of the Creation, in spite of Nature; all the Distinction was, that those Nature made so, could not pronounce Words, and the others rendered themselves so, by uttering no Meaning. I could not possibly allow, that the Obligation of joining in Society required any more of us, than to bury our Dislikes in Silence; to conceal a Truth, which, if known, may hurt, and can be of no Service, may be a Duty; but to pretend an Affection we do not feel, I esteemed criminal; and to express what we know will not, and what we did not intend should be believed, appeared to me an excessive Folly. The Disgust this little Incident gave me, made me attend less to the Conversation, and consequently more to the Persons of the Company; a Change that was not at all to my Ease; for I now found I had every one's Eyes upon me; where-ever I placed myself I was the principal Object; to move was to little Purpose, the Eyes might be different, but they were still alike fixed on me. The Gentlemen were more particularly troublesome in this Respect. If I sat down in hopes of hiding myself, it only drew them nearer lest any one should screen me from their Sight. My Uneasiness was visible in my Countenance; for I heard one Gentleman say to three or four others, "Come away, it is cruel to put any one so much out of Countenance." "That may be," answered another, "But it would be more cruel to myself to comply with a Bashfulness that adorns her."

All the Flattery with which Lord *Dorchester* had endeavoured to arm me against the Effects of such general Observations, had now no longer Power over my Mind; I could not persuade myself that I attracted the Notice of the Company by any thing but a Strangeness in my Air and Manner; and I was the more convinced of it by the contemptuous Glances of many young Ladies.

My Lord had informed me, that some ill-natured and some ill-judging People would despise others for their unavoidable Ignorance of the Follies of the World, tho' the Knowledge of them could have no good Tendency. These Signs of undeserved Contempt, gave me no favourable Impression of the Ladies, yet I liked them better than the rest of the Company: they looked less pleased indeed, but then they looked less at me, and that fully recompenced me for their Scorn.

I at last got Lord *Dorchester* to approve my going Home, and he immediately followed me, but found me so much humbled that I was quite dull. To cure me of my Humility was therefore much his Interest; and he laboured hard to persuade me into the Belief he had before tried to inspire; and to convince me, desired I would another Time observe the Difference between my Complexion and those of the rest of the Ladies; I was not so humble as to have overlooked that Circumstance; I had perceived a great Deadness in the best Complexions in the Room; and as I did not suppose there could be any thing very particular in mine, fancied it a strange Effect of the Light, till various Opportunities shewed me the contrary. This Advantage I could never attribute to any thing but having always kept such early Hours as Nature seems to have designed, having lived continually in the Air, tho' not much exposed to the Sun, and on so very spare a Diet, as by giving me the purest Blood imaginable, might communicate an extraordinary Clearness to my Skin.

I soon forgot the Uneasiness I had undergone; Lord *Dorchester's* Conversation banished every painful Thought, and the Pleasure he seemed to have received from my Appearance, recompenced me for what I had suffered for it.

Lady *Palestine* returned my Visit the next Morning; and invited Lord *Dorchester* and myself to dine with her the Day following, without any other Company. She was so easy in her Conversation, and courted my Acquaintance so politely, that, in a few Days, we became what the World calls intimate; that is, we saw each other often, and conversed with Freedom and Chearfulness. I found no Inclination to a real Attachment to her; she was rather amusing than engaging; she had a good deal of Wit, but Dissipation had robbed her of her Judgment. She was the Life of a Circle, but a dull

Companion *tête a tête*; and, as if she was sensible of this, she avoided them as much as possible, and delighted in a Crowd. Her greatest Happiness was a general Acquaintance, a Blessing to which she had attained.

CHAPTER XX

Your Ladyship perhaps begins to wonder that Lord *Dorchester* with the Views which you will suppose he had, would introduce me to a Woman of Fashion, where I might gain a Knowledge of the World; which, if it did not corrupt me, might frustrate his Designs by discovering them to me. That I may not leave this Improbability on your Mind, till the Course of my Narration clears it up, I will venture the Discovery, and inform you now, of what I long remained ignorant: For the Manner in which I at last came by the Knowledge you must wait till the Course of my Story leads me to it.

Lady *Palestine*, I have already said, was a Woman of Wit, and of considerable Rank; but her Fortune was by no Means equal to her splendid way of Life. At fifteen she was married to an old Man, who as he did not gain her Affections, could not greatly influence the Conduct of a Woman, who had been better instructed in Politeness, than in Prudence. Lord *Palestine's* Fondness, made her Mistress of herself from the Day of her Marriage.

The natural Vivacity of her Temper, and the Dislike to a Companion of an Age so ill suited to her own, led her into all the Dissipations which the gay World affords. Her Beauty, with the other favourable Circumstances of her Situation, attracted the other Sex; no Woman had more Admirers; naturally vain and lively, all received Encouragement, and few who strongly attached themselves to her, could complain of her Cruelty; however, as my Lord was pleased, the World was too obliging to take Offence. The Good-natured, in silence pitied her Errors; the Censorious, expecting a speedy Rupture from her bad Conduct, did not think mere Anticipation worthy the Attention of Persons accustomed to the more ingenious Exercise of Invention; and as the Consequences they expected from her Irregularity, made her less the Object of their Envy than Women of a less blameable Behaviour, they thought her an unworthy Subject of Discourse, and neglected her. Every one indeed called her imprudent, but were not the less desirous of her Acquaintance, since she gave Entertainments, had great Drums, and every kind of Diversion at her House.

Astrea,[1] with all her Virtue, were she now to come upon Earth, could not attract such Multitudes as a Card-Table.[2] People censure the Pleasures only of those who will not impart to others the Means of being pleased. If a Woman has Assurance enough not to be ashamed of Infamy, and a Fortune to afford every fashionable Expence; the World may blame her ill Conduct, but it will not desert her, while they censure her Behaviour they will Court her Acquaintance. I have learnt, that nothing is a Crime in polite Circles, but Poverty and Prudence. A Person who cannot contribute to the Follies of others, may perhaps be pardoned if she only complies with them; but if she attempts to be rational, she must not hope for forgiveness.

It is supposed, that Lord *Palestine* at last grew less infatuated than he had been; for at his Death, which happened when his Lady was about twenty-five Years of Age, he left her little more than her Jointure of 600 *l. per Annum*,[3] and his *London* House, Furniture, and Jewels. This appeared to a Woman of her Ladyship's Spirit, a poor despicable Pittance; it would have obliged her to have lessened her Pleasures; and if she had a proper Sense of the Consequences of retrenching, it must be allowed a serious Consideration; since the Splendor in which she had hitherto lived, had been the only Means of preserving her from Contempt and Neglect.

She could find but one Resource against the Evils that threatened her; as she was young, and in high Reputation for her Wit and Beauty, she thought it not impossible, for once, to reconcile Pleasure and Interest, and, accordingly, made those for whom she relinquished the Esteem of Mankind, give her the Means of purchasing their Civility, and outward Respect. She was too engaging to fail of Success in this Point: Her Wit and Politeness, for a long Time, excused the decay of her Beauty; and supplying by Art the depredations of Time, she was not destitute of Admirers, even when I was introduced to

---

1 "Starry maiden": the constellation Virgo, identified with Justice, and the last god to leave the earth.

2 The most popular card game, whist, was the height of fashion in the 1740s; on 9 December 1742, Horace Walpole wrote that it "has spread an universal opium over the whole nation" (*Horace Walpole's Correspondence*, 48 vols., ed. W.S. Lewis (New Haven: Yale UP, 1937-83) IX, 124).

3 Lady Palestine's jointure, the amount settled on her for the period of her widowhood, is several times less than that she requires to maintain her genteel standard of living. The '*l*' here, an abbreviation of the Latin *libra*, pound, is the eighteenth-century symbol for the modern £.

her Acquaintance, though she was then above fifty Years old; Fashion was a Charm of which Age had not robbed her, and continued to attract many Years after I knew her. But as this was not quite so universal a Magnet as Youth and Beauty, she found the Effects in a diminution of Lovers, and therefore was not averse to receiving Advantage from the Love of which she was not the Object.

Lord *Dorchester* had been one of her Train; more from Fashion and Indolence, than from Inclination; and as he knew Money had no more Charms for her than Love, he made little Scruple of acquainting her with his Passion for me, and of the Means he intended to persue. He wished to have me introduced into the World, as he thought it might both improve and amuse me; he knew not how to do this without running a Hazard of my learning more of it than was consistent with his Scheme, but by the Means of some Body who would concur with him in the Execution, and yet was on such a footing in the World, that her Acquaintance would not place me in a bad Light; for his Lordship did not chuse that any Person should have Reason to think ill of me, but himself. No one could be so proper for this Purpose, as Lady *Palestine*. She knew my Lord's Generosity too well to decline the Office, and complied with the Plan he directed, though she disapproved it.

She told Lord *Dorchester*, that, "in her Opinion, he would be more certain of Success by making me acquainted with all the Customs of Mankind; by treating *vulgar Prejudices* as they deserved; and shewing me how much more happy they were who set themselves above such *a low Way of Thinking*, than those *narrow minded People* who were governed by them. She offered to assist him in this Manner, which she esteemed much the best." But his Lordship differed in Opinion. He replied, "That what she said might be true, had I been educated in as great Ignorance of Vice and Virtue, as of the Customs of Mankind; but that on the Contrary, I was as much better acquainted with the one, as I was less so with the other, than those who are bred in the World. That he was convinced I should detest him, was I to perceive his Principles were less pure than my own; whereas he now had Reason to believe he had made some Impression on my Heart; and that as I was free from Suspicion, he could not but suppose he should find Opportunities from my Innocence and Love, which he might improve; and that all the Effects he wished from introducing me into the World, was, the dissipating my Thoughts, lest too much Reflection might teach me some Guard against him."

Lady *Palestine* had so great a Sense of female Frailty, she could not think Lord *Dorchester*'s Scheme absolutely impracticable, and readily agreed to obey his Commands; though an Intimacy with me was not very desirable, as it could not be cultivated in a Crowd. A gay Party at Supper was her greatest Pleasure, but in them I might have seen more of the World than was thought advisable, especially as Conversation was apt to take a free Turn at her Ladyship's House. However she sacrificed a few Hours to my Lord and me, excluding others. At her largest Assemblies I was judged safe enough; for though I there fell into Conversation with many People, especially the Gentlemen, for they were most watchful for Opportunities of speaking to me, and I was not more reserved to them than to my own Sex; yet Decorum secured me from the Freedom of Conversation, to which her Ladyship admitted them. She was likewise graciously pleased to carry me to public Places.

The first I appeared at was a Play. No one was admitted into the Box[1] to us but Lord *Dorchester*, who excluded all others that I might not confine the Emotions so new a Sight would raise in me. My Lord had often read to me some of *Shakespear's* historical Plays, and it was to one of these he carried me, never chusing I should go to any others;[2] and he gave me so poor a Character of the Performances of many of the other dramatic Poets, that I never felt a Desire of seeing them, tho' by the Play-Bills[3] I found there was great Variety.

Had my Lord's only View been by Entertainment, in this he would have acted judiciously; I have been convinced by Observation, that Plays and Novels vitiate the Taste: I allow many of them to be extremely diverting, some very fine; but by the Multiplicity of Events, mixed with a good Deal of the Marvellous; they learn the Mind a Dissipation even in Reading. The simple Chain of Facts in History, appear ill to a Person used to Wonder; as moral Truths, and sound Reason, do, to one who has been accustomed to the Turns and Quibbles of false Wit, the enchanting Jingle of Rhime, or the pompous Sound of high-flown Metaphors.

---

1 Enclosed accommodation, providing the most expensive and prestigious seats at the London theatres.
2 Shakespeare's most popular history play in the mid-eighteenth century was *Richard III*. Shakespeare's standing was far higher than that of any other dramatist, living or dead; Lord Dorchester's preference is not unusual.
3 Elaborately printed posters, providing detailed information about new theatre productions.

Not that I would exclude the Reading of such Authors as I mention. I am not insensible to the Charms of Poetry; perhaps was I more so I might not think it so unfit for young People. But I look upon it as dangerous, before Maturity has fixed some Degree of Taste, some Steadiness of Thought and Principle, as it is apt to render them ever after uninclined to such Studies as are useful, and of more lasting Entertainment. In short, I esteem such Reading as bad for the Mind, as high Meats[1] are for the Stomach; they may create a false Appetite, but will pall a true one, and make all proper Food appear insipid, till by long Use even they grow tiresome, and the true Appetite being vitiated, all alike disgust.

The very little I heard of such Performances pleased me for the Time; but being seldom, and of short Duration, they did not dwell enough on my Mind to lead me into any Comparison between the Entertainment they afforded me, and what I received from my common Studies; they amused without dissipating. Lord *Dorchester* dispensed them as a Cordial to my Spirits, when he perceived them inclined to suffer from the melancholy Reflections which would occur too frequently, as my Aunt could not be long out of my Thoughts. However, greatly as I had been entertained by the Plays I had heard, there was something so much more lively in the Representation of them on the Theatre as at first delighted me extremely. I had heard many of the Speeches much more to Advantage when my Lord read them; but in the Acting, the whole received such an Air of Truth, that I could scarcely disbelieve a Fact in it. This made my Agitations almost as strange as if I had been the Spectator of a real Tragedy. The Play was *Macbeth*,[2] and Lord *Dorchester* and Lady *Palestine* were sufficiently taken up in observing the Passions imprest on my Countenance. They told me, I might more properly be said to act the Play, than some of the Persons on the Stage. Indeed, I believe I was more fatigued with my part of the Representation; for when it was over, I found my Mind quite weary with the Agitation it had been in. Anger was one of the Passions that had been excited, for I could not bear with Patience the Noises that were sometimes

---

1 Meat such as game tending towards decomposition, favoured by gourmands.
2 Assuming that Ophelia saw a performance of *Macbeth* before 1744, it would have been in William Davenant's adaptation of 1674, which held the stage until David Garrick restored most of Shakespeare's text. Of all Shakespeare's plays, *Macbeth* was second in popularity only to *Hamlet* in the eighteenth century.

made; and was so intirely engaged that I could not utter a rational Sentence on any other Subject, even between the Acts: Nor did the Change of Scene change my Ideas: for after I went Home, they continued as much fixed on the Play, as during the Representation; and it was almost with Difficulty they at last gave place to Sleep.

CHAPTER XXI

Lady *Palestine* invited me the next Day to a private Party of a few Friends: I would modestly have declined the Invitation; for not being a general Friend to the Company, I felt myself unworthy of a Place among them, and expressed a Fear of being a troublesome Restraint on their Conversation. She smiled at this Notion, but insisted on my coming. I could not help anticipating, in my Imagination, the Pleasure I should receive from the Variety of Conversation so noble and extensive a Union must afford, where each Person could venture to declare every Thought, and give Vent even to their Follies. For I had been taught by my Lord, the Necessity of being guarded in what we say before any but most intimate Friends; and to this I attributed the extreme Triflingness of all the Conversation at which I had been present.

I went to Lady *Palestine's* at the appointed Time, and though there were fewer People than I had ever seen when she admitted Company; yet I was inclined to envy her so many select Friends; for there was about twenty in Number.

My Expectation being raised, I was all Attention; but, to my great Surprize, the Conversation extended no farther than the Weather; and their Engagements, during the Interval between their Arrival, and their being properly disposed to their separate Tables; for I then learnt, that even in *friendly* Societies, Cards were a necessary Ingredient.

Not doubting but Conversation would share their Time, I, by Turns, attended every Table, but found that the Game was the only Topick. One held the *cruellest* Cards, another the *pleasantest* Hand; those who won most Part of the Night, no sooner seemed to be threatened with a Reverse of Fortune, than they declared, "there was no playing against Lady such an one, she always won." Another equally unsuccessful added, "*Some People* had strange good Luck; for her Part, she found her Cards would sometimes be bad, but *some People* could make them win, whether they were bad or good." The Winners enjoyed their good Fortune in Silence, or told you how much they had lost the Night before. When it grew late, this select

Society broke up; and shewing, that Cards, not Friendship, had drawn them together, withdrew as soon as they arose from the Table; some exulting with the Reflection of having won their Friends Money, others out of Humour, at having lost their own, but none, I believe, so disappointed as myself, who had imagined a far different Entertainment; not having then learnt, that, a Party which does not, by its Numbers, deserve to be honoured with the Name of a Drum, is entitled a private Party of a few Friends; I suppose, by Way of expressing its *Insignificance*.

As I frequently met the same Company at Lady *Palestine's*, I soon became acquainted with many of them, especially of the other Sex, none of whom pleased me so well as Sir *Charles Lisdale*. His Person had no particular Charms; he was genteel, and looked like a Man of Fashion, otherwise plain enough. But he was extremely lively, had a great deal of Wit and Politeness, and shewed a particular Regard for me, by great Attention, Respect, and a constant Attendance; for he followed me about like my Shadow, and when I was present appeared insensible to every Person in Company. His Eyes seemed only given him to look at me, and his Ears to hear no Words but what I uttered, his whole Conversation was directed to me.

Ought I to be ashamed of owning, that I was pleased with Sir *Charles's* Behaviour? Does it shew a Spirit of Coquetry to like to be approved? Surely not. I thought not of Love, nor considered him as a Lover; but my Bashfulness found great Relief from perceiving him well disposed to be pleased with what I said: His Partiality made me less careful in weighing my Words, and this Ease rendered his Conversation particularly agreeable to me. There is great Satisfaction in having the Liberty of talking Nonsense, without incurring the Contempt of our Hearers; and, perhaps, People never appear to more Advantage, than when they dare give the Reins to their Imagination and Vivacity, and leave to others the Care of being wise.

Another Merit in Sir *Charles Lisdale*, was, that he did not surfeit me with Compliments, and when he made me any, there was always an Elegance and Variety in them; a Circumstance, of which the Conversation of many of his Sex could not boast. Their fulsome Flattery disgusted me; I could not listen to People who had foresworn all Truth. Besides, my Pride was offended in their supposing me so weak, as to believe what they said, and endeavouring to render themselves agreeable, by addressing my Vanity instead of my Reason, till I observed that they treated others a good Deal in the same Manner; for that they did not talk in quite so high a Strain to them, I imagined was from expecting less Credulity in Persons of more mature Years, and not so new to the World, as they must perceive I was. But Sir *Charles* taught me to divert myself with these ridiculous Compliments; and, after a Time, I began to find Amusement in their Folly.

I had one or two *Danglers*,[1] who were well stricken in Years, and afforded me more Entertainment than any; they deified me with so much Nonsense and Bombast, that I sometimes could scarcely understand them, and they would beg for a Smile, so much like a Street Beggar for an Alms, that my Generosity generally exceeded their Demands; for I was terribly apt to give them an ungrateful Laugh instead of a gracious Simper, which discomposed their Tempers still more than my Features, and excited a Resentment that was not soon cooled. However, whether languishing or angry, these antient Gentlemen were less disagreeable to me than many young ones, whose self-satisfied Air was more odious than their Nonsense. They seemed so sure of pleasing, that they could not but offend. We cannot well endure People who demand our Approbation as their Due, and look as if they would bully us into a Liking. A Lover, who would succeed, should not behave like a Highwayman, and attempt to obtain our Hearts, as he would our Purses, by only crying, Deliver.[2] They should consider, that as all the Fire of Assurance they can put into their Eyes, will not make them so dangerous as a Pistol; they may with less Hazard be resisted. They should, at least, accept our Hearts as a Favour; there is a Pleasure in obliging, which makes us love those who give us an Opportunity of exerting that Power.

I could perceive, that Lord *Dorchester* and Sir *Charles Lisdale*, did not greatly like each other. Sir *Charles*, I imagined, might be actuated by Envy, which I found was a common Vice in this Country. It seemed strange to me, that any one should envy when they might imitate, and thereby not only remove the Superiority that renders them uneasy, but love the other, whose Example led them into so happy a Path. No Person afflicted with an envious Disposition, can be ever happy; our Connexions with others, make us suffer by their ill Qualities; how unfortunate must we then be, if we feel Pain from their good ones.

Lord *Dorchester* was so superior to Sir *Charles*, that I could not suspect him of the same Vice; nor indeed, did I believe him capable of

---

1 Hangers-on; would-be lovers.
2 Alluding to the highwayman's conventional demand, "stand and deliver." Highway robbery was a danger to travellers in England throughout the eighteenth century.

it, could he have met with one superior to himself. But the last Reason I should have assigned for his Dislike was Jealousy; and, therefore, as I had supposed he had conceived some unjust Prejudice, I laboured to remove it, by giving Sir *Charles* the Praises I thought his Due, and wondered that the more I spoke in his Favour, the more averse my Lord seemed to him; this was very unlike his usual Politeness, which led him to see Charms in every Thing I approved. As he gave me no Reason for his Aversion, I was sometimes almost angry, and could not forbear telling him he was very unjust.

I found that I should have liked Sir *Charles* still better, if my Lord's Taste had concurred with mine. I could not but think mine was bad, since his would not give a Sanction to it; and if Sir *Charles* had not been too assiduous to leave it in my Power, I believe, I should have declined his Acquaintance; so much less agreeable was it rendered by my Lord's Disapprobation. But this could not be done without Incivility to Sir *Charles*; and not imagining it gave my Lord any Uneasiness, I continued to converse with him, which I could not do without great Pleasure to myself.

My Lord, at last, grew thoughtful and melancholy; he saw me seldomer, and oftener when he was with me, would be silent, or converse with little Connection or Chearfulness. If I expressed an Uneasiness at a Change of Temper, which I attributed to Sickness; he would make Answer, "that I could not possibly be concerned about him; but as he had no Merit but Love to engage my Heart, he could not complain, if I did not give him what he had no good Title to." If I exerted all the Eloquence of Tenderness to assure him of my Affection, and of my Anxiety for his Health, he would sometimes appear revived, and tell me, that "if I really had any Regard for him, he was well and happy." He would, perhaps, appear chearful for some Hours after; but if he left me in that happier State of Mind, when we next met the Air of Melancholy would be returned.

CHAPTER XXII

While Lord *Dorchester*, and consequently his *Ophelia*, continued in this State of Uneasiness, Lady *Palestine* desired me to go with her to an Opera. As Home became less agreeable, Dissipation grew more so, and I accepted her Invitation with Pleasure. I had a good Ear for Musick; and my Lord had given me the best Masters to improve it, though I had not yet made any great Proficiency, except in Singing; for, in that Branch, I had less to learn, Nature having given me a Voice, that your Ladyship (as well as many others, whom I must have allowed excellent Judges, even if they had not flattered me) has often said, did not require the Help of Art. As I was qualified to be entertained, it is not strange, that I was so, at a Time when Operas were in their highest Perfection.[1] Fashion had no Occasion to assist the Musick towards delighting me; but as I was a Stranger to Affectation, Extacies were not the Consequences of my being excessively pleased, and, therefore, I did not understand them in others.

My Attention was interrupted, by seeing a Lady who sat next me in a most languishing Condition; I thought her at her last Gasp, and did not doubt but she was going into a fainting Fit. The House being extremely full, was very hot; to this I attributed her Disorder, in which she seemed to have many Companions; but as she appeared in the greatest Extremity, she was the properest Object of my Care. Accordingly, in a Flutter of Haste, I applied my Smelling-Bottle to her Nose, fearing the least Delay might find her past Recovery. The Bottle was filled with very strong Salts,[2] and I was rejoiced to see their speedy Effect; for she recovered in an Instant, and opened her Eyes with a great Start, and a Look of Amazement; which might be expected from their sudden Operation. But I was extremely surprized, that instead of thanking me for my Care and Compassion, she looked excessively angry, and, in a most uncivil Manner and harsh Voice, asked me, what I meant by such Impertinence? She then gave Vent to her Rage in such a Torrent of Words, as raised my Opinion of my Salts, for having so immediately given such great Strength of Spirits to one before expiring, though the Effect was not very agreeable; for she did not leave me a Possibility of explaining my good Intention, nor should I have had Time to recover my Surprize, if the Salts had not taken a new Turn, throwing her into a violent Fit of Sneezing, which made very unlucky Breaks in her Discourse, and thereby increased her Anger. But *Musick has Charms to sooth a savage Breast*,[3] as I found, for her favourite Singer coming on the Stage, her Wrath subsided; and instead of the Words, impertinent, insolent, *&c. &c.* she could utter none, but oh the Charmer! the dear Creature! Ravishing! Enchanting! and all that our Language affords to the

---

1 Alluding to lavish productions of operas by Handel and others in the 1720s and 1730s, when the fashion for opera was at its peak.
2 A small bottle filled with smelling-salts, used by women as a restorative in case of fainting-fits, headaches, etc.
3 William Congreve, *The Mourning Bride* (1697) I. i:
   Music has charms to soothe a savage breast;
   To soften rocks, or bend a knotted oak.

same Purpose, with a Mixture of *Caro, Carissimo!*[1] Her Resentment was now buried in Admiration, and all her Senses absorbed by that of hearing.

While she was thus engaged, Sir *Charles* informed me, that Extacy of Pleasure, not Extremity of Pain, occasioned all those Languishments, which had excited my Compassion, and that her Anger arose from my having interrupted her Raptures, and, as she suspected, ridiculed them, by that Action. I think my Ignorance never raised so many Blushes in me, as on this Occasion; I was really overcome with Shame at my Mistake, till I reflected that she had most Reason to be so, since her Behaviour was foolish Affectation; mine only the Effect of reasonable Compassion.

This Incident, however, greatly interrupted the Pleasure I should have received from the Entertainment; and another, not less mortifying, was, that I did not see Lord *Dorchester* the whole Evening, till at my Return Home. I then found he had been at the Opera likewise, and could not forbear reproaching him for not being of our Party, especially, as he once found a Pleasure in going with me to every Place. His Answer was, that "He thought me too well engaged to have afforded him any of my Conversation, had he attempted to come to us; and, that it would not have been easy to have approached me, I was so encircled with Gentlemen."

I replied, that, "This was a poor Excuse to hide his Want of Inclination; for he must know, I would be engaged in no other Conversation when I had the Power of enjoying his; and that a Crowd must be great indeed, that did not leave one a Possibility of making Room for a Person whom we esteemed far above that whole Crowd." All the Answer I obtained, was so broken with Sighs, so unconnected in itself, and spoken with such an Air of Dejection, as touched me to the Heart, though it did not speak intelligibly enough for me to understand the Occasion of it.

In Pity to his Melancholy, I endeavoured to hide the Effect it had on me, and tried every Art to amuse him; I sang to him; I read to him; I attempted to lead him into Conversation; but all to no Purpose; when he looked most pleased with me, he seemed most oppressed; his Spirits were too much sunk to bear the Tenderness of his Mind, without an Increase of Dejection. When his Eyes expressed

---

1 Italian for beloved, best-loved man, although the words "Charmer" and "Creature" suggest a woman. The earliest citation of the phrase in *OED* is, surprisingly, 1857.

the utmost Fondness, they overflowed with Grief. I begged to know the Cause of his Sorrow, but he left me without satisfying a Curiosity, which arose only from Affection.

The following Day seemed to have made little Alteration in the State of Lord *Dorchester*'s Mind; but having promised Lady Palestine, to make Part of a very large Company at her House that Evening, we went thither at the proper Hour.

The Variety of Objects and Conversation, dispelled the Gloom which oppressed my Spirits before I left my own House. My Melancholy was not Proof against Sir *Charles*'s Vivacity, which even exceeded itself that Night, and the Evening passed away with great Mirth. I spoke several Times to my Lord, but could obtain little Answer. His Grief affected me; but still the natural Gaiety of my Temper supported by all that could flatter my Vanity or amuse my Understanding, was not to be soon overcome. But, at length, no longer able to endure the Sight of his Uneasiness, I determined to go Home if he would accompany me, in hopes that he would no longer conceal the Cause of his Affliction from Importunities arising only from the Desire of endeavouring to alleviate it.

I went up to him, told him I was going to retire, and begged to know when he would follow me.

Judge of my Surprize, when the Man whom I had never heard utter any Thing but the Words of Love and Tenderness; answered me in the sharpest Tone, "never, Madam; if you want Company, you have too good Interest with many in the Room to be denied theirs; you had better therefore change your Application; and may depend on not being impertinently interrupted by me."

My Amazement deprived me of Speech, and if it had not, it would have been of little Use; for he gave me no Time to answer him, leaving the Room as soon as he had done speaking. I was so much shocked I had not Power to follow him down Stairs, as I certainly should have exposed myself by doing, had I been able. As my Surprize abated, so my Grief increased; it overcame me so entirely, that I believe I should have sunk on the Floor, had not Sir *Charles Lisdale* perceived the Change of my Countenance and offered his Assistance, by which Means I left the Room and got into my Chair. He enquired, with kind Concern, the Occasion of my Disorder, but perceiving me incapable of either hearing or speaking, he supported me in Silence to, and attended my Chair to my own House, unseen by me till I was carried into the Hall. Seeing me surprized at his Presence, he excused it by saying, "he could not forbear accompanying me, lest the Motion of the Chair might make me still worse;

nor could he be easy without knowing how I was on getting home." But he found me so little better that he received no Satisfaction from this second View, and was still more alarmed when he learned from my Servant, that she had never seen me thus seized before.

Sir *Charles* intimated, that he could not rest without hearing how I did after I was put to Bed, but my Maid having more Consideration for me, than for his Ease, prudently told him, that any Noise might disturb me; upon which he said, that rather than run the least Hazard of that, he would endure his Impatience and Anxiety till Morning.

The only Relief I could not feel, was from being alone, that I might give an uninterrupted Flow to my Grief, which was indeed excessive. I had never before felt the Anger of one I loved; and had learned to think nothing but Tenderness and good Humour could fall from Lord *Dorchester's* Lips. Sir *Charles's* Servant watched the opening of the Door the next Morning, having been ordered not to knock, for fear of disturbing my Rest. Alas! my Night had all been spent in weeping. When my Servant informed him, that I was rather worse than the Evening before, having had no Sleep; he, who had a real Attachment to his Master, said "He knew not how to carry Sir *Charles* that Account, for that he had not been able to go to Bed all Night; and he feared such an Addition to his Anxiety might prove very hurtful to him." This, and the Enquiries after my Health, sent by such of my Acquaintance as observed that I was ill when I left Lady *Palestine's*, my Maid repeated to me; for perceiving that Grief was my Disorder, she endeavoured, as much as possible, to divert my Thoughts. These Attentions, from People for whom I had so small a Regard, in Comparison with my Love for Lord *Dorchester*, made me the more shocked at his not sending any Enquiry after me; tho' I thought he could not be ignorant of the Anxiety his Words must occasion. The Reflexion that I was in a new World, without a Friend, unthought of by him, increased my Affliction, as it gave me the worse Opinion of the Man who could thus wound a Heart so entirely his, when he knew I had no Comforter into whose Bosom I could pour my Grief, whose Tenderness could soothe, or Care redress them. Was every one more kind than this Man, who had ever before appeared so tender a Friend! If I had been guilty of any Fault to which my Ignorance had subjected me, for I was conscious of none towards him, might I not have expected an easy Pardon from one to whom I had forgiven so great an Injury as forcibly taking me from my Aunt, whose Temper could never make me feel such Agonies as his Caprice now gave me!

These were my Reflection the whole Day, during which Sir *Charles* called himself several Times at my Door to enquire into the State of my Health, desirous of a more particular Account than he could expect by a Servant. Towards Evening a Thought arose, that perhaps this great Change in a Disposition, which used to be unclouded, equally serene, and pleasing, might proceed from Distemper. The Possibility of this no sooner struck me, than I began to take myself to Task for complaining of him, when I ought rather to pity, nurse and attend him. I now arraigned my own Heart more bitterly than I had yet done his, and looking on my present Apprehension as most afflicting, prayed that from whatever Cause his Unkindness arose, it might fall on me alone, that I only might suffer, and he be easy tho' I was miserable.

To quiet the present Horrors of my Mind, I sent to his House to know how he did, and waited the Return of my Messenger with the Impatience of Distraction; which was rather changed than abated, by his bringing me Word, that my Lord had been abroad the whole Day. Notwithstanding my imaginary Disinterestedness, I severely felt this Indifference. Not once to enquire the Effect of his Behaviour! Not to comfort me with one kind Word! was an Excess of Cruelty; which made me think such a Heart as mine, capable of the deepest Impressions and strongest Sensations, very unfit to be in any degree linked with one who could be both so amiable and so cruel. Nor could Night give any Respite to my Affliction.

CHAPTER XXIII

The next Day reduced me to envy the Misery of the Day before, which I had then thought most deplorable. A Letter being delivered to me, the Sight of his Hand on the Superscription[1] revived my Spirits, and spread Joy over a Heart before immersed in Sorrow. I opened it with Impatience, to see in how kind a Manner he would at once sign both his and my Pardon. But, oh! Heavens! how was I disappointed! Your Ladyship, who never met with the like Trials, will, in imagining it, fall as short of what I felt, as I should do, if I endeavoured to describe the Shock I received at reading the following Lines:

"A Cold Address but ill agrees with the Love I have borne thee once, dear *Ophelia*, but it is suitable to the Sentiments I shall here-

---

1 The address.

after preserve toward her. Oh! *Ophelia*! you have by Deceit, I cannot call it Ingratitude, for I could not demand a Return, cured my Heart of a Weakness scarcely to be paralelled; but how painful is the Remedy: I have doated on you to Excess; and have been lulled into Happiness by the false Appearances of your approving my Love; but you have at last awaked me from this blissful Dream, and shewn me that Truth and Constancy are not to be found in a Female Heart in any Climate; that the Levity of your Sex makes them a Prey to the newest Lover, and prefer the fluttering of a Wit to the constant Attachment of an Affectionate Heart. If this Disappointment to my fond Hopes should make me miserable, it may punish me for my Folly, but my Resentment shall never render me criminal towards you. I have brought you from a fixed Habitation, introduced you into a Life of Gaiety and Pleasure, to the Charms of which you are sensible, if ever Woman was. Your Taste is so refined, and your Knowledge so much increas'd, that you would but ill relish the rustick Solitude of your former Cottage; I shall therefore remit to you 400 *l.* a Year,[1] which will enable you to live where you now are; and as soon as my Mind acquires a little Ease, I will so far extend a Regard, which, alas! *Ophelia*, I fear I shall always preserve, as to write you some necessary Advice concerning your future Conduct; for whatever I am, I must wish you happy, and that those who possess more of your Affections may adore you as I have done. I am carrying an afflicted Heart into the Country, unable to stay in Town after having resolved never to see you more. Your Humanity would make you pity, tho' you cannot love me, if you knew with what agonizing Pain I say, farewel for ever."

A slender Judgment of what I must have felt at the Perusal of this Letter, will serve to convince you that I was the greatest Object of Pity; regardless of the Presence of my Servants I could not forbear exclaiming, "Was it not enough to forsake me, but must he add Reproaches to his Cruelty! I practice Deceit! my Ignorance of such vile Arts renders it impossible, even tho' my Disposition was not so open that I speak my Thoughts as freely as they rise; and yet my Countenance expresses them before my Words can do it; and were I

---

1 Lord Dorchester offers to pay Ophelia an annual sum that would enable her to keep up an appearance of gentility but label her as a cast-off mistress.

to pollute my Tongue with a Falshood, would contradict it, and convict me of an Untruth. But they are all innocent; what then should hinder me from revealing them? And yet this Man accuses me of what he must know is a Stranger to my Heart. Arts and Concealments are for the inconstant and injurious; for those who can oppress the Innocent, and make the Friendless wretched by their Cruelty. Good Heaven! do I deserve this Character! would to God he could as justly defend himself from it!"

As soon as my Maid perceived me so far deprived of my Senses, as to give such free and unguarded Vent to my Distractions, she sent the Footman, who had brought the Letter, out of the Room, and was the only Person present during my Exclamation; to which a short Pause succeeded, and then I ran out of the Room, with an Air so frantic as greatly terrified her. She pursued me, and stopping me before I got out of the House, asked, "What I designed to do?" My Purpose was so full in my Thoughts, that I told her, "I was going to Lady *Palestine's*, to ask her where Lord *Dorchester* was? What he meant by quarrelling with me? and in what I had offended?"

She kept fast hold of me till she convinced me I was in a very improper Way to appear before so much Company as I must be sensible, if I reflected on the Hour, was then at Lady *Palestine's*: But to pacify me, in some degree, she went herself, and sending in a most pressing Message to her Ladyship, brought her out of Company to speak with her. All the Answer she brought me, was, that, "Lady *Palestine* was ignorant of every Circumstance, except that Lord *Dorchester* was gone out of Town." As soon as the Distraction of my Mind abated enough to give me leave to attend to the Effects it had upon me, I found myself extremely ill, and was soon unable to sit up. My Maid, truly alarmed at my Condition, sent for a Physician, who declared me in a high Fever, and ordered me to be kept in Bed. But the Pains that afflicted me, could not draw my Attention from my Lord's Behaviour. My first Resolution was to refuse the Income he offered; I would not give him room to think he had made me any Recompence for the Injuries he had done, or that it was in his Power to pay me for what he had made me suffer, first by tearing me from all my Soul could wish, and then by abandoning me in a strange Land, unfriended and unknown.

If my Lord's Inconstancy had deprived me of my greatest Good, I determined my own Spirit should discharge me from the lesser, if he thought me beneath his Friendship, I thought myself above his Charity, nor could his whole Fortune have given me the Joy I should have received from one Symptom of Regard. I had Money enough remaining to carry me back to my beloved Aunt, who grew more dear to me from my Lord's ill Treatment. From her tender and constant Affection I hoped to find Relief; in her Goodness expected to receive Consolation for the Faults of others, and, far from this bad Town, to learn to forget it, and its cruel Inhabitants, whose Minds are as variable as their Climate.

These Hopes and Resolutions were the Result of my Thoughts while I remained sensible; but, as to cure a Distemper by Medicine, which proceeds from Anxiety of Mind, is a vain Attempt, I grew, at last, so bad, that I was light-headed; to which I may attribute my Recovery. Want of Reflexion did what Reason could not effect; it quieted my Mind, and my Constitution received Benefit from it; for as Grief was the Cause of my Illness, the Loss of the Sense of my Affliction, left me to Youth and natural Strength, and my Fever abated. As soon as I recovered my Senses, I was apprized of my Danger, and once more saw Death without Terror. My Doctor assured me he had saved my Life; I could not have thanked him with a tolerable Grace, had I believed him, but my Credulity fell short of his Assurances: I was convinced my Distemper was beyond the Reach of human Art, and pressed him "to cease attempting a Cure that would afford him little Satisfaction, and me none." I was sorry his benevolent Disposition should throw away on me the Time which he dedicated to the Relief of Mankind. But when he was gone, my Maid told me, he would not part with a Patient so easily, as his Benefit was certain, tho' mine was doubtful, and came in a pleasing Shape; for he received current Gold in exchange for his Advice, and declared War to the Patient's Palate,[1] in Return for that Reward, which taken in the greatest Quantities was in no Danger of creating a Nausea.

When I found my Doctor mercenary, instead of charitable, I felt less Veneration for him; but no longer wondered Money was held in so high Esteem, since People thought they could purchase Health with it. Could I have flattered myself that would have brought me Ease of Mind, I should have been very rapacious, but, "Esteem and Love were never to be sold,"[2] and those were the Things wanting to my Peace.

---

1 I.e., Ophelia's taste ("palate") for dying.
2 Pope, *An Essay on Man* (1733-4) iv. 187-8:
    Judges and Senates have been bought for gold,
    Esteem and Love were never to be sold.

My Illness deferred the Execution of my intended Departure from *London*, but the Resolution continued.

All my Acquaintance sent daily Enquiries after my Health; Sir *Charles Lisdale* never called less than twice a Day. The first Person I saw was Lady *Palestine*, with whom I hoped to indulge myself with talking of my Distress; but my Spirits were so weak, that when she came, many past Circumstances crouded to my Remembrance, and I was choaked with Tears. She staid some time in Expectation of my growing more able to converse, seeming desirous to talk with me on the Subject most at my Heart; but finding no Amendment, was afraid her Presence, by agitating me so greatly, might do me harm, and therefore left me with a Desire that I would let her know when I was more able to see her.

Not understanding the Passion of Jealousy, I did not perceive any Signs of remaining Love in Lord *Dorchester*, or some flattering Hopes might have been my Consolation; I should then have seen, that the Man who wrote that Letter was not indifferent, of which I was now so well persuaded, that I never considered there was a Possibility of his being otherwise. What served to convince me the more entirely of it, was his never having yet made any Enquiry after me, tho' I had been so long and so dangerously ill. Seeing every thing in the worst Light, I did not consider that he might not know it. The continual Messages I received from many Gentlemen, with the more particular Enquiries of Sir *Charles Lisdale*, and Lord *Larborough*, a young Nobleman who always followed me about like a Shadow, a constant, rather than an agreeable Attendant; for he seldom spoke to me, made Lord *Dorchester's* Neglect appear the greater.

At first I imagined my Lord's Affection for me never real, or it could not so soon be entirely extinguished; but I now began to think even Humanity was dead in him. Good-nature would have suggested to him, but Friendship would have forced him to administer some Consolation to the Misfortunes of one whom he had introduced to Misery, tho' she seemed to have been placed by Fortune out of the Reach of his Inhumanity. It never once occurred to me, that he did not imagine I wanted any Consolation; and that from this Error arose all my Grief and his. My Afflictions seemed near an End; tho' my Fever was gone, yet I did not recover; I was pale and emaciated, had neither Strength to move, nor Spirits to speak, equally weak both in Mind and Body, and, had not a Ray of Hope at last shone upon me, I believe my Existence had not been of long Duration.

CHAPTER XXIV

As I was desirous of conversing with Lady *Palestine*, I sent to her as soon as I thought I had brought myself to see her with less Discomposure. Upon turning the Discourse to Lord *Dorchester's* sudden Departure from *London*, I frankly spoke the Sentiments of my Heart, and expressed my Grief as well as Astonishment at so immediate an Alteration. She told me, "She was well persuaded that Jealousy of Sir *Charles Lisdale* was the Occasion of it;" and she herself seemed to have some Suspicion of my giving the Baronet[1] the Preference. As I had always appeared without Disguise to my Lord, it was most incredible to me, that he could entertain any such Opinion; and my Earnestness, as well as my late Disorder, when she learned it was the Consequence of Lord *Dorchester's* Behaviour, were pretty sufficient Proofs to her Ladyship, that she had been under a Mistake. However, had they not been convincing, all Possibility of Doubt was removed before she left me. As we were sitting a Message was brought up to me from Mrs. *Belfast*, a Lady with whom I had become acquainted at Lady *Palestine's*, importing, that, "She was at the Door to enquire after my Health; and if I was well enough to admit her, would be extremely glad to wait on me." Not being fit to see Company, I had hitherto declined all Visits; but as Lady *Palestine's* Coach was at the Door, I thought I could not, without a manifest Affront, refuse seeing Mrs. Belfast.

The Lady was extremely intimate with Sir *Charles Lisdale*; and had no sooner done expressing her Concern at my looking so ill, than she began to tell me, "how very sensibly Sir *Charles* had been afflicted; and that he had engaged her to beg my Permission for his waiting on me, to congratulate me on my Recovery; and to receive his Cure from seeing mine, till when he could enjoy no Health."

Lord *Dorchester's* Behaviour had disgusted me with the Sex; and since Lady *Palestine* had given me Reason to think my Lord was jealous of Sir *Charles*, I was more particularly averse to seeing him. With more Sincerity and Positiveness than was consistent with good Breeding, I immediately refused to receive his Visit.

But Mrs. *Belfast* was too zealous an Advocate to be rebuffed by one Denial, and being extremely intimate with Lady *Palestine*, she

---

1 As a baronet, not a member of the peerage, Sir Charles is outranked by Lord Dorchester, who thus might find Ophelia's apparent preference all the more offensive.

said, "she thought her Presence need not prevent her from performing another Part of her Commission, if I refused the first." She then made a long Panegyric on Sir *Charles*, expatiated on the Excess of his Love for me, of his Uneasiness at being debarred my Conversation, extolled his good Qualities, his Understanding and Temper, and various Merits, which were unnecessarily enumerated to me who knew him; and ended with saying, that, "if I would not give him the Liberty of telling me how much he loved me, she was commanded to do it for him; and to let me know, that his highest Ambition was to be united to me for Life. If I would consent to marry him, my Happiness should be his sole Study; that he and his Fortune would always be at my Disposal; and he should think himself under the highest Obligation for the Felicity he must enjoy in an Union with me; that his Estate was very considerable, and I should myself direct the Settlements; for he could never esteem his whole Fortune, in any Degree equal to my Merits."

This Proposal startled me, it shewed more true Affection than all Lord *Dorchester's* Actions. To bind himself for Life, to give me the Command of his Fortune, was a strong Proof of his good Opinion. My own Reflections engaged me for a few Minutes, and those few served to shew me, that though I always esteemed Sir *Charles*, was delighted with his Conversation, and now felt myself sincerely grateful, yet I could not think of marrying him. This I told Mrs. *Belfast* in the plainest Terms, acknowledging, at the same Time, my real Regard for him, and my Gratitude for so generous a Proof of his Affection.

She endeavoured to prevail upon me to give a more favourable Answer, and so earnestly pressed for my Consent, that she convinced me, she was a warm Friend, and no bad Advocate: But, at last, assured of my Inflexibility, she went away, telling me, that, "she saw to what Sir *Charles* owed the Misfortune of a Refusal; had not my Affections been engaged, I must have accepted his Offers; but he had feared to find Lord *Dorchester* an Impediment to the Completion of his Wishes, and she grieved, that she must be obliged to give him so strong a Proof of the Reasonableness of his Apprehensions."

When Mrs. *Belfast* was gone, Lady *Palestine* asked me, why I refused a Proposal so much to my Advantage. I knew not well how to answer; my Heart, not my Reason gave the Denial, and its Emotions are not so easily described. All I had to say was, that, "I could not think of marrying him. I liked his Company extremely, was convinced of his Love, and grateful for it; that Marriage must give him such a Title to my Affection, as even Lord *Dorchester* could not disapprove, and could not imagine, interfered with my Friendship for him, the only Sort of Attachment he required, for he had never given me so strong a Proof of his good Opinion, as to think of me in the Capacity of a Wife."

Lady *Palestine* asked "If I was then determined to marry no Man." I replied, "Indeed, such was my Resolution. I was sensible from this small Trial, that I could not bear to look on any Man in the Light of a Husband except Lord *Dorchester*; and I wished only to live with him as a Friend, but those blessed Days were over; and, I had now no other Design, than to return as soon as my Strength would permit me, to my Solitude, and dedicate the Remainder of my Life to recompence my Aunt, for what I had involuntarily occasioned her to suffer."

I saw Lady *Palestine* listen to me with some Contempt. When I had done speaking, she, with a Sneer, intermixed the Words, *Girlish Passions, Foolish Constancy, Romantick Notions, imaginary Delicacy*; with her Answer; but I could have forgiven her a greater Affront, for the Consolation she had brought me, by attributing Lord *Dorchester's* Behaviour to Jealousy; though it seemed to me scarcely possible, yet my Despair seized this Glimmering of Hope. I once more opened his Letter, it corresponded with what she had said; and I now fancied some Sentences in it expressed a remaining Tenderness. But if this was the Case, I thought it strange that he did not enquire into the State of my Heart, and not build a Belief on Circumstances, when he might have had my Word for Information. It never occurred to me, that my Testimony must appear fallible, to a Man who had been used to see so much Falshood; and that,

> ———*Trifles light as Air,*
> *Are to the Jealous, Confirmations strong,*
> *As Proofs of Holy Writ.*———[1]

Three Days passed in reasoning on a Possibility, which was the Foundation of all my Comfort; till, at last, I began to say with *Solomon*, that "Hope deferred, maketh the Heart sick."[2] My Hopes were too slightly raised to support any Degree of Spirits for so long a Time, they grew faint, and would soon have vanished quite, and left me again a Prey to Despair, had they not been driven away by Cer-

---

1 Iago, in Shakespeare's *Othello*, III.iii.327-9.
2 Proverbs 13.12: "Hope deferred maketh the heart sick: but when the desire cometh, it is a tree of life."

tainty. In the Afternoon a Letter was brought me from Lord *Dorchester*; I imagined it contained the Instructions he promised me, yet opened it with a melancholy Satisfaction, as his Hand would endear the Contents, let them be otherwise disagreeable. But Joy broke in at once upon my Mind at seeing the most affectionate Address, followed by Words more tender. In the humblest manner, "he begged leave to wait on me, to ask a Pardon from me, which he could never give to himself, for a Behaviour so inexcusable, founded on an injurious Suspicion, too rashly conceived, and resented." He expressed so lively a Grief for the cruel Effects of it, that had I had Spirits to have retained Anger, I must have been pacified; he condemned himself in such Bitterness of Soul, that I could scarcely forbear resenting the Injury he did the Friend of my Heart, as I then again esteemed him, and was ready to think it the only Fault he had committed.

This Letter found me in so weak a Condition, that I had not till then been able to get down Stairs without Assistance; but such a Cordial is Joy, that I ran down to the Servant to enquire where his Lord was, who informing me that he was waiting impatiently at his House in Town, for my Answer, I told him I would not detain him till I could write; but desired he would acquaint his Lord, that I wished to see him as soon as possible.

The Servant was not long in carrying his Message, nor his Master in obeying it; few Minutes passed before the Flutter of Expectation was put an End to, by my Lord's Arrival. He entered the Room with a Confusion that deprived him of Utterance, and taking my Hand, with a Diffidence and Melancholy that hurt me, pressed it to his Lips. My Spirits overcome with the Agitation they had been in failed me, and I began to weep more like a Mourner than one in the Excess of Joy. My Lord accompanied my Tears with some of his, which seemed greatly to relieve him, and restore him to his Speech. "I cannot, my *Ophelia*," said he, "presume to ask your Pity, I am oppressed with the Consciousness of rather deserving your Hatred; but I am sure if you knew what I have suffered, and still suffer, your generous and gentle Nature would look on me, however blameable, yet as an Object worthy your Compassion, since my Punishment has been adequate to the greatest Offence, and if it could be expiated must be sufficient to wash it away. I thought it impossible to be a greater Wretch than I was while I imagined Sir *Charles Lisdale* possessed your Heart; but since I learnt from Lady *Palestine* the Injustice I have done you; and how grievously you have suffered by it, I have been ten thousand Times more miserable; the Paleness of your Cheeks, and the Languor in your Eyes, are Reproaches that rend my

Heart. To see you thus, is worse than being torn from you. O my *Ophelia*, can you ever forgive me?"

My Lord, indeed, appeared so very wretched, that I could not add to his self Reproaches; but, on the contrary, endeavoured to extenuate his Fault; I assured him "that if his Neglect had made me sick, his Kindness would be my Cure, that it had almost made me well already; and, that the Pleasure I now felt, compensated all past Pains, which would only serve, henceforward, to heighten all my Happiness by Comparison." But all I could say, seemed to increase his Grief, instead of alleviating it. He begged "I would be less generous, and said, my Goodness added to his Misery, in shewing him still more criminal in wronging, in afflicting, an Angel." I found by conversing with him, that he had desired Lady *Palestine* to observe my Behaviour, and discover my Sentiments; that she had written him Word of what passed in her Visit to me, which affected him so much, that he set out that Instant, and would not suffer the darkest, most stormy Night in the whole Winter to stop him in his Journey, so impatient was he to see me. The Moment he arrived, he went to Lady *Palestine*, to learn every Circumstance, more particularly than he could by her Letter, which both satisfied, and touched him still more sensibly.

He could not venture to see one whom he had so much injured, as he was pleased to think he had done me, without first asking Permission; but not having Patience to stay for his Servant's Return with my Answer, he met him half Way, which occasioned his Being with me so immediately.

CHAPTER XXV

I now found that nothing was so beneficial to the Constitution as Ease of Mind. A few Days passed in Happiness, made a greater Progress in my Recovery, than all the Medicines which the Physician yet had prescribed me. As Grief was the Cause of my Sickness, it was but natural that Health should be the Consequence of my Felicity.

I first now learnt to play the Hypocrite; my Lord seemed so tenderly anxious for my Health, and reproached himself so much for every Pain I felt, that when I was most ill, I durst not indulge myself in the peevish Satisfaction of complaining; perceiving that he suffered more by my Sickness than I did; for though I instantly forgave him, he could not forgive himself. Had it not been for the Consideration, that what has once been, may be again, and the Fear of my

Lord's relapsing at any Time into the same Sort of Whim, I should have been happier than ever; for he was now never an Hour in the Day absent. Even Sickness had its Pleasure; his Care and watchful Attendance turned Pain into Delight. I took Advantage of my Disorder to excuse my keeping at Home, that I might not lose my Lord's Company for those who I began to see acted upon Custom, solliciting what they did not desire, and begging for what they would not chuse to have granted. I had learnt that to be impertinent was civil, and thoroughly troublesome was being perfectly well-bred. I found that the Aim of the Complaisant was not so much to please, as to appear pleased, trusting to Vanity for rendering it mutual. In consequence of these Customs, I was too soon obliged to mortify myself and plague others, to avoid affronting them, though I deferred as long as my Health would leave me the Shadow of an Excuse.

The first Day I went to Lady *Palestine's*, I met Sir *Charles Lisdale* there, who seemed to have lost all Vivacity, which had rendered him so agreeable. He approached me with a very dejected Air, and used all possible Intreaties to persuade me to admit a Visit from him. When they failed, he expatiatied on his Passion with an Elegance and Appearance of Sincerity, that affected me, though not with Love. The very Thoughts of marrying him created a Kind of Dislike in me, which I did not feel before; but yet he seemed so seriously touched in all he said, that I was sorry to add to his Uneasiness. Endeavouring to comfort him, I assured him of my Regard and Gratitude, expressing great Pleasure in the Expectation of seeing him often at Lady *Palestine's* as usual; but he told me, that, "if I was absolute in my Determination, he must seek for Ease in Absence; for that he should be wretched with so poor a Return, unless my Cruelty could conquer his Passion." I could not help thinking the whole Sex distracted: To forswear any farther Acquaintance with me, if he could not have my Company at all Times, and fixed for Life, appeared to me as unreasonable, as if a Man was to kill himself, because he did not possess every Thing he wished in this World, refusing to enjoy the solid Comforts of Life, if some trifling Benefit was denied him. I was sorry Sir *Charles* was determined to avoid me; I thereby lost the Conversation of a Man I greatly liked and esteemed; and Lord *Dorchester* now appeared so easy about him, that I had no Reason to fear any Inconveniences should arise from our Acquaintance. My Lord endeavoured to account for his Jealousy from the general Inconstancy of both Sexes; but I could not think this a sufficient Reason for it, as Inconstancy towards him, could not be so well justified, as in many Cases; for by what I could learn, the general Practice of Deceit makes People appear so much better at first, than on long Acquaintance they prove to be, that to continue to love them, rather than cease to do so, should be termed Inconstancy. When the Merit disappears, the Object of a reasonable Affection is no longer the same, and Love like all other Structures, should fall, when the Foundation sinks: Our Love should follow our Esteem, and consequently no one can have a Right to the one, after he had forfeited his Title to the other. When the Deceit appears, by the Mask's falling off the Mind, the Man can have no better Demand upon our Hearts, than his Picture has; indeed, scarcely so much, as the painted Canvas is most innocent; but the daubed Hypocrite most criminal. Lord *Dorchester's* Virtues seemed to me too real and permanent to reduce a Woman to Change, and, therefore, I could not allow he had a good Excuse for his Suspicions; and I was fully determined to avoid exciting any for the future, by watching my Behaviour more narrowly, and not leaving my Vivacity under the Command of my Innocence, since that could not defend it from giving Offence. Sir *Charles* could no longer be an Object of Uneasiness; for after meeting him once more at Lady *Palestine's*, when he took a most affectionate Farewell, which I returned with all the Sincerity of my warmest good Wishes; he left *London*, giving out that, he was going to make the Tour of *Europe*.[1] He politely said, "in Hopes, by the Variety of Objects, and Dissipation, to banish me from his Mind." I could not think but this arduous Affair might have been contrived with less Trouble; and have been more convinced of it, since Experience has shewn me, that the Memory is not one of those hard Compositions, out of which, Impressions are so very difficult to erase; I have seen a Woman wash her Lover from her Remembrance, in less Time than she could get a Spot of Ink out of her Ruffle.[2]

Could I have brought myself to follow the Custom of being denied,[3] I should have been tempted to abate my civility to my Acquaintance. But the Practice of Falshood, however trifling the Circumstance, appeared to me a Thing of Consequence; it learns People to disregard Truth, and we cannot expect those whom we teach to lye for our Convenience, should forbear it when it may turn to their Advantage: It is corrupting the Minds of Persons who being

---

1 I.e., the Grand Tour, taking in the major European cities and places of interest; an essential part of a gentleman's education, it could last for up to three years.
2 A strip of lace, etc., used as an ornamental frill in clothing.
3 I.e., "not at home": not available for the reception of visitors.

in our Power, ought to be the Objects of our Care, whose Principles we should watch over, and improve by Precept and Example. Your Ladyship has observed, that my Opinion and Practice, are still the same in this Particular; though acknowledging the Inconveniences arising from it, but greater Evils cannot dispense with our Adherence to Truth. The Temptation was certainly never stronger than at the Time of which I am speaking: When Lord *Dorchester's* constant Conversation was a necessary Reward for what I had lately suffered; and yet I had less Liberty of enjoying it at Home than Abroad, as I was obliged to direct all my Conversation to my Visitors.

CHAPTER XXVI

Among other Places where I went after the Recovery of my Happiness and my Health, was the Masquerade. The Company beside Lady *Palestine*, Lord *Dorchester*, and Lord *Larborough*, who was become very intimate with my Lord, were Lady *Cambridge*, Lady *Rochester* and Miss *Baden*, of whom I shall give your Ladyship some little Account before I proceed with them to the *Hay-Market*.[1] Lady *Cambridge* claims the first Place, and far be it from me to rob her of a Precedency she would not have relinquished, no not in passing over a Dunghill, for her whole Estate. For the Honour of having been the first Woman, I believe she would soon have been contented to have resigned her Existence, and to have lain as long in the Grave, as our Mother *Eve* has. With all this she was courteous to Excess; for being persuaded that a Word from her was a great Honour to those who received it, and being of a benevolent Disposition, she generously bestowed that inestimable Favour on all she met. Humility was the Virtue, on which she particularly piqued herself; and to make it known to others, she lived in a perfect Convulsion of Civility, and had not a Limb or Feature, that was not as much overstrained by the Violence of her Endeavours, as her Complaisance. In the Height of these Agitations, one could as little know her Person, as her Mind, by the Courtesy she professed. No one so bitterly inveighed against proud Persons, telling you, that Pride was her Detestation. Convinced her Approbation stamped a Value on every

---

1 Weekly masquerades were held at the Haymarket Theatre, orchestrated by John James Heidegger, from 1717 until the 1730s; Ophelia and her company have tickets for one of these gatherings.

Thing, she would praise every Part of your Dress, in order to give a Dignity to Trifles. I never saw a Woman, who so truly laboured in her Calling, for Affability was her Profession: If it was in the Power of a Person one did not esteem to humble one, the Impetuosity of her Civility would have done it; for her Complaisance was an Insult, and her Fawning Insolence. They appeared only to her Inferiors; to her Equals in Birth, she was stately and imperious. Like the generous Lion, she would condescend to engage with an insignificant Plebeian, but would enter the Combat with a true heroick Spirit, if her Antagonist was of such noble Blood, as deserved her Notice, and defend her glorious Prerogative of Precedency, at the Expence of every Rule of good Breeding. Lady *Rochester* was a Person of sublimer Notions, than to dispute the Precedency I have given to Lady *Cambridge*. She was in Person tall and thin, formal in her Manner, and solemn in her Countenance. Her chief Employ was Reading, and the great Purpose of it to appear wise, not to be so. She acquired a Smattering in many Studies;[1] and having amassed a great Number of technical Terms, she applied them to all Subjects, whether proper or improper, and by *happy* Chance, they were generally misplaced. If a Ribbon was the Topick of Discourse, she delivered her Sentiments in mathematical Phrases; if she ordered any of her Family Affairs, which, indeed, was but seldom; for her Genius soared above such vulgar Things; she would borrow her Expressions from Metaphysicks, and talk of the "*Entity* of a Piece of Beef, the *Nonexistence* of a Pigeon Pye and the *heterogenous* Particles in Salmigondi;"[2] or changing Science, but still remaining Scientifick, would expatiate on the "Infinitissimals[3] in minced Meat." To describe an Assembly, she would call Astronomy to her Assistance, and Algebra must furnish its Quota of Words, to enable her to inform you of the Numbers that were at it. No Person could be mentioned, without reminding her of some one in Antiquity. If a Gentleman appeared inattentive, "he was as absent

---

1 Fielding's satirical portrait of the would-be learned Lady Rochester might have been a source for Lady Smatter, the judgemental leader of the "Esprit Party" in Frances Burney's *The Witlings*, a comedy she began writing in 1778. Lady Rochester's "Smattering" of knowledge might also have provided Burney with her heroine's name.

2 Metaphysics is the branch of philosophy dealing with first principles, such as being, identity, knowing, etc. Entity is existence, as opposed to non-existence; salmagundi is a cold dish made from "particles," small pieces of minced meat, vegetables, etc.

3 The term for a fraction approaching zero; Lady Rochester has switched from metaphysics to mathematics.

as *Archimedes*, when *Syracuse* was taken:"[1] if a Person expressed Concern at the great Prevalence of Vice "He was like *Heraclitus*, weeping for Follies he could not cure; and therefore, she advised him to inhabit a Tub, like *Diogenes*,[2] unless he would cease to expect Perfection in finite Beings, endowed with Free-Will and void of all Prescience; for that all Ages had been corrupt, and every Nation vicious, except some few;" which she would not omit to mention, any more than to enumerate the different Vices of all Kingdoms, beginning with *Cain's* Envy and Cruelty; and sometimes, scarcely sparing the Frailty of our first Parents.[3] If the Person whom she addressed, as would often be the Case, happened to laugh at the Inundation of Wisdom she bestowed upon him, she would observe, "that tho' *Risibility* was one of the most distinguishing *Characteristicks* of the human Species, yet as Laughter arose from Pride, it ought to be suppressed:" But if he did not compose his Countenance into proper Gravity on this Rebuke, she would declare him "as indocile as *Nero* to *Seneca's* Instructions,"[4] and therefore leave him. If a Man had an Impediment in his Speech, "he stammered like *Alcibiades*."[5] A narrow Passage was "the Streights of *Thermopylæ*;" and if any People stood at one End of it, she never failed discovering a *Leonidas*[6] amongst them. If a Lady whispered a Piece of Scandal, "she was more severe than the *Athen-*

---

1 Alluding to Plutarch's account of the death of Archimedes (c. 287-212 BC), the greatest mathematician and inventor of antiquity, during the capture of Syracuse by the Romans. He was, according to Plutarch, so engaged with working out a problem that he failed to notice the invading Romans, and thus met his death.

2 Heracleitus (c. 540-c. 480 BC), the Greek philosopher, became known as the "weeping philosopher," lamenting the nature of human life. Diogenes (c. 400-325 BC), the Greek Cynic philosopher, advocate of self-sufficiency and the natural life, supposedly lived in a tub in Athens.

3 Cain, the eldest son of Adam and Eve ("our first parents"), murdered his brother Abel in a fit of jealousy. Adam and Eve's frailty was their tasting the forbidden fruit, contrary to the will of God.

4 Seneca the Younger (c. 4 BC-AD 65) was tutor to the young Nero (AD 37-68), who became Roman emperor AD 54-68.

5 Alcibiades (c. 450-404 BC) was an Athenian politician. His stammering is mentioned in the life by Plutarch.

6 Leonidas, king of Sparta, was commander of the Greeks at the battle of Thermopylae in 480 BC. After holding back the Persian army at the straits of Thermopylae for several days, he was killed in a celebrated last stand.

ian Ostracism, from which the just *Aristides*[1] could not escape uncensured." If she was offended with a Fop, she declared him "more effeminate than *Sardanapalus*, and more indolent than the most inactive of the *Merovigienne* Race."[2] A Country Squire came by Chance into her Company, once when I was present, and she cried out, "He was more savage than the *Huns, Goths* or *Vandals*; and *Attila* or *Genserick* were polite in Comparison of that Barbarian."[3] If a Ball was mentioned, she would declare her longing Desire to see the *Salian* Dance; and grieve for the Degeneracy of Mankind in not reviving the Olympick Games.[4] A War was particularly fortunate for her, as she would from the smallest Skirmish, find an Opportunity of talking of the Battle of *Marathon*, of *Cannae*,[5] or some other, equally remote from the present Age; and of advising every General she saw, to a new Way of martialling his Army, particularly recommending to him, the Imitation of the *Macedonian* Phalanx.[6] She affronted seven young Ladies resplendently dressed, who were standing together, telling them, "they reminded her of *Ursa Major*,"[7] the Simile did not sound well, and they all frowned most uncourteously; but could not discourage her from addressing a Lady cloathed in Silver Tissue, on her "shining like the *Galaxy*." Folly as well as Vice, sometimes, is pro-

---

1   Aristeides (d. c. 468 BC), an Athenian statesman known as "the Just," made an enemy of Themistocles, and was ostracised in 482 BC. Ostracism, practised in fifth-century BC Athens, provided for the banishment of an unpopular citizen for ten years.

2   Sardanapalus, king of Assyria, was proverbial among the Greeks for effeminacy. The Merovingians, the first ruling dynasty of the Franks, retained power from the middle of the fifth century until 751. In its later years, the dynasty was notorious for its degeneracy.

3   The Huns, Goths, and Vandals, all enemies of ancient Rome, were regarded by Rome as barbarians. Attila was king of the Huns 434–53, and their most famous leader. Genseric or Gaiseric (c. 390–477) was king of the Vandals.

4   The Salian priests at Rome performed elaborate ritual dances. The Olympic games were held every four years at Olympia, in honour of Zeus, from 776 BC until they were abolished in 391. The modern revival began in 1896.

5   Marathon, on the coast of Attica, was the scene of a major Athenian victory over the invading Persians in 490 BC. Cannae, an Italian village, was the scene of a victory by Hannibal over the Romans in 216 BC.

6   An infantry formation created by Philip II of Macedon in 359 BC, and used to great effect by Philip's son, Alexander the Great.

7   The Great Bear, a constellation of the northern hemisphere.

ductive of Good to Part of the Society; thus her Ladyship's pedantick Vanity gave her a Right to the Praise given to *Lewis*, since it must be said,

That she the living Genius fed,
And rais'd the Scientifick Head.[1]

For flattering herself with a Notion of being a Female *Mecænas*,[2] as she would often indirectly call herself, she imitated his Bounty, if she could not rival his Judgment; and reconciled those two Parts of Man, the Mind and Body, which are apt to be so much at Variance, that where one is greatly attended to, the other generally suffers severely by Neglect.

Whether there is less Variety in good than in Evil, or that we are apt to be more concise in our Panegyrics than our Satires I know not, but few Words, tho' much Affection, will fall to Miss *Baden's* Share. Folly is extremely various, but good Sense is uniform, and from its perfect Consistency is soon described. I had not then met with a Woman whom I thought so agreeable as Miss *Baden*. She was several Years older than myself, and seemed well acquainted with the World, was sensible, polite, modest, and gentle, her Voice remarkably pleasing; and tho' not handsome, had a great deal of Sweetness in her Countenance.

Miss *Baden* was a good deal disposed in my Favour; so well inclined to each other I believe we should then have become intimate, had not Lord *Dorchester* discouraged it, and as much as possible interrupted our Acquaintance. As he had known her longer, I

---

1 I.e., Louis XV, in an epigram possibly by Jonathan Swift, "On the Hermitage at Richmond," ll. 1-2:
   Lewis the Living Learned fed,
   And rais'd the scientific Head.
   The epigram was one of several occasioned by Queen Caroline's commission of five busts for her grotto at Richmond in 1732; see *The Poems of Jonathan Swift*, ed. Harold Williams, 2nd ed. (Oxford: Clarendon, 1958) II. 662-4. It was first published in the *Gentleman's Magazine* 3 (April 1733), and reprinted in *A Collection of Epigrams* (London, 1737) II. 314. Laurence Sterne also alludes to it in *Tristram Shandy* (1760) II.xiv; see Thomas Keymer, "Scholia to the Florida *Tristram Shandy* Annotations," *Scriblerian* 34 (2001-02): 111-12.

2 Maecenas Gaius (d. 8 BC) was the most celebrated Roman literary patron, supporting Virgil, Horace, Propertius, etc.

could not doubt but she had Faults which had disgusted him, tho' I had not perceived them; and therefore avoided her to the utmost of my Power. The Reason of my Lord's objecting to her will be obvious to your Ladyship, to whom I need not say that he feared her Discernment, and the Frankness of her Nature, which must together enable her to see the Arts used to impose upon me, as well as the End designed by them, and induce her to discover the whole, to one whom a Woman of her Sense and Virtue must pity, for being too likely to become the Prey of Arts and Vices she could not suspect, and therefore was the less qualified to baffle.

In this Company I went to the Masquerade, which had been so described to me, as to raise my Curiosity very much; but in Absurdity it exceeded what my Expectation had formed of it. The motley phantastick Crew seemed to me more like what the Imagination represents to us in Sleep, when the Body is disordered, than any real Objects that ever appear before our Eyes; and I have often thought their Causes bore some Resemblance to each other. Dreams are generally the Effects of Excesses, or of feverish Heats; Masquerades are the Produce of a strange Excess of Fancy, an overheated Imagination, set to work by a wild Desire of Amusement.

The Variety of shocking Forms terrified me, till use had a little familiarized them; and I found that this Assembly, in the Opinion of most People, received its Terrors, not from masking the Faces, but unmasking the Mind. When I learned that the *English* were such great Enemies to Sincerity, that none dared practice it bare-faced, I allowed there was some Excuse for thus defending themselves from the ill Effects of so uncommon an Indulgence of that Virtue. I should imagine some Relaxation from the painful Exercises of Dissimulation and Flattery necessary; and might be productive of general Good. But the Divine Countenance of Truth is so seldom seen here, that if, by Chance, she does appear, she is often mistaken for ill Nature. Nor can one wonder at the Error; for she is, according to the fashionable Phrases, "One that nobody knows," "One that one never meets any where:" And therefore, if she will intrude, it is not wonderful, if she is so ill treated as to be forced immediately to withdraw. The Impression she leaves behind only serves to make her avoided like a Bugbear,[1] and ridiculed without Mercy; so generally rebuffed, that she can scarcely find Shelter in a Cottage; for she seldom meets with a very different

---

1 An imaginary being, invoked to frighten children, and hence any object of alarm or annoyance.

Reception, from the most sumptuous Palaces down to the poorest Hut; she may, indeed, perceive, that the Force of her Charms can be properly known only on long Acquaintance. There is a Severity in her Countenance which may please less, at first, than the alluring Sweetness of Falshood; but, in Time, her's is seen to be unfading Beauty; and tho' she may sometimes appear severe, is never morose. The whole Majesty in her Mein pleases, while it awes Beholders, who have any Taste for true Loveliness; and the longer her Votaries serve her, the more they are captivated with her Charms; Time increases their Love, and Familiarity raises their Adoration, an Effect not to be paralelled in any other Case. From the little Acquaintance People have with this Divine Goddess, they sometimes mistake one for her, who bears a small Resemblance to some of her Features, but so greatly heightned and bloated, that, to a distinguishing Eye, she is no more like her, than a *Saracen's* Head is like the *Venus* of *Medicis*,[1] and her true Names are *Brutality* and *Censoriousness*. This Ape of her Divinity, I believe, frequents Masquerades as much or more than she does. Accustomed to Excesses, People lose the Relish for the true Medium, and make but one Step from Flattery to Abuse.

Those who have fawned and cringed in a Drawing-Room, till after Ten o'Clock, will, before Eleven, under the Shelter of an antick[2] Dress and Mask, be lavishly dealing out their Impertinence and Incivility in the *Hay-market*. Observing this to Lady *Rochester*, she replied, "That she looked on a Masquerade as the *English Saturnalia*;[3] and as People of Fashion here were more abject Slaves to ceremonious Forms than the *Roman* Domesticks were to their Masters, it was but reasonable; that they should have their Days of Liberty to declare their Disgust with Impunity, and revile those they disapprove." I found her Ladyship so prejudiced in Favour of the *Saturnalia*, because of its Antiquity, that she made no Distinction between Freedom and Licentiousness.

I soon perceived that I should acquire more Knowledge of the true Dispositions of Mankind at three of these Assemblies, than by living three Months in the polite World; for it was the first Time I

---

1 Heads of Saracens, a general term for Arabs, Turks, Muslims, etc., were depicted on inn-signs. Venus de Medicis, a celebrated statue of Venus, was on display at the Medici Palace in Rome until its removal to Florence in 1680.

2 Grotesque, fantastic.

3 The Roman festival of Saturn, characterized by unrestrained merrymaking.

saw People in their natural Characters; the Mind was now apparent, the Face only hid; and, as the Company I was with, were much used to these Entertainments, they could see thro' the Masks, which would have concealed many of my Acquaintance from my less discerning Eyes, and by their Assistance I perceived the forced Prude indulging in Coquetry: the affectedly Grave giving a loose to Mirth and Pleasure; the fawning, pert, and impertinent; great Statesmen condescending to be trifling, and Philosophers to be foolish; all laying aside those Parts, which Interest, the Love of Power, or of Fame, induced them to act in publick.

Lady *Cambridge* was as new to this Entertainment as myself, never having been at a Masquerade before; and I could see the great Familiarity with which every one accosted her, with as little Distinction as they could the lowest Plebeian, greatly offended her Pride, and she could scarcely prevail on herself to conceal so much Nobility under a Mask. That I might be sure of the Cause of the Disturbance I perceived in her, I observed, that, "this Diversion seemed an Emblem of Death; it laid all Hearts open, and put an End to all Dissimulation and Pretence; and if the Resurrection was not so quick, I should be more on a Par with the rest of the World, since I was not one of the Number who durst not appear without an internal Mask, unless I had an external one to conceal me: That, like the Grave too, it levelled all Distinctions, and brought high and low on an Equality." Upon thus touching the tender Point, her Ladyship answered, that, "indeed she thought Masquerades could never long meet with Encouragement from Persons of Rank, unless they could find out a Method of distinguishing their Conditions." I proposed a Coronet on the Mask, as the easiest Method of fixing the Stamp of Rank and Fashion on those who could claim it. She was charmed with the Thought, and declared, "She would endeavour to bring her Friends into it; and if it once became general, she should be a constant Person at those Diversions, since, in every respect, but that leveling Quality, she liked them extremely."

A Masquerade, by no means, answered my Expectations, the Variety of Characters, which, I was told, were there personated, seemed to promise much Entertainment; but before half the Evening was spent, I found that Wit, the great Requisite to make them so, was a scarce Commodity; and that after the Wearer was once dressed, he thought as little of the Character he had assumed, as he did of the Propriety of it when he chose the Habit. Thus one sees a Harlequin limping with difficulty a-cross the Room; an old Woman skipping and dancing more nimbly than any of the Company; a *French Petit*

Maitre[1] pensive or sleepy; a Fortune-teller dancing a Minuet; a Bear exercising the Height of solemn Politeness; a Shepherdess bold and impudent; a Nun coquetishly frisky; a *Turk* drinking Wine, and a *Spaniard* easy, gay, and familiar.

Tho' Novelty has great Charms, yet I grew weary before the greatest Part of the Company: the lateness of the Hour contributed more than any thing to tire me.[2] I could not reconcile myself to the Custom of the civilized Part of the World of reversing the Orders of Nature, of sleeping the best Part of the Day, neglecting the Sun in his Brightness, and inventing artificial Lights to illuminate the Night. It was strange to me to find that People were never lively but when they should be at rest.

I was inclined to suspect them of a superstitious Regard to Midnight, especially when I reflected that the only Musick which was on any settled Establishment, and the only Lay Monitor, performed at that Time, and in the darkest Season of the Year; a Time, to Persons who keep regular Hours, the most unfit for Music, since there will seldom be much Harmony in the Minds of People waked out of a Sleep which was beginning to refresh them after the Labours of the Day, even tho' *Cecilia*[3] herself was to be the Musician.

The *Christmas* Monitor is better imagined, as he first rouses them with his Bell; and thus prepares them, with no small Solemnity, to listen to the moral Sentences,[4] which he has most ingeniously put into Verse. Not such, indeed, as the Muses inspire, and entitle the Author to the pure Streams of *Helicon*;[5] Ale being both his Inspirer, and his Reward; and instead of flying on the Back of *Pegasus*,[6] he creeps with a Crutch. This Institution I have often thought might be of great Use in a Religion, whose Doctrine was designed to fright from Sin by well wrought Terrors, rather than to encourage Virtue by Hopes. The awful Sound of his Bell, at an Hour to which Darkness and the Stillness of Night gives a Solemnity, would greatly heighten the Figures and strengthen the Metaphors, in a Discourse

---

1 Dandy, fop.
2 The Haymarket masquerades began in the late evening and ended the following morning.
3 The patron saint of musicians.
4 Sayings, maxims.
5 Mountain home of the Muses in ancient Greece; its streams supposedly inspired those who drank from them.
6 The mythological winged horse, representing poetic inspiration or genius.

formed to work on the Fears of our timerous Imaginations. Religious Hobgoblins as well as childish Bugbears, are but little believed in Sunshine. That great Luminary dispels Superstition as well as all other Clouds and Vapours; it clears the Understanding as well as the Sky; it nourishes only what is natural, banishing all phantastick Forms which are forced to fly before it, and take Shelter under the Shade of Night, when the Mind is more gloomy and less rational. Notwithstanding my Objections of turning the Night into Day, I was obliged, in great Measure, to conform to the general Custom, tho' never so far as to suffer it to deprive me of the Enjoyment of the blessed Sun, whose Presence had more Charms for me, than the Company of those who despised it; so that my Nights, not my Days, were abridged by these late Entertainments; and the next was obliged to make up to me for the Encroachments on the Night before, if requisite, which it seldom was, as I had been accustomed to take little Sleep.

CHAPTER XXVII

It was usual with Lord *Dorchester* and myself to take a Morning Walk, whenever the Weather would permit it, in the Fields leading to *Chelsea*,[1] which gave Rise to an Adventure so interesting, that I cannot forbear communicating it to your Ladyship, tho' it is foreign to the History I have engaged to give you of myself.

For several Days together we observed a Man, who, with Care, avoided the publick Path, tho' he walked in the same Fields. Curiosity, at last, tempted us to go up to him. His sickly and dejected Aspect excited our Compassion. Lord *Dorchester*, whose Humanity made him feel for the Distresses of others, tho' of such a Nature as he could never have experienced, was greatly touched with the Appearance of Wretchedness so visible in this Man. He was sitting down on the Trunk of a Tree; we seated ourselves by him; he attempted to rise, more from a Desire of flying Society, than from an humble Intention of giving Place to Persons who seemed more in Fortune's Favour than himself; but my Lord would not permit him to leave us. After asking several Questions about indifferent Things, and with great Difficulty leading him into Discourse, my Lord told him, that, "he might appear impertinent in thus forcing himself into his Acquain-

---

1 Chelsea Common, in the eighteenth century a large open space separating the village of Chelsea from London.

tance, but that Compassion, and a Desire to assist him was his Motive. That he appeared unhappy; and if it was not improper, we should be infinitely obliged to him if he would inform us what was the Occasion of it."

The poor Man shook his Head, and declined complying with his Request, saying, "Nothing was less agreeable to hear, nor to relate, than a Series of Distresses; that he made it a Rule never to talk of his Misfortunes, for if he met with bad, ill-natured People, they would dislike him for being wretched, and avoid him as if Misery was infectious. On the contrary, to Persons of Humanity he would not chuse to give even the Pain of Compassion." And, indeed, so much did he act up to this Declaration, that he could not be prevailed upon to give any Account of himself. My Lord finding he was not likely to succeed by Intreaties, endeavoured to draw him into the Subject; and taking the Hint from his Cloaths, which were a tattered Suit of Regimentals, began to expatiate on all the Hardships to which military Men are liable. Among the rest, he took Notice of the unhappy State of a disbanded Regiment. My Lord no sooner fell on this Topic, than it was very visible in the poor Man's Countenance, that he had hit upon the Cause of his Distress. My Lord perceiving this, dwelt on the Subject, and imagined all the Cases in which it could be most cruel; supposed many of these Men to have Wives and Children to maintain, out of a Half-pay,[1] which could scarcely afford Support to themselves; described the continual Sollicitation to Men in Power; and the Neglect and Indignities which, he said, Poverty was apt to receive. He then talked of the anxious State of a Suitor's Mind, elevated with Hopes, only to be sunk the next Moment in Despair. The poor Man could hold out no longer, Tears ran down his Face, and he begged of my Lord to say no more, for he had touched the String of his Misfortunes; crying out, with a kind of Agony, "I have too long suffered all, and more than you have described, and gone thro' the Scenes your Imagination has only drawn. Be grateful, Sir, to Providence, for never having afflicted you with such Misfortunes, for I perceive it has not, or you could not have dwelt on Circumstances of which the bare Recollection, tho' the Time of Suffering was past, must cut you to the Soul." Wound up to this Pitch it was easy to draw him into a Relation of Misfortunes, which had too entire a Possession of his Thoughts to be any longer concealed; but it was

---

1 Army officers not on active duty received only half of their regular salary.

some time before we could get him into a regular Narration. The Disturbance of his Mind made him repeat a confused Set of Facts, mixed with such pathetic Exclamations, as drew Tears from my Eyes. However, at last, my Lord composed his Spirits, so far, that he began thus:

"My Name, Sir, is *Traverse*, I was put into the Army as soon as I was able to carry a Pair of Colours,[1] which my Father, who was a Colonel, gave me; but dying soon after, and leaving me with nothing for my Support, but the Profits of my Post, and the Gratitude of his Friends, among whom he had spent his Fortune, it was not long before I experienced the disagreeable Parts of my Profession. My Father's Friends caressed me, indeed, and courted me into their Company, which was attended with Expences very inconvenient to me. I durst not, however, wholly neglect them, as I hoped a Return from their Friendship, the frail Dependence of People of my Profession, where Interest is the sovereign Disposer of every thing. But the first Opportunity I had of trying these Friends shewed me, that if Hope was a Pleasure, it was one I was likely long to enjoy. Every Vacancy in our Regiment raised it, and I got no Preferment to gratify it. Some Body or other was constantly put over my Head, tho' they sometimes could scarcely perform the easy Exercises practised among us. My Patrons[2] assured me they did all they could; but some great Power frustrated their Endeavours. However, they fed me with Promises of procuring me the next Lieutenancy. For some Years, I believe, their Intentions corresponded with their Words; but, at last, I found the highest Favours I should ever receive from them was being drawn into their Follies and Expences, little suitable to my Inclinations or Income; being treated with the little Ceremony of a Dependent, and obliged to please their Convenience and Pride, which led them to like having Gentlemen in their Train of Followers. Many would shew me as a young Man whom they had taken under their Protection, and whose Fortune they intended to push, having a great Regard for my Father; and never failed insinuating, that they conferred continual Obligations upon me. This greatly

---

1 I.e., receive a commission as an ensign, the lowest rank of infantry officer.
2 Fielding was probably aware of the notorious definition of "patron" in Samuel Johnson's *Dictionary*, published five years earlier in 1755: "one who countenances, supports or protects. Commonly a wretch who supports with insolence, and is paid with flattery." Johnson's own contempt for patrons stemmed from the neglect of Lord Chesterfield, to whom he had dedicated his *Plan of a Dictionary of the English Language* (1747).

mortified my Pride, as I was conscious of receiving none from them, unless they esteemed disagreeable Conversation as such. Finding I was not likely to be raised by their Interest; and that, notwithstanding I had been in several Engagements, and received particular Encomiums from my Officers, yet still I was passed by in every Preferment, as much as if it had been impossible for me to change my Post, I, at last, began to neglect them; and, in Despair, resolved to think no more of it, but to try whether Time would be a better Friend. Fortunately for me we had a new Colonel soon after this, who, understanding how long I had been in the Regiment; and having enquired into my Character, and the Reason of my remaining so long an Ensign, told me, I should see, that Merit had greater Interest with him, than the Recommendations of People in Power; and accordingly gave me the first vacant Lieutenancy. But he dying, in a short Time, I had no Opportunity of experiencing his farther Goodness, which, I am persuaded, would have led him to promote me in due Order. However, I was to owe the Obligation to a fairer Hand. Sometime after my Colonel's Death, I renewed my Acquaintance with a young Lady, which had been for many Years interrupted. During our Childhood, we had been almost continually together; but were separated by an Employment which called her Father into a foreign Country, from whence he was but just returned. I had not long visited at his House before I found a new kind of Uneasiness, which made me insensible to every thing that did not concern my great Wish, the longing I had to make my former Play-fellow the Companion of my Soul. The Recollections of our childish Sports, and all the Passages of our infant Years, created an Intimacy between us almost as soon as we met. Tho' she was handsome, Beauty was her least Charm; her Understanding was excellent, tho' Years and Experience could not be said to have improved it. Her Heart was as free from Blemish as it was filled with Virtues. Then, the numberless Attractions in every Look and Motion, were so far beyond Description, that I will be silent, tho' I could dwell on them for ever. I flattered myself with a Belief of a friendly Return of Affection from this Angel; but this was not sufficient. I ardently longed that she should conceive more tender Sentiments, tho' the low State of my Fortune would not permit me to endeavour to inspire them; as I considered it was the Means of making her the Companion of my Despair, of which alone I wished to act the Miser, and to communicate no Part to her. Accident, however, betrayed the Love I feared to reveal, and her Behaviour upon the Occasion served to bind my Fetters faster. Her Generosity charmed me to excess, and we soon enjoyed the enchanting Pleasure arising from Profession of mutual Love, with all the Warmth and Delicacy, that could be felt or expressed by People filled with a passionate Tenderness for each other, and blessed with frequent Interviews. We were so happy, we even forgot there was a Possibility of being happier; but the evil Star that presided at my Birth would not leave me long in this Situation. The Father of my *Caroline*, for that was my Angel's Name, died, and having seen the mutual Affection between me and his Daughter, and the Disadvantages which would arise to her from an Union between us, left her a good Fortune, but on Condition she should not marry me. Notwithstanding this cruel Usage, she (Miracle of Goodness) grieved for a Father who did not deserve it from her, and I was sufficiently employed in endeavouring to comfort her, tho' I was little able to bear a Circumstance which, I thought, must deprive me of all my Hopes; for I could not think of bringing her into a State where her Support must end with my Life, which had more than the common Chances of Mortality against it. But her Generosity disregarded these Dangers. She had a Sum of Money (the Legacy of an old Aunt) sufficient to buy an Exchange of a Company[1] for me. She pressed me to lay it out in this Manner; but I was determined against making that Use of it. It would, indeed, have made our Income more tolerable, but in case of my Death, she must have been left entirely destitute. After finding that her Generosity resisted all I could say to deter her from sharing the Fortune of such a Wretch as myself, (perhaps Arguments so contrary to the tender Sentiments of my Heart were not enforced in a persuasive Manner) I told her, that if she would venture to marry me, and to share my poor Commission, I should be the happiest Man on Earth, and would place her Money in such a Manner, that, after my Death it might be some little Dependance for her; but that I absolutely would neither lay it out, nor receive any thing from it while I lived. She seemed to consent, and we agreed to relinquish the Fortune her Father had charged with such heavy Conditions, and despise any Treasure when put in Competition with the Possession of each other. Various Accidents, however, deferred, for some time, the Execution of our Purpose; most of these Delays, indeed, proceeded from her; but my Confidence in her Truth and Love was such, that I could object to nothing she proposed, nor harbour any Suspicion of a Coldness in her

---

1 The money would be used to purchase a commission in another regiment, where a higher-ranking position was available.

Heart. The Liberty of spending, almost all my Time with her, constituted a State of Bliss, when she gave it some Interruption, one Day, by delivering to me a Captain's Commission; in the procuring of which she had laid out all her little Fortune. While a Friend (but an injudicious one) had been transacting this Affair, she had, on specious Pretences, deferred our Marriage, to avoid my having the Power of preventing her from concluding it. It was surprizing how well she had concealed the Knowledge of it from me. I have seldom been more sensibly hurt than at this Discovery of what she had done. She accompanied it with saying, that she could not believe one who was so entirely mine, whose Life and every Thought and Action depended so much on me, could ever remain in the World after I had left it; and therefore she had taken Care that I should enjoy the little Fortune had given her; but if she had had it in her Power to make me the smallest Reparation for the Injustice of mercenary People, she should think herself happy. Tho' I was overcome with her Generosity, yet my concern got the better of my Gratitude, and the first Thing I said was, That she had entailed Cowardice and constant Misery upon me; for I should be ever wretched with the Fear of what would become of her if I were to die. These sort of Conversations, when the Heart is so much engaged in them as mine was, are never obliterated from the Memory; but I find I ought often to check myself, for I am very tedious in my Narration. My Imagination was always too warm to suffer me to confine myself to a few principal Facts, when the slightest Circumstances were of such infinite Pleasure and Importance to me. However, I will suppress what passed between us on the Subject I have mentioned, tho' a thousand Things my *Caroline* said crowd to my Remembrance, and fill me with Rapture; but I will not allow Utterance to one, and only tell you, in few Words, that immediately after we were married."

CHAPTER XXVIII

"The Joy (continued the poor Captain) which I received from the Possession of my dear *Caroline* would have recompenced me for much greater Evils, than those I had experienced in Life. Every Day discovered some new Virtue in her Heart; Time even improved her Charms; and, however uncommon, what before Marriage was only violent Love and tender Esteem, grew in me almost to Love and Adoration. She was so good an Œconomist, that we lived very neatly on our small Income; and she appeared so entirely contented, that my Ambition was lost in Excess of Happiness. I scarcely thought of farther Preferment, nor felt the unjust Preference given to much younger Officers than myself. I saw Boys, qualified neither by Age, nor Experience for the lowest Posts in the Army, put over my Head, and could not find Disturbance enough in my Mind to produce one Murmur. I considered Providence had lavished its Blessings on me, when it gave me my *Caroline*; and so considerable was my Portion of Happiness, that I had no Title to ask for any Thing more, but ought to leave to others the poor Enjoyments of Preferment. Nothing could tempt me out of her Company, but an Endeavour to get some little Place for her, which might afford her a Support in case the Thread of my earthly Felicity should be cut. For this I importuned my *Friends*; for though I had but little Confidence in them, yet this Application seemed my only chance. My Success answered my Faith, I got nothing done, after repeated Trials, to remove this Burden from my Mind, which imbittered my Joy by so many painful Reflections, it almost made me a Coward. Death appeared to me, so encompassed with Terrors, that I have often wondered how I could hazard the Meeting of it, with tolerable Composure in the Field, when, in the Quiet of my own House, the least Disorder filled me with inexpressible Agonies, from the Apprehensions I had of its Increase. Though I have mentioned my Happiness as perfect, yet it was often interrupted by being obliged to attend the Army Abroad, and leave my Wife to mourn my Absence; but then joyful Returns succeeded, and recompenced us for past Pains. I often doubted, whether I could be justified in hazarding the Support of an inestimable Wife, and several fine Children in all the Chances of War. It seemed reasonable, that in Consideration of them, I ought to have sold out;[1] but, then again, it was ungrateful to my King, to have received his Pay so long, and leave his Service at the only Time I could be useful. It was true, I had suffered a great Deal of ill Treatment; but that was because my Obscurity hid me from his Majesty's Knowledge, and gave Persons of Birth still more obscure, though higher in Office, Power to behave towards me, as such People will ever do to the unfriended. But, I had still another Reason to keep and perform the Duties of my Commission. Such an Action would have branded me with the Name of Coward, and that, I had not Courage to bear; I could have given up my Life for my Family; but my Reputation was of more Importance to me, and without it I should have been a Disgrace, instead of a Comfort to them. I should

---

1 Disposed of an army commission by selling it.

have been unworthy of my *Caroline*; nor would she, I am convinced, as much as she was a Prey to tender Fears, have consented that I should have brought so great a Misfortune on myself, in order to remove the Chance of one from her. It is easy to imagine, the Peace gave us great Joy; we little foresaw the Consequences. We had now nine Children, the eldest not seventeen, the youngest under a Year old. My Health was much impaired by the Campaigns abroad; but I doubted not, that I should recover it, by the quiet and happy Enjoyment of the Company of my Wife and Children. Nor was I mistaken; by their kind Care and Attendance, I was grown much better, when I heard the fatal News of the Reduction of our Regiment.[1] I was greatly shocked at this unexpected Blow; by this Means, our Income was dwindled to so little, that it was insufficient for the Support of so large a Number. None of our Children were large enough to contribute much to the general Stock, by their most industrious Endeavours. I was too feeble in Body, and too weak in Mind, to give any Assistance. The most extreme Poverty, had it afflicted none but myself, would have rather served as a Spur, than a Depression to my Spirits; but when I reflected on the Difficulties into which I had brought my Wife, it overwhelmed me with Grief; nor could it be cured by the Patience and Chearfulness with which she bore this Misfortune. Her Behaviour, by shewing her Merit still more conspicuously, only heightened my Regret, that such Virtue should suffer. As fit to struggle with bad Fortune, as to grace good, she soon, by various Kinds of Work, found Means of increasing our Income, though the necessary Care of so large a family would not suffer her to gain enough to enable us to continue our Sons at School, which was a great Mortification, as we had always been desirous of giving them good Education, even though we should streighten ourselves for that Purpose, when our Income was the most plentiful. All the Service my Health could permit me to be of, was to turn Schoolmaster to my Children, that they might suffer as little as possible from our Poverty. Thus, by my *Caroline*'s Ingenuity and Industry, we were supported; nor, was I ever, for a Moment, able to perceive, that she either repined or grieved at being obliged to give this Assistance; on the contrary, she appeared to take greater Pleasure in it, than in any Amusements she had ever enjoyed. But, as if Providence had some wise and good Purpose in afflicting us, which, by this Means, was frustrated, she one Day, after returning Home wet quite through

---

1 The regiment would be dispersed, and the officers put on half pay.

her Cloaths, from a Place where her Business had called her, was seized, as we sat at Dinner, with a Stroke of the Palsy, which, at first, affected her Head, and deprived her of all her Limbs. However, she recovered her Senses, I may say, sooner than I did mine; for the Condition she was in, and the Occasion of it, left me very little Use of my Reason. The Physician who attended her, and was my good Friend, taking the greatest Care of her, without accepting any Reward, but the Pleasure of doing a charitable Action, declared, that he had no Hopes of her Recovery but from the Bath-Waters,[1] and offered to send with us, a Recommendation to one of his own Profession, who could well supply his Place in Care of her. You may imagine I did not hesitate a Moment, in my Resolution of sending her thither, notwithstanding the bad State of our Circumstances. I sold, directly, all the Furniture of our House, and every Thing we had, which could raise Money; taking, for my Children, a little Hole, which would just contain them; and leaving them under the Care of the eldest Son and Daughter (who were more prudent than their Ages promised) I, with my second Daughter, attended my Wife to *Bath*, where I had the Joy, in about two Months, to see her recover her Health and Limbs, excepting her Hands, which still remained so lame that she could not even dress herself. I never saw her so much affected with any Thing; she would have esteemed herself happy, could she have bought the Use of her Hand with the Loss of her Foot; for she looked on herself as a helpless Burden to a distressed Family. But, for once, I differed much from her, and rejoiced at the Seat in which the Distemper had fixed, if it would not quite leave her, as, by giving her the Power of using Exercise, I hoped, her Health might be preserved, which, in the other Case could not be expected. After a pretty long Trial, she was told there was little Possibility of her recovering her Hand; and the Weather growing fine, it was imagined Air might be of more Service to her. This, and the low Price of Things in the Country, made us determine to return no more to *London*; so enquiring for the cheapest Country in that Part of the World, we removed to the Borders of *Wales*, where we hired a small House, and sent for our Children, by the least expensive Conveyance. When we had been there some Time, I was induced to return to Town, in order to get some Redress, having been informed of a good Opportunity of attempting it; but found the Hopes that

---

1   The famous mineral waters at Bath, available for drinking at the Pump Room, were thought to cure a variety of ailments.

had been given me were very fallacious, and should have soon returned, had I not been seized with a malignant Fever, wherein, I verily believe, I must have perished for Want, had not my Physician assisted me, still more in the Capacity of a Friend than his Profession. I am now detained here, by some Business I am transacting for him, happy to have the Power of giving some little Token of my Gratitude. As my Recovery is yet but very imperfect, I come every Morning, to take a Walk in the Fields, for the Benefit of the Air, which I find is a Place much frequented, likewise, by this Lady and yourself, whom I have often observed." Here the poor Man ended his Story, which had detained us a long Time, even to the Encroaching on an Engagement of my Lord's; but he would not interrupt a Narration so hardly obtained. I could not forbear asking after his Wife, whether the Country had not done her Service. He told me, she was just the same as when she went into it, but, he thanked God, in very good Health; and that he had contrived to prevent her knowing of his last Illness. We parted from the poor Man with heavy Hearts; it lowered my Spirits for the whole Day, and filled my Lord's Thoughts for a longer Time.

CHAPTER XXIX

Lord *Dorchester* made very diligent Enquiry after our Captain, to know the Reality of what he said; for People who would not misapply their Bounty, must be on their Guard against what they hear, lest Truth should be disguised by Falshood, or clouded by Partiality. His Search proved to the Honour of the Gentleman's Veracity; for he learnt every Circumstance from other Hands. He was then not less earnest in procuring him Preferment; and, as there were many Vacancies, he got the Choice of two Commissions. The next Time we met our Captain, my Lord desired he would come to his House that Morning, and begged I would go along with him, that I might have the Satisfaction of seeing how the poor Man took the News of his Preferment. I should unwillingly have been absent from this Interview, therefore readily complied with his Lordship's Request.

At the appointed Hour the Captain came, and was brought up Stairs to us; the Surprize he had been at first thrown into, by so unexpected an Invitation to the House of one of my Lord's Rank, and, in a Manner which seemed to promise him some Benefit, still was visible when he entered. My Lord asked him, if he wished so much to be again in the King's Service, as to like going into the *West-Indies*. The poor Man answered, "that he really did not; for his

Health was so bad he feared he should not be able to bear the Change of Climate, and his Life was now of more Importance than ever to his Family, since his Wife was intirely incapable of gaining the Subsistence he could not leave her; which made him rather prefer his Half-Pay, than hazard a Life the Loss of which must bring so much Distress on those he loved to Excess. Besides, the Troops were to set sail so soon, that he should not have Time to bid his Family, perhaps, a last Adieu." My Lord told him, "he was sorry to hear this was his Way of thinking, having got a Majority[1] for him in one of those Regiments." Notwithstanding the Reluctance the poor Man had expressed to going abroad, yet he received this News with as much Gratitude as if it had been the very Thing he wished. "He acknowledged, his Obligations to my Lord were infinite; made many Exclamations on the Uncommonness of his Fortune, which had denied him all Assistance from People who professed themselves his Friends, had borne the Appearance of it for a great Number of Years, and had even given him a Right to expect they should be really such, by receiving Obligations from his Family; and now he had the highest Benefits conferred by one entirely a Stranger to him."

To this my Lord replied, that, "he wished what he had done, had suited his Inclination and Circumstances as much as he hoped it would." The Captain then endeavoured to hide the Regret which filled his Heart, for Fear of not appearing sufficiently grateful. He told my Lord, "the Obligation was equal, he had supplied all his apparent Wants; of the particular Temper of his Mind his Lordship could not be a Judge; he had done all that Compassion and Generosity could suggest, to make him happy; and, Sir," said he, "I hope, my Tears were the Effect of a poor Despondency; your Goodness has raised better Thoughts in me; the Change of Climate may repair my Constitution, and, I may, in a few Years, return in Health to my dear Wife and Children." However, so far was his Heart from the Chearfulness he endeavoured to express, that Tears ran down his Cheeks, in Spite of all his Efforts to restrain them; and finding himself unable to controul Emotions which he thought were a Kind of Ingratitude to his Benefactor; he just summoned up Strength enough to return him Thanks once more, and then went out of the Room.

No sooner was the Door shut than the Violence of his Grief found its Way, and, with his unavailing Endeavours to conceal it, I really feared would have destroyed him on the Spot. We had followed

---

1 The rank of a major.

him immediately, which heightened his Distress, as he wished to remain unseen. When he got into the Hall, my Lord desired him to accompany us into a Parlour, of which we opened the Door, and, thereby, presented to his View, his Wife and Children; my Lord having sent for them all up to Town, in order to give him this joyous Surprize, and to have the Pleasure of being Witness to it, and to procure a Meeting in Case he had chosen to go to the *West-Indies*. Even the beloved *Caroline* knew not half my Lord's Purpose. I was soon apprehensive we had done Harm by the Suddenness of this Interview; for the Captain fainted away instantly, and was so long a Time before he was brought to himself, that I feared the Joy had been too strong for his weak Thread of Life. His Wife seemed greatly terrified, and her Behaviour indicated the Affection which every Action of her Life had shewn. The Recovery of his Senses restored the general Joy; which increased to a great Degree of Extacy, when my Lord informed him, that he had the Choice of a Majority in a Regiment going to the *West Indies*, or to be a Captain of Horse here (having received the Promise of the latter, after he sent for his Family) which he now imagined he would prefer; adding, "to lessen the Uneasiness you seem under for your Family, here are Bills[1] to the Value of 1500 *l*. and I will furnish for you the House you shall take, let it be where it will." Their Joy rose to a Height that must have been painful; they looked on my Lord with Adoration, and gave Way to Raptures that would have forced a Heart the most insensible to the Sensations of others, to partake of theirs. How much my Lord did so, was visible in his Countenance; for I never saw any Thing like the Bliss expressed in it; he seemed to feel a more solid Delight than they did; and I can easily imagine he did so. I think their Satisfaction could scarcely exceed mine; but his must be higher, as he had the inexpressible Pleasure of having been the Cause of their Happiness, added to that of seeing it. Their Expressions of Gratitude were the most lively that could be, and they seemed not to know whether most to felicitate and caress each other, or to thank their Benefactor. They did both in a Breath, and were in an Agitation of Joy scarcely to be imagined, till on enumerating the Comforts he had thus bestowed on them, they all melted into Tears with Excess of Delight; nor could either my Lord or myself, refrain from joining with them. This, in some Measure composed them, and they began to take

---

1   The forerunners of modern cheques, bills were written orders to a bank to pay a specified sum on a given date to the individual named on the bill.

Leave of us with the most ardent Acknowledgments. The Captain asked my Lord Pardon for the Reluctance with which he received the first News of his Bounty; adding, "that he hoped his Lordship would excuse what was caused by the Love of his Wife, if he considered how very irksome any Gift would be to himself, that should oblige him to leave his Lady. For he could see from his Behaviour, as well as know it from the Charms Nature had bestowed on her, that he was a very strong Instance of conjugal Affection." He concluded, with wishing us to live to a happy old Age together, and they bid us Adieu, having raised Blushes in both my Lord and myself by their Mistake, and mine were increased by my Lord's watching my Countenance. I never before saw him do so ill natured a Thing, as to make any one suffer a Moment's Uneasiness even from Bashfulness.

I wondered why these People should imagine us married; as a Man may have many Friends, but can have only one Wife; the Probability was, in my Opinion against them; and I could no otherwise account for an Error that had so disconcerted us both, than from a Belief that it proceeded from the Appearance of more Affection in my Lord's Behaviour, than was usual between Persons united by no dearer Tie than Friendship. This Construction was too agreeable for me to perplex myself by seeking any other.

The Happiness I had of late enjoyed, was doomed to be of short Continuance. The Evening of the Day in which my Lord had given such Felicity, by his Generosity to the distressed Captain and his Family, I went to an Assembly; at my Coming from thence, my footman was not to be found, and, to avoid the Trouble of returning into a crowded Room, I got into my Chair, and went away without him. As my Chairmen were carrying me under a dead Wall[1] that was in my Road, they were stopped by some Men, who pulled me out of my Chair, and forced me into another, which they had brought for that Purpose.

The Place being little frequented, my Screams were not heard, and what little Courage Nature had bestowed on my Chairmen, was quite overcome by the superior Number of the Enemy, and I was carried off without Resistance.

Every Step increased my Terror; but yet conscious that the Shrilness of a female Voice must be almost as useful in populous Streets as a Weapon of Defence, I endeavoured to let down the Windows of the Chair, that I might the easier make myself heard. But this

---

1 A wall concealing the view of passengers on the road.

Attempt I perceived in vain: I then broke a Pane of Glass, but instead of receiving any Benefit thereby, I found that they were cased up with Wood on the Outside, I suppose to prevent the very Thing I intended. This Discovery, however, explained to me the sudden Darkness which had immediately followed the putting me into the Chair, and increased the Terrors, which the other Circumstances alone would have rendered sufficient.

However, unwilling to give up the Hope, of which I was thus in Reason deprived, I exerted my Voice to its loudest Key, flattering myself with a Possibility that it might be distinguished by some chance Persons passing close to the Chair, whose Compassion might lead them to enquire the Cause. But this Effort only served to spend my Spirits the more entirely. The Men who attended me, I imagined, kept every one else from coming within Hearing, and we proceeded without Molestation till we arrived at the House where we were designed to stop. The Chair carried me into the Hall, I was led into a dark room, and there left to my own Thoughts, with Subject for "Meditation even to Madness."[1]

It would be in vain, should I attempt to describe my Terrors; I had heard of Robberies and Murders; I was not conscious of having given such Offence to any one, as should incline them to perpetrate so horrid an Action; but then, so much Ceremony seemed unnecessary for a Robbery, which might have been performed with more Ease and Expedition. Thus I remained terrified and perplexed, fearing every Thing, yet fixing upon nothing, till I was almost distracted with my Apprehensions, from which, I was, at last, relieved, by seeing the Door open. The Terrors of Expectation were so increased by the Approach of the Danger which I feared, that, no longer able to support the Agonies it raised, Life forsook me, and I fainted away before I could distinguish for whom the Door was opened.

CHAPTER XXX

My Horrors did not end with the fainting Fit they had occasioned; I came to myself in Apprehensions no less dreadful than if certain Death had awaited me. Fear paints in very strong Colours; my Imagination represented to me armed Men, of most tremendous Mien

---

1 Calista, in Nicholas Rowe's *The Fair Penitent* (1703) V.i.21: "Here's room for meditation, ev'n to madness."

and merciless Behaviour; it cloathed them like the Murderers in *Macbeth*,[1] with the additional Terrors they would wear when one's self was to become the Victim of their Cruelty.

I could not immediately venture to look up, and when I did, it was not directly that the Appearance of a fine Woman, richly and gaily dressed, could dispel those dreadful Ideas from my Brain. However, her Endeavours to calm the Fears she had raised, at last succeeded; and when she perceived me, in some Degree, come to my Senses, she sat down by me, with a Countenance, which, under a Smile, tried to conceal, Dejection, Anger and Disdain; but so ineffectually, that at any other Time, every Glance would have discomposed and alarmed me; but I now beheld her with Pleasure; for however terrible a Woman's Rage may be to a Mind at Ease, yet her Face was more sweet than Mercy and Benevolence, when compared to the grim Murderers my Fancy had formed.

She left me some Leisure to recover my self before she broke Silence, during which Time I recollected her to be the Marchioness[2] of *Trente*, whom I had often met in my Visits, though she had never condescended to speak to me, and had always cast such disdainful Glances upon me, as made me not more forward to court her Acquaintance than she seemed desirous of cultivating mine; on the contrary, I used to keep at as great a Distance as I could possibly, flying her as if my Mind had some Knowledge of the Uneasiness I was to suffer from her.

At length, she began thus, "Though it may mortify my Pride to confess my Love to a successful Rival, yet my Design requires I should inform you, that I have long entertained a particular Affection for Lord *Dorchester*, and had once Reason to believe it was not without Return; though now his Views are more humble, and he confines his Desires to Objects easier obtained, I cannot longer endure to see him thus debase himself, neglecting a State of Happiness that might be as lasting as his Life; but, as I don't chuse to confer so great an Obligation as I should, by declaring my Care for him, I have taken this Method of consulting at once his Welfare and my own."

---

1   The three murderers employed by Macbeth in Shakespeare's *Macbeth*; they kill Banquo, Lady Macduff, and her son.
2   A marchioness, the wife of a marquis, holds the second-highest rank in the British aristocracy, of which the titles are, in descending order: Duke and Duchess, Marquis and Marchioness, Earl and Countess, Viscount and Viscountess, Baron and Baroness. The Marchioness of Trente is presumably a widow.

She then offered me an Income superior to that he gave me, on Condition, "I would promise, never, from that Hour, to see, to write, or send any verbal Message to him."

With great Warmth, I told her, "I would not enter into such an Engagement, could she reward me with the possession of all *Europe*; no, not to save my Life; because, I believed, I should not be able to perform it; and I would never make a Promise so contrary to my Happiness, as it would be bringing myself into an almost irresistible Temptation to break it."

"Wonderfully scrupulous truely," replied her Ladyship; "but how ignorant soever most People may be, you find my vigilant Endeavours to discover you, have not proved fruitless: And I must tell you, it would be more wise to accept the Proposal I have so generously made you, and to spend your Time in making Peace with Heaven, and rendering yourself fit for Death, with which our Mortality threatens us every Hour, than persist to glory in Wickedness, with such unparalleled Impudence."

I was so ignorant of the Marchioness's Meaning, that my Answer could not be very much to the Purpose; but it was spoke with that Spirit which such groundless, and, to me, unaccountable Abuse could not fail of raising in a Disposition like mine. Its Effect was natural; her Temper was combustible, and, consequently, being kindled by the Fire in mine, burst into Flame. She rose from her Chair in a violent Rage, telling me, "she would no longer give the Power of choice to so insolent a Creature, but by Force perform what I would not consent to; for she would convey me to such a Distance, that I should no longer see and bewitch Lord *Dorchester*."

I was very sensible of the Terrors of this Menace; but could not stoop to one whose unworthy Treatment of me gave little Hope of Redress from her Compassion; what Mercy can we expect from those who are void even of Justice. I told her with an Air of Indignation that still rendered me more qualified to converse with her, than I thought I could have been, that "I would never consent to my own Unhappiness, whatever her Power might inflict." Adding that, "it would not redound greatly to the Honour of Lady *Trente*, to have made a Woman unhappy, who deserved no Evil from her."

The Marchioness did not deign to give me any Answer beside a disdainful Smile, then turning to a Woman who was just come into the Room, but had kept a strict Silence, "*Herner*," said she, "take this Wretch under your Care. See she is well guarded, and that she has no Means of corresponding with any one, either before or after she leaves this Town. Watch her well on the Road, but never converse with her; for I could not forgive any Relation of mine, who should so far debase herself."

The obsequious *Herner* curtsied, and promised exact Obedience, and then they both departed, leaving me to my own Reflections, which were not much interrupted for three Days; for so long was I locked up in that Room, where was no Bed, by whose Refreshment I might alleviate either my mental or bodily Uneasiness.

A little Fire was afforded me, and a bare Sufficiency of meagre Food, little superior to Bread and Water. I have since had Charity enough to believe, her Ladyship thought Fasting and Mortification most salutiferous[1] for my Soul; of whose State, it seems, she had entertained no very favourable Opinion. My Door was never unlocked, but to let in the necessary Supports of my Existence, and all these Offices were performed with such silent Gravity, as gave a greater Air of Melancholy and Solemnity to a Situation, which, your Ladyship will allow, was in none of its Circumstances, very lively and agreeable.

My chief Attendant was a little Girl of ten or eleven Years old; who whenever she came in, startled at me, as if I had been a Monster. If I spoke to her, she would run away, and if I offered to snatch hold of her, would scream as if I was going to murder her. If she was obliged to pass me, she would take as large a Circumference to avoid me, as if she imagined I had drawn an enchanted Circle round my Chair.[2] I need not say, that my Mind was in a very uneasy State; I had a Love for Freedom which ill agreed with Imprisonment; and I hourly repined at having exchanged the Pleasures of Lord *Dorchester's* Conversation for the most odious Solitude, with no Object to entertain my Eyes, or raise new Ideas in me; denied the sound of a human Voice, or any Thing that might in any Degree divert my Thoughts from the Pains of my present Situation, or from the Fears of what farther Punishment might still be in Store for me. Without even the Means of exposing a Body fatigued with Want of Rest, and worn out with Grief and Terror. A Mind less painfully affected than mine, would have found some Difficulty in sleeping in an uneasy Chair; to me, it was so near impossible, that I had but a few Moments Respite from my anxious Reflections, the whole Time I was there. Nothing more distressed me, than the Notion of my Lord's Uneasiness at my

---

1 Conducive to salvation.
2 Fielding also alludes to the association between drawing circles, which were thought to have magic properties, and sorcery or witchcraft in *The Adventures of David Simple* (II.vi).

sudden disappearing; and I know not how I could have been supported under all the Perplexity and Perturbation of my Mind, had I not formed great Hopes of making my Escape, when Time should have abated the Rigour of their Vigilance. I thought I had so much greater Reason to be diligent in discovering the Means of getting from thence, than they could have for keeping me there, that, I must, at length, be able to effect it. I flattered myself, that my Lord's Search after me, would give me another Chance. I imagined he must hear of the Violence with which I had been carried away, and could not doubt, but his Affection would contrive to rescue me.

By these Hopes, I was kept from sinking into absolute Despair, and the Necessity of exerting some Command over myself, gave me Spirit to go through three Days of this painful Confinement, with more Fortitude than I could have expected. The third Evening of this my enforced Residence, Mrs. *Herner* made her Appearance, and told me, "We were to go into the Country the next Morning." I asked, "if the Marchioness was to be of the Party." To my inexpressible Satisfaction, she answered in the Negative, but added, "that I was to be guarded as carefully as if I was under her Ladyship's eyes. Though, perhaps, she might a little exceed her Orders in her Care for my Convenience; for, she could not but confess, my Person, and the Dignity which accompanied my Grief, without any Mixture of Rage or Impatience, had prejudiced her so much in my Favour, that, she was sorry she was forbid conversing with me."

I could not help thanking her for her Humanity; the least Instance of Tenderness was now particularly dear to me. The Comparison my Mind drew between her and her right honourable Cousin, represented her in most advantageous Colours. I immediately conceived Hopes of finding favourable Opportunities for my Escape, either in my Journey, or in my Residence with one whose Compassion might make her less desirous of detaining me, consequently less vigilant than the Marchioness.

Before she left me, I begged that if I was still to live with Mutes, she would give me a Book; with which she readily complied. Her Complaisance gave me no Reason to admire her Taste. I should have been very sorry to have had my Studies long under her Direction; however, simple as the Book was, I preferred it to the Chaos of my own Mind; and was less offended at the Folly of the Author, than I should have been at my own in so long a Series of Thoughts, as I was not inclined to blush for his Foolishness. Before the Marchioness went to Bed, she came into my Dungeon, to renew the Offers she had at first made, in hopes, I suppose, that my Captivity had humbled me; but, when she found my Resolution remained unshaken, she informed me, that, "I was going to a Family Mansion, which was so very dismal and forlorn, that it would make me repent my Obstinacy, and I might depend on spending my whole Life there, unless I would agree to the Terms proposed."

My Answer was, that, "Nothing could appear so dreadful to me, as losing the Conversation of Lord *Dorchester*, and leaving him in such Uncertainty, concerning the Occasion of it."

The Marchioness replied, that, "my rejecting her Offer, would not prevent the Thing I seemed most to fear, since she would take Care he should never more hear of me." Without any further Discourse, she left the Room.

THE

HISTORY

OF

OPHELIA.

PUBLISHED BY

The Author of DAVID SIMPLE.

In TWO VOLUMES.

VOL. II.

CHAPTER XXXI

Mrs. *Herner* and I set out at the very Moment she had appointed; for I soon found, that she was as regular as a Pendulum. I could have wished she had borne a more extensive Resemblance to a Clock; constant Ticking, indeed, might have been too much; but had she struck, though it had been only once an Hour, it would have been a great Relief to me; for I felt an ardent Longing to talk, convinced by her Sex and Age, that she was, by Inclination, loquacious, I hoped to vanquish her obstinate Silence, by the Force of Temptation; and, accordingly, asked her various Questions, and such as I thought might be most interesting, but without the least Effect, not a single Word in Answer could I obtain; and, at last, desisted in Despair; keeping the rest of the Day an inviolable Silence.

As I had, for a considerable Time, no Employ but gazing at my Fellow Traveller's outward Form, I will make your Ladyship my companion in it, by describing her to you. Mrs. *Herner* was a little Woman near fifty Years of Age, very thin and brown; with a very long Nose and Chin, hollow Cheeks, wide Mouth, scarcely any Eyebrows, and light grey Eyes; which, however, were not void of a Sweetness, denoting some Portion of good Humour in the Mind that animated them. Dejection and Humiliation appeared in her whole Aspect; her Air, and every Look, were prim and demure.

I once saw Mrs. *Herner* before I was taken Prisoner by her Cousin, and then learnt a little of her History, which I shall impart. Mrs. *Herner* had originally a moderate Fortune, and, on the Death of the Marchioness's Mother, who was her Cousin-German,[1] and intimate Friend, she took the Marchioness to live with her, being moved to Compassion by her being left intirely destitute of a Provision. Mrs. *Herner*, from the Time she first became possessed of her Fortune, lived above her Income; and though she perceived the Principal was every Year decreasing, she had not Prudence to retrench. The Rank in which she lived, gave fair Opportunity to the Marchioness's Charms, to win her a more lasting Provision than she could have received from Mrs. *Herner*; accordingly, before she was eighteen, the Marquis of *Trente* saw her, and becoming truly enamoured, married her; but lived a very short Time after raising her to the Rank and Fortune, which gave Birth to her uncontrouled Insolence.

---

1 First cousin.

Mrs. *Herner's* Fortune lasted a very few Years beyond this Marriage; and, by a strange Fatality, she spent to the last Shilling before she attempted to lessen her Expences. When she had no longer Means to support them, the Marchioness seemed to hold out the Hand of Consolation to her, inviting her Home; but the poor Woman soon found that Pride, not Generosity, offered her this necessary Relief; for the Marchioness made her exchange Poverty for Wretchedness. She esteemed so highly an Act she was bound in Duty to perform, that lest Mrs. *Herner* should be less sensible of the Weight of the Obligation, she refreshed her Remembrance continually, and expected, in Return for her Charity, that she should undertake the Care of her Family, and comply with every Inclination her Ladyship should condescend to signify. Her Passions, were extremely violent, and never appeared in such full Lustre, as when her unhappy Cousin was the Object, for as she had no other Dependence, she knew she must endure all.

Thus the poor Woman, for a Subsistence, sold herself to the most abject Slavery: But she was too proud to take any other Means of gaining a Support. *Pride that licks the Dust,*[1] she had, but no true Spirit; for to pacify the Marchioness in her Furies, she would descend to the meanest Flattery, and was ruled by a Frown or a Nod. From a continual servile Compliance with the Will of another, she lost all Liberty of Thought, of which only one's own Meanness can deprive one. She entirely forgot the Method of pronouncing the Word No; her Language was composed of nothing but Expressions of Assent and Affirmatives; and she would contradict her own Senses, as often as her violent and capricious Cousin, happened to err. So accustomed to obey, she scarcely could find out Terms that would express her Refusal of the Liberty she dared not grant me. I sometimes mistook her Negatives for Consent, and should not have discovered my Error, had she not checked me, when I was going to act in Consequence of it.

In this *lively* Manner did we travel for three Days, without Accident or Interruption. But, the Night of the third, as I was beginning to undress myself, after having sat a little Time meditating on my deplorable Situation, I was alarmed with the Cry of "Fire, Murder, Rape, Beast, Brute, Savage!" The Clamour I could distinguish to come from Mrs. *Herner's* Room, and thinking myself bound in Duty

---

1 Pope, *Epistle to Dr. Arbuthnot* (1735) I. 333: "Wit that can creep, and Pride that licks the Dust."

to assist even my Enemy, I ran to try what I could do towards her Relief. When I entered, I perceived her with a double Towel round her Head, by Way of Night-Cap, in a short ragged Bed-Gown, standing by a Bed, in which was a Man who held fast by one Corner of her little Jerkin.[1] I did not comprehend the Motive for this Detention, consequently knew not the Cause of her Fear; but sensible that I alone was not sufficient to rescue her from the Arms of this Giant, I attempted to open a Door in the Passage, in order to call in more useful People, but found it locked, the Consequence of my Goaler's[2] Care of me. Had I not been of a most charitable Disposition, Resentment might have prompted me to let her suffer by the Means she had taken to prolong my Captivity; but I conquered the Impulse, and taking the Key out of her Pocket, let in our Hostess, and some of her Servants, who, like myself, had been attracted by the Noise.

Our Landlady I found more equal to the Task than I was; she soon rescued the timerous Virgin, telling the Gentleman with a very sonorous Voice, that, "She wondered he, who was a *Justice of the Peace and Quorum*[3] should so disturb a quiet Family; for her part, she would not suffer such *normous*[4] Behaviour in her House, not even by his *Honour's Worship*."

He, with a Voice that denoted much Sleepiness, replied, "Woman hold thy Brawling; I have not disturbed thy cursed House; I was sleeping quietly when that Wench waked me. She has a Mind to coy it a little now, but the Jade was willing enough to come to Bed to me before I asked her. I did not want Company; but I scorn to disappoint a Woman; and I shall have her still for all thy Clamour; for I know she is kind at Bottom."

At this Declaration, Mrs. *Herner* screamed out, "O save me! Preserve my Honour! Do not let the wicked Wretch come near me;" and caught up a Candle to light her in her Flight. Being obliged to pass by the Side of the Bed, in order to get to the Door, the Man had a much more perfect View of the affrighted Fair than he had before, whose Appearance, I must confess, was not very alluring; for her Lips were greased with Tallow;[5] her Eyes done thinly over with a dark coloured Ointment, and the Rest of her Face covered with thick

---

1 A short jacket or waistcoat, often made of leather.
2 I.e., gaoler, variant of jailer.
3 An archaic term for Justice of the Peace: a magistrate presiding in a county town.
4 I.e., enormous, in the archaic sense of monstrous, shocking, outrageous.
5 A fatty substance, rendered from suet, normally used for making candles.

Cream not quite dry; and through some "Chinks which Time had made"[1] in her Bed-Gown, her yellow Skin shone resplendent; so like Gold, through a netted Purse, that it could charm nothing but a Miser. He beheld her with Astonishment for near a Minute, and then, with all the Appearance of Scorn and Distaste that his Countenance could wear, which was better suited to such Expressions, than to any of a gentler kind, he cried out, "Wicked Wretch; not so wicked as to want thy Company, thou Witch, thou Monster, full Light would better have obtained thy Release than all thy Struggling. Have such a Hag as thee by my Side! I had rather have Fowler or my Crop Horse[2] for my Bedfellow." This Adventure shocked me strangely; there seemed an Enormity of Wickedness in this Man that amazed me; but yet, when he had thus addressed a Figure, which had surprized me almost as much as it had done him, I could not restrain a Smile. As I was near the Candles, he perceived it, and looking at me (after the short Preface of an Oath) "That's a pretty Lass, Faith," said he, "and looks good-natured and merry. I love a hoddy[3] Girl hugely, that will make one laugh, and laugh with one, and share a Pot of good October,[4] when a Man has no better Company; such a Wench is worth fighting for; and, I will have her instead of thee, thou Succubus,[5] who art nothing like a Woman but in thy Brawling." I was not more valiant than Mrs. *Herner*, but being much more nimble, I ran out of the Room with the utmost Speed. Not unmindful of the Opportunity of the double Escape I had to effect; and as desirous of getting free from Woman as from Man, and I ran through the Door I had opened, and got into the Yard; but was there overtaken by Mrs. *Herner*, in Fresco[6] as before, with the rest of the Family at her Heels.

1   Edmund Waller, *On the Divine Poems* (1686):
    The soul's dark cottage, battered and decayed,
    Lets in new light through chinks that time has made.
2   "Fowler" (meaning bird-catcher) is probably the name of the gentle-man's dog. His "crop-horse" would have cropped hair, probably for reasons of style.
3   Healthy, pleasant, cheerful. *OED* cites this passage to illustrate the term.
4   Ale brewed in October.
5   A demon or evil spirit in female form, thought to have sexual intercourse with sleeping men.
6   Figuratively, with her "paint" (tallow, ointment, and cream) still wet; painting in fresco involves applying water-colour to freshly laid plaster, so that the colours penetrate and become fixed (*OED*). There is also a play on another sense of "fresco" as cool, fresh air, alluding to Mrs. Herner's being scantily clad.

As soon as I disappeared, she recollected the Desire I might have, and not finding me in my Room, was as clamourous at my Escape, as she had been about her own Detention. Without staying for an Increase of Cloathing, she ran after me; and, it is no Wonder that, unincumbered by the Weight of Dress, she overtook me, whose Flight had been retarded by not knowing where to go. I cannot pretend to say, what Vengeance I might have taken at being thus disappointed of my Purpose, had not the Servants of the Inn revenged my Cause with some Success, by hooting at her Figure, and bursting into such immoderate Peals of Laughter, that our Hostess, at last, thought it incumbent on her to resent it; and with a shrill Pipe, cried out, "What do the Villains mean? Must you affront a Gentlewoman truly? Did you never see a Woman in her Smock[1] before? If Madam's Lips are chapped and her Eyes sore, what's the Matter of that, it is no Body's Business but her own, sure! such fine Tallow as we burn, would not disgrace the Mouth of the first Dutchess in the Land; it is as sweet as a Nut, and much more *healinger* than all their *curous* Salves.[2] As for her Eyes, why Eyes should be black, should not they? and what signifies whether Outside or In, or Inside or Out, its much the same Thing."

This eloquent Oration a little suspended the Laugh; but they took in no more Matter for Mirth, that the Time might not be lost, staring without Interruption at the Object of it; for the good Landlady, determined Mrs. *Herner* should hear how well she defended her Cause, kept fast hold of her, till her Flow of Oratory ceased. When we were conducted up Stairs, I was again locked up till Morning, and then I attended Mrs. *Herner*, to whom another Room had been given. At Breakfast, our Landlady came to pay her Compliments of Enquiry after the Health of the poor affrighted Lady, which was not a little impaired by the Night's Adventure, her Fears lasting longer than her Danger; for she told us, it communicated itself even to her Dreams.

As she condescended to talk with our Hostess, though not to converse with me, I learnt the Occasion of the Disturbance, which was no other than a small Error in the Gentleman whose Intellects were a little troubled by too hard Drinking, in Celebration of a Fox Chase, in which he had been engaged that Day; for in going up Stairs to Bed, he had mistaken Mrs. *Herner's* Room for his own, and taken Possession of it.

---

1   A woman's undergarment; a shift.
2   I.e., curious (fine, exquisite) healing ointments.

In the Course of this Conversation, I found nothing had so sensibly hurt Mrs. *Herner*, as the Squire's affronting her Charms. When she had heard our Hostess's Account, she said, that "Indeed, by his strange boisterousness, she, at first, suspected he had drank a little too much but did not find out till afterwards, how totally he was deprived of his Senses; of one Sense at least, for the Man was certainly blind. The Hurry and Bustle that ensued, she supposed, had increased the Effects of the Liquor; for he seemed in full Possession of his Judgment, at first, only his Passions were a little too much elevated, to bear with proper Composure the View of Temptation." Thus attributing to the Fumes of Intoxication, the honest Impulse of Nature, which made Disgust the Consequence of a full View of her Person.

Mrs. *Herner* hinted, that it was incumbent on him as a Gentleman to ask Pardon for the Outrage he had committed. "So I told him, Madam," replied the Landlady, "and what think you he answered to this? Why, truly, taking me very short, and swearing like a Trooper,[1] he said, 'not he, he should ask no Pardon, nor make no Defences; he had made the Gentlewoman a very civil Proffer, she might not receive the like of many a Day; and, he thought, if she believed him in earnest, she had more Reason to come and thank him, than he to ask her any Pardons.' Oh! Madam, he is a sad ribaldry Gentleman," added the Landlady.

I saw Mrs. *Herner* could have excused the Warmth of the good Woman's Resentment, which led her to so faithful a Repetition of the Squire's Words, but, with some Change of Colour, she, at last, sagaciously observed, "that every one had a Sense only of the Charms of their own Species. She never heard of a Bat that preferred the elegant Pheasant to its own leather-winged Race, nor of a Hedge Hog, that was not fonder of its own shapeless Kind, than of the beautiful Peacock."

Our Conversation ended with Breakfast, and we left the Inn to proceed on our Journey, that now drew to a Conclusion; which, as I had received a strange Notion of the Confusion in Inns, from what I had experienced, would not have been a disagreeable Circumstance to me, had I not flattered myself, that from it, some Opportunity of an Escape might arise.

---

1 The earliest use of this phrase cited in *OED* is in Richardson's *Pamela* (1740), in which the heroine writes of Mrs. Jewkes, "she curses and storms at me like a Trooper" (180).

CHAPTER XXXII

Our Landlady had entertained us with an Invective against Drunkenness, (though her Complexion bore some Tokens of less Inveteracy against that Vice) which employed my Thoughts for Part of the Day. Nothing I had seen in this Country more astonished me, than that, for so trifling a Pleasure as Liquor could afford, any one should relinquish Reason, that best Gift of the great Creator. It is inconsistent with the Pride of Man, thus to destroy the Source of all his Insolence and Presumption. But the Terms in which this Vice was reproached offended me. "The debasing themselves to the Condition of Brutes," was an Expression I thought very unjust. Perhaps, many, even when not intoxicated, have no Right to be inrolled in so honourable a Class; but when deprived of all Sense and Reason, surely they ought not to be compared to that Generation, who act conformably to the Will of their Creator, and to their Rank amongst the animal Tribes. Some, indeed, by living amongst Mankind, lose a little of their native Temperance, and acquire bad Qualities; such is the Force of Example! void of Knowledge of Good and Evil, they are qualified to walk in the Way ordained for them, but not to resist the Infection of the grand Corrupter, Man.

There is nothing so mean, as People who are artificially insensible; Vegetation produces more useful Materials; a Tree, for Instance, properly manufactured, supports a Passenger, fills up a Gap, or if, worn out by long Service it should be condemned, it blazes to warm us, fulfils its Part, and is a useful Member among created Beings, in comparison of a Man addicted to Drunkenness. But, perhaps, your Ladyship will think I put an Affront both on you and myself, by exclaiming at so undeserving a Subject, unworthy of employing your Thoughts, and my Pen; therefore, I will leave it for my Journey, which, ended the Evening we left our turbulent Inn. We arrived at the Marchioness's Castle, a little before it was dark, which afforded me an Opportunity of seeing it, though the View did not greatly conduce to my Satisfaction.

We first passed a Moat, over which was a Bridge so impaired by Time and Damp, that it threatened us with no small Chance of visiting the Frogs, who inhabited underneath. I could not help thinking, that they saw us approach, and taking us for the Successor of their former King, the hoarse Nation was once more ready to croak "God save King *Log;*"[1] but I afterwards found the Noise was usual, and only the Result of Numbers, from which among Frogs as well as Men, a general Hum arises.

The Castle was then tottering with Age, and may now, perhaps, by the irresistible Arm of old Time, be levelled to the Ground; therefore, I shall speak of the Fabrick only in the past Tense. The Rooms were extremely large, wainscotted with Oak, which was turned almost as black as Ebony; and all the Light that entered was from small Casements, with a larger Proportion of Lead and Iron than Glass. The Chimneys were as big as the Arch of a large Bridge. The Beds were higher than some Rooms, and all the Furniture large and clumsy, except the Chairs, whose Seats were stuffed with admirable Art, being harder than a Tennis-Ball,[2] and rising in the Middle in Imitation of a Pyramid.

The Hall was hung round with a most uncomely Representation of the Marquis of *Trente's* Ancestors, except in two Slips,[3] which were filled with Rolls of Parchments of a prodigious Length, bearing, in the Figure of a Tree, the Genealogy of the whole Race: If a poor Babe died in its Birth, its Memory was still preserved, under the dignifying Representation of a little Twig; but, a Miscarriage was honoured no farther than in being marked, as a Knot in the Trunk. I could not but admire this Care, lest Vanity should die for Want of Food, where few Flatterers could come without feeling their Consciences so affected by the Solemnity of the Place, as must have reduced them to speak Truth. The Garden was not, in Extent, equal to the Size of the House; but what there was of it, was laid out in narrow Gravel Walks, then over-grown with Weeds, bordered with Box, and ornamented in Quarters with Yew Swans, Laurel Bears, Holly Dogs, and Box Chickens;[4] their Colours happily variegated by

---

1 Pope, *The Dunciad* (1728) I. 259-60:
     Loud thunder to its bottom shook the bog,
     And the hoarse nation croak'd, God save King Log!
2 Tennis balls, used in the game of real tennis, were smaller and harder than those used in modern tennis. In Swift's *Gulliver's Travels* (1726), Gulliver, caught in a Brobdingnagian hailstorm, complains of receiving "such cruel Bangs all over the Body, as if I had been pelted with Tennis-Balls" (II. v).
3 The ledges beneath narrow, elongated windows.
4 The birds and animals sculpted from trees and bushes resemble those ridiculed by Pope in an essay on gardens first published in *The Guardian*, no. 173 (1713) and reprinted in his *Prose Works* (1741). Pope here describes a "Catalogue of Greens to be disposed of by an eminent Town-Gardener," which includes a serpent, a dragon, a bear, a hog that has grown into a porcupine, and a pig.

the dead Branches, which made up about three Quarters of the Animal; to the great Ease of the Gardener, who was, thereby, saved the Care of watching over this his Creation, lest their Shapes should be destroyed by the irregular Growth of some luxuriant Branches. The Wall of the Garden was almost the Extent of our Prospect. We were not in the Season for Flowers; but had all the "Perfumes of *Arabia*"[1] been dispersed about the House, they could not have got the better of the Stench arising from the Moat.

You may imagine that our Situation was better suited to the Dark, than to the Day; but, in this, you are mistaken; for the Horrors of the Night exceeded all the dismal Prospects the Sun could shew us. With the Twilight our Concert began. The first Performance was a great House-Dog, that would suffer no Noise but his own, incessantly howling or barking. Every Hearth was full of Crickets, who chirped the live long Night, but had none of those lively Notes, which *Milton* celebrates as the Sound of Mirth.[2] The old Towers of the House were filled with Owls of every Sort, who, by their hoarse Hooting, and their shrill Shrieking, bore no inconsiderable Part in the Concert, of which the Froggery[3] made the Base. These vocal Performers were accompanied by all the Modulations of a bleak Winter's Wind, which gathering in various Passages of that rambling House, made a continual Whistling, even in the mildest Weather, roared in the Chimneys, and blew in at a thousand Crevices in the shattered Wainscot.

Dismal as this Scene must appear, I found, that had I not retained very strong Affections for absent Objects, I could have been happy even there, if every Face had not worn an Air of Wretchedness. Excluding the suffering Hours of Reflection, I was the only Person in the Place that did not appear in such a deep and settled Despondency, as made me fear that I should, at some Time, find all the Family hanging in their Garters;[4] as I had learnt, that, it was no uncommon Thing in this Kingdom, for People to sign their own Passports into the next World, as soon as they are tired of this.

A general Melancholy run though every Species; there was a

---

1 Lady Macbeth in Shakespeare's *Macbeth* V.i.48-9: "All the perfumes of Arabia will not sweeten this little hand."
2 Alluding to Milton's *L'Allegro* (1632), in which Mirth is celebrated for her tunefulness.
3 A colony of frogs.
4 I.e., hanged by their own garters: lengths of silk tied below the knee to hold up stockings, worn by both women and men.

Monkey[1] who was so infected by his Situation, that he might have walked chief Mourner at a Funeral; a Parrot who, ceasing to be articulate, uttered no Sound but that of a piteous Sigh. The Servants had slit a Magpy's Tongue, in order to make it as conversible as themselves,[2] but had never been able to teach it any other Words than heigh-ho! The Kittens were there, from the Hour of their Birth, more serious than old Cats, who have, in other Places, been the inseparable Companions of antient Virgins. There was not a Lamb, Colt, or any other Creature, however youthful, that did not walk with more Solemnity than an Archbishop in a publick Procession.

Poor Mrs. *Herner* was full as miserable as myself or any of the Inhabitants: Grief had so relaxed every Muscle, that there were none but long Faces in the House. Mrs. *Herner's* fell away very fast, and, I dare say, had we stayed a Month longer would have come up to the general Standard. I cannot but confess, I felt mine lengthen considerably; tho' I was treated with great Lenity by my Goaler, who kindly studied my Ease and Convenience, as far as the Place would permit; but kept as strictly to her Vow of Silence, as if it had been the Road to Salvation. The greatest Indulgence she could grant me, was, in giving me Leave to frequent a Library, wherein I found some good Histories. Here, when I could banish Reflection, and the Regret which was the Consequence of it; I could, for some Hours, enjoy the Pleasures of Society, and forgetting the lonely Solitude to which I was confined, could transport myself to Scenes of Hurry and Tumult, and amuse myself with a constant Course of Novelty. But it was seldom I could bring myself into a proper Temper to taste this Pleasure; and the seldomer, as the Dampness of the Place, joined with Vexation and Anxiety soon affected my Health.

The Country around us was all Quagmires and Bogs, which rendered it impossible to take any Exercise at that Season of the Year, except in the melancholy Garden; and though I had no Objection to walking "With the Beast, Joint-Tenant of the Shade"[3] yet I could

---

1 Monkeys were sometimes kept as pets by people of fashion. One such is Mrs. Orgueil in Fielding's *David Simple, Volume the Last* (1753), who declares that "she could not have wrote such a cold insensible Letter, even if she had lost her Monkey" (VI.ix).

2 Magpies were kept as pets and taught to speak; slitting the tongue was thought to improve the bird's pronunciation.

3 Pope, *An Essay on Man* (1733-4) III. 151-2:
Pride then was not; nor Arts, that Pride to aid;
Man walk'd with Beast, joint Tenant of the Shade.

not extend my Love of Society to the Reptile likewise, and the Garden was so over-run with Frogs and Toads, that it was impossible to walk there, without having Multitudes of them for Companions. This total Want of Exercise, I suppose, had some small Share in impairing my Constitution, having been always used to a contrary Way of Life: I was so sensible of suffering from it, that nothing but Experience could convince me, that there was no Possibility of going beyond the Moat; however, having been almost swallowed up in a Bog, and giving my Guard (for I was not permitted to stir without one) a violent Cold, I had no great Inclination for any further Attempt; and less still was any one inclined to accompany me.

We had not been many Days in our Solitude, before we received a Visit from Mr. *South*, a young Clergyman in the Neighbourhood; a very well bred, sensible, and worthy Man, of an exceeding good Family, and educated suitably to it; but being the younger of many Brothers, he was glad to accept of a Living[1] near this Place, though the Manners of the neighbouring Gentlemen were not agreeable to him. However, he conversed less with them than with his Books, and the Poor of the Parish, whom he much visited in order to instruct and guide their Minds, and learn and relieve their Necessities; for he denied himself many of the Gratifications of Life, in order to communicate to others, the Conveniences and Comforts which they could not afford themselves. He sacrificed his Money to their Indigence, and his Time to their Instruction; acting the Part of Schoolmaster to the Children, as well as that of a truly spiritual Guide to their Parents. From one of such a Disposition every Visit must be welcome; and I could perceive, was not less so to Mrs. *Herner* than myself; for she pressed him to repeat them, which he did as often as his Leisure would permit; for to a Man who so laboriously performs his Duty, a large Parish is almost a constant Employ; and, though we might soon perceive, and, I was afterwards more fully convinced, that his pleasantest Occupation was visiting us, yet would he not suffer it to break in upon his Duty.

I have already observed, that Mr. *South's* Visits were agreeable, and your Ladyship will not think this so improbable, as to require any farther Assurance of it; but what will you say, if I own, that the Love of Talking rendered other Company eligible, who had no other Recommendation than taking the Embargo off my Speech, and suffering me to export a few Thoughts, with which I was overstocked? Depraved Appetites are apt to have strange Consequences; the Love

---

1 A position for a clergyman that provided an income and/or lodging.

of talking, to those with whom we cannot converse, argues great Depravity of Mind, and the Result of it was, that I rejoiced at the Arrival of some country Neighbours of whose intended Visit we had Notice before they came, and as they were Characters new and strange to me, I will give you the Account of them, which I learnt from Mr. *South* after their Departure, as some Excuse for my being diverted with them, for Novelty is allowed a Right to entertain.

CHAPTER XXXIII

The Marchioness of *Trente* was rendered a Person of great Consequence to the Sportsmen in the Neighbourhood, by the Possession of a very extensive Manor. And to the Desire of courting her Favour we owed the Visits we received from three; by Name, Mr. *Rumford*, Mr. *Darking*, and Mr. *Giles*. The two first were preceded by their Wives, the latter by his Wife and Sister; for the Gentlemen[1] did not think a Visit to two Women a sufficient Recompence for giving up their usual Amusements, and therefore, hunted all the Way between their House and ours, which separated them from their Families, who came early, to shew their Desire of being good Neighbours. Mrs. *Giles* and her Sister[2] Mrs. *Martha Giles*, sat next me, and the former[3] being of a communicative Temper, was grown so very intimate with me, that when the Gentlemen came in, she was making me the Confidante of her political Sentiments, beginning by an Enquiry after the new Pamphlets that had been lately published; "for that, the Nation was now in such imminent Danger of losing its Liberty, that she could not help being very desirous to peruse all the Schemes proposed towards redressing the Grievances we laboured under;" adding that, "an additional Inducement was the Hope that some of them might convince her Sister, into how many Errors she was led by her Attachment to a Monarchical Government, which entirely blinded her to all the Blessings of a Republick.[4] Miss, would you

---

1 Corrected here from "Gentleman" in the first edition, as in the 1763 Dublin edition, the *Novelist's Magazine* edition, and the 1787 London edition.
2 I.e., sister-in-law.
3 I.e., the latter, Martha Giles.
4 Mrs. Giles's republicanism is unusual in mid-eighteenth-century England. The radical pamphlets she recommends are of the kind collected by the Commonwealthman Thomas Hollis, who, from 1754, made substantial donations of such material to British and European institutions and, especially, to Harvard College.

believe," continued this female Politician, "that she is so strangely prejudiced, as to detest the Character of the great, the glorious *Oliver Cromwell*, and will not allow, there is any tolerable Reasoning; or indeed, any Thing but impious Blasphemies, in the admirable Books written to prove, that killing a Tyrant is no Murder.[1] She grieves with all the Solemnity of Affliction every thirtieth of *January*, and is as inconsolable, as if the Person she most loves, was just expired. Then, Miss, she is proportionably elated on the fatal Day, wherein the glorious Thread of *Cromwell's* Life was cut;[2] and old and asthmatical as you see her, sings and dances like a distracted Thing; nor has Complaisance enough to me, to conceal the least Part of her Joy, though she knows, my Soul is then overwhelmed with Sorrow. Never believe me, Miss, if her Room is not hung round with the Pictures, in her Phrase, of the blessed Martyrs, and yet really, in other Things, Sister *Giles* is a good Sort of a Woman; and, were it not for these Prejudices, which she has imbibed from the servile Notions of those that educated her, I should have been very happy in her Friendship; but ignorant of the Charms of glorious Liberty, she is as little able to bear my more extensive View of Things, as I am to endure her Narrowness of Mind."

Mr. *Giles*, it seems, knew his sister too well, to be in Doubt of the Subject on which he saw her so very loquacious, and cried out, "What, you're teizing Miss with your Politicks, I suppose; What the Devil have Women to do with the Nation! You want a Petticoat Government, I warrant? Was I King, I would make an universal *Salick* Law,[3] that should not allow you the Government of your own Lap-Dogs."

"Really Brother," replied Mrs. *Martha*, "you but expose yourself by declaring your Aversion to the most interesting of Subjects.

---

1   The most famous of books justifying the killing of tyrants was Milton's *The Tenure of Kings and Magistrates* (1648), one of the works that Thomas Hollis was promoting in the 1750s and 1760s, and which would certainly have been known to Fielding, who alludes frequently to Milton's poetry and prose. She would also have known his *Eikonoklastes* (1649), republished by the republican Richard Baron in 1756; see Tom Keymer, "Marvell, Thomas Hollis, and Sterne's Maria: Parody in *A Sentimental Journey*," *Shandean* 5 (1993): 20-21.
2   Charles I was executed on 30 January 1649; Oliver Cromwell died on 3 September 1658.
3   I.e., Salic Law: a law excluding women from dynastic succession, originally of the French monarchy.

However meanly you may think of my Sex, I must inform you that my Views are nobler than your's, and if you are contented to move in no higher a Sphere than the Dominion over your Stable or Dog-Kennel, I find my Genius leads me to reflect on the best Manners of ruling a State; I cannot help being anxious to see how Things are ordered at the Helm."

"Helm!" exclaimed the Squire, "Steer your Family; see if you are Pilot enough to guide that in its proper Course. Go to your Distaff, the proper female Sceptre.[1] However trifling you may think the command of my Dog-Kennel, I would not trust you the Government of it, though I had not so valuable a Bitch as Mopsey, who deserves the Care of the greatest Man in the Nation."

With a Look of the most sovereign Contempt, as disdaining to return an Answer, she turned her Back to him, and whispered me, "This is always his Way, Miss; would it not provoke a Saint? But this is the Consequence of having an Understanding more cultivated than the illiterate Neighbourhood one has the Misfortune to be born in, People totally ignorant of the Policies of Nations. Their Pride will not allow one any Peace. He does not treat Sister *Giles* with any more Ceremony, and, between you and I Miss (but one would not have those Things repeated) she once resented this Behaviour so much, that they were going to part upon it, and she and I were to have lived together, removing to some Place where we might have conversed with Persons of more refined Understandings. But while they were bartering about the Terms of a separate Maintenance, a political Dispute arose between her and myself, which convinced me so fully of the Impossibility of ever bringing her to Reason on that Subject, that I declared against living with her, and a Reconciliation between them ensued."

I know not when my political Friend would have done talking had she not been interrupted by Mrs. *Darking*, who came up to me, and enquired after the reigning Diversions in *London*; expressing great Joy at seeing one, "who was come from among Christians, and compassionating me, for having left them for a Land of Brutes."

Mrs. *Herner* before any Company came, advised me, on no Account, to mention my being brought thither by Force; but to pretend, that, a Desire of accompanying her, during her Stay there, was

---

1   The squire's witticism plays on the resemblance between a distaff, literally a cleft stick for holding wool, used as symbol for women's work, and a sceptre, the ornamental rod used as a symbol for (usually masculine) authority.

my Motive. Though I was sensible my Taste would not receive much Honour from this Concealment, yet, as it was my Interest not to offend her, and I perceived no Advantage likely to accrue from refusing to comply, I told her, that, as far as Silence would give my Detention the Air of Choice, I had no Objection; but she must excuse my intimating a Falshood, much more my telling a palpable Untruth. I now found she took this Office on herself; for upon hearing Mrs. *Darking*'s Condolances, she told her, "I was not worthy of her Pity, since I had been so kind as to give her my Company from the Desire of retiring from the Hurry of *London*."

This gave Mr. *Darking* an Opportunity of Exultation, crying out, "There's a wise young Woman now! So much Wisdom in Youth, is marvellous. What a happy Man her Husband will be, if Marriage does not alter her as much as it did my Fool. See *Betty*, how much a *betterer* Figure that young Gentlewoman makes than thee do with all thy Whims, thy Figaries,[1] and nonsensical Fancies and Whinings."

Mrs.[2] *Darking* answered with an indolent Air, "that, the young Lady would be a better Judge of her own Taste, when she had lived a little among Brutes." With a contemptuous Smile and significant Glance, which very intelligibly told him, he was signified under the last Word of her Speech.

This Lady I afterwards learnt had been bred in Town, where, for a Punishment of his Sins, Mr. *Darking* was called by a Law Suit, in which he was engaged with a Gentleman who had hunted and killed a Hare in his Manor.[3]

While he was in *London*, he met with this Lady, who, destitute of Fortune, lived with a Maiden Aunt, of a Temper by no Means easy, and whose sole Support was an Annuity. The Necessity of finding some more certain Provision, made her omit no Endeavours to please; and so general were her Views, that her Sentiments changed with every unmarried Man's Opinion; whatever he seemed to like she immediately became.

---

1 I.e., vagaries.

2 Corrected here from "Mr." in the first edition, as in the 1763 Dublin edition, the *Novelist's Magazine* edition, and the 1787 London edition.

3 Mr. Darking's eagerness to prosecute those who hunt game on his land resembles that of Squire Western in Henry Fielding's *Tom Jones* (1749). When young Tom is found to have shot a partridge on his estate, Western "complained of the Trespass on his Manor, in as high Terms, and as bitter Language, as if his House had been broken open, and the most valuable Furniture stole out of it" (III. ii).

This conformable Disposition led her to declare a Detestation of a Town-Life, whenever Mr. *Darking* was in Company; and so successfully did she expatiate on the sweet Innocence and tranquil Regularity enjoyed in the Country, that he was convinced her Conformity to the Gaieties of *London*, was a painful Necessity, from which she sighed to be delivered. He had been a good deal captivated by her Beauty, from the first Time he had seen her, and this amiable Disposition compleated her Conquest. But still warily determined to be certain of the Happiness which he was inclined to think must be the Consequence of his possessing such a Wife, he examined into her Knowledge of Family Affairs, and was charmed to hear her talk of the inspecting a Dairy, and the well ordering a Family, as the greatest Pleasures in Life, and as Things in which she was well skilled. All his Doubts being dispelled, he ventured to make his Proposals; and thro' meer Œconomy overlooked her Want of Fortune. He had been early taught that wholesome Precept, that "A Penny saved, is a Penny got;"[1] and, learnedly arguing on that Principle, convinced himself, that so good a Housewife was the best Treasure, since no extraordinary Settlements were demanded in consideration of a Woman's Virtues; and therefore, his Estate would not be tied up as if he married a great Fortune; and, from hence he drew a Conclusion in her Favour, that "Money saved, was Money got."

Mr. *Darking* was not made to wait long for the Lady's Consent, they had Proverbs on their Side, as much in Recommendation of a speedy Marriage, as he had; there was no Text on which the old Aunt was more eloquent than "That Delays are dangerous;" "Those that will not when they may, &c. &c." "A Bird in the Hand is worth two in the Bush,"[2] and some others to that Purpose; mortifying Experience having so fully convinced her of the Justness of them, that she rivalled the renowned *Sancho Pancho* in retailing of Proverbs.[3] As soon as Mr. *Darking* was married, he conducted his Bride to the Country for which he had sighed; where he found that Reflection is so infallible a Source of Wisdom, that he might have acquired

1 Proverbial since the 1660s. The hero of Henry Fielding's comedy *The Miser* (1733) also uses the expression (III.xii).
2 The three proverbs are all of medieval origin. The second, in full, is "He that will not when he may, when he would he shall have nay."
3 The rustic Sancho Panza, squire of Don Quixote, the eponymous hero of Cervantes' satirical romance *Don Quixote de la Mancha* (1605, 1615), has a rich store of proverbs that he retails as he accompanies the knight on his adventures.

some from his favourite Amusements, which would have taught him, that the Fowler never spreads the Nets after having caught the Birds. All the Snares she laid for him, appeared henceforward useless: Art was now disclaimed, she freely shewed her Dislike of every Thing she had declared herself fond of, laughed at his Friends, despised his Neighbours, detested Country Entertainments; never thought of Œconomy, but to shew she scorned such Trifles and low Offices, and grew vapoured[1] and peevish.

Mr. *Darking* was not so blinded by Love, but that he grew outrageous at this Disappointment; for, however blind *Cupid* may be represented, the hymeneal[2] Torch lights him so well, as to render him admirably quick-sighted to the Faults of a wedded Mate. *Cupid*, as your Ladyship must have perceived, in many Instances, before he becomes linked with *Hymen*, is generally as different from what he is after that Union, as a Bee and a Serpent: In the first State, his whole Application is to gather Sweets from every Thing; there is not a Circumstance but he can make to produce something valuable; but, after this melancholy Change, he as industriously collects Poison; and, in the smallest Trifles can discover baleful Qualities. If I was to undergo a Metamorphosis, it should be of a Bee into a Serpent, as an allegorical Description of the Transformation of a Lover into a Husband; a more dismal Change than that of the industrious *Arachne* into a Spider, the melancholy *Philomela* into a plaintive Nightingale, or any other that *Ovid* celebrates.[3] But to put an End to a Digression, which, no one, from her own Fate, has so little Reason to make as myself, I shall return to this ill-matched Pair.

As Mr.[4] *Darking* was not blessed with Delicacy of Voice or Manner, his Rage broke forth into Sounds so harsh, and Gestures so alarming, as greatly terrified the gentle Lady, and made her determine to endeavour to comply with his Inclination. But, during the

---

1 Suffering from the vapours, defined in Johnson's *Dictionary* as "diseases caused by flatulence, or by diseased nerves; hypochondriacal maladies; melancholy; spleen."

2 Wedding; from Hymen, the Greek god of marriage.

3 In Ovid's *Metamorphoses*, a fifteen-book Latin epic poem, Arachne and Philomela are among the various characters who undergo transformations. Arachne, an industrious and ambitious weaver, is turned into a spider; Philomela, who had been raped and had her tongue cut out, is changed into a nightingale.

4 Corrected here from "Mrs." in the first edition, as in the 1763 Dublin edition, the *Novelist's Magazine* edition, and the 1787 London edition.

Trial, his Dairy was spoiled through Neglect and Ignorance, his Family and Visitors half-starved; for which, he received no other Apology, than "How should she guess that the vulgar robust Animals would devour whole Hecatombs,"[1] and all Regularity banished from his House; the Order for Dinner being often forgot till the Time it should have been ready.—He tried to make her useful by the same Means, as he had brought her to attempt to obey him, but finding it easier to fright, than to alter her, he gave her up as incorrigible; desiring her to resign the Management of his House, and keep within the Confines of her own Apartment.

Not long after this, Mrs. *Darking* proved with Child, which restored her to her Husband's Favour, as it shewed her of some Use. She perceived, by his Behaviour, how much he was interested in the Fate of the unborn Babe, and therefore, made it the Means of acquiring some Indulgencies, which otherwise would not have been granted to her. She daily encroached on the Liberties thus obtained, till, at last, she ventured to express a longing to lie-in in *London*, which, if disappointed, she feared, might prove fatal to the Child. Mr. *Darking* would have been truly alarmed, had he believed, it could be marked with the Representation of any Part of a Town, he so much hated; but, never having heard of that Effect from any such longing, he refused to comply, swearing, "no Child of his should breathe that pernicious Air; he had suffered enough by going thither to make him careful to be the last of his Family who should ever run themselves into any such Scrape." But finding his Lady sickened, from the Steadiness with which he had adhered to this Resolution, he began to be under some Apprehensions for the consequences; so to make her easier, he promised to carry her there, as soon as she was recovered from her Lying-in. This Assurance kept up her Spirits so well, that it enabled her to bring into the World a fine Boy, who was joyfully received by his Father; but the Journey to *London* expired at the Child's Birth. It was a Promise Mr. *Darking* never meant to keep, nor could he be induced to perform it by her falling ill on the Disappointment; her Health was no longer of Importance.

She had several more Children, but found that her Pregnancy was not to meet with the same Indulgencies after the valuable Heir apparent was born. Mr. *Darking* had the Children brought up wild. Though the two youngest were Daughters, yet he would not permit

---

1 Literally a large number of animals, sacrificed in a religious ritual; here, a vast amount of food.

a Maid Servant to come near them, except just to put on their Cloaths; the greatest Part of their Time was spent in the Stables, and the Stable-Boys were their Play-Fellows.

The poor Wife, who was in the contrary Extreme, being the Excess of Delicacy, and thought a Girl ought not to set Eyes even on a Baby, that was not of the *Feminine Gender*, looked on Compliance in this Point as criminal, from which arose a never ceasing Contest between her and her Husband, whereby the Children were the innocent Sufferers. Each ordered them to rebel against the commands of the other; she chastised them, if they obeyed their Father, and he (as he called it) *trounced* them, if they complied with their Mother; till, by the double Application of that great Instructor, the Rod, they soon grew so exceeding wise, as to despise both their Parents, learning from each the other's Foibles and Errors, much sooner than their own Understandings could have discovered them.

Mrs. *Rumford*, the only Lady that now remains unmentioned, was much better suited to her Situation. Nature seemed to have formed her for the Care of her House and Dairy; and had not Mr. *Rumford* declared her to be the Wife of his Bosom, one might have taken her for his Cook or his Dairy-Maid; though Poetry has been so much the Friend of the latter Class,[1] that to have guessed her one would have been no small Compliment. She was as much charmed with my supposed Love of the Country as Mr. *Darking*, and was very eloquent in Behalf of the Pleasures of Domestick Business. My Regard for Truth would scarcely suffer me to receive the Praises given me with so little Reason, and I believe, I should not have permitted them to continue in their Error, could I have prevailed on myself to have exposed any one to so much Contempt, as I imagined Mrs. *Herner* must have incurred, from being convicted of telling a voluntary Lie.

CHAPTER XXXIV

A very considerable Part of the Company yet remains unmentioned, though perhaps were the Men to direct, I might have given them the Precedency. These were the Squires faithful Companions, their Dogs, who followed them into the Room, which they entered with

---

1 Alluding to the pastoral tradition of celebrating dairy-maids, exemplified in John Gay's praise of Marian in "Tuesday," *The Shepherd's Week* (1714):
Marian that soft could stroak the udder'd Cow
Or lessen with her Sieve the Barly Mow. (ll. 11-12)

a loud Cry of Halloo, Halloo! that, at first, greatly alarmed me; but seeing no Emotion in the Countenance of any other Person in Company, and finding Mrs. *Martha* did not suspend her Cares for the Nation, I was sensible my Fears must be groundless. Mrs. *Herner* knew too well the Regard due to these Dogs to expel them her Dining Room; the Consequence of which was, its being so filled with them, that there was no moving without treading upon one, falling over another, and making Confusion among them all, they snarling and growling at every one who was so unlucky as to tread on them; while the Squires, to increase the Clamour, cried out, Ware *Hector*, ware *Juno*![1] according to the Names of the Dogs in Danger.

Dinner at last appeared; at the Sight of a Sirloin of Beef, the Squire set up what I found they called, the dead hallo,[2] and cried out, "to-un Boys, to-un; the best Beast in *Christendom*, though he would give but a scurvy Chase;" and while the Ladies were ceremoniously adjusting the important Article of Place,[3] sat themselves at the Table, observing, that, "the first Cut of a Sirloin of Beef, was better than the finest Compliments in the World." As soon as Dinner was ended, the Chase was celebrated, the Stag once more run down, all its Arts for Escape remembered, the Victory of the Dogs sung in songs of Triumph, every Victor receiving his distinct Praises and Caresses. When the Stag was killed in Story, as well as in fact, and all the Songs on the Subject had been sung, with Voices that equalled the hoarse Thunder; one of the Gentlemen whispered another, "let's roast the Parson," to which his Neighbour replied, sealing his Approbation with an Oath, "I will begin to run the Rig[4] on him." And, accordingly, much Impertinence was applied to Mr. *South*, by Way of Wit, which he received with great Insensibility, only giving them

---

1 "Ware," an abbreviation for "beware," was used as a warning cry in hunting. The dogs are named after Hector, the bravest of the Trojans during the siege of Troy, and the Roman Juno, the wife of Jupiter and goddess of marriage and childbirth.

2 A hunting term, but not in *OED*, which gives "view-halloo" as the cry raised when a fox breaks cover. The "dead hallo" (or halloo) is presumably the cry raised to greet the death of the fox. In *Tom Jones* (VII.iii), Henry Fielding discusses Squire Western's prowess in hunting cries: "He was indeed a great Master of this Kind of Vociferation, and had a Holla proper for most Occasions in Life."

3 I.e., in what order they should be seated at table, according to the elaborate rules of social precedence.

4 Play a prank, ridicule.

two or three very cutting Answers in Return; but his Wit being too refined, and too just to be comprehended by them, Mrs. *Herner*, who I began to perceive was more than commonly affected with Mr. *South*'s Merit, thought it Time to retire, asking him to drink Tea with us. He readily consented, and rising from Table with us, they cried out, "fine Parson! efaith, always stick by the Women. Nay, thou hast a good Taste, she's worth a Chace!" "but take Care, thee does not catch a Tartar,"[1] added Mr. *Darking*. Every one understood me to be the Person hinted at in this Speech, which rendered me the more glad to leave these ungentlemanlike Gentlemen. As soon as we were out of the Room, they set up another Hallo, crying, "Clear, clear!" which informed us, that they were not less rejoiced at our Absence, than we were at having got rid of such irrational Society.

Mr. *South* told me, that we had judged very well in retiring so soon, for the next Step towards driving us out of the Room would have been their entring into such Discourse as no Women of Modesty could without great Impropriety sit to hear. This greatly astonished me, I did not suspect any Person of such Brutality; I thought Politeness was not requisite to teach People Decency; common Sense alone, I imagined, might shew that it was brutal to say, what any one ought not to hear. But more still, have I been since surprized, at finding this Vice, for I cannot give a Breach of so amiable a Virtue as Modesty a gentler Name, was too common in Circles that call themselves polite; but surely without Reason, since nothing can be so contrary to Politeness, as an Offence against Decency. Our Visitors did not leave us, till the Gentlemen were so far overpowered by the Potency of Mrs. *Herner*'s good October, that they were with Difficulty set upon their Horses; but those Animals, much superior to the Brutes that rode them, conveyed their unworthy Loads safe Home.

Your Ladyship, perhaps, by this Time, may find it easy to be tired of such Company, therefore, will not wonder if I did not wish them to repeat their Visits often, as, when they ceased to be new, they must become more dull than Solitude.

After a Month spent in this old Castle, I began to grow impatient of Confinement, and almost to despair of making my Escape; but my Uneasiness was still greatly increased, one Morning, by Mrs. *Herner*'s shewing me a Letter from the Marchioness, in which, she related to

---

1 I.e., take care not to be caught, rather than catching, since Tartars were proverbial for their strength.

her, as she termed it, "the happy Consequence of removing me out of Lord *Dorchester's* Sight." She there informed her, that "he looked melancholy for a few Days after my Departure; but soon began, by Degrees, to recover his Gaiety, and with it, his Inclination towards her. Convinced, by Experience, how little he liked Reserve in a Woman he loved, she had not endeavoured to conceal the Sentiments of her Heart; and they so well agreed with his that, in a few Days, they were to be married, waiting only for the necessary Preparations." She then proceeded to say, "that she was no longer under any Uneasiness concerning me, a thousand Instances having assured her that Lord *Dorchester* was become totally indifferent towards my future Fate, and had even expressed himself glad that he was delivered, he knew not how, of one who began to grow burdensome to him. But yet, as she pitied my Youth, and was sensible how hard it must be for an unexperienced Girl to resist such a Man as Lord *Dorchester*, it grieved her Heart (*too full of the Milk of human Kindness*)[1] to think I should be left quite destitute of a Subsistence; exposed to the *wide World* and all its Villainy, which might lead me into Courses that would prove the Destruction of my *precious Soul*. She therefore could not forbear giving Way to the Overflowings of her *Humanity*, *Generosity*, and *Compassion*, in offering me the same Income which she had tendered me before I left *London*, if I would bind myself, by a lawful Contract, to relinquish it, if I came with 40 Miles of *London*, or of his Lordship's Country Seat; for tho' she was no longer jealous, yet she could not bear to see Lord *Dorchester's* Happiness interrupted, by the whining Complaints or Reproaches of a Woman who would call herself ruined by him, tho' her own Frailty was most in Fault."

The Shock this Letter gave me was, at first, inexpressible, I could not support the very Sound of Lord *Dorchester's* Indifference. I knew not how to believe he was weary of me; I thought no one could dissemble so well, for he had appeared more fond of me, more delighted with me than ever, but just before this cruel Separation. My Mind was in too great an Agitation to return Mrs. *Herner* any Answer. She seemed to pity me, for my Distress was very visible, and would have bestowed upon me a Lecture on Patience and Resignation, had she been allowed the Liberty of Speech; but after a very eloquent

---

1 Lady Macbeth in *Macbeth* I.v.16-17: "Yet do I fear thy nature: / It is too full o' th' milk of human kindness." Fielding also quotes the phrase in *The Adventures of David Simple* II.ix.

Beginning, she was stopped short by recollecting the Marchioness's Prohibition, and observed, "her Compassion had led her into Forgetfulness."

I was never so well pleased with Lady *Trente's* Commands, as on this Occasion; a Person who is deeply afflicted, can but ill bear the dull insipid Nonsense of an insensible Preacher; when the Heart speaks loudly, who can listen to a Discourse dictated by a cold Imagination. I prevailed on Mrs. *Herner* to give me Lady *Trente's* Letter; and, after having renewed the first Agonies of my Grief by a second Perusal, a plentiful Flood of Tears came to my Relief, and so far quieted my Mind, that I began to discover Reasons to suspect the Truth of this Account. I was little disposed to believe the Marchioness was so very full of the *Milk of human Kindness* as she pretended, nor that one who had so little Consideration for the Ease of my Body, and the Peace of my Mind in this World, could have so tender a Regard for my Soul, and my Happiness in the next. The Desire of buying my Absence from Lord *Dorchester*, was a suspicious Circumstance; and I thought this all might be a Fiction formed on a Supposition that my Aim was to marry my Lord, and therefore I might the more readily comply with her Proposals, if I could be persuaded all Possibility of the Completion of my Hopes were at an End.

This Scheme, like all others that are built on false Foundations, could not answer the Intent. My Views were narrower, and more humble; I thought not of Marriage; to preserve his Friendship and enjoy his Conversation, was the utmost Extent of my Ambition; and this I flattered myself I might do, should another Woman become his Wife. But I must, in Sincerity, confess, that the Notion of his marrying, was most tormenting to me. To be his Friend while no one had a stronger Tie on his Affections, satisfied my Wishes; but if he had a Wife I was sensible I ought to resign, even the Desire of retaining the first Place in his Heart. This was a Self-denial that required a stronger Mind, or weaker Affection than I possessed.

The declining State of my Health would have rendered me little able to support the Anxiety of my Mind, had not the Hopes I conceived, that the whole was a Fiction, proved a most reviving Cordial to my Spirits. This restored me to Life, tho' not to Ease; but my Fears and Doubts made me more grieved than ever at my Captivity; and as my Impatience for the Means of escaping from this Prison was increased, it was mortifying to me to give an Answer to the Marchioness's Proposals, which would rather quicken than relax Mrs. *Herner's* Watchfulness. This, I knew, must be the Consequence of a Refusal; but obliged to declare myself, what could I do? My Desire of Liberty inspired me with Courage enough to dare any Thing but a Violation of Truth; there I was still a Coward, for I could not think myself justified in repelling Wickedness by Wickedness. The Falshood of others could not be a Sanction for it in me.

Mrs. *Herner*, at last, broke thro' her Vow of Silence, in order to use all the Arguments her Understanding could suggest, and her Inclination strengthen, to persuade me to accept the Conditions offered me. The Goaler, in this Case, led as melancholy a Life as the Prisoner, and she longed, almost as much to be dismissed from her Charge, as I did to be out of her Power. The poor Woman was half dead of the Vapours, and, I believe, would not have survived it, had not Mr. *South*'s Company afforded her Relief; for whenever he appeared she was as happy, as Envy of the particular Attention he paid to me could suffer her to be; and tho' I would not, in general, recommend Jealousy as very conducive to mental or bodily Health, yet it certainly would be of great Service in a Situation that stagnates the Blood, without some such animating Passion to continue its Circulation.

I could not but confess it was pity, that, "one who spoke so well, should ever speak in vain;"[1] but what Success could attend it, had she been endowed with the most persuasive Eloquence? An Orator places his Hopes in moving our Passions, and to make them of his Party is his sole Aim; it is no Affront, therefore, to her Rhetoric, that it should fail, when it was directed against the most invincible Passion. After the good Woman had talked herself hoarse, I repeated what I had first told her, "That no Offers could tempt me to sell Lord *Dorchester*'s Friendship; but if I was permitted to judge for myself, and found him, in reality, as indifferent as the Marchioness represented him, I should fly far enough from one whose Inconstancy must render the Sight of him painful, without putting her to any Expence."

I thought her Ladyship in a great Error, when she supposed Poverty might prove so dangerous to the State of my Soul; I did not comprehend her Meaning; and as far as I had been able to observe, Luxury led People into more Vices than Necessity. Experience had then shewn me that,

---

1 Pope, *The Rape of the Lock* (1714) IV. 131–2:
It grieves me much (reply'd the Peer again)
Who speaks so well shou'd ever speak in vain.

The Devil grown wiser than of Yore,
Tempts Men by making rich, not poor.[1]

I was under no Apprehension that want of Virtue could be the Consequence of want of Money, and, therefore, saw no sufficient Inducement to accept any, from one who had so cruelly injured me.

CHAPTER XXXV[2]

Mr. *South* had omitted writing to us for more Days than usual, having, as we learned, been prevented by a Friend who had spent a little Time with him; but during this Increase of my Anxiety, he came one Morning to Breakfast; his particular Enquiries after my Health, shewed me, that he perceived an Alteration in it. The Day being fine we went together into the Garden, where we had not walked long, when he intimated a Desire to speak with Mrs. *Herner* alone. His Countenance had shewn Confusion, his Thoughts wandered, and his Conversation had been strained and unconnected from the Time of his first coming in. I pitied him, from a Belief that he laboured under some Uneasiness, and Pains of the Mind could not then fail of exciting my Compassion. I was now more convinced that he had some Distress to impart; and having heard him whisper his Request for a private Audience, I walked from them, and thinking myself at a sufficient Distance, sat down at the Bottom of an old Yew Tree, which Time had rendered hollow, and frequently served me for a well sheltered Seat.

But, as the God of Laughter would have it, Mrs. *Herner* brought her Gentleman to a Bench full in my View.[3] I observed her Eyes rather twinkling than sparkling, every Feature wore a Smile, and she had pulled up her Head till she was as upright as a May-pole.

After they were seated, and she had blushed, drawn down her Handkerchief, stroaked her Ruffles, pinched her Apron,[4] and played

---

1   Pope, *Epistle to Lord Bathurst* (1732) ll. 351-2:
    But Satan now is wiser than of yore,
    And tempts by making rich, not making poor.
2   This and the next chapter are misnumbered "VI" and "VII" in the first
    edition. For a discussion of this odd error, see Introduction, above, 14-15.
3   This scene is the second of three illustrated by Corbould for the 1785
    Novelist's Magazine edition; see Appendix C below.
4   Handkerchiefs were neckwear, folded diagonally, draped around the neck
    and knotted in front in a breast knot. Ruffles were ornaments attached
    to the sleeves of a woman's gown. Aprons could be worn as a decorative
    addition to a gown.

over all the pretty Airs of Confusion, finding he did not break Silence, she, as I could perceive, with great Hesitation and Difficulty, enquired his Reason for desiring this Interview; her Words were breathed in a Voice too gentle for me to hear, but her Manner explained them.

Mr. *South* did not seem to speak with more Facility, nor in a Sound more audible, I could not divine his Meaning, but saw him confounded, and in a Tremor; however, the first Effort passed, he grew more easy; but in Proportion as his Countenance expressed greater Pleasure, her's shewed less. His Eyes petitioned; but as his became more tender and humble, her's shot forth fiercer Rays, her Cheeks glowed with a higher red, and losing all that sweet Complacency of Feature with which she at first listened to him, she rose, from her Seat, and Anger giving Strength her Voice, I could very distinctly hear her thus address him: "Is this the mighty Secret for which you wanted a private Audience? You did well, indeed, to desire it private; such an abject Thought should be known by as few as possible. In Love in so short a Time! and with a Baby Face, a little white and red, and perhaps some pretty Features! A Child, not able to know the Duties incumbent on a Wife, and the Mistress of a House! To marry her would disgrace your Family, contaminate your Profession, dishonour your Cloth, and bring certain Ruin on yourself. Such willful Blindness deserves not a Guide, but I will be one to you, and preserve you from the Perdition you court." Mr. *South* interrupted her at this Expression of unwished-for Regard; I could not distinguish his Words, but he had the Air of a most melancholy and humble Suppliant, which proved unavailing, for Mrs. *Herner* again broke forth. "Fye, fye, is it seemly for one, whose Example and Preaching should teach the World to mortify and deny themselves, to overcome their Passions? Is it decent for such an one, to chuse a Wife for little transitory Beauty? What will a People say when you are exhorting them to Abstinence; but that, after having provided every Gratification for yourself, after indeed abstaining from all that is less tempting, and thinking it Virtue; you triumph over them who practice less Self-indulgence, tho', perhaps, more lawfully? Does not your Profession teach you to search after more sublime Beauties; those of the Mind? Moral Charms alone should be regarded by a Minister of our sacred Religion. Has not the wise *Solomon* told you, *That Favour is deceitful, and Beauty is vain, but the Woman that feareth the Lord, she shall be praised*? Does he not say, *That the Price of a virtuous*

Woman is above Rubies?[1] Such you might have found," softening her Voice, "You might have met with Women who have been tried in the World, like Gold in the Fire, and passed thro' it unsullied; whose Minds are formed by a Competence of Years, and their Hearts purified by Knowledge and Care; who have been taught by Experience to value true Merit;" (casting Glances at him, which she designed should be languishing, but seemed more expressive of Stupidity;) "one qualified to be Friend, Companion, and Helpmate; one who would nurse you when sick, obey you when well, and live up to a true Sense of her Duty; and all this with Rank and Family that would not have debased you in the Eyes of the World. This, I say, you might have found." And here she stopped, as if to see whether a Description she meant for her own Picture, would warm him to any kind Thoughts of the Original; but he, with some Indignation in his Countenance, answered, "I think I have found it all in your Friend; I have too much Faith in Physiognomy to doubt it; her's expresses every thing that is amiable in the most legible and charming Characters." "I see what you are," interrupted Mrs. *Herner*, with a Voice still louder, than before, "The Man gets the better of your Divine Soul; we may now no longer wonder, that the Sheep wander out of the right Path, since the Shepherd himself goes astray; and tho' obliged to purify human Nature, is sinking to the Brute, and not only withdrawing himself from his Obedience to Religion, but even to Reason. While you are thus a Slave to your Appetites," continued she, "you are below the Beasts of the Field, and as such, not fit Company for me; but I shall take Care to lead Temptation out of your Way, since you have not sufficiency of Virtue to resist it. You shall no more see this painted Baby,[2] this fleshly Idol, now the sole Object of your Devotion." With this Menace she left him; nor did he endeavour to detain her, but seemed all Amazement.

I sat still, in Hopes of remaining unobserved. I suspected myself to be meant under the flattering Appellation of painted Baby, that pernicious Evil she had been describing, and had no Desire to reverse her Sentence, tho' I esteemed the Man. But passing by the Place where I sat, he perceived me, and coming up, with great Confusion in his Manner, would have sat down by me. I had been

---

1 Proverbs 31.30 and 31.10.
2 Doll.

detained there too long, from a Desire of being concealed, and was grown very cold, therefore chose to walk. With great Difficulty he stammered out, "He had been entreating Mrs. *Herner* to offer him and his Fortune to me. He feared I should accuse him of Presumption if he attempted to make so poor an Offering without the Mediation of a Friend; but she had reduced him to it, for he had no Hopes of her Assistance." He then gave me an exact Account of his Fortune and Income, saying every thing that was tender, generous and delicate on the Subject, with such Fear and Humility, that I was grieved at being obliged to humble him still more, by a Refusal, which, however, I endeavoured to palliate as much as possible. "I acknowledged the Obligation his good opinion conferred on me; assuring him of my Esteem, but that I could not think of Marriage; were not this a literal Truth, he might be sure I should not except to his Offer; for my Situation was extremely unhappy, but I could not change it for the married State, tho' I was there a Prisoner, most unjustly seized by Force, and detained against my Will with the utmost Vigilance and Care."

While I was uttering these last Words, Mrs. *Herner* appeared, and with a Degree of Rage, not natural to her Disposition; but Jealousy can work Wonders, inquired, "What I meant by remaining in the Garden?" commanding me to go into the House. I was so shocked with the Concern I had given Mr. *South*, which he seemed rather to endeavour to conceal than to shew, that I was glad to obey her; but he catching hold of my Hand, entreated me to finish what I was saying, and explain a Mystery which filled him with Astonishment. I easily understood that by this he meant the Imprisonment I had slightly touched upon; but I could not make a farther Explanation before Mrs. *Herner*, nor did she give me Time; for telling him, that, "It was unbecoming a Minister of the Gospel to give way to his Passions," she led me into the House, out of which I was not suffered to stir that Day.

Mrs. *Herner* had never beheld me with such Looks of Anger as she gave me after this Affair; she was frequently in Tears, and made me partake of her Sorrow, by being the Victim of her ill Humour. Her Jealousy added so much to the cruel Effects of the Marchioness's Commands, that I was so strictly watched (at a Time when I more than ever longed for Liberty in order to examine into the Truth of Lady *Trente*'s Letter) that three Days passed before the Gardener, who had been bribed into Mr. *South*'s Interest, could give me the following Letter.

"Madam,

"Tho' you deny me the Hopes of Reward, you have not deprived me of all Pleasure, since you cannot be so cruel as to refuse me that of attempting to rescue you. To know that you are detained by Force, is sufficient to excite my Endeavours to deliver you from your Imprisonment; and happy shall I esteem myself, if in this I can succeed, tho' it be attended with the greatest Misfortune to myself, the never seeing you again. As soon as you are in Safety, I will implicitly obey your Commands, even tho' they should require me to leave you for ever; more blessed with the pleasing Recollection of having contributed to your Happiness than any thing but your Hand can make me; in your refusing which I have not a Pretence to accuse you of Cruelty; it is but Justice, since I can plead no other Recommendation to your Favour than the necessary Consequence of knowing you, and the being with the sincerest Respect, and warmest Affection, and Admiration, your most devoted,
                    obedient Servant,
                    Henry South."

This letter, at the same Time, afforded me Pleasure and Uneasiness. I had been observing all the Servants, in order to find out among them an Eye of Pity and Humanity for one distressed, as they must perceive me to be, in Hopes of contriving my Escape by their Assistance, could I prevail on them to give me such essential Proofs of their Compassion. This Event shewed me, that the Gardener, who was the last in my Thoughts, must be the Foundation of my Scheme. I had little Reason to suppose he thought of me; but the Office he had undertaken for Mr. *South* proved he was accessible in some Avenues to his Heart; and from what I had learned by Conversation, I imagined Avarice to be the Quality most likely to stand my Friend; to this, therefore, I resolved to have Recourse, and fortunately was provided with a Sum sufficient to gratify such a Motive, in one whose Terms were not very high.

But still I had many Difficulties to encounter. I could not recompence him for the Loss of his Place, which must prove the Consequence of being known to have assisted me in my Escape; and yet where to go without a Guide, if I got clear from the Castle, I knew not. These Considerations distressed me. They might have been obviated by putting myself under Mr. *South*'s Protection; but how could I make a Man of his Worth subservient to my Interest, and disappoint him of the Reward which no Generosity could prevent his hoping from such a Service, tho' it might not suffer him to press what he would think, in Gratitude, his Due. I could not procure my own Gratification but by his Disappointment; and my first Resolution was to write him an Answer, which I will, as nearly as my Memory will permit, repeat to your Ladyship.

"How ardently soever I may wish for Liberty, I cannot consent to receive it from one to whom I can make no Return. No Captivity can be so grievous to me as the Sense of Obligations which it will never be in my Power to repay. I must intreat you not to deliver me from my Imprisonment, to fetter me with Ingratitude; nor to add any farther Proofs of a Regard I so little deserve. Your generous and kind Intentions can never be effaced from my Memory; nor shall I ever cease to wish your Happiness and Prosperity may be equal to your Merit, and the just Sense I have of it: I can never give you a Right to expect a Heart which it is not in my Power to give, and to which your Merits alone are too good a Title."

When I delivered this Epistle to the Gardener, he informed me that Mr. *South* had made several unsuccessful Attempts to see me, and finding them vain, had applied to him to deliver me his Letter, adding many other Things in order to move my Compassion, by the Uneasiness under which he represented him, or to please me by describing Symptoms of an Affection in Mr. *South*, which from my Readiness to enter into a Correspondence, I suppose, he thought very agreeable to me.

I listened patiently, for fear of offending a Man from whom I hoped to receive the Blessing of Liberty; but did not dare to venture a Hint of my Design at that Time, lest it should be delivered to Mr. *South* with my Letter, and I be obliged to him, contrary to my Inclination.

I had the good Fortune to meet with the Gardener alone the next day: He told me he had given my Epistle to Mr. *South*, who seemed so sorry, poor Gentleman, it grieved his Heart to see him. Time was too precious for me to suffer him to spend it in expressing his Compassion; I therefore offered the Bribe I intended, and promised Secresy and Prudence.

The Man seemed strongly charmed with the Sight of the Gold, which I exposed to his View, in Order to strengthen the Temptation, and engaged to answer my Hopes, if it could be contrived without his being discovered as a Party in it, and assured me of using his utmost Endeavour to effect it. We agreed on an Hour of meeting again, when he should be able to impart his Success; I charged him to keep the Affair a Secret from Mr. *South*; and we parted with a great Increase of Content on both sides, he enjoying, in Imagination, the offered Gold, and I my Liberty.

CHAPTER XXXVI

Mrs. *Herner's* Vigilance would not suffer me to hear the Gardener's Success at the Time appointed; but I was too industrious in seeking an Opportunity of speaking to be long prevented, and I had the inexpressible Joy to learn that he had formed a practicable Scheme. I listened, with Eagerness, to every Particular; but when I found my first Step was to be on a Ladder, I confess I trembled. As the Doors were all most securely locked every Night, he told me "he saw no Hope of my escaping that Way, and the Rooms being very high, I was raised so far from the Ground, tho' I lay only on the first Floor, that he had no Ladder that would reach above half-way to my Window. This induced him to associate a young Carpenter in the Execution of his Scheme, whom he found as sensible of the Charms of Gold as himself. They agreed to join two of their longest ladders together, and thro' Favour of the Night place them at my Window, from whence I was to descend into the Garden. The same Means were to be used to convey me and themselves over the Garden Wall, the Key of the Garden being delivered every Night to Mrs. *Herner.* Horses were to be ready in waiting, and the young Carpenter was to be my Conductor till I arrived at a Town where I could procure an easier Way of Travelling."

The Gardener had in Charge, after having conveyed the Ladder over the Wall to carry them into the Carpenter's Shop, there to disunite them, to avoid Suspicion, if a Search was made, and then returning over the Part of the Wall, which some private Excursions had taught him to climb, he could go into his own Bed-chamber, without any Impediment, as the Windows of it opened into the Garden, and it was on the Ground Floor.

This Scheme, he assured me, nothing could frustrate but a Noise being made in the Execution of it, which must alarm the Family.

I thought they shewed me more Care of themselves than of me; to descend from so great a Height, down a pieced Ladder, in a dark Night, appeared very terrible in my Eyes, and riding on Horse-back, a Thing I had never attempted, and that too in Darkness, was not less dreadful; but my Desire of Liberty was so strong, that it overcame my Fears, and I punctually observed all their Directions. The appointed Hour found me watching at my Window; my Guide was punctual, and with trembling Steps I left a Place I detested. But my Joy was greatly clouded with Fear, till, after riding the whole Night, at break of Day I arrived at a Town, where I was informed I might get more suitable Means of Conveyance. The Night had favoured my Project no other Way than wrapping all Nature in Darkness, and all the Inhabitants of our Castle in Sleep; for the Rains beat, and the Winds blew; and when I got to the Inn I was entirely wet thro' my Cloths, my Body perishing with Cold, and my Heart chilled with Fear. My Guide had lent me a great Coat; but the Rain had penetrated that long before we arrived at our Journey's End; and it became only an additional Fatigue to me, by the great Weight it acquired from the Rain it had imbibed.

In this Condition I would have proceeded on my Journey, tho' I was almost dead, had not the Landlady insisted on my going to Bed, to receive some Refreshment from the two Things I wanted, Warmth and Rest. I was as little able to contend with her Advice, as to pursue my own Intention; and thro' Weakness, more than Inclination, obeyed. Before I retired to my Room, I would have dismissed the young Carpenter; but he positively refused to leave the Place till he had seen how I did after my Rest. This humane Attention surprized me, in one to whom I was a Stranger, as I had not met with the like from People who had more Reason to regard me; and I could not but feel myself obliged to him for this Action, tho' I was afraid he might open his Heart with the Liquor the Inn afforded, and betray the whole Affair. I did not fear it should be by that Means frustrated, but I could not like to be the Subject of Discourse among such a Set of People.

These Thoughts, however, could not disturb the Rest I so much wanted; and after a Sleep of some Hours I awaked greatly refreshed, and determined to prosecute my Journey directly. While the Chariot was getting ready, Breakfast was brought me; and with it came my Guide to enquire after my Health. I thanked him for his good-natur'd Concern, and expressed a Fear that I had inconveniently detained him from his Business; but he assured me that was of no Consequence, adding, "I durst not, for my Life, my Lady, have left you, till I could give a *betterer* Account to Mr. *South*; alack, I warrant he will be main glad to hear you set out from the House so pure *hoddy* and *sprack*;[1] he will have fretted *hugeously* at the Night's being so bad; for he was so *timbersome*[2] about your being cold that he made me take his warmest great Coat for to put about you."

Surprized at this Address, "I enquired what he meant by Mr. *South*; I apprehended he knew nothing of my Flight?"

---

1 Brisk, active, alert, smart. *OED* cites this passage to illustrate the term.
2 Dialect for "hugely" and "timorous."

"Ah, Lard, do you think naw,"! continued the Carpenter, "our silly Heads could have fancied this fine Plot our own selves? No, no Master Gardener knowing Mr. *Parson* to be your Sweet heart, went and told him what you had said to-un, and *as how* you had ordered that he should not be telled of it. Mr. *Parson* bid-un not say nothing of having let-un into his *Conferdence*, and having sent for me, and tried as whether I was willing to act my Part; what do he do but write us the Plot down, come to my House and see that I had fastened the Ladders tightly together, that they might not throw you a Fall; lent me his own Horse, because it is as quiet and as sure-footed as one of us Christians, and then gave me this Letter for you. My Mind gives me, that this will tell you all; but I does love to tell News, so I was bent on telling you all myself."

I opened the Letter with a Mixture of Curiosity and Uneasiness. It contained but few Lines, which were to acquaint me, that, "To prove he deserved a better Opinion than I entertained of him, when I imagined he would want a Reward for any Service he could render me, he had done every thing in his Power to Favour my Escape, and would have guarded me in it, had not my Charge of Secresy to the Agent I had chosen, as well as my Letter to him, plainly shewn that his Presence and Assistance would be highly disagreeable to me. That, he wished he could have contrived to have set me at Liberty with more Ease to myself, but hoped Success would amply recompence me for every Difficulty." He ended by the warmest Wishes of Happiness, adding, "that he would not ask for leave to be a Spectator of it, by begging Permission to wait on me in *London*, fearing that I was so averse to him, that he could not enjoy that Pleasure, without its being painful to me; and he would rather suffer the most sensible Affliction all his Life, than give me an Hour's Disquiet; nor was he worthy to know the Occasion of my being confined in that old Mansion; and indeed he should be afraid to learn it, was not his Despair already arrived to the utmost Excess."

I should have thought myself inexcusably ungrateful, had I not written a few Lines to return my Thanks for his generous Assistance; to which I added an Assurance, that I should be always glad to see him, whenever his Affairs would permit his coming to *London*; but, thro' Inadvertency, forgot to give him a Direction which might enable him to find me. With this Letter I dispatched my Guide, and got into the Chariot.

Tho' my Situation was easier than before, yet my Mind was far from enjoying Peace; every Step that brought me nearer *London*, increased my Anxiety; I trembled to enquire what I wanted to know, and the meer Possibility of finding the Marchioness's Account true; for I often flattered myself, that it could scarcely be called a Probability, made me wretched. The only Source from which I hoped to receive any Consolation was returning to my kind Aunt and her peaceful Cottage; her wise Instructions, and tender Indulgence, I hoped, might, in Time, heal my Mind, and restore me to something like Tranquility; for real Peace, I believed, would never more enter my Heart, should this fatal Change prove real. If Indifference were to incline Lord *Dorchester* to avoid me, yet Justice, I thought, must lead him to inform me in what Part of the Kingdom my Aunt inhabited, a Circumstance he had hitherto kept from my Knowledge. These were the Reflections of my most melancholy Hours, which grew more frequent as I approached the Place where I had so ardently longed to be. My Apprehensions increased so fast, that fair Hope could scarcely find Time to smile on my black Imaginations.

Between this Anxiety of Mind, and the Fatigue of my Journey, I was not half animated when I got into Town; but as I could not forego my impatient Desire to see Lord *Dorchester* while a Spark of Life remained, I ordered to be driven to his House, and made the Coachman let me out before the Servant (in less Haste than I was) came to the Door, and I was ready to enter, as soon as it was opened.

I enquired for Lord *Dorchester*, with an eager Wildness, which I saw surprized them; one answered, "he was not at home,"[1] while another went into the Parlour, and, I could hear, pronounced my Name. My Lord's Voice soon informed me, that it was to him he spoke; for he, rising suddenly from his Seat, as I could plainly distinguish, cried out, "Good God! is it possible! where is she!" but with a lower Voice added; "Why should I ask where she is? I can never see her more. Keep her from me, and bid her avoid the Man whom she has so cruelly injured, and fear the Effects of his Resentment."

As soon as he spoke, I exclaimed with the Eagerness of Distraction, "I hear, I hear his Voice! Why do you refuse to let me see him?" and endeavoured to force my Way into the Room where he was, but the Servants stopped me, and held me fast. This was not long necessary; for his Words more effectually deprived me of the Power of Motion, and for some time afforded me Relief, by reducing me to, almost, a total Insensibility.

---

1 I.e., not receiving visitors, whether physically present in the house or not.

When I recovered my scattered Thoughts, I desired to have a Chair called; the Servants unwillingly obeyed me, being moved with the Condition I was in; they would have persuaded me to wait a farther Recovery; and when they found all they could say was unavailing, each intreated me to permit him to see me safe home; but I equally rejected them all, charging them not to offend, on my Account, so good a Master, who, it was plain, would be displeased with any Regard shewn to one whom he was determined to abandon. "They insisted, that they were sure he could not be angry at the Respect and Concern, which they must be Brutes not to feel for me, whatsoever he might think proper to do himself." But I would not suffer any of them to attend me, tho', I confess, I received some Satisfaction from seeing they retained a Regard for me, independant of their Master's. Gratitude will give us Pleasure, whatever Heart pays us that valuable Tribute.

CHAPTER XXXVII

I directed my Chair to Lady *Palestine*'s, from whom I hoped to learn the whole of the Affair between Lady *Trente* and Lord *Dorchester*, which, from his Behaviour, I more than ever believed; but Pride would not suffer me to ask any Questions of his Servants, tho' in such Particulars they are generally well qualified to give Information.

At Lady *Palestine*'s I was told, she was not at Home. I knew she never went abroad at that Hour; and, being well acquainted with the fashionable Paradox of a Lady's being abroad when she is at Home; I replied, that I was sure she was denied, and therefore desired the Servant would return and tell her my Name. He complied, but brought me back Word, that, "my name could be no Recommendation to me while my Conduct was so indiscreet."

Rejected a second Time I had not Courage to go to any other of my Acquaintance, especially, as her Ladyship was the only one with whom I was on an intimate Footing; but ordered to be carried to my own House, where I hoped to be screen'd from such Indignities, and perhaps to get some Light into this undeserved ill Treatment; for such, I thought, I had a Right to call these Affronts, since Indifference could not excuse Brutality; nor did I suppose that my forced Absence could be attributed to my Dishonour. I was insensible to the suspicious Air it bore, and thought it should have excited Pity, not Resentment in the Hearts of those that loved me. I imagined they might be apprehensive for my Safety, and pity my Fate, but not blame my Conduct. Since I became better acquainted with the World, I have been sensible that they could not be called unjust in the ill Opinion that they conceived of me, tho' they proved in an Error; when People can judge only by Appearances, a Mistake may often be unfortunate, without being blameable.

But as, at that Time, my Ignorance prevented my looking on the Treatment I received in this Light, I was not free from Resentment; especially against Lady *Palestine*; she had hurt my Pride; my Lord had wounded me in my Affections, and Grief did not leave me Spirit enough to be angry with him. It was not in the Power of any other Person to afflict me, for, *Where the greater Malady is fix'd, the lesser is scarce felt.*[1] My Mind was so little capable of any Increase of Uneasiness, that it received no Addition from finding myself excluded, even from my own House. The Chairmen knocked a considerable Time at the Door, till they were convinced Nobody was at Home, and ask'd me where I chose to be carried.

This Question, indeed puzzled me, tho' it could not add to my Distress. I was afraid of attempting to get Admittance into any other Place, lest it should be refused me, and being little able to think, was long sat down there, before I could recollect a House where I might hope to be received. At last I thought of a Milliner whom I had used, and directed them there.

This Woman very readily accommodated me with a Room, and would have favoured me with her Company, had I not entreated her to leave me to myself; for in such a State of Mind the Sight of any Person was irksome; it must have laid me under some Restraint; for my Pride would not suffer me to declare that I could be so much affected by one who felt nothing for me but Indifference; and I was afraid of mentioning Lady *Palestine*'s Behaviour, since her Scorn might prove an Example to the Milliner; for the Little love to ape the Great. It was not till the next Day that I became able to resolve or execute any thing. I then determined to write to Lord *Dorchester*, justifying this Course from all Imputation of Meanness, by persuading myself, that to shew I was blameless was a Duty I owed to my Reputation. Inconstancy appeared to me the more criminal, from my having no Idea of it. I supposed it a Crime almost unparalelled, and knew not that Custom was thought so great an Alleviation of the Offence, that it was treated by the World as one

---

1 Lear in Shakespeare's *King Lear* III.iv.8-9. Fielding quotes the same lines in her *Remarks on Clarissa* (1749) 43.

of the smallest Frailties to which human Nature is subject. Your Ladyship will, therefore, not wonder if some Resentment was mixed with Grief. But I found it easier to humble my Pride than to mortify my Affection.

Had I perceived that Appearances were against me, I should have thought myself obliged to make all the Submissions which could have been required of me, if I had been really in the wrong, for who can be secured in such Cases from mistaking the Truth? But without this Excuse for my Condescension I wrote to my Lord a short Account of my Imprisonment, adding, that, "I hoped he would not partake of the Marchioness's Aversion to me; and he might be assured that I should not return even an unfriendly Wish for the Injuries I had received from her; for whoever was his Wife I must look on with Respect; and, if she pleased, with Affection; and, indeed, if she made him happy, must feel that Gratitude towards her, which a Person deserves, who confers upon us the greatest Blessings in Life; for in that Rank I should always esteem his Happiness, however his Heart was estranged from me." I then begged, "if he no longer wished to see me, he would instruct me where to find my former Solitude, and not detain me in a Place which was become more lonely to me than my Cottage."

I forbore, as much as I was able, any strong Expressions of my Grief; if his Affection was gone, I did not wish to move his Pity, and my Concern was too tender to suffer me to make him any Reproaches.

As soon as I had written my Letter, I sent it by one of the Chairmen who had brought me to the Milliner's. This Man, either moved with Compassion for one he saw so deeply afflicted, at an Age when Grief might reasonably have been thought far off, or actuated by the less laudable Motive of hoping to find Advantage from attending on a Person whose Affairs appeared so confused and complicated, that a menial Assistant might be requisite, came early in the Morning to ask if I had any Commands. Whatever was his Motive, the Effect was convenient, I wanted a Messenger, and gladly employed him. His Sagacity convinced him that my Letter was of Importance to me, and, without my saying any thing to that Purpose, assured me he would return with the utmost Expedition.

I believe the Chairman kept his Word; but to impatient Expectation Time seems to move with leaden Pace. The Hour-Glass empties slowly to those who watch every Sand that falls thro' it. This was the Case with me; the fleetest of the Creation, had he been my Messenger, would have appeared slow to my Impatience. From the

Instant the Chairman left me, I expected his Return, and would not believe my Watch, it marked the Progress of Time so tediously, in Comparison of my swift Imagination. After what I thought a long Absence, the Man came back; I had scarce Courage to ask the Success of my Letter, and was damped by seeing none in his Hand; but calling all my Fortitude to my Aid, I stuttered out something like an Enquiry, to which he replied, Lord *Dorchester* was at Home, and the Servant carried in my Letter, but returned immediately with it in his Hand, saying, his Lord refused to receive it, and commanded him, "never to bring any more Messages or Letters from me, unless he wanted to incur his Displeasure, and entirely destroy all Hopes of his Recovery of Health or Ease." With this Answer the Chairman was returning, when the Servant overtook him, desired the Letter, and that he would acquaint him where I was to be found; bidding him, "present his Duty to me, and assure me that he would make farther Trials to bring me an Answer; and if he could not succeed, I should receive my own Letter safe, with an Account how he had proceeded."

Nothing could be more shocking to me than to find my Lord would not even read my Justification. Indifference alone could make him void of all Curiosity about me; therefore I had little Hope from his Servant's good–natur'd Intention; I knew if the Sight of his Hand had not dispelled any Pique I had conceived against him, the strongest Arguments from another must have been unavailing; I should have discovered more Eloquence in the least significant Letter of the Alphabet written by him, than in all the Words another Tongue could have uttered. Had I entertained the least Hope of succeeding by his Servant's Intercession, my Pride was too much humbled to have felt any Mortification at being reduced to make use of such an Intercessor, but I confess I blushed to think how low I was fallen. I now strongly experienced this infallible Truth,

She must be humble who would please,
And she must suffer who would love.[1]

And yet I continued blind to my own Passion; I suspected myself of no tenderer Affection than Friendship, of which I had so high an

---

1 Matthew Prior, *Chloe Jealous* (1718) ll. 19–20:
    She shou'd be humble, who wou'd please:
    And she must suffer, who can love.

Idea that I readily reconciled every Pang I endured to my exalted Notion of it. If I compared the Sentiments of my Heart with what was generally called Friendship in the World, it only served to make me despise what others professed, not to suspect my own. A common Effect of a Comparison between ourselves and others; any Difference that appears to our own Opinion, generally turns to our Advantage, and gives us Opportunity of bestowing some Self Applause upon our own Perfections.

CHAPTER XXXVIII

I had been for some Hours devoted to Despair, when I beheld Lord *Dorchester* before me. I was so buried in Thought, that I had not heard the Door open, but the Sight of him put all my Reverie to Flight. He eagerly embraced me, and thanked Heaven, he once more had me in his Arms. Sudden Joy overcame me, and deprived me of the Power of Speech. During my Silence, he "begged Pardon for his Insolence in refusing to see me, but that convinced I had voluntarily fled from him, he thought it mean as well as imprudent, to trust himself with the Sight of one, from whom he was endeavouring to wean his Affections; a painful Trial which had cost him many Pangs, and yet proved totally unsuccessful. The same Motive," he said, "induced him to refuse my Letter, which he confessed, he repented the next Minute, and should have called back my Messenger, had he not been restrained by the Fear of exposing himself to his Servants, and being despised for his Meanness. This Consideration prevented his asking any more Questions concerning me, the Day before, but he could no longer maintain the same Command over himself, and on some other Pretence, calling the Servant who had brought him my Letter, he enquired what Messenger I had employed."

This gave the good-natured Footman an Opportunity of describing the Condition into which I was thrown by his refusing to see me, and all that passed on the Occasion. Seeing his Lord moved by the Account he gave him, he ventured to express his Wonder at his Lordship's having rejected my Letter, for "he was sure I could not be in the wrong, since it was plain to perceive that I did not expect such Treatment as I had received the Day before; and had none of that Confusion in my Countenance, so impossible to be hid by one who fears the Reproaches of a Person she has injured." Lord *Dorchester*, without seeming offended at the Liberty he took, replied, that "if he had supposed Miss *Lenox* could have justified herself, he would, at least, have read her Letter; and, indeed, could not but accuse himself of great Insolence in having refused to see her, when she had favoured him with a Visit, or to receive what she had done him the Honour to write, but that Anger had got the better of the Respect due to her."

The Servant not perceiving that Pride might be his Lord's strongest Motive for retaining some Appearance of Regard for one whom he had taught every Person belonging to him to respect, was encouraged by the Manner in which he spoke of me, and told him "the Chairman had left my Letter, therefore the Means of repairing what he thought an Offence, was still in his Power." Observing that he looked rather disconcerted than angry; he brought it, and laying it on the Table before him, went out of the Room, while my Lord continued in an anxious Uncertainty what Course to take. He owned, that, "had his Servant staid he could not have prevailed on himself immediately to have opened the Letter, so strong was Pride and Resentment; but when he found himself alone, every other Consideration vanished before his Hope, weak as it was, of seeing me justified by my own Defence." But, continued he, "When I had read your Letter, the Affliction expressed in it, untinctured either with Resentment for the Inconstancy of which you suspected me, or the Meanness of one who cannot feel an Injury; and the cruel Treatment you had received on my Account, as I gathered from the Circumstances you related, gave me the tenderest Concern, at the same Time that it relieved me from a State of Misery, to inspire me with the most lively Joy. I could not restrain my Impatience, but instantly repaired to your House, with such Haste and Eagerness in my Steps and Countenance, as attracted the Attention of every one that met me. I perceived it plainly, but could not command either, nor on such an Occasion, bestow a Thought on the Opinion of the Multitude. But when I hoped to receive the Reward of my Haste by the Sight of you, I learnt that you were not there, nor could your Servants give me any further Information, than that a Neighbour told them, a Chair had stopped a considerable Time, at your Door the Day before, and finding no one at Home, at last, went away. I reproved them for their Negligence in leaving the House empty with more Warmth and Bitterness, than I believe any of my Dependants ever saw me use; and now had no Chance of finding you, but in the Possibility of my People's having learnt where you were. In order to make this Enquiry, I returned Home with as much Speed as I had left it, and had the Satisfaction of hearing where you lodged. Add to this, my Joy in finding you, my dearest *Ophelia*, the Delight of knowing you think me worthy of Pardon. Relate to me every

Circumstance of what has befallen you. Compleat my Felicity by giving me Hopes you still retain an Affection for me, or if you do not, forbear to tell it me: Deceive me into Happiness, and Hypocrisy will for once be a Virtue." Alas! I replied, "I never had less Occasion to act the Hypocrite, if this is all you require. Though I have thought your Treatment of me cruel, I could not resent it. My Heart was too much your's to be angry; it could only grieve. But surely, it was a melancholy Recompence for all the Pain I had suffered by my Absence from you."

Lord *Dorchester* used all his Power to soothe me, and in Justification of what he had done, informed me, that Lady *Trente* wrote him a Letter the Day after my being carried off, to inform him, that, "she had overheard Miss *Lenox* concerting with a young Gentleman, the Night before, the Means of running away with him; and considering all the Precautions necessary towards concealing him from his Lordship's Resentment and her from his Search. That she did not hear of the Day that was agreed upon, therefore thought she could not too soon give this Information as there seldom passed much Time between the forming such Schemes and the Execution of them, and knowing none of my Friends, but his Lordship, she believed herself obliged in mere Charity to acquaint him with it, as it might give him the Power of preventing the young Lady's Ruin."

This ingenious Epistle found Lord *Dorchester* in the utmost Anxiety, and the Agreement it bore to my Disappearing, persuaded him of the Truth of it. A Prophetess who could fulfil her own Predictions, would be very injudicious, if the Fact did not correspond with her Words. He went directly to her House to enquire more particularly into the Affair, which she confirmed to him by many corroborating Circumstances of her own Invention; and expressed herself "vastly concerned, that she did not apprehend how soon it was to be executed, since it might possibly have been prevented, if she had acquainted him with it at the Instant she overheard us." Lord *Dorchester* wanted to discover the Gentleman, but she would give no particular Description, telling him, "she could not satisfy a Curiosity which might endanger a Life she so highly valued, as she feared he intended to call the Person to Account."[1] When ever he

---

1 I.e., challenge him to a duel, which would be fought with swords or pistols. Although duelling was illegal, gentlemen were expected to issue challenges when offence was given by other gentlemen; not to do so would be to invite accusations of cowardice.

pressed for this Information he could obtain nothing but Expressions of her Attachment to him (of which, though not a vain Man, he was not ignorant before) and Invectives against my ill Conduct; telling him "it should make him indifferent to my Fate, for no more could be required of a Guardian than a Parent would perform, who on such Provocation most abandon their best beloved Child, and leave her to receive the Punishment she so justly deserved."

Lady *Trente* procured many Interviews with Lord *Dorchester*, by pretended Informations that might assist him in finding me out, the only Means she could discover of bringing him to her House, and therefore her working Brain was continually employed in inventing them, and every Time she saw him, she omitted no Endeavours to attract him; but mixed so many bitter Accusations against me, with the Language her Love dictated, that she only increased his Dislike to her. He thought the Love could not be delicate or generous, that took a Pleasure in giving Pain to the Object of it, whatever Benefit she might hope would thereby accrue to herself.

Having sufficiently informed each other of all that had passed during our Separation, we spent the rest of the Evening in rejoicing at its being, at last ended; but my Lord declared, he should never more think me safe out of his Sight, nor knew how he should venture to leave me for an Instant. There appeared an Increase of Tenderness in him, which silenced all my Repinings at what I had suffered. Some Disasters give a Relish to good Fortune, and little Reverses quicken Affection.

CHAPTER XXXIX

I did not return to my own House till the next Morning; the Hurry of my Spirits had a good Deal disordered me; and as all Places are agreeable to the happy, I chose to remain that Day at my Lodgings; one great Reason, I believe, might be an Unwillingness to lose any of my Lord's Company, by the Interruption we should have received from removing my Habitation.

My Lord *Dorchester* grew extremely uneasy when he perceived that my ill State of Health was more lasting than my Anxiety. We had both flattered ourselves that Happiness would have cured me; but I believe my Constitution had suffered as much from the unwholesome Situation of the Marchioness's Castle, as from Vexation, and therefore Ease of Mind was not sufficient to recover me. He made me consult a Physician, who declared *Tunbridge* Waters[1] the most probable Remedy, but as it was yet too early in the Year to drink them, he gave me some Medicines for present Relief, with but indifferent Success.

My Lord determined to carry me to *Tunbridge*, as soon as the Season would permit, and engaged Lady *Palestine* to be of the Party, which I then looked upon as an obliging Attention; without any one to countenance and direct me, I must have been extremely at a Loss, in a Place so new to me; but I have since perceived, his Motive was to prevent my becoming intimate with any Person, who not being so well instructed, might have frustrated his Views.

In the Interim, my Lord's principal Care was, finding me out a Variety of Amusements. I was carried to every Place where there was any Novelty that might divert me, but none made so great an Impression on me, as a Collection of Curiosities, and *Bedlam*,[2] both of which I was shewn. I proposed great Pleasure from the first imagining, I should there see every Thing that was uncommonly beautiful; and was greatly disappointed to find, that on the contrary, the Collector seemed to have been actuated by a Pique at Nature. For if she happened to swerve from her general Laws, to contradict all Order, Beauty and Use; the mishapen, unformed Mass became to him more valuable than her fairest Productions. He had spent his Life in Search of Things, from which most People would have run away, and had cherished what would have frighted others. I found he was the general Parent of Monsters, the grand Nurse of Abortions, and equally the careful Receiver of those who were born dead, or died of old Age, declaring War with the Earth, by defrauding it of its due Tribute, the Bodies of the deceased. The latter indeed, I was informed had not been performed by his own Art, he having robbed *Egypt* of half

---

1 Tunbridge Wells in Kent, about 32 miles southeast of London, was a newly fashionable spa resort in the mid-eighteenth century. Its chalybeate spring waters were being promoted as superior to those of Bath, its older rival. The Tunbridge season was in summer, unlike that of Bath which was in winter.

2 Bedlam was the popular name for Bethlehem Royal Hospital, a hospital for the insane from 1547 to 1815. The patients were notoriously illtreated, and until the 1770s the hospital was open as a place of public entertainment.

its *Ptolomies*,[1] and yet without a moral View in shewing how poor a Load is the Body of a King. One might say with *Anthony*,

> *Lie there thou Shadow of an Emperor;*
> *The Ground thou coverest on thy Mother Earth,*
> *Is all thy Empire now.*————[2]

I was carried next to *Bedlam*, where I was surprized to find so few Persons confined in a Place, which I was told had been appropriated to the Reception of such as were deprived of their *Reason*, for I myself had seen a sufficient Number to have filled it, whom I should have judged well qualified.

It was strange to me, that no Person should be thought to deserve Confinement, but he whose hurtful Actions proceeded from mistaken Notions. While he, who is prompted by *evil Intentions*, who acts in open Defiance of *Religion Virtue*, and *Reason*, and endeavours to form a Happiness for himself in destroying that of Society, shall be imitated by a few, approved by many, and tolerated by all. He shall be suffered to enjoy Liberty, who from a false Pride reduces himself and Family to Beggary and Shame; he, who prostitutes his Principles, and tramples Honesty under Foot, in order to gain Honours, shall be received into Society, while the poor Wretch who innocently fancies himself a King, shall be shut in a dark Room. Denied the Light of the Sun, which graciously *shines on the just and the unjust*.[3]

I received great Consolation from seeing so much Happiness among a Set, who, above all others, seemed to claim our Pity, and was glad to find, that the Lunaticks in *Bedlam*, as well as those that live more at large, could say that, *there is a Pleasure in being mad, which none*

---

1 The Ptolemies, a Greek dynasty, ruled Egypt from the death of Alexander the Great in 323 BC until the Roman conquest in 30 BC. The collector has acquired a horde of their mummified remains. In a chapter entitled "Monster-Mongers and Other Retailers of Strange Sights," Richard D. Altick recounts the eighteenth century's fascination with monstrosities of all kinds, including those displayed by the collector here. See *The Shows of London* (Cambridge: Harvard UP, 1978) 34–49.

2 Mark Antony in John Dryden's *All for Love* (1678) I. 216-8:
   Lie there, thou shadow of an emperor.
   The place thou pressest on thy mother earth
   Is all thy empire now.

3 Matthew, 5.45: "He maketh his sun to rise on the evil and on the good, and sendeth rain on the just and on the unjust."

but Madmen know.[1] And, I am not sure, the former have not the larger Share of it. He who madly believes Felicity to consist in Things which when attained, would give him more Pain than Satisfaction, he who aims at Impossibilities, and searches for what cannot be discovered, has just Reason enough to feel Disappointment, but not to conquer the Turn of Mind which led him into the vain Pursuit which occasioned it.

On the contrary, in *Bedlam*, the ambitious Man is a King, and with fancied Majesty, struts as proudly in his wretched Rags, as if cloathed in Coronation Robes, and his Head is as easy as if graced with a Diadem. The Miser, in his dirty Cell, believes himself possessed of Mines of Gold, and rejoices in his Store. The gay Man enjoys imaginary Pleasure, and fancies Variety, while his Life passes in a dull Sameness, Day after Day. The Politician here beholds the Success of every Scheme, he new moulds the State, wages bloody Wars, effects the greatest Revolutions, and becomes the Ruler of the World, without stirring out of his little Cell. Here the Author's Imagination reconciles the two Things he before found most irreconcileable, Wit and Riches, and enraptured, enjoys a Consciousness of superior Genius. The vain Woman in Spite of Age, or Small-Pox, perceives an Admirer in every one that beholds her; and the finical Beau fancies Finery in his Filth. Where every Thing is imaginary, the Pride and Vanity of the Undertaker assures him of Success, nothing but Reason will convince an obstinate Man, that his Genius can be conquered, and his well-laid Scheme baffled.

I was not long permitted to enjoy the Consolation I received, from finding, that Misery was not always the Portion of the Mad; for we were soon carried to another Part of the Hospital, set aside for those who were afflicted with imaginary Wretchedness. This, indeed, was a dreadful Sight; for tho' the Causes were fantastick, the Sufferings were real. There was something too shocking in this Scene, to tempt me to make a Stay of many Minutes in it. We left it as soon as we could, but yet I thought the Lesson it gave, might not be useless to a Mind capable of Reflection. Should it not teach Mankind to endeavour to bring their Passions under the Directions of Reason? To fix their inconstant Minds, and expel every fantastick Whim, lest they should gain Strength from Time and Encouragement, till they

---

1 Torrismond, in John Dryden's *The Spanish Fryar* (1681) II.ii.114–5: "There is a pleasure sure / In being Mad, which none but Madmen know!"

arrive at the dreadful Excess of which *Bedlam* affords so many Examples? If People once suffer themselves to deviate from Reason's Path, who can pretend to fix any certain Bounds for their misguided Steps; and when the Consistency of Action which she should constitute, gives Place to every Whim of a capricious Mind, it is wonderful that they should wander on till they arrive at Distraction. The Pleasures, Honours, and Misfortunes, of those who are denominated rational Beings, are generally imaginary; they frequently rejoice at what is no Benefit, and grieve for what is no Evil; they eagerly pursue trifles which are not worth a Thought, and neglect Matters of the highest Importance: In short, they will labour Years, to obtain Pleasures which last but a Day, and, for a Moment's Gratification, will give up the Happiness which shall continue through all Eternity.

I cannot help thinking your Ladyship lulled into a sweet Slumber, by my moralizing on this Scene; but, indeed, you must excuse me, for it made so deep an Impression on my Mind, that I can never recollect it without falling back into the same Train of Reflections, which I then made upon it, and for which, a longer Experience of the World, has only served to give me a greater Scope. In Consideration of this Indulgence, I will promise, if possible, to avoid all such Offence for the future, and the better to effect it, will carry your Ladyship to a new Place, passing over in Silence the Remainder of the Time I spent in *London*; for as it afforded little beside Matter for Reflection on Customs to which I was a Stranger, I may be apt again to turn Moralizer. I must depend on the Actions of others for making my Narration more agreeable to you, than a long Series of my own Thoughts, which are nothing but a Composition of *witty* Observations that, would make any good-natured Person weep the Poverty of the Imagination, that gave Rise to them; *lively* Remarks that would prove better Soporificks than all the Opium in *Turkey*; Dissertations *moral, religious,* and *entertaining,* from which, after much Yawning, you may learn, that it is right to do Right, and wrong to do Wrong, that Friendship is better than Enmity, and that it is wiser to please than to offend. These great Truths I shall leave to be taught by Persons, who love sporting on an old Sentiment in thread-bare Words; avoiding as much as I can, the Produce of my own Brain; in Hopes of affording you more Entertainment by collecting Exoticks, than from any Plants that arise from so bad a Soil as my Imagination, which is not very fertile of any Thing but Weeds.

I must not, however, omit one Affair which was transacted before we left *London*. The Marchioness of *Trente* was so enraged at Mrs. *Herner's* having left me a Possibility of escaping, by which her

Schemes were frustrated, and she exposed, that she refused to see her at her Return to *London*, where Mrs. *Herner* went, as soon as she found I was irrecoverably lost. A more lamentable Effect of the Marchioness's Displeasure, then the withdrawing the Light of her Countenance, was her refusing to maintain her any longer, in which Denial, she abused her in the most opprobrious Terms that Rage and Insolence could suggest. In this Distress, Mrs. *Herner* applied to many of her Friends, but found that, few People's Compassion extended farther than Words and Condolances, as for more effectual Consolation every one shifted her off to another, as more able to assist her; like *Gay's* Hare, she received nothing but Advice to apply to others; *The Sheep's at Hand, and Wool is Warm.*[1] I suppose she thought I might harbour some Resentment against her, in Consideration of the Part she had been employed to act towards me; at least, saw no Reason to expect I should do for her, what those who called themselves her Friends, refused; so that I only heard by Chance, that she and her Neice had quarrelled, but the Occasion of it was unknown. Lord *Dorchester* had advised me to conceal the Marchioness's Behaviour towards me, and Mrs. *Herner* had not declared it, fearing to exasperate her still more.

Though I was as little disposed to esteem Mrs. *Herner's* Disposition, as to be grateful for the Office she had undertaken, yet I could not be insensible to her Distress. "A brave Man struggling with the Storms of Fate," is the noblest Work of God,[2] and deserves our Admiration; but a mean Man is still his Workmanship, and, when afflicted, demands our Pity. I told my Lord, how much her Misfortunes affected me, and the more as I was, though not blameably, the Occasion of them. I found his Heart was not less penetrable than mine; he compassionated her, and said, "he could not bear, that any one should be made wretched, by an Event, which restored his Happiness. He answered me, that I might be easy on her Account, for he would take Care she should have the Means of being so; but thought it right that, if possible, they should be procured from Lady *Trente*, who, at least, deserved that Punishment."

---

1 John Gay, *The Hare and Many Friends* (1727) l. 48. The speaker is a goat, one of the hare's many false friends who give her useless counsel that will fail to protect her from danger.

2 Conflating two quotations from Pope: *Prologue to Mr. Addison's Tragedy of Cato* (1713) l. 21, "A brave man struggling in the storms of fate"; and *An Essay on Man* (1733-4) IV. 248, "An honest man's the noblest Work of God."

Lord *Dorchester* accordingly went to the Marchioness, and told her, that, "she must know, he was well acquainted with her Treatment of me, and that, she might expect to have it made publick, and to become the Topick of general Discourse, if she would not agree to settle an Independency on Mrs. *Herner*. Not that he was at all oblig-ed to that Lady's Intentions, who had been a vigilant Goaler, but because he pitied the Woman." Lady *Trente* was shocked at seeing my Lord; but this Proposal soon turned the Blush of Shame into the higher Red of Anger. He found her invincible Spirit scarcely to be subdued by the Pride of Reputation. She would indeed, after a short Resistance, have consented to receive her Aunt; but my Lord had undertaken the poor Woman's Cause, and thought he should but half relieve her Distress, if he exposed her to her Neice's ill Usage. He therefore insisted on a Settlement of 200 *l. per Annum* for her, find-ing no Hopes of such an Allowance, voluntarily, as he thought her Relation to the Marchioness, and her past Merits deserved from her. At last, he succeeded; got the Settlement drawn up, and delivered it into the Hands of the overjoyed Mrs. *Herner*.

CHAPTER XL

Lady *Palestine* delayed our going to *Tunbridge*, for more than a Fort-night after Lord *Dorchester* wished me there. He was desirous of my drinking the Waters as soon as the Weather would permit; but her Ladyship did not apprehend she should receive sufficient Pleasure from watching my Recovery, to reconcile her to the Place while it continued empty. She did not give this as her Reason for deferring her Journey, but put it upon Business, which, in a Woman who had no Business but Pleasure, told it as plainly, though more civilly, than if she had said it in express Terms. By this Delay, the Place was pret-ty full when we got thither. We arrived late at Night, but the Love of Company determined Lady *Palestine* to appear the next Morning, and she insisted on my doing the same. I had been accustomed to Evening Crowds, but to be introduced into one so early in the Day, was quite new to me, and so little agreeable to me at a Time when my Health made me rather languid in a Morning, that I wondered it should ever be a Practice among a Society of Invalids.

The Musick which played while the Company remained upon the Walks pleased me; but I have laughed at myself since, for the Reasons I assigned for it. I imagined, it was intended as a Part of that Course which was to restore the Sick to Health; and medicinally designed to promote Chearfulness, to remove the Gloominess acquired in the Night, enliven the Languor of a sick Person's Morning, to divert their Thoughts from their Infirmities, and give a Turn to their Spirits. Not contented with this Reason alone, as some of the Musick seemed too loud for the trembling Frame of an Invalid, I suspected it was also intended to drown the Complaints of the sick, as Drums and Trumpets are used in Battle, to prevent the Groans of all the wounded from being heard by the rest, who might be intimidated by them. Imagination often makes us attribute to Design what is really the Effect of Chance,

And learned Commentators view,
In Homer, *more than* Homer *knew.*[1]

But I am still of Opinion, that though this may not be a Reason for the Musick's playing, it is a good Consequence arising from it; for I observed, that if it ceased for a Moment, I heard a hundred Voices, too weak indeed, to contend with the shrill Violin, or the hoarse Violoncello, uttering promiscuously the Words Jaundice, Palsy, Gout, Rheumatism, with the Names of almost every other Disease incident to human Nature; with so minute a Detail of the Symptoms of each, as increased the Evil in the Sufferer's Imagination, and lowered the Spirits of the Hearer; and all in such a Confusion of Tongues, that it was impossible to appropriate to each their respective Complaints, but served to convince me, that all Distempers were there assembled. This filled my Mind with a Kind of Horror, and I was almost ready to believe I made one in *Holbein's* Dance of Death.[2]

I was for some time amused with the Variety of Characters this Place afforded, and with the Vanity and Envy so apparent in many, which I make no Doubt often delays the Benefit that would otherwise be received from the Waters. A pretty Woman afflicted with the Jaundice, whose Spirits have been sufficiently depressed with the Cloud of yellow spread over her Charms, has been seen to grow visibly of a deeper Dye by the Persecution of a Rival Beauty, who, to complete the Triumph of Health and Bloom, would always sit next her. It was common to see a young Lady with bright Eyes, and resplendent Complexion, place herself close by a pale and languid Spectre, and with Pleasure considering the Contrast; or a giggling

---

1 Jonathan Swift, "On Poetry: A Rapsody" (1733) ll. 103-4.
2 Hans Holbein the Younger executed a famous series of woodcut engravings, "The Dance of Death," in 1523-24. They depict a series of figures, from high to low, being forced to take part in a dance with skeletons.

Girl, crowding a dejected Invalid, who might have sat for the Image of Patience on a Monument.[1]

The Variety of Behaviour in this various Company, was not less entertaining. I was often diverted with observing a Meeting between a delicate Town Lady, and a robust Northern Lass; the Contempt in each of their Countenances, sufficiently proved the Self-Satisfaction of both. The easy Assurance of a Person much accustomed to Company, and the timerous Sliness[2] of a Country Girl, who never before was five Miles distant from the Family Mansion, makes no bad Scene, the one advancing with intended Affability, while the other, with innocent Fear, retires from the forward Thing, whom she suspects of some bad Design.

When I had so often observed these Movements of the Mind, that they grew old to me, they ceased to entertain, and I became very much tired of the Rooms, except on Ball-Nights. I loved Dancing; and Lord *Dorchester*, or Lord *Larborough* (who followed us down to *Tunbridge*) were my Partners. I found more than ever the Inconvenience of being the Subject of Observation; I could neither sit nor walk in Peace. Every Motion was constrained by perceiving myself continually stared at. In a Morning, indeed, I was less observed; sick People have not then Spirits enough to be impertinent: My Lord said I owed it to the Paleness of my Complexion, for Sickness had robbed me of my natural Colour; though the Heat of the Room in an Evening, would, in a Degree restore it. Lady *Palestine* used to be out of Patience with the Uneasiness she saw me under at being looked at; and would tell me she never envied me so much; I have been ready to reply that, "perhaps she thought a very exact Examination could discover only Beauties in her, whereas I was fearful that such strict Observation must rather enable them to perceive Defects in me, which, in a transient View, might be overlooked."

I wished myself less at Leisure to remark the Actions of others, the impertinent Effect of Idleness; and growing extreamly tired of sitting by a Card Table without having the least Knowledge of the Game there played at (which however so fixed Lord *Dorchester's* and Lady *Palestine's* Thoughts on their Cards, that I had no Conversation with them) I was tempted to try my Fortune at a Game at Chance, then much in Fashion. As no Skill was required, I thought I might

---

1   Viola, in Shakespeare's *Twelfth Night* II.iv.115-6:
    She sat like Patience on a monument,
    Smiling at grief.
2   I.e., slyness.

succeed as well as others; Fortune has been said to favour Fools,[1] and at Play, I was an absolute Ideot; therefore, had some Reason to hope, she would prove propitious.

I went Home the first Night, Winner of two or three Guineas, and was very well entertained. Play, by keeping up an eager Attention, amused me much, and soon awakened in me the Spirit of a Gamester. I regularly attended the Table every Night, but constantly with bad Success. This did not discourage me; but on the contrary, convinced my Luck was changed, I continued till I had not a Shilling[2] left; fully expecting that every Stake would bring me back a Part of what I had lost. I was now in a disagreeable Situation; I reproached myself for my Folly, and not being able to supply the Expences of going abroad, was obliged to spend my Evenings at Home. This was not very easy, for Lady *Palestine* loved no Place that was not crowded, and my Lord was engaged in a Party, which, he knew not how to leave; I was obliged therefore, to practice a constant Resistance to the pressing Instances they continually made me, to accompany them. It was with Regret, I did what seemed so very obstinate and disobliging, as to persist in saying, I did not chuse to go, when they so earnestly intreated it; but I was too much ashamed of my Folly, to own my Reason; besides, that it would have been making my Lord pay for it instead of my self. To be so long deprived of his Presence, was very painful to me; if I had gone to the Rooms,[3] there were Times when he was not fixed to a Card Table, and I then used to enjoy his Conversation; but now I did not see him for three long Hours together. He too regretted the same; and, at last, began to account for my Obstinacy from his own Imagination.

One Day he was extremely melancholy, though he seemed as fond of me as ever, if not more tender; but it was accompanied by such an Air of Dejection, that I forgot the Emptiness of my Purse, and thought of nothing but him.

Having a Dread of his jealous Temper, I considered whether this Change could be attributed to it. I recalled to Mind, every Circumstance of my Behaviour; whereby I dissipated all Fears of that Sort. I had been so very cautious of giving him Offence, that I had avoided the Acquaintance of all Men, and had not even given a civil

---

1 "Fortune favours fools": proverbial since the mid-sixteenth century.
2 There were twenty shillings in a pound; "not a shilling" thus signifies almost no money at all.
3 The pump-rooms, where the spa waters were drunk.

Answer to those who spoke to me; or thanked them for such Civilities as People have an Opportunity of paying at a publick Place. To do this had been a great Force on my Disposition, which is naturally free and gay; but I had suffered too much not to conquer it.

Unable to guess at the Reason of the Depression of my Lord's Spirits, I begged him to tell it me, and with some Reluctance, he said, "It is cruel my dear *Ophelia* to persecute you any more; I am sensible if I am unhappy, it is not with your Intention; your Behaviour shews me, that you are unwilling to make me so; though it afflicts, yet it obliges me; and by raising my Esteem, increases my Affection, while it proves the Abatement of your's. Do not imagine, I mean to reproach you; you are not unjust, though I am unhappy; our Inclinations are not in our Power; if yours were, I am persuaded I should retain the same Portion I once enjoyed. You look surprized, but pardon me, my dearest Angel, if I impute your Resolution of not going abroad, to a Desire of conquering some Impressions made on your Heart, which in publick you fear would be increased. I can assign no other Reason for your resisting our Importunities, and thus turning us loose in a Place of Gaiety and Dissipation; nor for the Confusion and Disturbance which is visible in you, when we endeavoured to get you with us, and the Thoughtfulness in which I often perceive you. I admire the Efforts you use to conquer this new born Inclination; it is worthy the Goodness of your Heart, which would make you grieve to render any one so unhappy as you know I shall be made by the Loss of your Affections. I have nothing to complain of but my own Defects, which prevent my keeping a Heart that so generously endeavours to remain mine. I almost pity you for possessing Virtues, which increase a Love your Humanity would wish to diminish; you are far above the low Pride of desiring to preserve an Affection you cannot return. My kind, my good *Ophelia*, tell me, with your natural Sincerity, if I may hope, that, by thus avoiding my powerful Rival, I begin to recover the Heart I was in Danger of losing." All this he uttered with so much Melancholy and Tenderness, that I could have shed Tears for his imaginary Misfortune. My Astonishment at this unaccountable Whim, was beyond Expression. I cried out, "What will not a jealous Fancy suggest! How fertile is its Invention! Oh! my Lord, how ingenious are you to torment yourself! Who would imagine, that all your Suppositions have no other Foundation than my staying a few Days at Home! Consider how susceptible you are of Fancies that afflict you; had I been eager to go abroad, I should have given Rise to some of these Kinds of Suspicions; by chusing to stay at Home, I have done the same; can nothing but a total Indifference to every Thing, give you the Ease of Mind I wish you? I have much of it in my Heart; but Youth and Vivacity will not suffer such Coldness of Manner. I then assured him that, so far from having found any one whom I was disposed to like too well, I had not even seen a Man that was agreeable to me." But all I could say, would not convince him. He replied, "This was the Answer of my Humanity, not of my Truth; that I thought Conceal-ment justified by the Ease it might give him; and in short, he would not believe, that his Fears were groundless, if I would not tell him the Reasons of my leaving off going abroad, when he imagined it was grown more agreeable by my having got into a Party at a Game, of which I seemed very fond." I then told him that, the Truth was, "I had been so foolish as to lose too much Money to like it any longer." "That," replied his Lordship, "is no Reason why you should not go abroad as you did before you played." Thus he perplexed me, by not readily accepting my Reasons, till at last, I was reduced to tell him, "That, I thought it would be more prudent to take the Hon-our of the delicate, wise, and generous Sentiments, upon which he had supposed me to act, than to own frankly, that I was so very great a Fool, as to lose every Shilling I had at Cards; and, by that means, had been obliged to keep House for want of Money to defray the necessary Expences of going abroad."

I looked sufficiently silly, I believe, when I made this Confession, but when I had thus mortified myself, it was hard that my Lord would scarcely credit it. To give a particular Description of my Folly, was a sufficient Punishment for it, but I found this necessary in order to convince his Incredulity; so with some Blushes, I told him, "that my first ill Luck made me desperate, and I lost all my Money in try-ing to recover Part of it."

Lord *Dorchester* laughed so heartily that he put me almost out of Humour, and quite out of Countenance; but he soon acknowledged this to be so natural and so common, that it was extremely credible; and declared himself overjoyed to find that my Money, and not my Affections, had been won. He would have repaired my ill Fortune, by giving me much more than I chose to accept. "He begged, I would not controul my Inclinations, for he could furnish me with a considerable Sum yearly, without any Inconvenience to himself, and could trust to my Prudence for not exceeding it."

I could not forbear returning him Thanks for an Indulgence, in Reality so blameable, but telling him, that, "he was willing to build his Dependance on a very weak Foundation, as my past Folly too plainly shewed," I assured him, "I was sufficiently disgusted with Play, and would never again begin any Thing, to which my Prudence found it difficult to put a Stop."

My Lord seemed so happy in having learnt the Cause of my Retirement, that I could not but think, I was peculiarly fortunate in having the Power of giving so much Pleasure by the Discovery of my Follies. But this suspicious Turn in his Temper appeared to me very strange; I thought it an unaccountable Narrowness of Mind in a Man so generous in other Respects.

I wondered he should suppose Friendship should be so soon conceived or ended, since either appeared to me a Work of Time. One might see Merit in an early Acquaintance, or in some unguarded Moment, discover Faults, which for a long Time had been concealed, but the Effect could not be so speedy; natural Indifference, or habitual Fondness require Time to conquer them. However, as this Covetousness of my Affection proved the Value he set upon it, I was not inclined to complain of the Consequences, but thought myself made for the Destruction of his Virtues, since only in his Behaviour to me, had he ever swerved from the most extensive Generosity and tenderest Humanity.

CHAPTER XLI

During my stay at *Tunbridge*, I saw many bad Consequences attend Gaming, but none are worth communicating, except one, which was so ludicrous, that as it soon became publick, it grew a general Entertainment. A Country Gentleman, a few Years before, had married a young Lady, with whom he made an Agreement before Marriage, that she should never go to *London*; to which, as liking the Man and his Fortune, she readily consented. After a pretty long Stay in the Country, she began to grow a little tired of her Solitude, and could not forbear using some Persuasions to prevail on her Husband to be more complaisant after Marriage, than he was before. A strange Endeavour certainly, but he being a good-natured Man, was sorry to refuse her earnest Request; though as their Estate was small, and they had a pretty large Family, he could not reconcile it to his Conscience. However, as her Desire grew very strong, and her Importunities frequent; he, at last, told her, that, "an Expedition to *London* was too expensive to agree with their Finances, but if she could save up an hundred Pounds, as she had the sole Care of the Money, he would go with her to *Tunbridge*, and stay there as long as it lasted."

Thus encouraged in her Œconomy, she abridged their own Table, starved the Servants, and was indefatigable in her Endeavours to scrape up this happy Sum.

This, in a Year's Time she accomplished, and, with great Joy, acquainted her Husband with it. He had suffered a little by the Change which this Sparingness had produced in the Entertainment of himself and his Friends; but that had never mortified him so much, as the Knowledge that the Sum was compleated. He was fond of the Country, loved the Sport it afforded, and had besides great Part of his Estate in his Hands, for the good Management of which, his Presence was absolutely necessary. However, he would not disappoint his Wife, or break his Word; so the Day was fixed, and they went thither accordingly. They placed themselves in the first Lodgings they could find, but as they were very bad, it was agreed they should change them for better the next Week.

Now our Lady was in high Bliss, and that all her Time might be filled up, was abroad from Morning till Night. The Husband was not fond of any of the Diversions going forward there; and found the Weariness natural to People at first coming to a Place where they have no Acquaintance, and where the Manner of Life is quite different from what they have been accustomed to, or liked; but he did not despond, as he hoped to get into a little more Society and Hospitality when they had a better Apartment.

Accordingly, at the End of the Week, he desired his Lady to give him the Bill in which they had brought their Money, that he might get it changed, and then they would go and take good Lodgings, and settle themselves in a comfortable and handsome Manner. The meek Wife was a little confounded, and deferred her Compliance, saying, "it was Time enough; their Lodgings would serve very well another Week, and then they should have better Choice, as in so fluctuating a Place many People would be gone by that Time," with many other Pretences to delay it. But the Husband shewing her Reasons were not sufficient, persisted in his Request.

This increased her Confusion to the greatest Degree; at last, with downcast Looks, conscious Blushes, and fluttering Voice she cries, "my Dear, I have changed the Bill." "Oh! very well," answered the Husband, "it will save me the Trouble of doing it, but give me a little Money that I may provide us with such Things as we want." The poor Lady grew still more distressed, and was reduced to whisper, "I have no Money," "I beg your Pardon," answered he, "I understood you had changed the Bill. Come, give it me then, and you shall have some presently. I assure you, *Molly*, there is no living at this Place without Money." "You are right," answered the penitent Wife "I have changed the Bill." "Well, well," replied the Husband, "I am very stupid to be sure, this thick Air has affected my Senses, and I can understand nothing. First, I fancied you said you had changed the Bill; and then, that you had no Money. I do nothing but blunder. Come, my Dear, let's go and seek for Lodgings. Our Cousins of *Penn-Hall*, came last night. My Uncle *Crump* writes me Word, he shall be here to Morrow; and my Aunt *Jones* is expected every Minute. We must invite these Friends to Dinner. I would not have them think we are grown fine Folks, because we are in a fine Place, we must not forget our Relations. I love to live well every where with my Family." "My Love," says again, the abashed Lady, "Indeed, you do not blunder. I beg your Pardon, but," and instead of finishing her Sentence, a few Tears trickled down her Cheeks. "What is the Matter with you, *Molly?*" quoth the Husband, "why, you are a Riddle, I think. Come, speak plain, and never cry. Why you know I am never angry. You are my good Wife, and I love you, say what you please, for I cannot bear to see you vexed."

"You are too good my Dear," replies the Wife, sobbing grievously, "but it must come out, so I may as well tell you at first, my Love, that I have lost."————Here the Tears flowed again. "Oh, you have lost your Purse, have you?" answered the Husband, "why I am sorry for you, it is hard, you should lose any Part of what you had saved with so much Care, and I wish I could afford to make it up to you; but we will have it cried,[1] if an honest Person has found it, he will restore it undiminished, but to be sure, there are more Rogues than honest Men here; so the Chance is against us; however, if we do not recover it, you are so good a Manager, that we shall do very well some Time on the rest. We must live a little more sparingly, that is all."

"Alas! Alas!" cried she, in an Agony, "there is no Rest to live upon. We have nothing of which to be sparing." "What" says he, "had you all the Money in your Purse? That was unlucky indeed, and I am afraid, will make it more difficult to be recovered; for there are People whose Honesty would have resisted twenty Pounds, who will not be Proof against an Hundred."

"It was not lost so neither, my dear Husband," replied the Lady, "I will confess the whole Truth, if my Tears will but let me. You must know then, the first Night I went into the Rooms, I saw a great many People at a pretty Play; it seemed the easiest Game in the

---

1 Announced publicly, by a town crier.

World. Some very civil Persons made Room for me, and I could not see why I should not play as others, so I sat down, and began by winning; but before the End of the Night, I lost a good Deal, and was obliged to get the Man belonging to the Table to change my Bill. The next Morning I endeavoured to win it back again, and did in Part. At Night I thought I might win the whole; but instead of that, I lost more. I was ashamed to let you know it; but intended as soon as I could get back all I had disbursed to play no longer, and to settle all Things with you." Here her Sorrow grew very clamorous, and with much Difficulty she sobbed out, "in trying to win it, I lost it all to ten Guineas." At this melancholy Conclusion, the weeping Dame was quite inconsolable but the Husband not sorry to have a good Excuse to return Home, where his Affairs required his Presence "begged her to make herself easy. That he came only to divert her, and as she had had her Diversion, he was perfectly well pleased, and as much so, that it was done in a short, as a long Time. That he would pay for their Lodgings, and their Journey back; he had just heard a Coach cried that was going to their Part of the World; and he would secure it directly, for them to return in, intreating her to be under no Concern." Thus he got her safe Home to his great Satisfaction; nor was the Lady so mortified as one might imagine, being well out of a Scrape she feared, would have greatly offended her Husband. She thought herself much obliged to him for an Indulgence which he found very easy, as the Event of their Journey was as agreeable to him as it could be, in procuring him a speedy Return.

Though in one Folly I was kept in Countenance, if Companions in our Weaknesses can have that Effect; yet my Ignorance and Want of Thought had Consequences of such Importance; that if I could have pleaded Precedents for my Errors, it would have offered me no Consolation.

The Diversions of the Place brought me into Scrapes of which I had no Notion before: That which most alarmed me, arose from a Ball.

At the Beginning of the Evening, I was asked to dance by a Gentleman, with whom I had no Acquaintance. Having been a good deal indisposed all Day, I had determined not to dance, and saw nothing in this Stranger, that should conquer my Resolution, with which I acquainted him, and he chose another Partner. Toward the End of the Night, being pretty well recovered, a lively Tune inspired me with an Inclination for Dancing, and Lord *Dorchester* being by me, offered to be my Partner, which was an additional Inducement, and accordingly we began; but I had not gone down many Couples,[1] before I was stopped by the Gentleman I refused, who addressed me with saying, "I had not used him like a Gentleman, in dancing after I had told him, I did not chuse it."[2]

His Countenance wore such visible Marks of Anger, that he startled me very much; but I answered very innocently, "That, what I said was the real Truth, when he asked me, I did not chuse to dance, but that I afterwards altered my Mind."

To this he replied, that, "the Change he supposed was occasioned by being asked by a different Person, had Lord *Dorchester* been in his Place, the Refusal would scarcely have been given."

I was insensible to any Affront being designed in this, I thought what he said extreamly probable, though it was not then Fact, and with great Simplicity assured him, that "he was mistaken, for that when he asked me I would not have danced with any one, though I allowed, to have had Lord *Dorchester* for a Partner, might have been a stronger Temptation, as my Intimacy with him must make him more agreeable to me."

The angry Man grew more ireful, and replied, "Beauty could not excuse Insolence," adding, that, "he did not at all doubt, but I was intimately acquainted with his Lordship, who, in Return for the Intimacy, should teach me how to treat Gentlemen of Fashion." He continued some Time in this Strain, repeating the Word Intimacy with a Sneer, and so strong an Emphasis, that I thought it had offended him, but did not imagine he meant more by it than I had done.

My Lord did not hear it with the same Indifference. He came up to him, and told him, "it was not acting the Part of a Gentleman to insult a Lady, who ignorant of the Customs of Balls, having never been at one before she came to *Tunbridge*, could not properly be said to offend against a Ceremony she knew not. He in a Whisper,

---

1 In country dances, couples were ranged in order, with the top couple choosing the dance. During the dance, this couple moved down the aisle formed by the other dancers, i.e., "going down the dance." They would then return to their place while the next couple went down the dance.

2 Ophelia's blunder here anticipates that of the heroine of Frances Burney's *Evelina* (I.xiii): see Appendix G below. Both are ignorant of the convention by which a woman who refused to dance with a man, without previously being engaged to another partner, should not dance for at least two further dances. The parallel was first noted by Clementina Black; see Appendix D below.

offered to defend my Intention, and justify his Right to me as a Partner, when and where he pleased; being as ready to do it, as to correct his Impertinence and insolent Insinuations. And," continued he, "a Man of Courage would chuse to attack one, rather than to affront a young Lady, from whom none but yourself could resent any Behaviour, tho' he might feel it most sensibly." Lady *Palestine*, who was within Hearing, cried out to me, "what have you done! You have occasioned a Quarrel which may become fatal to the Life you value above all others." Her Words filled me with Terror and Confusion, I could not comprehend her Meaning fully, but was so extremely affected, that Lord *Dorchester* begged her to be silent, and desired I would permit him to lead me Home.

He could not have made a Request with which I should more gladly have complied. I feared I knew not what for him, and consequently for myself; if he was with me, I thought us both safe; I wished to carry him from a Place which, from what I could learn, I had made dangerous, and hoped to receive from him, an Explanation of what Lady *Palestine* had said to me. She followed us immediately, and made me understand the Nature of the Affront I had given, and the Danger that resulted from it. The agonizing Fears which now agitated my Mind, rendered me incapable of receiving Consolation from my Lord's Assurances that the Quarrel would pass over without further Consequences. I could not be persuaded that they were not solely designed to ease my Apprehensions, and therefore dared not venture to believe, what the next Day might prove too fatally untrue. I blamed him for his Anger, telling him, that, "if I had done a Thing that was wrong, I deserved a little Incivility in Return, and that he should not have resented Expressions, which were not too severe a Punishment for an Offence against Custom, though the Error arose from Ignorance, not Design: Since People in the polite World, profess being guided by Fashion rather than by Reason, I could not stand, excused by what is not here a Rule of Action, nor be justified by Truth where of all Places, it is least allowable in a polite Circle." I was shocked to find that Decorum and Politeness required that I should have palliated my Refusal with his, and not have owned a Preference so very reasonable and so little affronting, that the Gentleman might have flattered himself it proceeded only from being acquainted, with Lord *Dorchester*, and entirely unacquainted with him, a Circumstance which must greatly lessen the Pleasure of Dancing with him, however agreeable he might be to those by whom he was better known. But as such were the Laws of Custom, I thought my Error should have been acknowledged, and the Gentleman's Anger unresented.

Any Danger that threatened Lord *Dorchester*, appeared to me in its utmost Terrors, but nothing could affect me so much as the Apprehension of being the Occasion of an Action, which if not fatal to his Life, must be so to his Virtues, and consequently to his Peace. Duelling, to one unprejudiced, must appear so criminal, so contrary to every Branch of Morality and Religion, that I could not bear my Lord should have the most distant Intention of committing it;[1] that alone I thought a sufficient Crime to sully the Purity of his Mind for ever. His not perpetrating his Design could not make me easy; that he should have ever harboured the least Thought of it, was an insurmountable Affliction to me, who valued his Integrity as much as his Life, and was as tender of the one, as of the other.

Lady *Palestine* laughed at my esteeming so criminal, an Action which she "called *spirited* and *honourable*, and almost requisite to the Perfection of *a fine Gentleman's* Character, in which Courage was the most necessary Ingredient." Not considering that a Defiance of the Laws of God deserves a far worse Name, and can never, to a well judging Mind, wear the Disguise of any Virtue. Her Sentiments raised an Abhorrence in me, which my Regard for her could not suppress, but I received some Satisfaction from finding my Lord did not differ much from my Opinion, but owned that, "the properest Object for true Courage was the Resistance of a Custom which contradicted the divine Will; and that Duels proceded from a Degree of Cowardice which is always most moved by present Danger, and therefore had stronger Fears of the Censure of Mankind, which is a Punishment immediately inflicted, than of the Wrath of God, whose Effects may for some Years be suspended. He confessed, that when he had ever been in Danger of fighting a Duel, he was always sensible his Motive was a Want of real Valour, which he esteemed, but knew not how to acquire."

CHAPTER XLII

Though the Night put an End to a Conversation in which we were not likely to agree perfectly, as our real Sentiments differed, yet it could not afford me any Rest. The Opinion my Lord had expressed of Duelling, in a great Degree, abated my Fear of any such Event; but

---

1 The objections to the custom of duelling expressed here resemble those made in the "Concluding Note" to *Sir Charles Grandison* (1753-54), in which Samuel Richardson describes challenges to a duel as "those polite *invitations to murder.*"

yet as he confessed his own Weakness, at the same Time he acknowledged the Crime, I could not think the Safety of his Person certain,
and was sensible, that his Mind was not less contaminated, but rather
more so, from the Sense of the Ill which he had thought of committing. I trembled for the Man who could regard his Fellow-Crea-
tures more than their great Creator; and suffer the most pernicious
Custom to banish *Religion*, and even plain *Morality* from his Breast.

Immersed in these Reflections, the Morning found me; my Heart
was too much oppressed to suffer me to think of Rest, I had not
even entertained a Thought of going to Bed, but after having sent
away my Maid, had yielded myself up to my Meditations.

As soon as my Lord was up, which I learnt from a Message he sent
to enquire after my Health, I went to him in his Dressing Room,
rather to confine than to converse with him, for I could not think
of letting him go out of the House, unless I could have accompanied
him, which was by no Means proper, for the Agitation of my Mind
and Want of Rest, had made such Alterations in my Countenance,
that I was not fit to be seen. My Lord had an Air of Thoughtfulness,
which increased my Fears. Indeed my Conversation was not fit to
remove it, but even Lady *Palestine*'s Vivacity was ineffectual. He was
serious but not disturbed; his Thoughts took a graver Turn than
common, but were not at all confused. This gave me some Hope that
the Alteration which alarmed me, might arise only from the Sense
of the Rashness, he had been guilty of; I could not believe that a
Man while under the actual Intention of a Crime could possess any
Composure of Mind. Confusion and Terror I imagined to be the
necessary Consequence of criminal Designs; and therefore, received
some Consolation at perceiving none of those Symptoms of Guilt in
him. Though I could not obtain a Promise from him, that he would
not fight with the Man who had made me so wretched, yet he said
every Thing that he hoped might make me easy, but the Want of that
Assurance weighed heavier in the Scale of Fear.

A Visit from a Gentleman with whom I knew him to be intimately acquainted, obliged me to withdraw; for my Eyes were so
swelled I was ashamed of being seen, but I entreated Lady *Palestine*
to keep Sight of my Lord, an Office to which her own Fears inclined
her. When I retired to my Chamber, I began, as was my Custom
when afflicted with Vexation, to lament my having been taken from
my Retirement; but my Thoughts soon took another Turn, on
reflecting how severely my Lord might suffer by having brought me
from thence. The Punishment that threatened him extenuated his
Offence, and I only grieved, that he was not born there with me;

that he had not likewise been placed in a Solitude where Death was under God's immediate Direction, and none could pass into another World, till the Almighty had dismissed them from this, and opened for them the Gates of Eternity.

Above an Hour had passed in these Reflections, when I was raised by the Entrance of Lady *Palestine*, who had such Consternation in her Countenance, as struck Terror to my Soul. My Fear turned me to a Statue, I could neither speak nor move; but she rendered all Enquiries unnecessary, by telling me that, soon after I withdrew, Lord *Dorchester* desired her "to step out of the Room for he had a little Business to transact with his Visitor." As he had long employed this Gentleman in some Affairs, she was not surprized at the Request, but complied with it. She long waited in Expectation of being told they would be glad of her Company, supposing the Business that had required her Absence, could not last long; but finding her Expectation not answered; she attended more carefully, and could not hear any one in the Room; upon which she entered, and found it indeed empty.

She thought it so impossible that Lord *Dorchester* should have evaded her Care, that she was going to seek for him in the House, when she observed, on a Shelf against the Door, a sealed Packet, which she had not perceived before she withdrew, and, as she imagined, put there as the safest Place, there being no Buroe or Drawer in the Room. Pen, Ink, and Paper on the Table whereon we had breakfasted, shewed her they had been used. She found the Packet was directed, by Lord *Dorchester*, for me.

Drawing very melancholy Conclusions from these Circumstances, she was greatly shocked. She brought me the Packet, which I opened as soon as I was able, though I rather expected to learn more certain Grounds for my Fears, than any Thing that could abate them. And, indeed, my Grief received a very great Addition from the Contents, which were a Will, as it said made for greater Security in Conformation of one he had left in *London*, whereby he bequeathed me his whole Fortune.

This Proof both of the Danger that threatened his Life, and of the Strength of his Affection, had so melancholy an Effect upon me, that I fell into Fits; from which Lady *Palestine* found it so difficult to recover me, that she left the fruitless Trial to my Servants, and gave her Care where she hoped it might be of more real Service.

She made all possible Enquiry, in order to find which Way Lord *Dorchester* had gone; but not being able to get any Information, she knew not how to contrive Means of having him pursued, which was her Intention. From this Perplexity, she was, at length, relieved by a Gentleman, who, by a Desire of avoiding Company and taking a quiet Walk, had chosen the least frequented Places and, in the most retired Spot, found Lord *Dorchester* and his Antagonist fighting. It was not without Difficulty he parted them. My Lord had received no Hurt, but his Adversary was wounded in two or three Places, but not mortally; my Lord's Aim being to disarm him, without giving any considerable Wound.

The Gentleman, whose Presence had been so fortunate, waited on Lord *Dorchester* Home, who, on his Arrival found me in a Condition that revenged me for the Fright he had given me, by occasioning equal Fears in him. The Obstinacy of my Disorder made him send for a Physician, whose Assistance he hoped might relieve me. Whether the Art of this Son of *Æsculapius*,[1] or my natural Strength might more properly claim the Honour of my Cure, I will not pretend to say, but one or the other wrought my Recovery.

The first Object I beheld was Lord *Dorchester*, who, standing at my Bed-Side, was watching the Symptoms of Amendment. Joy and Perception now seemed but one. To see him safe filled me with Transports, which Words could not have expressed, at a Time when I had more at Command, but at that happy Instant I was speechless, not being sufficiently recovered. However, Silence did not conceal my Joy; I embraced my Lord with a Tenderness that surprized him; he has told me since, that, till then, he knew not half the Impression he had made on my Heart; though he had long perceived I loved him with a stronger Affection than I myself imagined.

The grave Doctor's Countenance expressed so much Surprize, that it did not pass unobserved by me, but attributing it to his having outlived the lively Sense of Joy, so natural at my Time of Life, I thought it no Reason for me to confine the Vivacity of Sensations as innocent as if they had been chilled by old Age, and therefore did not conceal the Transports of my Heart. Since I became better acquainted with the World, I have been inclined to believe that I incurred the old Gentleman's private Censure; but as Secresy is full as necessary in that Profession, as Knowledge in Physick, he did not publish a Behaviour which I supposed he thought indecent.

As soon as I was quite recovered, the Doctor was dismissed, and Resolutions were taken for our leaving *Tunbridge* whose Waters had removed the Complaints which brought me thither; and I had now

---

1 I.e., a doctor, so named from the Roman god of healing.

no Disorder remaining, but what was the consequence of my Fright, and would be cured by Ease of Mind. I had, therefore, no Occasion to stay longer; Lord *Dorchester* did not like to remain where he was, continually exposed to hear his Conduct canvassed; and your Ladyship will imagine it could not be agreeable to me, to listen to an universal Discussion of my Inadvertency, since the Consequences of it made it appear almost criminal.

Lord *Dorchester* left the Place in two Days, but Lady *Palestine*, on Pretences to which I was obliged to submit, detained me there above a Week after him; but I have since learnt that this was concerted between them, to avoid giving Room for the Increase of Reports which began to spread, of a mutual Attachment between my Lord and myself; which would have received great Strength from our leaving *Tunbridge* together.

CHAPTER XLIII

After Lord *Dorchester* left *Tunbridge*, the Place grew very tiresome to me. I had nothing to do, but to observe the various Follies of the Companies and to study Vanity, which I perceived suffered Alteration rather than Diminution by Time. The Woman, who in her Youth, placed her supreme Joy in the Flattery of the other Sex, and in the Number of Partners she had at her Command; when Activity is no longer in the Legs, and Age has stiffened the Joints and sunk the Spirits; in short, when Pertness has undergone its usual Transformation into Dulness, and an old Age of Cards succeeds a Youth of Folly,[1] a plentiful Supply of Gentlemen of her Party becomes the Object of her Ambition; and the Contention between her and her Cotemporaries of the same Taste, will be as great as their Envy, while they were rival Beauties. The Appearance of a Man of Quality just arrived awakes an equal Impatience in both to add him to their Party, while he, wavering between the Importunities of each, keeps them in a Suspence that increases their Enmity. At the Beginning of a Season a private Gentleman finds himself of Consequence; but has the Mortification of perceiving that he dwindles in their Esteem on the Arrival of a Nobleman, who in his Turn becomes neglected, if one of higher Degree can be had to supply its Place; for the Vanity

---

1 Pope, "An Epistle to a Lady: Of the Characters of Women" (1735) ll. 243-4:
  See how the World its Veterans rewards!
  A Youth of Frolicks, an old Age of Cards.

of these Ladies is so voracious, that notwithstanding the Party is full, they are so eager to raise the Dignity of it, that after dropping the Plebeians one by one as they gather Patricians, the Nobility, at last, become obliged to each other for their Release; thus a Duke sets an Earl at Liberty, the Earl a Viscount, the Viscount a Lord, as the Lord did a Baronet, and he before the untitled Gentleman.

Nothing appeared to me more strange than the Love of Precedency. I have often been diverted to see how much Pains a Lady would take to walk first out of a Room where Laziness would have inclined her to remain; and last into another, where she was so little wished, and so little Pleasure attracted her, that she could not have come too late. In this Particular I gave great Offence when I first went to *Tunbridge*, and while I took Place of those who had a real Title to it, I received only cool Contempt for my Want of Breeding, and they would drop the Acquaintance of the *vulgar Thing*. But having gone before a young Lady whose Right of Place was disputed, she pursued me with such Swiftness, and asserted her Prerogative so forcibly, that she threw me down a Flight of a dozen Steps, thereby impressing my Want of good Breeding strongly on my Mind; and the Sense of it being kept awake by my Bruises, I afterwards became so cautious, that nothing but a Desire to escape some impending Danger could have induced me to have taken Place even of a Milliner. With no small Entertainment have I observed a young Lady whose Father had not been long ranked among the Nobility, break off in a Story she was eagerly telling, the Subject being herself, and leave her Honour and Glory imperfectly celebrated in order to get out of the Door before the daughter of a new made Peer, whom she saw going towards it. While her Mother at a few Yards Distance was prolonging her Discourse with all possible Impertinence, that she might leave the Room at the same Time with the newer Peeress, and have the Pleasure of asserting her Prerogative.

But the last Day of my Stay at *Tunbridge*, I was taken off from this Employ of the idle, the impertinently critical Observations of others, which render them almost as destructive to Society as those who are buried in Mischief. Lord *Larborough*, who by Lord *Dorchester's* Departure, was become my Partner in Dancing, and my principal Companion in Conversation, gave me a more affecting and more interesting Subject for my Thoughts. He had long professed a great Friendship for me, and for some Time, had added to the Appearance of it, by the most minute Attentions, and those flattering Distinctions which insensibly gain the Esteem and Regard of a young Person. I conversed with him with all the Freedom and Confidence of

Friendship, not more pleased with him on his own Account, than from knowing my Lord's Affection for him.

From the Time Lord *Dorchester* went away, Lord *Larborough* never mentioned him without a seeming Perplexity, and when I would indulge myself in giving him the Praises I thought his Due, he would turn the Discourse, and drop little Hints, which at the Time, passed without my Notice, though his Unwillingness to dwell on the Subject most pleasing to me, rendered his Company less agreeable.

The Day before we left the Place, Lord *Larborough* appeared very uneasy. I could not forbear enquiring the Reason of it, to which he replied, that "the Thought of going away distressed him."

I asked, "What could attach him to that Place, since he appeared to have no Intimacy with any Person there, and was not of so trifling a Disposition as to take any great Delight in the pitiful Amusements it afforded, or to compare them with the more solid Pleasure arising from the sincere Friendship and Conversation of a Man whose Mind was full of Variety, whose Wit was inexhaustible, his Judgment solid, and his Learning extensive; of which no one could be so sensible as himself, since he had an Understanding capable of perceiving and tasting his Friends Excellence, and saw him when confident in his Affection remove all Restraint and Disguise."

Lord *Dorchester's* Name would have been an unnecessary Addition, Lord *Larborough* could not doubt his being the Man I meant, and accordingly answered that, "he wished Disguise was less requisite to support the good Character of many People. Had that never been banished, the Conversation of the Man I so highly esteemed would have been more delightful to him, and he should not have been obliged when he admired the Understanding, to have grieved that the Heart had shared so little of the Perfection too lavishly bestowed on the other."

I could not hear Aspersions so contrary to my Sentiments without Resentment, and expressing myself warmly on his venting such injurious Insinuations, he replied, "he was every Way unfortunate if he had incurred my Displeasure by a slight Expression of the Indignation, nothing but Affection for me had raised. Had the Part of Lord *Dorchester's* Character he reflected on, concerned any other Person, he should have beheld it with the same Indifference he did the Views of his other Friends, but since his Resentment had excited my Anger, he should never more touch on the Subject, which, indeed, he knew not how he came to do at all; he could curse his Tongue for giving Way to the Sincerity of his Heart; and hinting at Secrets, which my Lord's Confidence in him, had bound him by stronger Ties to conceal, than his Affections for me could offer for discovering them; he begged me to forget what he had said, and never let one Thought rest on his inexcusable Inadvertency." Fortunately, though I am not naturally very curious, this made me so; "I desired he would tell me plainly what he meant," but he excused himself from complying. As I pressed him still more earnestly, he more absolutely denied me; till, at last, I gave up in Despair. As if his Resistance was wearied out at the same Time with my Importunities, but in reality, as he did not design to keep the Secret, he was then reduced to declare that "he was not able to disobey my Commands, that I was absolute Mistress of him, and he wished he could say of his Fortune likewise, which he would lay at my Feet, if it could in any Way alleviate the Sense he feared I should have of the Treachery he was going to relate." By the Force of this Preparation, I began to tremble before he commenced his Narration; but every Word increased my Horror; he began in the following Manner. "I must previously acquaint you, that it is very customary for Gentlemen to live with Women as if they were married, without being so; which has this Convenience, that they can leave them whenever they are tired, or see another they like better. You have, by great Care, been kept ignorant of this Custom, lest it might frustrate his Lordship's Intentions, by raising your Suspicions of them, for all his Hopes of Success, depend on the Strength of your Affection, joined with unsuspecting Innocence. To shew what his Desires are, he waits impatiently to find some Moment, when your Virtue shall be off its Guard; this he may reasonably expect, while you are in no Apprehension of an Enemy."

Here I could not suppress an Exclamation suggested by my Hatred to such Principles, but cried out, "what a Basis for so vile, so treacherous an Intention! Can Love and Innocence be turned into a Means of Ruin by the Person who ought most to protect them."

"Every Thing," he continued, "has hitherto been so well ordered, that no one suspects you are not a Woman of real Fortune, otherwise Innocence could not have preserved you from Infamy; for all People would, on the Knowledge of your being thus maintained at his Expence, judge you guilty of the worst Returns. A Fate you must expect, whenever Chance shall disclose the Secret, which sooner or later will happen."

It is impossible to express what I felt during this Narration. All I had ever suffered, the Fear of every Evil, the Persuasion of his Inconstancy, were trifling Pains to the Thought of such Baseness in a Mind I had esteemed the Seat of Virtue. I could better endure an eternal

Separation from him, than thus to find him a Stranger to Goodness, my Surprize, and my Detestation at all Lord *Larborough* had told me, was so great, that I could express it only by involuntary Signs. I was struck dumb with so amazing a Discovery. To this succeeded Reflections on the Probability of it. My Love for Lord *Dorchester* seized on this only Hope with Eagerness, and I declared that the Account I had listened to, was past Belief; and he having concluded with offering his House and Protection, and assuring me of the Greatness of his Affection, I added that, "I could easier imagine that the Love he professed had the Consequence I observed to be so common in his Country. Jealousy and a Desire arising from it of getting me from him, who, till my last Breath, must be cherished by me, as my dearest Friend, than give Way for one Hour to so injurious a Suspicion of him, in whom I had experienced and observed the best Qualities our imperfect Nature admitted." Lord *Larborough* was piqued at my Reply, he told me "if I chose to nourish the Error I was in, he had no more to say; but perhaps, the Prospect he had drawn, was not so shocking to me, as he had imagined it would be; if I was desirous of searching into the Truth of what he had said, he would convince me, whenever I pleased."

This Proposal startled me, it gave an Air of Truth to what he had related, which I could have wished not to have found in it; but in a Doubt of such Importance to me, I could not rest, therefore begged to have it cleared up as soon as possible. He then informed me, "that there was an easy Method of discovering the whole the first Evening he should spend at my House with Lord *Dorchester*, after I got to *London*; I had nothing to do, but to excuse myself soon after Supper, on Pretence of the Head-Ach, and a Desire of going to Bed, but instead of doing so, to conceal myself where I might hear all that should pass between them." I came into this, so anxious was I to know the Truth of this dreadful Account, though it appeared to me dishonourable for me to listen to what one is not intended to hear, yet surely, if ever excusable, it was so in my Case. If Lord *Dorchester* was so very criminal as Lord *Larborough* represented, I could not expect an honest Confession from him, and a Denial of it tho' sincere, would not have entirely conquered my Suspicions, or consequently have restored either my Happiness or his; which depended, in some Measure, in my Confidence and Ease of Mind. If in disowning such Intentions, he denied the Truth, my Situation was too dangerous to remain safely in it. Besides, if a disinterested Regard was so uncommon in this Country, I perceived that though I should keep my Innocence, I must lose the Reputation of it, which, next to it, ought to be a Woman's first Care. To be obliged both to leave him, and conquer my Affection, was, indeed, a Task too hard for my weak Reason; but I flattered myself, that if this should prove true, my Friendship would be turned into Contempt; I loved him for the Appearance of Goodness and Truth, which he ever wore; if he proved different from what I believed him, the Love founded on that Belief ought to change; I hoped it would not outlive the Object, as I could not reflect on the Virtues I thought he possessed without recollecting they were prophaned by being made a Cloak to Vice and Injustice. I waited with Impatience for the Hour in which we should set forth on our Journey, fearing, yet wishing to learn what Truth there was in Lord *Larborough*'s Accusation. I was not without Hopes of finding it a Fiction, but yet when I recollected every Circumstance of Lord *Dorchester*'s Behaviour, my Apprehensions were increased. If Mankind were what Lord *Larborough* represented them, I had, indeed great Reason to suspect my Lord's Views were such as had been described to me; but I was unwilling to let my thoughts dwell on so cruel a Probability, and set out from *Tunbridge* with a Mind so divided betwixt Hope and Fear, as is, I believe, more painful that the worst Certainty, for Anxiety is a more grievous State, as it is more turbulent than Despair.

CHAPTER XLIV

As we approached *London*, Expectation of the Event made me full of Trouble, and with great Reason, since it was to determine my future Happiness or Misery; cruel Uncertainty! the greatest Misfortune certain and present, could not exceed the Torment of the anxious Fears that then oppressed me. My fluttering fond, but honest Heart, was robbed of Peace, and scarcely hoped ever again to enjoy its beloved Tranquility. I had no Occasion to feign myself sick, alas! I was so in Reality; my Strength, my Colour, almost my Life had failed me, from the Time my Ears had received the killing Narration. Could I have distrusted Providence, or repined at its Almighty, and, however obscure, its just Decrees, I should have complained of my hard Fate, in thus being tossed about by more uncertain Things than Winds and Waves, the Inclination of a fantastick merciless Race of Mortals.

How does Distress heighten Devotion, which in Prosperity is apt to grow languid; with what ardent Zeal did I address the Almighty, and to his best Will resign myself; prayed for a Continuance of the Happiness that fatal Day had interrupted, or if that Petition was presumptuous, and I might not dictate to his Wisdom, which watches over all his Works, I only begged that I might preserve untainted the Virtue he had given me, improve the Portion I was born with, and not live to see myself swerve from his most righteous Laws, but that his Grace would still vouchsafe to protect the Creature of his Power, the Dependent on his Mercy!

When I arrived, I found Lord *Dorchester* waiting for me at my House. He perceived I was very ill, and seemed greatly concerned at it; my Illness excused my conversing, for which, indeed, I was but ill qualified. He tried with his enchanting Tenderness to soothe my Pains, but I was now acting the Hypocrite, complaining of my Head, while my Heart was the only Sufferer; and that was more distressed than relieved by his Care and Fondness. The Scene was difficult for me to support, and I was glad when Lord *Larborough* came in. As soon as Supper was over I left them, but went into a Closet, the Door of which I had purposely set open. I was no sooner in Appearance gone, than Lord *Dorchester* began to express the great Uneasiness he was under at seeing me so ill, as he was afraid it might be the Beginning of a Fit of Sickness. Lord *Larborough* took this Opportunity of bringing on the Discourse he aimed at. "Indeed my Friend," said he, "I am not surprized at the Greatness of your Apprehensions, to be robbed by Death of the Fruit of all your Schemes, all your Attendance, Generosity and Love, would mortify a Man less passionately fond than yourself."

"If you do not wish to be troubled with a very bad Companion all this Evening," replied Lord *Dorchester*, "mention not the Word Death. The Thought of her Suffering any Pain, is more than I can support, without a considerable Diminution of Spirits. But, whatever happens, I can never think I have been unrewarded for any Thing my Love has made me do, if it has hitherto rendered her happy, which I flatter myself it has done. Her kind and innocent Marks of Affection would recompence me for any Pain or Trouble, whereas my Care of her has been my greatest Joy."

"Well," answered Lord *Larborough*, "I will no farther affront your Generosity, though I cannot flatter you so far as to say you have acted through a mere Love of that Virtue. If those Godlike Qualities were to be found unmixed among Mankind, I should sooner expect to see them in you than in any one; but, in Truth, my Friend, Sense[1] has

---

1 Here signifying sensuality, rather than reason.

had as great a Share in the Direction of your Actions as Sentiment; pray which has been most gratified?"

"As for Gratification," said Lord *Dorchester*, "Sentiment has had much the best Time of it. *Ophelia* is certainly above us Mortals, she never condescends like Goddesses of old, to divest herself, for one Moment, of her Divinity; and for any Hopes of Amendment I can see, I may worship my Deity till the End of my Life, without finding her once propitious to her Votary's Wishes."

"I am afraid," answered Lord *Larborough*, "you understand the Arts of Love less than those of any other Kind, or you could not now be as far from your Hopes, as when you first took her from her Solitude."

"I believe," replied Lord *Dorchester*, "I may practice the Arts of Love with less Skill for having so much of the Reality. I have so true an Esteem and Respect for her, that I reverence her Virtues and her Understanding, while I adore her Person; those aweful Sensations are great Retarders of a Lover's Progress; but yet I flatter myself with a different Opinion from yours. I cannot help thinking, I have made a considerable Step towards Success. I have gained her Heart, my Lord, and I take that to be the sure Road to her Person. It is impossible a Woman should always resist both her Love and her Lover; they must prevail in Time, how great soever her Prudence may be, or I shall never believe Woman was made out of the Rib of a Man, and yet differ so much from our Natures: I already begin to suspect that Miss *Lenox* sprung from another Creation, and was made out of some more icy Composition than the rest of Woman-Kind. But yet, trust me, however cold she may naturally be, her Tenderness for me, my passionate Love for her, with that Innocence which takes from her all Suspicion, consequently all Fear of having the Object of her Affections watching for a complying Moment, must, in Time, yield me the Reward for my long Services and Disappointments. I am certainly a Coward, for I have not yet ventured to attempt any Liberties which a Vestal might not permit. When my Spirits are at the highest, and I think my Passion no longer to be hid, there is a Purity around her, such aweful Purity in every Look and Word, that I bow to Virtue, and worship it in her fair Form. There is more Innocence in her Caresses, than can be found in the Coldness of any other Woman. Instead of encouraging my Hopes, they damp them while they charm me; and shew the best Affections in such Beauty, that I cannot forbear calling myself a Villain, for not being more like her." "And pray," said Lord *Larborough*, "by what Means do you make Peace with yourself?"

"By reflecting, that if she loves me, she will remain very happy," replied Lord *Dorchester.* "Marriage is of human Invention; for was it a necessary Ceremony we must be all Bastards, as we have no Reason to believe *Adam* and *Eve* had the Sanction of the Priest for their Union. Their's was the Wedlock of Hearts, the true Matrimony of Affection, I and my *Ophelia,* will, like our first Parents, love by our own and Nature's Licence, with more Warmth, more Tenderness, Sincerity and Constancy, than the obedient Servants of the Church, the Slaves of Custom can boast. We will love to the End of our Lives, always assured of each other's Affections, by unabated Assiduity and Tenderness. Necessity shall have no Hand in our Union, for I will make a Settlement on her, which shall render her perfectly independent of me. We shall be linked only by Love, and therefore cannot doubt of the Strength of the Chain while neither breaks it."

"A most noble Rapture truly," interrupted Lord *Larborough,* "since eternal Constancy is your Scheme, why not marry? Surely Wedlock should only terrify the fickle?"

"Have I not often told you," said Lord *Dorchester,* "with how much Justice I dislike Matrimony? The ill Fate of all my Family in that State, has created an insurmountable Aversion to it in me. Besides, I am more unfit for it than any Man, as being so fearful of losing the Affections of one I love, that I could never be easy while it was her Interest to live with me. It is true, I know, and love *Ophelia's* Sincerity, but I am equally acquainted with my own Temper; I could fear her Truth and Openness of Heart should be corrupted by our vile Customs, she might give herself to me in Marriage out of Prudence and Interest. I would receive her as the Gift of Love alone. Her Heart must give her to me, and mine receive her as the pure Votary of Love; mine and mine only, exclusive of all prudential, all lucrative Views. This is the truest Bliss my Heart can know. But in the midst of all this glorious imaginary Felicity, comes across this painful Question, Oh! my Friend, when can such Virtue be subdued? I fear she is exalted above human Weaknesses, though to leave the Disposal of herself to the Priest, rather than to her Heart, would be only Compliance with servile Custom, and not Virtue, which can never be the Gift of a foolish Ceremony; it consists in Constancy not Words; and we will be more constant than licensed matrimonial Couples, who love from Duty; whose Passions are so cool, they ask Leave to burn, requiring the Sanction of a cold, withered, insensible Priest, to whom all powerful Nature is made to relinquish her Sway. *Ophelia* ought more than any one to obey that first Parent, who has lavishly dispensed to her, her best Gifts. She who still enjoys her natural Innocence, who has made uncommon Progress in the Knowledge of all Good, and yet remains as ignorant of Evil as on the Day she was first numbered among the Species she was born to eclipse, has no Occasion to be confined to political Rules, made to keep those in order who have not a better Guide within their own Minds."

"Pray," answered Lord *Larborough*, "do not treat all the rest of Women-Kind with such Contempt. The Ignorance you boast of is not meritorious; if it is you are the Person who should have the Honour of it. Is there any Virtue in not knowing the Evil she has never seen? You have spread the Veil which has concealed it all from her Eyes; and then like a true irrational Lover, admire her for not seeing what was not visible to her. Her Part is natural; your Contrivance is all that can create Wonder, and I can never think of it without Surprize. However, I cannot imagine it possible to continue this Ignorance, where Matter for Instruction is so frequent as in this Town, and to which some of the Acquaintance you have introduced her, are not Novices."

"You must have been wrapt in cold Indifference all your Lifetime," replied Lord *Dorchester*, "or you would know that nothing is impossible to a true Lover. A short Acquaintance with her Principles, shewed me the Necessity of preserving her from all Suspicion of my Design. The only Method was to keep her in Ignorance of the Ways of Men in this enlightened Corner of the World. From the dull Simplicity and Innocence in which she was bred, the least Shadow of Vice of any Kind shocks her, by which I was convinced her Prejudices in Favour of lawful Unions must be great. This excited my Invention, and I considered all Ways of keeping the Difference of our Manners from her Knowledge. I instructed her Servant, but without imparting my Reasons to her; and as I furnished her with Books, I have carefully excluded all by which she could form a Notion of any Customs, that might raise Suspicions in her Mind, and this I have found possible without retarding any useful Improvement of her Understanding. When the Heart does not dictate a Probability of Evil in others, the Owner is easier deceived into a good Opinion of Mankind than you imagine. I had a Desire of bringing her into the World, thinking it would amuse and make her happier, which, next to my own Happiness in one Point, is my first Consideration; but here was my great Difficulty; how to prevent her seeing, when the Object was before her Eyes, puzzled me. However, having great Confidence in female Invention, I opened my whole Scheme to my Cousin Lady *Palestine*, who, I knew, would willingly assist me, as she is one of *Cupid*'s best Friends; and, like a good Woman, has so equal a Love for her Neighbour and herself,[1] that she is glad to help them in any Way wherein she would be industriously gratified. She, in this Respect, lives up to the golden Rule, and does to others, as she would they should do unto her.[2] This made her fit for my Purpose. The Art she has had to keep herself in high Fashion, and be caressed by the World, and even by such whose Behaviour and Character give one Room to believe that the Merits I found in her, were of no Use nor Recommendation to them, made her Acquaintance proper, for my honest, my innocent *Ophelia*, at the same Time she was useful to me. I esteem the Purity of my Angel's Heart, and the Goodness of her Principles too highly, to introduce her into Company that might pervert either. It would be impolitick to lessen the Merits of the Object of our Affections in so essential a Point, in order to gain the Possession of their Persons. I have had great Reason to be pleased with my Choice: Lady *Palestine* has excelled herself in the Management of this Affair; and some fortunate Circumstances have assisted our Design. Miss *Lenox*'s great Unhappiness at being observed and looked at, which was the necessary Consequence of her appearing in publick, was of excellent Service to us. We advised her to be silent as to the Place of her Birth, and all the Passages of her past Life, and this on Pretence of saving her the Pain of universal Observation, which otherwise, by their Novelty, would be excited. She complied; the rest has been our Care. You know we have reported her a Relation of mine, of a large Fortune, left by a dying Father to my Guardianship."

"By these little Deceits, her Reputation has hitherto continued unblemished. I verily believe the Envy of the World, would by this Time have spent a little of its Venom in Slander, had any other Woman been in her Place; but the Innocence and Openness of Heart expressed in her Countenance, damps all Suspicion, and disarms Scandal of its Sting."

"I have likewise contrived to prevent all Intimacies with any of her own Sex, except my useful Cousin, least conversing with them, might overthrow my Scheme. I was some Time ago, a little uneasy at a great Disposition I perceived in her towards Miss *Baden*, who was not unwilling to cultivate her Acquaintance, I could not wonder at either; without seeing all the bad Qualities which many possess, the

---

1 Leviticus 19.18: "Thou shalt love thy neighbour as thyself."
2 The "golden rule" in Matthew 7.12: "Whatsoever ye would that men should do to you, do ye even so to them."

Good in Miss *Baden's* Disposition, shines so clearly that it could not escape the Observation of *Ophelia*, who sees by the Light of Reason, that best Distinguisher of Truth. An Intimacy between them seemed natural, and I feared the ill Effects of it; but my Uneasiness was perceived by my lovely Charmer, and, I believe, a kind though silent Compliance with it, put a Stop to all Increase of Acquaintance.

"I found she construed my Dislike into Jealousy. She has not the least Notion why we should be jealous but of our Friend's Affections, and in that Case, it must be equally excited by Man or Woman, who seems likely to share them with us.

"I began now to have fewer Apprehensions than ever of her learning the Customs of our Sex. Time and Success have hardened me; but instead of it another arises, which is what I have already mentioned, that I shall never find the unguarded Moment, I have so long waited for. To declare my Intentions, or give her Reason to find them out, would be losing all my Hope. My sole Dependance is on the Frailty of human Kind, and she seems to be void of any. I thought I had only a Woman to resist me; who would have expected that an Angel should be hid in a Cottage, while we frail Mortals inhabit Palaces?"

I had now heard too much, my Doubts were turned into the most painful Certainty, and I could not stay to listen to more of a Conversation, every Word of which gave fresh Pain to my Heart. So I retired out of another Door, and went to my own Room.

CHAPTER XLV

Upon retiring to my Chamber, I found some Ease from the Liberty of indulging the Sighs and Tears which I had been obliged to suppress, while I was so near the Cause of all my Grief: I was the whole Night incapable of every Thing but lamenting my unhappy Lot, in being among a People with whom I was so unequally matched. The Violence of my Affliction persuaded me that I hated the Man who had occasioned it; but as Dejection succeeded to Distraction, for by no other Name can I call my first Emotions, the Necessity of leaving one whose Aim was my Destruction, informed me more certainly of the true State of my Heart. I found it still repined at the Thought of absenting myself from him, whose Presence ought to have raised Detestation in me. But this only served to determine me the more strongly to fly from that Place, where I no longer could be safe, since I was myself my Enemy; and resolved if I could not command my Heart, at least to punish it.

The Past might give me some Room to hope Success for the Future, but I would not trust to a Confidence which oftener destroys than saves, while Diffidence is a wise Preserver, and the best Defence of the weak. To stay till we are sensible of our Frailty, is remaining too long, I was desirous to prevent the Sense of it, and not run the Hazard of being obliged to reproach myself for my own Weakness.

Convinced that I was unhappy, I was, however, determined not to be criminal, and I could not hide from myself the Danger to which my open and artless Temper must expose me, when I had so deceitful and designing an Adversary. The Contest was too unequal to venture; but it seemed to me as dishonourable to attack the artless with Art and Deceit, as to attempt the Life of one who is not armed for his Defence. I wondered at the Ingratitude that could wish to turn a Woman's Affection into the Means of making her wretched, and rob her of the Pleasure of being esteemed, and of the Heartfelt Joy arising from the Consciousness of deserving to be so.

I was fixed in the Resolution of leaving my House, and of concealing myself from Lord *Dorchester*, till I could contrive my Return to my Cottage, where I might seek for Peace and endeavour to forget a vicious Race, whom I had known only to suffer by them. I thought it would not be safe to attempt this immediately, as I could not doubt but my Lord would take all possible Means of discovering my Retreat; and, suspecting my real Intention, would more diligently watch the Road. Where to conceal myself I knew not; but had no Hopes of Safety among those who were acquainted with me. I had now learnt to distrust every one, and my too fond Heart found some Resource in believing no Man was less an Enemy to Virtue, than Lord *Dorchester*.

The following Night I fixed for my Elopement, with which I dared trust Nobody, but was to transact it without any Guide or Adviser but Resolution and Fear.

Lord *Dorchester* called several Times in the Morning, but I did not rise till Noon, in order to avoid seeing him, till I had acquired a sufficient Composure of Mind to enable me to converse.

In the Afternoon he came again as I expected, I feared his Sight, though he had more Reason to fear mine, the guilty only have Cause to tremble; but the great Change which was to succeed this Visit, made it appear dreadful to me. I had endeavoured to practice some worldly Arts; I thought it was strange if I had lived so long here without acquiring the Power of Dissimulation; I tried to conceal my grieved Heart under a smiling Countenance, that I might not either puzzle my Lord, or give him Room for Suspicion. But I had esteemed my own Abilities too highly; I was less improved than I could have wished.

Lord *Dorchester* at first coming in, addressed me with inexpressible Tenderness, and Concern for my Health. The Variety of Emotions from the Joy I felt in the Proofs of his Affection, which would have made even Sickness delightful, with the Pain that attended the Thought of the bad Designs it had given Birth to, and yet how much I must suffer in relinquishing the greatest Happiness of my Life, overcame my Resolution, and brought such a Crowd of Images to my Mind, as drew a Flood of Tears from my Eyes, which never ceased flowing for a Quarter of an Hour together, during the whole Evening. My Lord appeared greatly concerned at these Signs of Grief, and was importunate to know the Reason of them. I could only attribute them to Distemper, and, according to the Fashion of the Place, complain of my Spirits. This did not make him easy; he declared, he could not forbear suspecting some hidden Cause; and by the many Assurances of his constant and increasing Affection with which he endeavoured to remove my Melancholy, I perceived he imagined me a Prey to jealous Fancies. I was glad his Thought took that Turn; for I was in great Fear, that my Weakness in thus shewing the Situation of my Mind, might have created better grounded Suspicions; especially at his going away, which was not till very late. I had not Power to tell him it was Time he should leave me, and he was not inclined to make that Discovery himself; but at last, the Watchman forced him to observe the Hour, and Care of my Health induced him to obey its Call to Rest. I was determined this should be the last Interview I would ever have with him. The Thought that I should never see him more, had so violent an Effect on my depressed Spirits, that, as soon as he was out of the Room, I fainted away. I believe it was not long before I recovered my Senses. I found myself in his Arms, and my Maid rubbing my Temples, while he was holding a Bottle for me to smell to.[1] He had, as I afterwards learnt, returned on the Noise I made in falling, and finding me on the Floor, called to my Maid to assist him, in bringing me again to Life. The Joy I felt from the Tenderness of his Behaviour, on my coming to myself, was ill suited to my Intention. It was long before he would leave me, but the second Parting was not so bad as the first. To get quit of my Maid, I was obliged to go to Bed. As soon as she was out

---

1 This is the third of three scenes illustrated by Corbould for the 1785 *Novelist's Magazine* edition; see Appendix C below.

of the Room, I dressed myself anew, and sat down to write to Lord *Dorchester*, to the following Purpose.

My Lord,

"As little as a Man can deserve to find a Place in the Thoughts of one on whom his Views have been so ungenerous and low, yet I cannot forbear informing you, that a Discovery of your base Designs, has rendered it necessary for me to fly you. Was my Pride equal to my Love, I should be ashamed, that in our last Interviews, I discovered so much Sorrow in parting with one who never had any true Affection for me. But why should I blush at not suspecting Intentions in you, which I thought no Heart had been bad enough to harbour? My own made me a Dupe to the Appearance of yours. It was not difficult for me to believe, that the Generosity, the Tenderness, the Esteem you appeared to have for me, were real. Though I deserved little of it, it seemed to me less injurious to suppose you mistaken than deceitful. The Understanding of the wisest Man may err, but I did not imagine the Heart of any one could be so corrupted. I own, that at this Moment, I still repay in real Fondness, all the Arts you practice to make me believe it mutual; in the Midst of my Resentment my Love is as strong as ever. I am sensible you have for ever destroyed my Happiness; I can never enjoy a Moment's Comfort absent from you. The happy Composure of my Mind is turned into Distraction; my Constitution is not equal to the Sorrows that attack it. But this is not my Grief. I am the Creature of Providence, and must without repining wait its Decrees; if without Ingratitude I might wish to lose the Life it has given me, I should pray for Death as the desirable End of a miserable Being. One Effect I would gladly hope my Sufferings may have on you. Let them shew you how wretched you aimed at making one who deserved not to receive so much Evil at your Hands. Think what Torment the Success of your vile Arts must have given me, since to avoid the Chance of it, I can without Hesitation reduce myself to so great a Misfortune as leaving the Joy of my Life, your Company! Let this deter you for the Future, from leading others into the same unhappy Circumstances. I wish an Amendment of your Principles for your own Benefit; for I feel a sincere Pity for the Ignorance you must live in of the greatest Pleasures, those arising from a truly affectionate, generous, pure and honest Heart. As for myself, it can no longer be of farther Consequence to my Peace; I shall not even know what passes here, I will not remain among a People to whom I am so ill suited. Opinion had raised you almost to a Deity; finding you fall so far below what even a human Creature should be, I can't help doubting myself also, and, therefore, will never see you more. I will return to my little Cottage where I shall behold no Actions but what are just and consistent; where Innocence is no Temptation to Vice, nor made a Means towards the Possessor's Destruction. In that dear Solitude, my Love will be repaid by Affection, by the only worthy Object of it, and our Hearts united with Sincerity and Truth. There I lived, blessed indeed, in Innocence; all that was dear to me within my Sight; I had nothing to regret, nothing to sigh for, no Thought, no Wish to suppress; actuated by Virtue, with Virtue alone I loved my single Friend; happy in knowing no more, I enjoyed a constant State of Contentment. Think my Lord from what you have taken me, and what Misery you have brought on her, who, notwithstanding all Distance, the Impossibility of seeing you again, and the great Reason she has to hate you, must ever remain attached to you in the tenderest Manner! This is your Doing, this the Effect you call Love! This the Reward of Mine! But why should I reproach you, when I cannot resent as I ought? I am too little Mistress of myself to write more. Heaven preserve you! may you never feel Remorse enough to give you equal Pain to that I endure! I would have your Heart improve by Reason, and not by Suffering. Once more accept my Prayers, my best Wishes; you are the only Object I have for them, I myself excluded, since all I ought to wish for, is a total Forgetfulness of you, and if I cannot part with your Image, Misery is attached to it. If you can help it, do not quite forget me, think of me, as one who has such an Affection for you, as in the great World cannot be equalled; think of me as anxious for your Happiness, while I am suffering by you; who could receive any Evil by Self-Condemnation rather than part with you, rather than once say Adieu. But it must be so; the God you have offended, forgive and bless you."

This Letter was not written without Torrents of Tears, with which my Paper was so blotted, that it was scarcely legible; but the Interruptions my Sorrow gave, took up so much of the little Time left me, that I had not Leisure to write it over again, and if I had, I might not have mended it. As soon as it was finished, I laid it where I imagined it would be found, though not the first Moment I was missing. I then put as much Money in my Pocket as I thought requisite. Without scrupling to save myself at the Expence of the Person who had reduced me to the Want of such Assistance, I took no more than I believed necessary; if I had, it would not have been so justifiable. I loaded myself with Linen and other Things that I might want, and could conveniently carry. The Jewels, Watches, Trinkets, and every Thing valuable, I put up with the Money in my Bureau, and inclosed the Key of it in the Letter to my Lord. Grief purifies the Heart. So much had it lessened my Vanity, that Things which in Possession, had given me a foolish Pleasure, were now of no more worth in my Eyes than a Piece of Glass. By this Time Day began to dawn. I stole down Stairs, and unbarring the Street Door as gently as I could, I went out. I got through that, and the adjacent Streets, as quick as possible, and walked a great Way, before People were stirring, without knowing where I was. I went into the first House where Lodgings were to be let, and the People up, and hired a Room, well satisfied with my Situation, because it was at a great Distance from that I lately lived in, and from my Lord's House. I learnt I was in a Part of the City,[1] and took a back Room that I might run no Hazard of being seen from the Street. The People where I lodged were quiet and civil, and too busy to be very curious.

As soon as I had hired my Chamber, I shut myself in it, and indulged my Grief with greater Freedom than I had yet ventured to do. The Tears which had only fallen gently down my Face as I walked through the Streets, for I could not confine them entirely, now came with double Force, and did not cease till I grew so weary with the Agitation of my Mind, Want of Rest, and a Walk far too long for my decayed Strength, that I fell asleep for some Hours.

This refreshed my Body, but could not relieve my Heart, that remained the same, or rather acquired new Strength only to grieve with more violence.

I grew very ill by Night, and kept my Bed for two Days. From that Time my Health began to mend, and I became somewhat more composed.

CHAPTER XLVI

Lord *Larborough* had placed Spies upon me, by which Means he learnt the Place of my Abode, and came the Day after my Escape; but I was not able to see him till the latter End of that Week, and was then but very unfit for Company. He addressed me in the most affectionate Manner, "lamented my unhappy Fate, and the unworthy Hands into which I had fallen: Applauded my Resolution in leaving Lord *Dorchester*, and admired my Innocence. He ardently wished he could have saved me from the impending Danger which threatened

---

1 I.e., the City of London, then as now the centre for commerce, which lay to the east of the City of Westminster, where people of fashion lived.

me, without making my Happiness a Sacrifice to my Virtue. You heard," said he, "Lovely *Ophelia*, how I endeavoured to shew my Friend, that he ought not to be averse to marrying you. I had done much more at other Times; I have represented to him the great Charm of your Innocence, which should preserve itself by disarming all bad Designs. I proved to him an Alliance with you, could not hurt his Pride, since it must do Honour to a Man of any Rank. It could not excuse the Fears he expressed of Matrimony, as your numerous Virtues secured him from every Evil that can attend the State of Wedlock. In Point of Interest no Man could be so bigotted to Money, as to think it comparable to your Worth. Others might bring him Gold, you would make him Possessor of more Wealth, of a nobler Kind of Riches, than *Peru* or *Mexico*[1] could yield. These are the Arguments I have used to persuade him to marry you. But his Notions are so depraved, that all I could say made no Impression on his Mind; indeed, it was vain to hope it would; if his Love and the fairest Miracle of Virtue, could not dispose him to Justice, how should my Arguments have that Power? They could not be so prevalent as every Look, every Word and Action of the innocent *Ophelia* must have been, to any one who had the smallest Seeds of Virtue in their Breast; I should have believed the most debauched Man living could not have harboured a momentary Thought against the Virtue which appeared so amiable. Pardon me the Blasphemies I uttered against you in the Conversation you overheard. They all agree with my real Sentiments, my Heart bled for what you were suffering, while I treated his Opinion so highly, but I was obliged to put that Force on myself, to make him more openly declare Sentiments, which I would have given my Life to have changed into such as would have been agreeable to your Wishes, and due to your Merits. It was with the utmost Difficulty, I performed my Task, and prosecuted a Discourse which tore my Heart by friendly Sympathy with your's."

This elaborate Speech of Lord *Larborough's* surprized me a little; it seemed so honest and affectionate, that during some Parts, I believed his Disposition was suitable to his Expressions, but he mixed so much Flattery with his Panegyricks on my Virtue, that I told him, "I hoped, I had, indeed, enough to preserve me from committing any criminal Action; but where was the Miracle of this?

---

1 Alluding to silver, of which the Spanish colonies of Peru and Mexico were major producers.

Thousands would do the same. If it preserved me from Censure, I had all I could require from it; but I saw I no Reason to commend me so highly for having only done my Duty, and that merely when one Virtue was concerned; a small Portion to be proud of, when we ought to be possessed of so many; he could not have given me more Praise, had I acted up to the Laws of general Perfection. In behaving differently from what I had done, I should have been very criminal; but I could scarcely think myself quite justified, unless I had that proper Love for Virtue which would make me hate the Former of vile Schemes, as well as induce me to avoid him; whereas I had not arrived even at Anger. Grief possessed my whole Soul, and left no Room for any other Sentiment. I still loved to Excess the Man to whom I owed my Sufferings; and while I fled from him, and resolved never again to see him, I endeavoured to excuse him, and blame only Education and pernicious Custom, which had, by corrupting his Principles, rendered me a most unhappy Woman." My Tears flowed almost incessantly, Lord *Larborough* joined in them, and wept too, till I grew convinced of the pure Friendship he possessed. He frequently exclaimed against "the Baseness of a Man, who could mean me ill, and with all the Appearance of Sincerity declared, how incapable he should have been of such Behaviour, had he been blessed with my Love; he would have adored me with a pure Devotion, have looked on *Hymen* as his tutelar Deity, and have esteemed himself the happiest of Mankind if I would have conferred an eternal Obligation on him by becoming his Wife."

Many more Things he said to raise his own Character, and blacken Lord *Dorchester*'s, which served only to encrease my Affection, as I grieved as much for my Lord's Depravity, as for my own Sufferings, independently of the Connection between them.

All Lord *Larborough* said, was uttered with such an Air of Tenderness, and mixed with so many Expressions of Fondness, that, at last, I began to think his Sentiments were beyond those of Friendship, which I thought I must detest in a Country where People can be led by Love, to do Actions so unworthy of themselves, and so inconsistent with the rest of their Character. I was fully convinced of it, when after finding Fault with my Lodging, and lamenting "that I who ought to receive the Services of Mankind, (for he mixed the most fulsome Flattery with every Thing he said) should be void of necessary Attendance and Convenience, he sollicited me to accompany him to one he would find out for me, where I should be served in a Manner worthy of me, and all possible Care taken to alleviate my Grief, and assist Time in conquering it." This Proposal startled me. I told him, "that Flattery was no Means of pleasing me. I looked on it in no better Light than as an indirect Accusation of an insufferable Vanity and Folly, since it shewed an Expectation of being believed. That in a Country where Benevolence and Justice reigned, I might, indeed, expect so much of the Service of Mankind, as tended to that mutual Defence,[1] due from all Fellow Creatures to each other; but as here Money only obtained that Assistance, which Humanity should give, I had little Title to any, nor the least Occasion for those venal Services, which I had been accustomed to perform for myself. If Reason and proper Indignation could not conquer my Affliction, I feared it was beyond the Power of any Thing else to perform it. But that his Lordship's Offer surprized me; he seemed to have forgot that he was inviting me into a Situation which I had learnt from him, was so unusual in *England*, that it was always thought criminal." He replied, that, "he allowed the Truth of what I alledged, but he would remove all Objections from the malicious Censures of Mankind, by keeping every Circumstance concerning me so private, and ordering his own Visits so prudently, that no one should have Room to suspect that I was not wholly Mistress of myself, and every Thing belonging to me." I told him that, "hitherto I had been only unfortunate, what Imprudence I had been guilty of, must be laid to the Charge of unavoidable Ignorance; but if I was to accept his Offer, I should esteem myself greatly blameable. I thought it was wrong to act contrary to the Customs of the People among whom we live, unless in Contradiction to their Vices. Want of Concealment argued a Degree of Guilt, and whether arising from Vice or only Folly, it was our Duty to avoid it. Nothing more was required to render me unhappy, than to be obliged to make a Secret of my Thoughts and Actions. Besides, I made no Doubt but the Suspicions of Mankind were founded on Experience and Probability, which was a sufficient Reason to induce me to avoid giving Cause to them. That in my Opinion a Woman who did one imprudent Thing premeditately, gave good Grounds to suspect her of more, and was guilty, at least, of being the Cause of all the Untruths People thought and said about her, which was a greater Load than I chose to have on my Conscience. That I was determined to appear guiltless, as well as to be so, and therefore would continue where I was, or change only to some Place of my own providing."

---

1 Presumably a misprint for "deference," but not corrected in any subsequent edition.

He spent no small Time in endeavouring to persuade me, that "necessary Concealments could be no Pain to any one blessed with the Consciousness of Innocence." But I, at last, convinced him, that I would not consent to it. It was with Difficulty I prevailed on him to leave me to my own Thoughts, though it was really late at Night. I cannot say they were to his Honour. The Treachery I had discovered made me now as suspicious as before I was the contrary, which must naturally tend to the Disadvantage of Lord *Larborough*, since nothing could give me more Reason to believe he harboured some bad Design, than his Endeavours to draw me into a Way of Life of which he had told me the Impropriety, when it served to get away from Lord *Dorchester*. Could I forbear suspecting them of being equally culpable? It was happy for me, that they were so, for as I fear Humanity would not have been of so much Service to me as Lord *Larborough's* Jealousy and Desire to get me into his Power, I could not attribute what he had done to any other Cause, since he could wish to lead me into Part of the Evil from which he had strongly represented the Necessity of my flying. I had Reason, however, to thank Heaven, that the bad Intentions of one ill Person thus saved me from the Dangers threatened me by another, equally my Enemy; and could not hate Lord *Larborough* for his Sentiments, since they turned so much to my Benefit. But I feared I might find him some Obstruction to my Departure, and without that Addition I had too many Impediments, and no one to assist me. I dared not trust any Body, and had a Mind too ill at Ease to take any Measures for myself. I could only grieve for my Misfortune, incapable of forming a rational Thought towards redressing them. How often, in my Wishes for the friendly Relief of Death, was I checked by the Remembrance of my kind Parent, the Nurse and Instructor of my Youth! But for the Consolation I hoped my Presence would afford her, the Grave would have been my sole Desire, for that alone I thought could bring me Ease; but I preferred the suffering any Evil to the Increase of the Pain I had already involuntarily given her, and this Consideration controuled my ardent Wishes for its kind Hand.

When Lord *Larborough* found neither Persuasion nor Flattery could prevail upon me to put myself into his Power, he tried whither Fear would not be more his Friend. He pestered me every Day with his Visits, and invented new Stories to alarm me. At one Time he pretended, Lord *Dorchester* had discovered where I was, and therefore "thought his Service might not be unexceptionable in procuring me some safer Asylum." But I told him, that, "being less known in the Town than his Lordship, I could more securely perform that

Office for myself;" fully determined to conceal my new Habitation with equal Care from both. I gave Orders to the People of the House to admit no one that wanted to see me, and tried every means to prevail on Lord *Larborough* to leave me, that I might seek another Lodging, for in one Respect he had succeeded, he had frighted me extremely. But, notwithstanding my most pressing Intreaties, and a good Deal of Uncivility, for my Patience was exhausted, yet he would not go away till Night; and then finding no Enquiry had been made after me, I was pretty well convinced the whole was his own Invention.

Another Day he informed me I had got into a House of ill Repute, opening to me a Scene of Iniquity, as appeared to me entirely incredible, and I frankly told him, "it was impossible there should be such Monsters in the Form of Women as he represented, but I was, above all, sure my Landlady was not of that Kind, the House being extremely quiet, she having little Company, no young Person belonging to her; and beside depending on a Shop for her Support, which must render the infamous Trafick he mentioned contrary to her Interest, since it would put a Stop to her lawful and honest Trade."

I grew at length so disgusted with a Man, who could endeavour to increase the Agony of my Mind, out of such base Views as these various Falshoods more and more convinced me actuated him, that I could scarcely endure his Presence. While I believed he exposed Lord *Dorchester's* Designs out of real Humanity, I honoured him. Virtue is a Man's first Friend, and his Regard for it is never put to a severer Trial than when its Interest clashes with the Schemes of those whom he most loves, and therefore he who gives it its true Preference, is greatly to be applauded. But Lord *Larborough's* Motives made his Behaviour treacherous, and the Discovery of them turned all the Gratitude I had at first felt towards him, to Providence, who had a better Right to it. To that was I indebted for my Safety, which was secured by meeting with two Men whose Views were equally base, and both alike fixed on me. In the Moments of my most excessive Grief, I reflected on this as a Blessing, and all my Soul was filled with Gratitude, when otherwise my Wretchedness might have tempted me to an impious Repining, that guiltless, and contrary to any voluntary Steps of my own taking, I should, by various Degrees, be led to the Misery I endured.

I hoped that Despair, might at last, incline Lord *Larborough* to assist me in my Return to my Cottage, but I had vainly flattered myself, he would not even give me any Advice, as to the Manner I should contrive it, and instead of removing the Difficulties that lay in my Way, took a Pleasure in starting new ones. All the Benefit I reaped from a Behaviour which he called ungrateful, was an Abatement in the Frequency of his Visits; and, that I confess, was some Reward.

CHAPTER XLVII

For a Fortnight after I escaped from Lord *Dorchester's*, I had lived without seeing any one except Lord *Larborough*. But the People where I lodged, having as much Pity for my Melancholy, as they had Leisure to feel; were, at last, so pressing with me to drink Tea with them, that I could no longer refuse it, though I was not very fit for Company.

They had been so obliging as to order their Servant to admit no Body, in Compliance with my Desire, but before we parted, by Mistake, she brought in a Visiter, who, the Maid knowing their Regard to him, imagined it must be agreeable. It was so indeed to me, for it proved to be Mr. *South*.

His Behaviour when I was Mrs. *Herner's* Prisoner, had created in me so much Esteem, that I often begged my Lord to give him the first great Living in his Gift, which should prove vacant, and he had promised me he would do it.

As desirous as I had been of remaining concealed, I could not be sorry to see Mr. *South*. He seemed rejoiced to meet with me again, and asked Leave to wait on me the next Morning; very much puzzled by the Way I appeared in, as it differed greatly from the Rank he imagined me of, by Things he heard after my leaving his Neighbourhood. I was not without my Reasons for being glad to have some private Conversation with him. I had sufficient Proof that he was fit to be trusted, and hoped with his Assistance, to get soon from *London*.

He had not been long with me before I communicated to him the Difficulties of my Situation, and told him, that "although I had once rejected his friendly Offers of contriving my Escape, I should now be highly indebted to him, if he would order my Journey for me, in the Way he thought most safe from Discovery. That I hoped, Lord *Dorchester* had taken for granted, that I was returned to my Aunt before that Time, and therefore would have no Suspicions of finding me on the Road; but that to prevent it more certainly, it might be best to go round by some Country[1] that did not lie directly in the

---

1 I.e., some part of the country: countryside.

Way." He was greatly affected with my Distress, and tried all the Power of Persuasion to compose my Mind. He offered to go to Lord *Dorchester*, in order to learn whether the Certainty of being unable to succeed in his Intentions, might not make him glad to marry me. But this I absolutely refused, I had Pride enough to think one with his Principles did not deserve me; but there were Considerations of still more Weight. The Account he gave of his Aversion to Marriage, and the Impropriety of his own Temper, for that State, gave a Woman Reason to fear she might not be happy as his Wife: I had already undergone the worst Part of the Pains of Separation, it would have been very simple to subject myself to suffer it all over again, when by living longer with him, my Affection was still increased; for with all his Faults, I saw him amiable beyond Expression. Besides, as well as I loved him, I would not have turned Beggar, no not even for himself. What Happiness could I have expected from a Love which I thought his Actions proved was not founded on Esteem! Marriage would not make me see it in a different Light, as I could not but know the Desire of it arose in him merely from ungovernable Passion, not Principle, and, I must, therefore, always fear his repenting it, as he could not believe me more worthy of being for ever united to him than before I left him.

I was so positive in the Point, that Mr. *South* did not at all insist on the Execution of his Offer, but, on the contrary commended my Spirit, and appeared extremely pleased with it; the Reason of which I did not find out till the next Day, and then admired the Generosity of his Mind, in having been so ready to undertake an Office, wherein he certainly could not wish to be employed.

In the second Visit he begged, I would forgive his renewing the Offer I had once refused of the whole Service of his Life and Fortune. He pressed it in the genteelest and tenderest Manner imaginable. I told him, "I was very sorry he had still a Wish depending on me, which I could not grant; but that I was absolute in my Determination to return to my Aunt, and on no Account could think of marrying a Man whom I did not love better than any other in the World." He replied, that, "he knew his Misfortune in that Respect; but would never repine at it, if I would but grant him the second Place in my Esteem, and give an Opportunity to his sincere Affection, to make him, in Time, happy in the Possession of my Heart." He added, that "the Delicacy which made me averse to Marriage in the present Situation of my Mind, was a sufficient Assurance that if I was married to him, I would join my Endeavours to his, to get the better of a Love which my Principles would not suffer me to encourage; he would wait those happy Effects with Patience, and with Gratitude acknowledge, the present Blessing of being united to me; which he should prefer to the Possession of the whole Heart of any other Woman." In this Manner did he importune me long, and very reluctantly believed, that I was immoveable on this Subject. I grieved to afflict him, but what could I do? I could not marry him, it was better, therefore, to repress his Hopes at once. This Topick made him so little fit for other Conversation, that during this Visit, I got no Intelligence with regard to my leaving *London*.

The next Day he seemed easier than when he left me, and agreed to assist me as expeditiously as possible. We determined that I should take a Coach to myself, and go through *Northamptonshire* into *Oxfordshire*, and then strike into the Western Road.[1] And he promised, that the Day following he would seek for one. I wished him less slow in procuring the Means of my Departure; could I have transacted it myself, I should have proceeded with more Haste. If an unhappy Person could be so inhuman as to receive Comfort from perceiving others were so as well as herself, I might have found some Consolation the next Morning from a Scene to which I was Witness. I happened, by Chance, to be in a little Room belonging to the People of the House, that had a Door and a Window into the Shop. I saw a very pretty Lady making some Purchase there, when at once I heard her scream; and a Gentleman, whose Face I could not see, express great Satisfaction at meeting her. Her Surprize gave him Time to reproach her, for "having so long avoided him, refusing both his Visits and his Letters, denying him all Opportunity of justifying himself, for an Event, in which she must acknowledge he was not to blame." She struggled to get from him, and begged, he would let her go, but he held her Hand so fast, that she was obliged to hear him protest the most violent Passion, and assure her, that "he had taken all proper Measures to bring her to the appointed Place, but had been strangely disappointed in having another Lady brought instead of her."

Your Ladyship may imagine, that one whose Heart like mine, was filled with Love, would be attentive to any Thing that had the least Relation to it; but I became still more so on what the Gentleman

---

1 This circuitous route, designed to cover her tracks, would take Ophelia northwest from London to Northamptonshire, then south through Oxfordshire until she arrived at the Western Road, the main road from London to Bath and Bristol. Heading due west from London would be much shorter, but would allow pursuers to follow her more readily.

said. By her Endeavours to get from him, I, at last, saw his Face, and perceived it was the Person to whom I had been carried in my Way to *London.*

The Lady declared she would raise an Outcry if he did not go farther from her, and leave her at Liberty. My Landlady then spoke very sternly, and desired he would not trouble any one in her Shop, but let the Lady alone. He no sooner let go her Hand, than she ran to the Street Door, but was stopped by his placing himself between her and it. When she found an Attempt to get from him that Way was vain, she turned short, and seeing the Door which opened into the Room where I was, she sprung with such Force against it, that not shutting very well, she broke it open, and had bolted it on the Inside, before her Lover could reach it.

Seeing me, she begged I would protect her, and keep her from that Man. I carried her up Stairs into my Apartment, the Door of which I fastened, and left the Gentleman to the Disposal of my Landlady. The poor Lady was no sooner eased of Part of her Fear, than she fell into a Fit, which greatly alarmed me, but I durst not open the Door to call any one. When she came to herself, she burst into Tears. Her Case, in some Degree, resembled mine, which made me accompany her in weeping.

She begged me again, not to let the Man from whom she had fled, come up Stairs. I told her, "I had once ignorantly been her Protector, and that now I would be so designedly." I then informed her, that I was the Person who had been carried to his Lordship's House when he expected her, and gave her an Account of my Reception, and what succeeded it.

She seemed to receive some Satisfaction from finding herself with one who knew some Part of her History, but expressed her Astonishment at seeing me in such an Habitation, having, as she said, "understood that I was a Relation of Lord *Dorchester,* and from the Disturbance he had been in, she could suppose no other; and yet the Place in which I now lived, was not at all proper for any of his Family."

So many Circumstances in what either said, touched some tender Part of the other's Heart, that more was expressed by Tears than by Words. They were the only Answers I made to her Expressions of Surprize, till I found she misconstrued them, by her telling me, that, "she feared Lord *Dorchester* was not Proof against Pride and Beauty, which together, made Men do very wrong Things. She had had a better Opinion of his Lordship, his Behaviour to her deserved eternal Gratitude; but she was afraid I had not an equal Obligation to him. She assured me, she pitied me sincerely, for that my Youth and the very great Amiableness of his Lordship were strong Excuses, if I observed a different Behaviour for the Future, offering me any Kind of Assistance in her Power, and exhorting me to a regular Life." These Suspicions raised my Indignation; I could not forbear answering with great Warmth that, "her Opinion injured me greatly, and it was cruel, by such an Imputation, to add to the Affliction I was under."

She begged my Pardon in the handsomest Manner, made all Kind of Submissions, and excused herself so well on the Probability of the Thing, that I forgave her, and complied with her Request in relating to her, in as few Words as possible; the Occasion of the Difference she saw in my Situation. She shewed a very real Compassion for me, and offered to take me Home with her, to her Aunt's, where they would carefully conceal me. But "I entreated her, not even to mention me to that Relation, as it must redound to my Lord's Dishonour; and I thought myself so safe, where I was, that it would not be advisable to change my Abode." Her Fear lest her Lover should have set Spies at our Door, made her glad to remain the whole Day with me; during which I learnt, that her Father had faithfully kept the Agreement made with him by Lord *Dorchester*, and her Aunt had behaved very kindly to her; but that she had been obliged to make herself an absolute Prisoner ever since she came to Town, having never been able to venture into any publick Place, or large Company, for fear of meeting that vile Man from whom she had been so fortunately delivered. "Not," she added, that "she apprehended any other Harm from seeing him in publick, but the keeping alive a Passion, which it was necessary to her Peace to extinguish; she owned she had not been able to do it, which made her extremely unhappy; and had occasioned her suffering excessively during that Interview between them, to which I had been a Witness."

Her Lover omitted no Means of seeing or writing to her, after he found where she was gone. He attempted to visit her continually, but always received a Denial at the Door; he contrived a thousand Ways to convey Letters to her; he often had them directed by other People, in hopes that not knowing the Hand, she would open them, but being constantly on her Guard, she never read one, though for any Thing she knew, some of them might be from other People; but the only Means she had of certainly avoiding to receive his Letters, was to accept none, but such as were in the Hands of her usual Correspondents. Her Care had answered so well, that she never before met him.

It was plain from his Discourse, that he imagined her Behaviour proceeded from Resentment at not having been carried to his House. I found she was as weak as myself; she was still very much in Love with him, and appeared extremely unhappy, though she said, she was grown easier before this unlucky Interview. She told me, "her Intention, was to persuade her Aunt to live in the Country, where she hoped, by Absence and Reason, to conquer this unfortunate Passion. For she took no Joy in Society, nor did it afford the least Relief to her Spirits. I once," added she, "by Chance met his Wife, who seemed not less unhappy than myself, and I felt almost equal Pity for her. Instead of looking on her with the Dislike generally borne a Rival, I conceived a Kind of Love for her as a Fellow-Sufferer, and could not forgive myself, for having, perhaps, been a Means of creating Part of the Uneasiness, which appeared in her Countenance, though I had innocently offended against her; her Lord being the cruel Injurer of both."

By enquiring into his Character, she learnt, that his Lady was a Woman of very great Fortune, whom he married in little more than a Year before he came into her Father's Neighbourhood, having gained her Affections by a very assiduous Courtship, to which her Riches alone had tempted him.

The Similitude between this young Lady's Fate and mine, disposed us well towards each other, and, before we parted, we should have been glad to have agreed on a Means of Meeting again, but I dared not venture to her End of the Town, nor could she come where I was, without Danger of meeting the Man, she wished to avoid, as he might probably hope that a Love so tender as he knew her's once was, would, when her first Anger was abated, relent on what he had said, and that she would come again, where she might hope another Time to see him. These Considerations obliged us to take a final Leave, only she insisted, on my informing her by a Line, when I should be got safely out of Town, which she advised me to attempt cautiously, but resolutely, tho' she owned, she was sorry Lord *Dorchester* should have any Cause to grieve, for notwithstanding his having acted an unworthy Part, yet her Gratitude for the great Benefit he had conferred on her, made her wish him not to suffer by it; adding, that, "I must allow, this was due to one who had preserved her from being the unhappiest Wretch on Earth; but yet she should be very sorry that he should commit a wrong Action, who had deserved so much Honour from having prevented another from doing one." We exchanged mutual good Wishes, and parted.

How much are the Orders of Providence perverted! Our Affections seemed given as the Sources of Happiness, but by the bad

Qualities of Mankind are frequently made the great Springs of our Misery. While they correspond with Virtue, they alone give us a Notion of true Bliss; but when once they are connected with various Kinds of Vice, how wretched do they make both the vicious Person, and those who are the Objects of their ill-founded Affections!

CHAPTER XLVIII

The next Morning, when Mr. *South* went to hire an Equipage for me, as he had promised, he perceived a Man sauntering in the Inn-Yard, who observed him while he was making the Bargain, and followed him at a Distance at his Return. Mr. *South* fearing it might be some Spy of Lord *Dorchester*'s, went Home, instead of coming to me. He learnt of the People of the House where he lodged, that after he was gone in, the Man enquired his Name, and some other Particulars. He was so cautious lest the Place of my Abode should be discovered thro' his Means, that he would not stir out of his Lodgings till the following Day, but he had not been long with me, before the same Person came after him, having been directed from his House with a Message from Lord *Dorchester*, desiring to speak with him then, if he was at Leisure. This surprized us, as they had not the least Acquaintance, and made us suspect that, upon laying Circumstances together, his Lordship thought Mr. *South* might be able to give him some Information about me.

I was desirous of moving my Habitation directly, that he might be able to say with Truth, he knew not where I was, but he differed from me in this, he said that, "Lord *Dorchester* had no Power over me, nor could a Man of Honour attempt to use Force to prevent my pursuing my intended Journey; that he would take Care I should have the Liberty of a free-born Woman, and not be detained by any one. If his Lordship kept so strict a Watch, I should scarcely be able to get off undiscovered, and therefore, it was better to do it openly and boldly; offering to see me safe to the End of my Journey." As his Profession obliged him to some Dependence on the Favour of those who could assist in his Preferment, and as I hoped, Lord *Dorchester* would perform the Promise he had given me, I rejected this Proposal, very unwilling to do him an Injury in return for the Obligations he had conferred on me, by thus neglecting his own Interest for my Good. He replied, that, "he could never receive so much true Satisfaction from any Thing, as from doing me Service; that he should have only this one Opportunity of enjoying so great a Gratification, which, since I could not be prevailed with to make him happy, would be always reflected on by him as the darling Moment of his Life," and that "it would be the highest Cruelty to refuse the Acceptance of his best Services, the Recollection of which, would sweeten all his future Cares or Pains, and as I could give but a very imperfect Account of the Place from which I had been taken, he could not venture me with any other Guide than himself." He left me without waiting for an Answer.

His Resolution distressed me, I could not bear to be detrimental to his Interests, though I was convinced that with Truth, he said, they weighed less with him, than the Pleasure of doing one friendly Action; but such Generosity should meet with an equal Return, and I would not in this, have given Way to him, could I have avoided it: But his Absence robbed me of the Power of resisting his kind Intention, and, indeed, the Difficulty of finding out the Place to which I was to be carried from the very imperfect Hints I could give, was so great, that there was some Danger, that none but so very assiduous a Friend would have taken the Pains to have sought it out, which he intended to have done, while I remained on the Borders of *Wales*, till he could direct the Vehicle in the right Course. I was impatient to know the Occasion of Lord *Dorchester's* sending for him, and yet it should have seemed of little Importance to me. My Departure was determined. If he would have fixed me out of his Power, and complied with my Terms, which the Censoriousness of this Country, founded on the dissolute Manners of the People, would have required to make me acknowledged as innocent as I was, I would not have staid. I could not accept an Obligation which I never would return. The Customs of Mankind, and the different Opinion I had of my Lord, to what I formerly entertained, rendered it impossible for me to live with the same frequent Intercourse, and perfect Confidence, which till then had been the Source of all my Joys. Without that, what Charms could any Place have for me? The more I reflected, the stronger was my Resolution to fly it, as I would the Pestilence, lest the Contagion should reach me, and I be infected with their Immorality.

While I was in the midst of these Reflections, I heard some one coming up Stairs to my room; full of Expectation of Mr. *South*, I ran to the Door to meet him, but how great was my Surprize at seeing instead of him, Lord *Dorchester*! I cried out, and sunk into a Chair, my Strength failing me. He was in too great a Rapture to think of the Effect his sudden Appearance had on me. How far above Description were his Transports on seeing me again! He embraced me with an Eagerness, which, however innocent I once thought it, his own Words had instructed me too well to suffer; and the Desire of repeling the Familiarity, I believe, recovered me sooner than I should otherwise have been. All he said, were incoherent, passionate Expressions of his Joy. My Sensations were more silent; I was as unable to speak as he was to preserve any Regularity in what he said. Love, Resentment, Grief and Fear, divided my Heart; each alike strove for Utterance, and therefore rendered me dumb; till he cried, "speak to me, my Charmer, my Angel, speak; no Words can be so cruel as this Silence. Your Voice must delight whatever Subject you chuse, but let it not be a harsh one; pity and forgive a Man, whose whole Bliss is centered in you. Will you, can you, pardon me?"

"Can my Forgiveness be of any Worth," I replied, "to one who could long harbour a Wish to make me so criminal, that I could not have pardoned myself? If it was of Value, why would you desire to rob me of it, to whom it must be of most Consequence."

"Upbraid me not," answered he, "with Errors that make me wretched. If you knew how much I deserve your Pity, Forgiveness must succeed your Compassion. All my Life shall be devoted to extenuate my Offence. Actions proceeding from the truest, the purest Love, shall plead the Excuse of my injurious Designs, believe my Word, I have never broken it; I will not rise from your Feet, till you assure me of my Pardon." "Rise then, now, my Lord," said I, "Anger maintains much shorter Possession of my Mind than Grief, I can suffer, but not resent. From my Heart I forgive all the Misery you have inflicted, and the greater still which you intended me. I forgive you your constant Endeavours to create a Love in me, which could only tend to my Unhappiness. I will not exclude even this last Pain, this Interview, which tears my Heart: It is your inflicting, and, therefore, I will receive it with Patience; but I had hoped to be settled in Peace without undergoing any new Conflicts; I would not have troubled you in the Search of Tranquility; a blessing hard to find, for a Heart so fond, so tender, as mine; one that is by you, taught, all the Anguish that the highest Degree of Sensibility can give. It was before I knew you in the entire Possession of Rest and Peace, had no Wish ungratified, no Fear, no jarring Passions to torment it. This dreadful Change, I pardon you, and while I am seeking in my Solitude for my former Ease, I will pray for your Felicity, and Tears shall wash away all Resentment, I might be happy if they could drown Remembrance too."

Tears eased the Rack I was upon,[1] and gave my Lord Time to

---

1   Alluding to the rack, an instrument of torture used to stretch the joints of its victim, which was frequently used on prisoners until and during Elizabeth's reign, but not thereafter in England.

desire me not to talk of returning to my Cottage, for it was uniting Death with the healing Sound of Pardon. "If you love me" continued he, "can you wish for such a Separation? You have now no Reason to fly me, I have no concealed Design. I was, indeed, greatly prejudiced against Marriage, but you have removed it all; I now look on it as a State of Bliss, if you are my Companion in it, and pray for it more devoutly than ever Martyr did for Heaven. Indeed, I have had my Martyrdom; no Tyrant could inflict a Torment beyond what your Absence has made me suffer. What bitter Accusations have I not made against myself, for permitting Prejudice to get the better of the truest Love that ever possessed the Heart of Man. If you are only indifferent, mere Pity will move you to comply. If you do not hate me, you will consent to become my dear, my wedded Wife directly; you will relieve my Mind from its present Sufferings; and put it in my Power to make what Recompence I can for the Trouble I have caused you."

"That I love you," I replied, "I am much too well convinced by painful Experience; but you have so forfeited my Esteem, that I cannot comply with your Proposal. I could not be happy if I was married to you, consequently should not make you so. Your Passion for me is the same it was, all the Difference is in the Companions of it. While accompanied by Hope, you know how little I was obliged to you for it; now Despair has taken its Place, it has blinded you, and I will believe you think your Affection all you say it is, but was your Despair to cease, you would find your Mistake too late, after we were both made Sacrifices to the Deception. I have lost all my Confidence in you, and detest the rest of your Nation. I will go where I shall be secluded from Mankind, where Virtue makes every Action open and intelligible; there I am capable of living happily, without learning the Arts that here hide every real Thought. If this Resolution is painful to you, make it likewise beneficial; trust me, so corrupt a People cannot be taught Virtue, but by Suffering. Affliction will purify a Heart perverted by Education and Custom; it takes off the Varnish from glaring Vices, and shews them in their own dark Colours. If you really suffer, consider to what it is owing, learn to hate Vice, which as certainly carries its Punishment, as Virtue does its Reward along with it. But why should I think you can suffer long enough to do you any Good? Your Heart is not made like mine, therefore I cannot judge of it." "Can you," cried my Lord, "kindly shed these Tears to part with me, and yet accompany them with so cruel a Declaration of your Intention?" He omitted nothing that he thought could prevail with me, and so far did he succeed, that had I known how much I should have been affected I would not have staid to hear him, for I could not have believed my Reason strong enough to resist my own Agitation of Mind, and the Distraction he appeared in. He saw my Distress, but receiving Hope from it, cruelly continued his Persuasions. I would have left him, but he held me fast, protesting he would never let me go till I promised to be his Wife. He offered me the Disposal of half his Fortune to make me less dependant; but when our Ease of Heart depends so entirely on another's Love, what Freedom can Money give us?

I know not whether I could for ever have refused to comply, but happily for me, his Reason failed him, before he had sufficiently conquered mine to get my Consent; his Spirits were so oppressed, he became quite speechless, and almost senseless. I was half distracted, but as soon as he began to come out of this Fit, to avoid prolonging a Scene so difficult for me to support, I left the Room, though not without taking a kinder Farewel than seemed consistent with a Desire never to see him again, which I begged, while with Tears, I kissed his Hand. He had only Power to look up at me, with dying Eyes, swimming in Tears. Thus I left him: But how hard it was to do so, none can know, but those who have loved as well, and gone through as severe a Trial.

I shut myself into another Room, there to give Way to the Distraction of my Mind, which was so excessive, that when Mr. *South* came, I was not capable of attending or speaking to him. He was greatly touched, and endeavoured to soothe and compose me; but finding it impossible, he went away, unable to support the Sight of me in that Distress. The next Time Mr. *South* came, he found me more capable of hearing what had passed after Lord *Dorchester* sent for him.

He told me, that my Lord was waiting for him, and as soon as the Servant introduced him, asked, with the utmost Impatience if he could impart any News of Miss *Lenox*? Mr. *South* expressed some Surprize at his Lordship's applying to him, who alledged for the Reason of it, "the Knowledge of the Regard he had for me, and the Reason I had to place a Confidence in him, which made him appear the properest Person to whom I could have Recourse, in a Situation, where, without the Assistance of one more accustomed to the World, it must be very difficult to conduct myself. That this Probability, was turned into almost a Certainty, by the Account of one of the People whom he had in Pay at every Place in Town, where Equipages were to be hired, to prevent my getting away from it without his Knowledge." This Man told him, "he had seen a Clergyman hire a Chariot which he had looked at, and seemed to prefer to the rest, for having Canvasses to let down before the Glasses,[1] at least he could guess no other Reason for the Preference he gave it, as it was rather the worst Vehicle there. That upon this, his Spy followed him to his Lodgings, and learnt his Name. My Lord then, in the most affecting Terms, conjured Mr. *South* to tell him where I was."

He answered, that, "he did not know, though he was obliged to Chance for finding me out, but that he must beg to be excused giving an Information that might make a Resolution more difficult to execute, which was already almost too hard for a Woman who, except Virtue, loved nothing so well as his Lordship."

My Lord said, "he hoped they were not inconsistent; he would not have asked him for any Information of which he designed to make a bad Use. He had no other Wish but to marry me, and wanted to see me, to obtain my Consent, together with my Forgiveness for what was past, and hoped, it might be gained, as he had only mentally offended, and would devote his Life to make me Reparation." He added, "that he could not live without me, and should gratefully receive me on my own Terms, if I pleased, that very Day, for no Time was early enough for his Impatience."

Mr. *South* offered to come and tell me his present Sentiments, but my Lord begged he might not defer seeing me, and prevailed on him to direct him where to find me.

After Lord *Dorchester* left me, he sent again for Mr. *South*, who found him in a Way, that the Description alone moved my Heart too much at. He begged Mr. *South*'s Assistance in his Endeavours to prevail on me to desist from my Purpose of never seeing him again.

Mr. *South* promised he would give it him, but added, that, "if my Love for his Lordship could not prevail, he feared all other Advocates would prove very weak. That, if I was able to persist in my Resolution notwithstanding the Distress I saw him in, in the Interview, which, he imagined would have ended in our Union, he did not flatter himself he could make me change it."

I told him, he "had undertaken an unsuccessful Cause; that his Expectations of the little he should be able to effect were so well founded, I need give no other Reasons to persuade him to desist from a Persecution with which, however obstinately, I had determined not to comply, yet to resist, was very painful to me."

That I might be removed from these Obstructions to my intend-

---

1 Curtains, covering the windows.

ed Departure, which I feared would grow too strong for my Resolution, I desired Mr. *South* would procure me an Equipage for the next Day, without imparting to my Lord the Suddenness of my Determination. He promised to fulfil my Request. I wished myself in some Place where my Lord could not find me, for I feared I should not be Proof against another Interview, though I was fortified by the full Belief that I could not be happy with one so defective in his Principles, on the Goodness of which must depend the Felicity of all those small Societies; as Esteem is a necessary Foundation for a lasting Love: I could not believe this Change in him arose from an Amendment of Heart, but from Despair of Success in his former Schemes, and was convinced it would therefore be Madness to unite myself, for Life, with one who had no better Motive; for no Suffering can equal that of being married to a Man of whom one has a bad Opinion.

As soon as Mr. *South* had reported his small Success, Lady *Palestine* was sent, by my Lord, to try, whether she could prevail. Your Ladyship may imagine, I did not give her a very cordial Reception. She took no Notice of it, but addressed me with Fondness, and began to combat my Intention by setting before me all the Happiness that attended my Consent to marry my Lord. Instead of endeavouring to excuse his Faults, she only said slightly, that no other Man would have preserved so blameless a Behaviour, and proceeded to shew an Union with him in the most pleasing Light. Her Aim was to bring my Affections to her Side of the Argument.

I did not let her go on long, but told her, "it well became one who could condescend to connive at, and assist such villainous Designs, as had been harboured against me, to endeavour to prevail by the Force of Passion, against the Reason which ought to subdue it, but that I was not to be moved by Arguments so wrongly applied, and uttered by one from whom every Thing must appear in a suspicious Light, and who would disgrace even the Cause of Virtue by defending it. Without saying much more, I affronted her, and freed myself from her Importunities."

Lord *Dorchester* came soon after; but I heard a Coach stop, and fearing it was him, hid myself so well, that though the House was diligently searched, they could not find me. After that he sent me a Letter, but I did not chuse to give him more Arms against myself, so sent it back with a Desire he would leave me in Peace.

Before I had Time to compose my Spirits, Miss *Baden* was brought up Stairs. I was greatly surprized to see her, but my Heart was so great a Stranger to Pleasure, that I could not find Words to express what I felt at her Visit, so soon as she did the Occasion of it. "I am come," said she, "to plead a Cause, in which I find so many others have been unsuccessful, that although to be employed might raise my Vanity, it ought to create Fears in me, that all my Endeavours will prove fruitless. My Regard for you, the Pleasure I have always imagined I must find in your Friendship, and Pity for one whose Distress would move a harder Heart than mine, makes me wish for Eloquence enough to prevail in my Suit." She proceeded to tell me, that she had had a Visit from Lord *Dorchester*. As soon as he came in he told her, that, "though he had never before had the Honour of waiting on her, yet he trusted in her good Nature for his Pardon, when she knew that he had placed all Hopes of the Happiness of his Life in her."

He related to her, every Thing that had passed between him and me, from the Time of his first seeing me till his last Trial, by Lady *Palestine*, of prevailing on me to lay aside my Intention of returning to my Aunt. He added, that, "he knew I had a good Opinion of her, and he had never seen so strong an Inclination in me to any other Person; he, therefore, hoped she might be more successful, if she would kindly undertake his Cause."

I told her, "it was a bad one, and I wondered she would engage in it." She replied, "that I ought not to expect consummate Virtue among a degenerate People; that it was scarcely possible to find a Man who had any Scruples in Regard to his Behaviour to Women. She gave me a thousand Instances wherein the Men of the best Characters had failed; telling me, they esteemed Matrimony as so entirely a political Institution, that though each might approve of it in Society, many did not like it for themselves. That they looked on the Life of a Woman who lived with them without being married, as generally most happy. That my Lord, in the Care he had taken of my Reputation, had shewn a Delicacy and an Affection for me, of which few Men were capable, that, in every other Virtue, he was as nearly perfect as a human Creature could be. She told me, how much I ought to allow for the Force of Custom and Education; these had both tended to make him look on Chastity as a very small Virtue, for that it was even made the Subject of Ridicule in such Men as were possessed of it."

In short, she said so much in his Excuse, that, although I could not allow that Custom should so far overcome Truth, I found some Satisfaction in thinking him less criminal, but still saw him too much so, not to resist all her Importunities, and she was obliged to submit to my Obstinacy.

I should be deficient in Sincerity, were I not to confess that Miss *Baden*'s Persuasions a little staggered my Resolution. I sometimes was inclined to doubt whether Lord *Dorchester* could be so much to blame, since she undertook to excuse him, and whether I might not be allowed to forgive one I loved so tenderly, since a Woman who had no such Motive could so easily acquit him. But I soon became sensible this was the Dictate of my Passion. Bad Examples and pernicious Habits, had, in a Degree, perverted Miss *Baden*; the Frequency of Vice had deadened her Sense of it; but I had no such Excuse; Custom had not confounded my Ideas of Right and Wrong, and therefore to have united myself with a Person whom I knew guilty of Vice, was, in a Degree, to become vicious; and I could not have a stronger Reason to avoid it than Miss *Baden* herself furnished me with, for since a Woman of Virtue could, by Example, have her Principles so much perverted, the Danger I should run by marrying Lord *Dorchester* was obvious; and to put ourselves in a Situation that must hazard our Integrity, is a great Proof that it is not at that Time sufficiently strong. I very frankly told Miss *Baden* how much more prevalent I found her Example than her Arguments, for that, "she could urge no Reasons which would so strongly induce me to live with Lord *Dorchester*, as her being capable of urging them would deter me from it, since she thereby shewed me the Danger that arose from a Communication with Mankind; for I should fear, that my Principles might be corrupted by the same Means that had perverted her's. Therefore all she could say, only proved to me the Necessity of flying Mankind, if I designed to hold fast mine Integrity as long as I lived."

Miss *Baden* smiled, without any Appearance of Resentment at what I had said, and only answered, that, "she saw I was determined to make no Difference between excusing the Guilt of others, and accompanying them in the Crime, and since I was resolved to retire from the World, in order to avoid becoming as bad as she was, she found she had little Chance of carrying back any Consolation to Lord *Dorchester*;" and the Night being far spent, she took Leave of me.

CHAPTER XLIX

My Mind had been too much agitated in the Day, to allow me any Rest at Night. The various Attacks that had been made on my Passions, had cost my Reason so much Labour to resist, that I had not Strength enough to compose my Spirits, which, when Mr. *South* attended me the next Morning were in a State little different from what they were when he left me the day before. He imagined Night would afford me but little Relief, and therefore came the earlier, out of a kind Desire to divert my Thoughts, if he could not alleviate my Uneasiness.

Before the Hour the Chariot was ordered, a Letter was brought, which I perceived, by the Superscription, was from Lord *Dorchester*. The first Impulse was to return it unopened, to avoid giving fresh Pain to my Heart; but before I could put the Thought in Execution, it gave Place to a tenderer Consideration. I feared by such a Proceeding, I might add to his Uneasiness; and this, in a Point that could do me no essential Harm, was ungenerously preferring my own Ease to his, and since I was just going to execute a Resolution which affected him so much, it would be cruel to encrease it unnecessarily. I therefore opened the Letter, and, to my great Surprize, learnt from it, that, "he left *London* before Break of Day, in order to proceed directly to my Aunt's, having Hopes of obtaining her Mediation in his Favour, which he flattered himself might have more Weight than any other Person's had yet had."

Nothing could have filled me with greater Astonishment. To expect so good a Woman should plead in the Excuse of Vice, appeared to me extremely absurd; but the Consequence of this Step was the preventing my Journey; since had I prosecuted it, I must have met him on the Road, or found him there; neither of which would have been at all agreeable to my Purpose. The best Scheme I could now form, was to leave my Lodging before he could return to Town, and remove into some obscure House in the Suburbs. And that as soon as Mr. *South*, who kindly undertook this additional Trouble, could learn that he was come back, I should set out directly on my Journey. We were not without Hopes, that as my Lord had taken his usual Retinue with him, the Person employed to watch his Arrival in *London*, might learn some Particulars of the Situation of my Aunt's House, that would serve to direct us, and save a very difficult, and, perhaps, a very tedious Search after it.

My travelling Equipage was sent away, and every Thing settled for my Continuance at my Lodging, till I imagined Lord *Dorchester* might be coming back; for I liked the people of the House too well to leave them while I could avoid it. Their Humanity endeared them to me; they had gathered so much Light into my Situation, by Circumstances that had fallen within their Observation, that I thought myself obliged to acquaint them with a little more, lest they should have received Impressions that might make them discontented with my continuing in their House. This Mr. *South* performed, and though he told them very few Particulars, yet their good Nature appeared very conspicuously on the Occasion, and their greatest Wish was to amuse me. But in this they could not succeed so easily, as in making their House perfectly convenient. To relieve the Anxiety of my Mind, was reserved for others, who, for the Time they were with me, did it effectually, and inspired me with a Joy, which, on my own Account, I could not have felt.

Sir *Charles Lisdale* came to Town two Days after Lord *Dorchester* left it, and not finding his Lordship, went to Lady *Palestine's*, where he heard my whole History, and, desirous of seeing me, was directed by her to my Lodgings.

Sir *Charles* came directly to my Lodging, and sending up his Name asked Leave to wait on me, a Permission I readily granted, and he was brought up Stairs with a young Lady who I perceived to be a Daughter of Captain *Traverse*, and consequently received her with Pleasure. I was glad to observe more Chearfulness in Sir *Charles's* Countenance, than when we last met. He accosted me with saying, "He was come to claim the Friendship I had once offered him. That Time, Absence, and Despair, had made him more reasonable, and brought him to see that he was presumptuous, in aiming to possess me, and not thinking that my Acquaintance and Conversation was more Happiness that he merited." I told him, "mine would be greater, if he would cease to flatter, an Effect, which I might hope from the Improvement of his Reason, of which he boasted, since it must make him know, that in what he said he far exceeded the Truth, and might incline him to believe, that he likewise exceeded my Credulity."

He answered, that, "I had much mistaken the Office of Reason, if I imagined it had altered his Opinion of me, it had only made him more sensible of his Demerits, which shewed too much Inequality between us, to give him the least Room for Hope. But," continued he, taking the young Lady, who accompanied him, by the Hand, "let me beg your Friendship for one who has kindly soothed my Griefs, and turned my Disappointment into Happiness." I was overjoyed at these Words; I gathered from them that they either were already, or were to be united. I embraced and congratulated her with Transport. She had so favourable a Prospect of Happiness, both from Sir *Charles's* good Qualities, and the Affluence of his Fortune, that nothing could give me more Pleasure; she blushed, in Appearance, from Excess of Satisfaction, and looked up at him with so much Love and Gratitude as charmed me. I could not remain long without expressing a Desire to know how this Union was brought about, which seemed to me as impossible as any Thing could be. Sir *Charles* assured me he would gratify my Curiosity, which he did in the following Words.

"When you deprived me of all Hopes of obtaining your Affection, having no longer any Pleasure or Interest in Society, my only Aim was an absolute Retirement, till my passion should be so much moderated as to allow me to endure Company, and to enable me to be fit for it. To secure such a Retreat it was necessary to chuse some Place where I was not known. This led me to the Borders of *Wales*, as the most promising for the Solitude I sought. It answered my Hopes. I found a little Cottage situated to my Wish, for every Thing around it appeared as desolate as my Mind. Lest I should be troubled with Visits from any Gentleman in the Neighbourhood, I concealed my Name, and passed for a Man driven thither by Poverty and Distress; a certain melancholy in my Air, created this Report, and I would not contradict it, for nothing could better favour my Temper. None are so sure of Neglect as the Poor; they may enjoy an absolute Solitude in the most populous City, therefore it is not wonderful, if no one broke in upon my Time and Reflections. However, I had not been there long, before I became acquainted with Captain *Traverse's* Family, whose Circumstances appeared to correspond with mine. Little inclined to extend our Thoughts beyond ourselves, we were made known to each other, only by sitting in the same Pew at Church, without which Circumstance, perhaps, we should have remained ignorant that there was any unhappy Persons in the Neighbourhood, besides ourselves. After we had been obliged to speak civilly to each other, by these Means, he one Day invited me to go Home with him, after Church. I liked the Manner of his Behaviour, and was well disposed to accept his Invitation. Towards Evening, he asked me if I would drink a little Milk," adding, "it might seem an odd Question, but it was the only Offer he could make me, having neither Tea nor Wine, for they were too expensive for Persons in his Circumstances,[1] who wanted all the little Money they had to furnish them with more necessary Things. I was greatly pleased to see with what Ease they denied themselves the small

---

1 Fielding also emphasizes the cost of tea and wine, both luxury items, in *The Adventures of David Simple*, in which the hero lodges with a woman who "indulged herself in drinking Tea, Wine, and in such Expences as a Man in his way [her husband] could not possibly supply, notwithstanding all his Industry" (I.viii).

Indulgence which the lowest People enjoy. I would gladly have increased their Income, but I feared to make myself suspected of being less poor than I was thought, which I wished to avoid, till I knew whether they were to be trusted. Finding them very agreeable, I used frequently to visit them, and they often returned it. I received great Pleasure from their Society, and was more charmed with them, as my Acquaintance with their Tempers and Conduct increased. This young Lady particularly, I found so amiable in her Disposition as, joined with her Beauty, to make me feel all the Regards of a Friend towards her. She shewed the same Attentions to me, nor were her Parents offended with our innocent Affection. She was always employed either in attending her Mother, taking Care of the Family, or working for them. I admired the Alacrity and good Sense, with which she performed her different Duties, and became her Companion in many of them. With very great Difficulty I prevailed on the Captain to suffer me to join my little Family with theirs, on Condition I should pay half the Expences of the whole. He objected, that this was more than my Share, and that he feared there was great Similitude in our Circumstances. However, at last, I succeeded, and we became one Family.[1] They let me bring Books there, and those that were at work would often listen to me while I read aloud; my lovely *Fanny* most of all, tho' when we were alone the Time was seldom given to Books. I used to lament at my Misfortunes, communicated to her the Passion with which my Heart was filled, concealing none of the Truth but my Name and Fortune, leaving her to imagine that my ill Success proceeded from my Poverty. With how much good Sense, she would endeavour to shew me the Necessity of conquering my Love! With what gentle Sweetness would she try to comfort me! How tenderly did she join with me, in my Complaints, and endeavour to soothe them! It is impossible I can ever recompence her for the excessive Goodness she shewed me. I am afraid her kind Behaviour tempted me to teize her the more with my Uneasiness. I felt so much Pleasure in being comforted by her, as led me to encourage my Distress.

"I had not long made Part of this amiable Family, when Captain *Traverse* went to *London*. You already know what drew him thither, and the ill Success of his Solicitations, as well as the unexpected

---

1 A similar arrangement is made at the beginning of *David Simple, Volume the Last*, in which two families—David and his wife, Camilla, together with Valentine (Camilla's brother) and his wife, Cynthia—form a household and share living expenses.

Blessings which Lord *Dorchester's* Generosity bestowed upon him. I had undertaken to supply his Care over his Children's Studies, during his Absence, which proved an agreeable Amusement to me, as I did not act the Part of a School-master long enough for it to lose the Pleasure of Novelty. Any Thing new gave a Turn to my Thoughts, and was, thereby, of Service to me.

"Lord *Dorchester's* Letter broke in upon the Peace I began to acquire, by robbing me of all my Companions. His Character sufficiently convinced me, that he had some generous Design in sending for them, tho' he hinted it but darkly in his Letter. This could not recompence me for their Loss, as I was myself able to relieve their Distresses, and was determined, after being longer acquainted with their Merits to have made them easy. My *Fanny* promised not to let a Post pass, without acquainting me with the Event of their Journey, and was as good as her Word. The Joy and Gratitude expressed in her Letter, made me envy Lord *Dorchester* the Pleasure of having conferred so noble an Obligation on People who had Hearts to feel it so sensibly, and esteem it so justly. The Captain's Convenience would no longer suffer them to live at so great a Distance from *London*, they therefore hired a House about twenty Miles from it, which his Lordship furnished very genteelly for them. As my *Fanny* and I kept up a very constant Correspondence, I was frequently solicited to forsake my desolate Solitude, and once more make Part of their Family. At first Melancholy was more powerful than their Persuasions, and I resisted them; but I soon began to accuse myself of Obstinacy, and, on their assuring me that they lived extremely retired, I consented, and went to be a Witness of, and consequently a Sharer in the Happiness, at which none can arrive, who have not before felt the cruel Distresses they had endured.

"But I had not enjoyed this Satisfaction many Days, before I was taken ill of a Fever. My *Fanny* was now my constant Friend and tender Nurse, and seemed to forget the general Happiness in a humane Concern for what I suffered. My Fever increased, till I grew so very ill that it appeared proper to send for a Physician. He thought my Life in great Danger, which Declaration made my fair Nurse inconsolable. The Affliction in which she appeared, touched me excessively I fancied I saw in it a softer Passion than Friendship. No one can be truly sensible of the Pleasure of being beloved, but he who has felt all the Pangs of an unsuccessful Passion. The Hopes I had formed increased my Regard and Esteem for her; and, one Day, as she was sitting by my Bed-side, I told her, that, her incomparable Goodness had conquered the Grief with which my Heart was filled, when I first knew her, and had taken the Place of a Love I thought eternal; therefore she must not wonder, if henceforward I complained of no Passion but one for her, and I should esteem myself very happy if she would take her usual Pains to comfort me. She looked stedfastly on me, and then calling to my Servant, who was at the other End of the Room, she told him my Senses wandered, and desired him to repeat the last Medicine. I assured her, that they were never more perfect; and, after some time, convinced her that I spoke my real and sober Sentiments. She then burst into Tears, and begged I would not say any Thing that might increase her Affection, or make my Company give her more Pleasure, at a Juncture when it was very uncertain how long she should enjoy it. This kind Reception of my Declaration rendered me incapable of obeying her; and my melancholy Situation so softened her Mind, that she returned it in the most endearing Manner. I would not discover my real Circumstances, desirous to try her Affection to the utmost. Her Joy appeared very sincere, indeed, on being assured I was out of Danger. The Progress of my Recovery gave her as much Satisfaction as her Satisfaction did me. I continued my Addresses to her; but I found her Return less tender, as I grew better in Health, which made me tell her that I wished myself sick again. However, I had no real Cause of Complaint. I perceived she put some Constraint on herself, to alter a Behaviour which she thought justifiable only during my Illness, when mere Compassion required a Shew of Tenderness.

"As soon as I got well, I proposed to marry her. She begged me not to think of it, for she could not possible agree to add to my Distresses by making me poorer; and thought we then lived happily in the innocent Assurance of each other's Affection. As this was an Objection I could easily remove, it did not make me alter my Design, but before I confessed my real Name, I was desirous of trying the Degree of Estimation in which I was held by Captain *Traverse*, by making my Proposal of becoming his Son-in-law, before he was acquainted with my Fortune. But while I was preparing to put this Scheme in Execution, my Thoughts received a new Turn. My Sickness had prevented me from having much Conversation in the family, but now, being well enough to associate with them, I was talking with the Captain on the Change in his Affairs, when he mentioned Lord *Dorchester*'s Lady. Having left him a Batchelor, I was curious to know who she was, perhaps the more so for the Jealousy I had always entertained of him, thinking that I perceived, he was favoured by you. The Description they gave me, and the Raptures they were all in when they mentioned your Beauty, and every Circumstance of your Behaviour, convinced me my happy Rival had triumphed. Though I thought my Passion over, yet I own I was so much affected by this News, that I could not contain myself. I had grown easy by looking on you as a Being far above us, one designed to be adored, but not possessed, one to whom all Mankind, as well as myself, must pay an unavailing Worship, and submitted patiently to the general Fate; but I found, I could not bear to think another enjoyed a Happiness I believed above a Mortal.

"My dearest *Fanny* will suffer me to report this, as my Emotions were too visible not to be perceived by her, who cruelly made me ashamed of my Behaviour by the most generous Tenderness. She guessed you were the Woman whom I had often described, while she was the Confidante of my Passion. Instead of reproaching me for harbouring in my Breast the Sparks of any other Love than her's, she used all her Softness to comfort me, while she tenderly grieved for my Misfortune and her own. Thus was I cured of my Relapse, and in a few Days, restored to my Peace of Mind, ceasing to envy Lord *Dorchester* his divine *Sacharissa*, and happy in my lovely and tender *Amoret*.[1] Her Father declared he could refuse me nothing, but advised us not to marry; however, finding us resolved he consented. I then gave them all an exact Account of my Circumstances, which you may imagine did not abate the Satisfaction then reigning in the Family. I remained with them at their Country House till two Days ago, that I ventured to come and congratulate you and Lord *Dorchester* on your Union. You may imagine how much I was surprized to find it was not compleated, but could not forbear coming hither to introduce to you my *Fanny*, who made me the happiest of Men about a Week ago, by becoming my Wife. And now, Madam, like all other Romances, mine must end with Wedlock; but permit me to hope, we shall never be so much tired of each other, as you must be of us both in this long Story."

Sir *Charles* was much mistaken, for I was never less so. I was overjoyed at acquiring two amiable Friends, and at seeing him so happy. For once I reflected with Pleasure on the Inconstancy of Mankind, since it had been so fortunate to him. I ought not to confine the Happiness of it entirely to Sir *Charles*, as I have received so much from it myself; for the Friendship which has ever since subsisted

---

1   Alluding to Sacharissa, the heroine of several poems by Edmund Waller; and Amoret, "Of grace and beautie noble Paragone," in Edmund Spenser's *The Faerie Queene* (1590, 1596).

between me, Sir *Charles*, his Lady, and her amiable Family, I have always esteemed one of the most pleasing Circumstances of my Life.

CHAPTER L

I hope your Ladyship now thinks it Time after so long a Digression, to return to Lord *Dorchester*, for I should be sorry to carry you so tedious a Journey, without you undertook it willingly; and yet, having little to say of myself during this Interval, I am under a Necessity of doing it, lest I should seem to have put in Execution the Lover's Wish, and appear to have "annihilated both Space and Time to make two Lovers happy."[1] Lord *Dorchester* travelled most expeditiously to my Aunt's Cottage. He found her reclined on a Couch, the Serenity of her Countenance changed into the most dejected Air, and her fresh Complexion into a sickly pale. He came so gently to the Door, that she did not hear him till he was entering the Threshold. As soon as she saw him, she started up, and, with Eyes that shot forth Impatience and Anger, but not without a Mixture of Joy, cried out, "Where is my Child! Where is my *Ophelia*."

The Alteration Lord *Dorchester* perceived in her, awakened so severe a Sense of the Injury he had done her, that he was distressed and confounded, and could utter no more then "she is well; forgive me, Madam, forgive me!"

"Thank Heaven," cryed my Aunt, with Hands and Eyes lifted towards the Heaven she thanked, "my Child is well!" and then bursting into a Flood of Tears, sunk down on the Couch, where she remained sometime, not too much affected to utter now and then a grateful Ejaculation, which would force its Way in Spite of the Tears that almost suffocated her.

My Lord was too much moved to interrupt her till this painful Excess of Joy was abated, and then could do nothing but ask her Forgiveness for all the Uneasiness he must have given her, protesting his Desire of making her all possible Reparation. "As the first Proof of it," said she, "let me know whether you give me a Possibility of pardoning you, by having the least Title to it. Inform me of every Particular, since you robbed me of my dear Child, the Delight and only

---

1 Alluding to two lines quoted in *The Art of Sinking in Poetry* (1728), by Pope, Swift, et al., ch. xi:

    Ye Gods! annihilate but *Space* and *Time*,
    And make two Lovers happy.

  The original source has not been identified.

Support of my Life? But before you enter into a Detail which may take up Time, first tell me where she is? What is her Situation, and whether she still does Honour to the Care I took to instruct her in the Precepts of Religion and Virtue, that I may be better able to listen to the rest?"

In these Points, Lord *Dorchester* gave her full Satisfaction, and then proceeded to relate the whole in Order, only was at a Loss how I became acquainted with his Design. He endeavoured to excuse himself on Account of his Prejudices against Matrimony, and expatiated on his Objections to it, concluding, by telling her, that "his Love had conquered them all, and to be united to me was the Wish nearest his Heart; and that I had hitherto been inflexible, and, more merciless than Heaven, would not pardon the sincere Penitent." "You could not have said any Thing which could have given me so sincere a Pleasure" replied my Aunt, "since this proves my Neice's Principles to be such as I wish them. Heaven, indeed, forgives the sincere Penitent, but then the Heart is there laid open, and the Sincerity of it is well known. *Ophelia* cannot have the same Assurance of your's; even yourself cannot; we often mistake the Effects of disappointed Passion, for real Virtue. If the Innocence and unfeigned Piety of so fine a young Creature could not change your Heart, how can one suppose any thing else will have that Power. You tell me she loves you, therefore may be sure her Passions plead in your Favour, and could her Reason give a Sanction to them, she would concur with your Wishes. That it has Strength sufficient to conquer the Instigations of her Love, and the Persuasions of her Lover, raises her in my Esteem, and gives me a Pleasure that almost repays me for what I have suffered on her Account. Does not this noble Command over herself, this steady Adherence to every virtuous Principle," continued she, "make you blush at the Remembrance of your Design, to debase so much Excellence? A little Reflection, my Lord, will shew you, the false Principles on which you have founded your Objections to Matrimony. Are you of so perverse a Nature, that a Conformity to the Laws of God and Man, must rob Society of all its Charms? And must the Conversation of one who loves you, lose all its Merit, as soon as it can be enjoyed without a Crime? Surely no Man can be so abandoned as to own such depraved Sentiments! You are, it seems, disgusted with the Behaviour of many Wives; would you therefore to mend a Woman's Conduct, learn her to despise all Ties, human and divine? And to render her an amiable and valuable Companion, instruct her in Vice? Is that a Means of teaching her, to acquit herself of the Duties of Society, and the tenderer Obligations of more intimate Connexions. Another of your Arguments against Marriage is little better than a prose Paraphrase of,

> Love light as Air, at Sight of human Ties,
> Spreads its light Wings, and in a Moment flies.[1]

With all the abandoned Rhapsody of voluptuous Vice. You talk of Freedom and Equality, in a Situation which entirely abolishes both. What can render a Woman so much your Slave, as having given up her fair Fame, and *that sweet Peace that Goodness bosoms ever*,[2] to gratify your mean Passions? Where then is the Equality between you? You have in your Power every Pleasure but Self-Approbation, and, perhaps, the hardened do not want that, while the Woman has nothing left her but your Love, which it is more her Interest to keep, even by little despicable Arts, than it could be in any other Situation. As soon as Reason begins to return, in what Light do you imagine, she herself must see the Man who has robbed her of every Blessing in Life? Must she not grow uneasy under such Circumstances, and detest the ungenerous Mind that could draw her into an Action, whose Consequences were to her so grievous, and to him so trifling, that unless Honour makes him rather than desert the Woman he has ruined, endure the Effects of her afflicted Heart, and the Fretfulness which naturally arises from it, he is under no worldly Disadvantage."

Lord *Dorchester* listened with all the Humility of a School-boy to his Monitor,[3] and gave her no Interruption but, with a doleful Face, and a simple Sheepishness that he never felt before, cried now and then, "very true, Madam, right, Madam, to be sure, Madam," and such like Sentences of mild and bashful Approbation; till my Aunt thought it cruel to humble him any longer, into such a sneaking repentant Boy. When she ended her Sermon, he assured her, that he was perfectly convinced of the Truth of all she had said, and protested, with an Air of Sincerity that almost convinced her, that "if he might have the free Choice, whether he should have her Neice for his Wife or Mistress, he should not hesitate a Moment, but prefer

---

1 Pope, *Eloisa to Abelard* (1717) ll. 75-6:
    Love, free as air, at sight of human ties,
    Spreads his light wings, and in a moment flies.
2 Milton, *Comus* (1634) l. 368: "And the sweet peace that goodness bosoms ever."
3 A senior pupil in a school, assigned to keep order.

that State which should secure her from the Censure of the World, and the Reproaches of her own Conscience." He abjured his past Errors, shewed the Fallacies which had given Rise to them, and confuted his own Arguments so much more forcibly than my Aunt could do, that she was touched with his Candour, and grieved for the pernicious Education and Examples, which had created any Blemishes in a Mind that seemed naturally virtuous and upright. When he had succeeded thus far, it was not very difficult to move a Heart by Nature tender, and softened by Affliction. The Excess of his Grief excited her Compassion, and Pity had some Share in making her promise to accompany him, though when she did it, she imagined her only Motive was the desire of seeing me. During their Journey, his Distress prevailed on her to undertake to obtain his Forgiveness. He did not doubt, but my Regard for her, and the high Opinion I had both of her Judgment and Principles, would make me submit to her Persuasions, especially as he was too sensible they corresponded with the secret, though suppressed Wishes of my Heart. When they arrived in *London*, I had, according to the Plan I had formed, left my Lodging, and to save my kind Landlady the Pain of telling a Falshood, did not acquaint her with the Place which I intended for my Asylum. Mr. *South*, to avoid being importuned to discover my Abode, changed his Habitation likewise, and chose one whom he could trust, to watch Lord *Dorchester's* coming to Town. His Spy performed his Office so well, that he heard it the Night of his Arrival, and was told by him, that he saw my Lord hand a Lady out of his Chariot.

Mr. *South* asked me, "if I did not imagine from this, my Lord had succeeded, and, in Reality, brought up my Aunt?" I could not believe, there was a Possibility of her giving such a Sanction to his past Conduct; however, I wished to be entirely certain: I dared not, indeed, consent that Mr. *South* should venture to Lord *Dorchester's*, lest by watching him, my Retreat might be discovered as it was before, but told him, that as they would naturally go to my old Lodgings, if my Lord had really prevailed on her to accompany him, we might gain some Intelligence from thence. Mr. *South* went thither accordingly the next Morning, and learnt, that, "Lord *Dorchester* and a Lady, whom they found by their Discourse, was my Aunt, came there as soon as they entered *London*, and asking for me, were under the greatest consternation at hearing I was gone from thence." The good Woman told them my Motive, but, at the same Time assured them, she knew not to what Place I was removed. Upon this Information, they went away much disappointed, after having promised her any Reward if she could contrive a Means of finding me out. She told them, "she wanted no other Inducement to do that, than the Pleasure I should receive from seeing an Aunt, I seemed to love so tenderly."

As I was at a very great Distance from my old Lodgings, Mr. *South* thought that to go back to me, would be robbing me of some Hours of Joy, and therefore instead of returning, went to Lord *Dorchester*, where he found his Lordship and my Aunt, concerting Measures for finding me. The Sight of him was most welcome to the former; with Delight he received him, and intreated him, "to inform an anxious Parent and the still tenderer Anxiety of a Lover, where I was?"

As this was the Intent of Mr. *South's* Visit, he immediately complied, and offered them to guide them to me. The Equipage was sent for, and stopped at my Door, sometime after my Impatience for the Account I expected Mr. *South* to bring, had fixed me to the Window, in Hopes of seeing him arrive.

At the sight of my Aunt, I ran to meet her; and we received each other with an Embrace from which the Spectators thought we could never be disengaged. I had already felt how much the Imagination falls short of the Reality in Sorrow, I now found it as poor a Mirror of our Joy. The Extacy I was in, at seeing one so inexpressibly dear to me, far exceeded the Force of Fancy, and a long Time passed in rejoicing at the Felicity we felt, before I took Notice of the Person who accompanied my Aunt.

My Lord looked on me with Tenderness and Grief, but with an anxious Timerousness that rendered him silent. My Aunt observing it, as soon as we could think of any Thing, but the Joy of meeting, told me, "she had undertaken to plead, what I should think a bad Cause, unless I would allow Repentance washed away Sin." She then proceeded to say, "she thought Lord *Dorchester* had suffered so much he deserved to be forgiven." I objected all I had before said to myself and others on the Occasion. I arraigned his Principles and Conduct with more Severity, I believe, for finding he had an Advocate, for I felt a Satisfaction in hearing him a little excused. My Aunt's Arguments were much the same with Miss *Baden's*, and would not have proved more efficacious, had it not been easier to influence my Heart, than to convince my Reason. Her Opinion gave a Sanction for my yielding; I could call my Weakness obedient; an Opportunity of so agreeably deceiving myself, staggered my Resolution, and I began to listen with Pleasure to the Apology my Aunt made for him.

As soon as Lord *Dorchester* had perceived me wavering between Reason and Love, to strengthen the Party of the latter, he attacked me with the most persuasive Importunity. Though my Heart felt every Syllable he uttered, yet my Mind was too much agitated to suffer my Memory to retain what he said, all I know is, that every Word, every Look, every Action of his, spoke too much to be expressed by any other. Such powerful Eloquence was not to be for ever resisted; unable to bear a longer Continuance of the Scene, I cried out, "you have conquered all my Resolutions, dispose of the Remainder of my Life as you please, my Happiness is in your Hands, I may repent, but I find, I must comply!"

Lord *Dorchester's* excessive Joy made me feel that Pleasure in my Consent, which Reason had denied me. My Felicity was perfect in seeing I had made him happy; I was insensible to any Dangers, with which my Peace was threatened by his Principles, while I had the infinite Satisfaction of imparting Happiness to one that was dearer to me than myself; I felt I was unworthy of a Thought, mine were all engrossed by him, every other Object seemed beneath my Care, and if he was happy, I believed I must be blessed.

As soon as his Lordship's Extasies were a little over, my Aunt turned toward him and said, "My Lord, I have done all you asked of me; I have suffered Compassion and that weak Sympathy, which I believe all feel for the Pains of Lovers, who have themselves known the Pangs of Love, to conquer my Opinion. I have persuaded the only Joy of my Heart, and Blessing of my Age, to an Union with a Man, whose Principles I always looked upon as an infallible Source of Unhappiness to the Woman whose Fate must depend upon them. I never saw any Thing but Repentance succeed a Marriage with a Rake, and yet Compassion for you, and, indeed, for my Niece, whose Fondness for you is but too visible, through all the Resolution she has assumed, has made me plead your Cause, and prevail in it. I feared for her, the Grief which would have succeeded the sharper Pains of Separation. I, who have felt it, know how hardly Life is supported under a Load of Sorrow. I pitied you for having a worthy Mind so corrupted. Can you do less, my Lord, than reward *Ophelia's* Love and my Compassion, by preserving the Principles you now profess, and by keeping the strictest Guard over yourself, lest you should again deviate from the Path of Virtue? I know you are not absolutely a Rake, and therein I place my Hopes."

Your Ladyship may imagine Lord *Dorchester*, was not sparing of his Promises. He defended himself from the Imputation of a Rake, though he confessed, his Principles had been very defective, and gave her every Assurance that could make her easy; and what is more extraordinary, he fulfilled them all, and rendered the Rest of our

Lives a Scene of Bliss; though I confess, it was not immediately I could depend on my own Happiness. I feared Reverses, which would be more severely felt for the Felicity I enjoyed. But Time banished my Apprehensions, and taught me, that a Mind naturally good, may be clouded for a Time, but will recover its original Lustre, and shake off the bad Influence of vicious Examples, and the erroneous Opinions of the fashionable World, if it has the good Fortune to suffer sufficiently by them. But as that does not happen so often as one could wish, for the Reformation of Mankind, and it is difficult to know when a Person has been sufficiently punished to effect their Amendment; mine was a dangerous Trial, and, I think, my Imprudence in making it, deserved a Punishment rather than a Reward; which has increased my Gratitude to Heaven for a State of Happiness I by no Means merited.

Lord *Dorchester* to gratify himself in his darling Pleasure of doing Good, procured a very considerable Preferment for Mr. *South*, and behaved with the utmost Generosity to my Aunt; he settled a very handsome Income on her, and to gratify both her and me, made such Additions to her little Cottage, as gave us the Power of accompanying her thither, where we spent three Months in every Year, which, in the Opinion of us all, was the Time when we enjoyed the most perfect Happiness, as we were there free from Interruptions.

Lord *Dorchester* was very desirous of knowing how I became acquainted with his Designs on me; but I made his giving a solemn Promise never to ask any Questions concerning it, one of the Conditions of our Marriage. I feared his Resentment against Lord *Larborough*, had he been acquainted with the Part he acted, and should have been very sorry, if Lord *Larborough* had suffered by making a Discovery that was so fortunate for me; besides that Lord *Dorchester* might have been exposed to his Share of Danger, had a Quarrel ensued. Lord *Larborough* was, I believe, under no small Apprehensions on finding what Turn the Affair had taken, but I seized the first Opportunity of making him easy, by giving my Word, that, "I would conceal every Thing he had done in Consideration of the Obligation he thereby conferred on me, and that he might rest in perfect Security in that Particular."

He returned me many Thanks, assuring me that, "he would ever gratefully acknowledge it; and, to prevent all Possibility of giving me any future Offence by a Passion he was unable to stifle, he would, by Degrees, break off his Intimacy with my Lord, and avoid me as much as he could." This Resolution he steadily executed, and before he died, which was two Years after my Marriage, he had almost entirely dropped our Acquaintance. After his Death, as no Danger could arise from it, I acquainted my Lord, with what he had too strict a Regard to his Promise to have asked of me, telling him all that passed between Lord *Larborough* and myself, which he said, "rendered his Lordship rather the Object of his Gratitude, than of his Anger, since the happy Effects of what he had done, excused the Intention."

Having obeyed your Ladyship's Commands, I shall now lay aside my Pen, without making any Apology for being so circumstantial, since Obedience to your Orders made me so; but shall grieve in Silence, that it was not in my Power to render this little Work more worthy of her who is to honour it with a Perusal. If I have in some Places repeated Compliments, which lay me under an Imputation of Vanity, I hope you will consider it as the unavoidable Consequence of telling one's own Story with the Sincerity you required; and as a necessary Thing, in order to keep up in my Reader such an Idea of my Person, as may represent me more worthy of her Attention, which you might have thought thrown away on a Dowdy,[1] and deprived me of the Honour of subscribing myself,

Your Ladyship's
Most obedient,
Humble Servant,

OPHELIA DORCHESTER.[2]

---

1 A shabbily dressed woman.
2 The final word of the novel emphasizes the heroine's change in status. As the wife of a peer, Ophelia uses the signature Ophelia Dorchester; she would be addressed, or referred to, as Lady Dorchester. Fielding does not reveal Lord Dorchester's rank in the peerage. He cannot be a duke, since dukes are always so described, but could be any one of the four lower grades: marquess, earl, viscount, or baron.

Appendix A: Contemporary Reviews

[Shortly after its first publication in March 1760, *Ophelia* received short reviews in *The Monthly Review*, 22 (April): 328 and *The Critical Review*, 9 (April): 318, and a one-line notice in *The British Magazine*, 1 (April): 140. *The Monthly* and *The Critical Reviews* were the two leading literary magazines of the day. *The British Magazine*, newly founded by Tobias Smollett in January 1760, gave most novels the same brief attention that it gave *Ophelia*. All three reviews were published anonymously, and the identity of the reviewers has not been determined.]

1. *The Monthly Review* (April 1760)

In an Advertisement prefixed to this work, we are told, the Editor was obliged to Fortune for the manuscript of this History; which, it is hinted, was unknowingly purchased in an old buroe. I have not been able, continues the Advertiser, by any enquiry, to find out the Author, or the Lady to whom it is addressed; but I hope I shall not give offence to either of them by the publication; for if the story be fictitious, in all probability it must have been designed for the press; as it is unlikely any one should put their invention on so laborious a task, merely for their own amusement; and if the story be real, it is pity adventures so new and entertaining, should be buried in oblivion; especially, when they and the reflections scattered throughout the book, are as well calculated for instruction as amusement.

Now, whether the history be true or false, if it be fact that Fortune did thus put the Editor in possession of the copy, it matters, in our opinion, very little, whether the Author, or the Lady, be offended, if the public in general are pleased or instructed, by its publication. But as it does not follow, that every performance which is designed for the press, is worth printing; so, for any great instruction or amusement a Reader of taste and discernment will meet with in the perusal, the manuscript might as well have still remained in the buroe: neither do we think that a more lumping pennyworth, because this happened to be thrown into the bargain. We do not mean, however, to cast a too rigid censure on the taste and judgment of the ingenious Editor; whom the singularity of the accident might, very possibly, not a little influence to partiality, in favor of this literary Foundling.

2. *The Critical Review* (April 1760)

The author of this performance would seem to have *the Female Quixote* in view;[1] but the character of Ophelia is supported with less humour. The novel, however, preserves that delicacy peculiar to female writers; and we may venture to say it affords as much entertainment, and harmless recreation, as most productions of this kind.

3. *The British Magazine* (April 1760)

Delicate, natural, and tolerably entertaining.

---

1   Charlotte Lennox's *The Female Quixote* had been published in 1752. For the links between it and *Ophelia*, see Introduction, above, 21.

Appendix B: Material added to the Dublin Edition (1763)

[In 1763, the prominent Dublin bookseller James Hoey, Jr., published a new edition of *Ophelia*. This edition, published at two shillings, 8.5 pence for two volumes bound together, or two shillings, twopence sewn,[1] offered a large saving on the price of the London edition, six shillings. It was, moreover, described on the title-page as "the second edition, with additions." Such a claim might be taken as a promotional device to attract purchasers. In this case, however, Hoey was as good as his word: the Dublin edition contains the passage below, inserted near the end of chapter two and more than doubling that chapter in length. There is no evidence to suggest that Fielding was in any way responsible for the new material, or even that she was aware of its existence. The names of characters, printed in capitals in the Dublin edition, are printed in conventional fashion in the present transcription.

The Dublin edition is extremely rare: ESTC lists copies only at the British Library and the National Library of Ireland, Dublin.[2] The British Library copy has been microfilmed for Research Publications, *The Eighteenth Century*, reel 5344, no. 1. Still rarer is an earlier Dublin edition, published by James Hoey, Jr., in 1760, without the additional material: ESTC lists a single copy only, at Trinity College Library, Dublin.]

My aunt would frequently beguile the time, with reciting the history of some of her intimates in the earlier part of her life: one of her narrations, in particular, made a strong impression on my memory by the entertainment I received from it; and, as the story may afford your ladiship the like amusement, I shall insert it just as my aunt, who was well acquainted with the parties, related it to me.

---

1   See James Raven, *British Fiction 1750-1770: A Chronological Check-List of Prose Fiction Printed in Britain and Ireland* (Newark: U of Delaware P, 1987) 212. The information on the price of the Dublin edition comes from an advertisement for the book in another of Hoey's publications, the 1763 Dublin edition of Margaret and Susannah Minifie's *The Histories of Lady Frances S——, and Lady Caroline S——*.

2   Raven (212) also lists a copy supposedly at the University of Illinois, Urbana, but this is an error.

"Euclio who at the age of fifty, was as remarkable for his avarice, as others are at eighty, was equally distinguished for the most steady adherence to all his resolutions, and having determined to marry his son Pamphilus to Melissa, a young lady of great fortune, and by no means defective in personal accomplishments: Pamphilus, who knew his father's temper, thought himself reduced to the sad alternative, of either being obliged to marry against his inclinations, or being dis-inherited by a tyrannical parent. Melissa indeed had merit sufficient to make any other man happy; but the affections of Pamphilus were pre-engaged; the beauteous Sophia had entirely captivated his heart, and though greatly superior in person and qualifications to Melissa, had one defect, for which he knew no merit could compensate in the opinion of his father, who had often declared that he looked upon marriages for love, as the strongest examples of the folly and indiscretion of youth. So ardent was the love of Pamphilus, that he preferred the interest of his passion to every other consideration, and immediately married Sophia in private; resolving to defer his mar-riage with Melissa upon various pretexts; and in the mean time, endeavour to procure from his father, by stratagem, that consent which he could not hope for from his parental indulgence. Accident made the first care superfluous; Melissa, being at that time obliged to go into a distant country,[1] to visit her grandmother, who had been given over by the physicians. The young gentleman therefore deter-mining to avail himself of this favourable opportunity, had recourse to the advice of Eudoxus, who, though a batchelor, and a man of a philosophical disposition, had often shewn himself able to direct both husbands and lovers. He had been all along privy to the passion of Pamphilus, whose father had a great esteem for him, for Eudoxus was of such a disposition, that his conversation appeared equally engaging to persons of the most opposite tempers, and his acquain-tance was equally sought after by all. Pamphilus and Eudoxus in con-cert, soon formed a stratagem, which tho' not very promising in appearance, proved in the end productive of the desired effect. It was agreed that Eudoxus should present Sophia, to Euclio, as the daugh-ter of an intimate friend of his who had lately been obliged by an unfortunate affair, to retire beyond sea, and had left her to his care, intreating him to do his best in order to procure her an asylum. The old gentleman readily granted his request, and Sophia was intro-duced to him by Eudoxus: no sooner did Euclio salute her, but the

---

1 E.g., a different part of the country, not another country.

awe with which she was struck, at seeing her husband's father, whose consent to their marriage she almost despaired of obtaining, made her fall into a swoon, from whence being recovered by the care of Euclio, Eudoxus, Pamphilus, and her maid Estiphania, who all exerted themselves with equal concern in her behalf; the old gentleman seeming to discover some curiosity, to know what this accident could be owing to; Estiphania said archly, Lord sir, do you think any one could embrace such a gentleman as you without emotion? This pleasantry however was justly applied; for it appeared soon after, that Euclio, at fifty, was coxcomb enough to think a fine woman susceptible of a passion for him. The old gentleman, was indeed capable even then of catching the amorous flame, and soon so plainly discovered his inclination for Sophia by his behaviour, that the following verse of Tasso, may be properly applied to him,

> *Concerto hor' pargoleggia, a vecchio amante.*
> Canto 2.
> *Turns boy, and plays the lover when in years.*[1]

This was not taken notice of by Sophia, whose respectful behaviour was by Euclio looked upon as an indication of love; Pamphilus and his friend, were overjoyed at perceiving this, thinking that it could not fail of proving highly advantageous to their scheme.

"It seems indeed highly probable, that it owed its success to this very circumstance; Euclio having at length so far yielded to his passion, as to discover to Eudoxus his design of proposing marriage to Sophia: the former told the old gentleman, that he did not doubt, but the father of Sophia would be overjoyed that so advantageous a match should offer for his daughter; but seemed to insinuate that the disparity of age might possibly render the young lady averse to it. Seeing, however, that Euclio, like the Moor of *Venice*,[2] had too good

---

1 Torquato Tasso, *Jerusalem Delivered* (1575) V.lxxiii:

   Vincilao, che si grave e saggio avante,
   Canuto hor pargoleggia, e vecchio amante

   [Vincilao who, previously so solemn and wise
   white-haired now, plays the child and the old lover]

   Canto five, in which the quotation appears, is misnumbered "2" in the Dublin edition.

2 Shakespeare's Othello; the full title of the play is *Othello, the Moor of Venice.*

an opinion of himself, to draw from his own weak merits, the smallest fear or doubt concerning the lady's affection; he promised to sound her, and prepare her for an interview with him. He accordingly made a full discovery to Sophia, in the presence of Pamphilus, of all that had passed between Euclio and him; and it was agreed by all three, that there could not be a properer time for Sophia to confess the whole truth, to ask his pardon, and beg to be received into favour by him. It was however judged proper, that Eudoxus should continue to appear ignorant of Sophia's marriage with Pamphilus, and should affect surprise, when made acquainted with it. These preliminaries being adjusted, Estiphania was dispatched to the old gentleman to inform him, that her mistress had something of importance to impart to him; Eudoxus having just before returned, and given him to understand, that he had sought for Sophia every where, and not being able to find her, concluded that she was gone out to pay a visit. Euclio having just after heard the message delivered by Estiphania, answered in a transport of joy, that he would be proud of the honour of receiving her mistress's commands. The interview was not long delayed; an interview which to both parties appeared to be of equal importance; and was in both, attended by the throbbings of hope and fear, though the flutter in old Euclio's breast, seemed to spring chiefly from the palpitations of hope, that in the breast of Sophia from the bodings of fear. The latter began the conversation, and said with a low and interrupted voice of timidity,—Sir, I hope you will hear me with indulgence;—to which Euclio immediately replied, with a vivacity not usual in him,—Madam, you can say nothing that will not be highly acceptable to me.—I never, Sir, continued she, aspired to the honour of being admitted into your family; and if the choice—Here, Euclio thinking that she dived into his design, answered briskly—Madam, it is my family, that will be honoured by your alliance, which would reflect a lustre upon the noblest family in the land. Sophia not yet sufficiently encouraged, began to lament that the smallness of her fortune, seemed to lay an obstacle in the way of her happiness; whereupon Euclio, whose sordid avarice had been succeeded by the most gallant sentiments; assured her in the warmest terms, that he thought beauty and worth more than sufficient to attone for the want of fortune, especially as his estate was an ample provision for both. He continued to discant with so much earnestness, upon the little weight that should be laid upon wealth in love-affairs, that Sophia thought this the favourable moment to proceed to the eclaircissement; and throwing herself at Euclio's feet, owned her marriage with his son, and in the most pathetic terms implored his favour and forgiveness. So great was the surprize of Euclio, that he never once interrupted her, but stood motionless as a statue, until she had made an end of speaking; and then paused for some time, with the utmost perplexity visible in his countenance. At length, he said with some confusion, Madam, I do not complain of you, but the disobedience of my son deserves the severest punishment. Sophia hereupon, pleaded his cause with the most tender eloquence, and the old man, seemed at last to begin to relent. When men are once prepossessed in favour of a person, they seldom immediately pass to the extreme of hatred; in like manner as when they have once conceived a resentment, though upon unjustifiable grounds they are not often suddenly reconciled. Euclio was so far affected by the remonstrances of Sophia, that he yielded in some measure, and said, Madam, if I forgive Pamphilus, it will be entirely upon your account, and not upon his. Pamphilus, who from the anti-chamber, had heard all that had been said, entered just at that juncture, and throwing himself at his father's feet, implored his blessing and forgiveness. Sophia in the same posture, seconded his entreaties; the old man, whose passions had been thus gradually wrought to the highest pitch, burst into tears, and giving them his blessing, wished heartily that their union might prove lasting and happy. Having afterwards informed Eudoxus of what had passed, the latter affected great surprise, but at the same time acknowledged that the match between Pamphilus and Sophia, was much more suitable on account of the equality of their age; this Euclio readily acknowledged, and having by paying his addresses to Sophia, so far divested himself of his former character as to lose sight of his avarice; he now totally dropt it, by acknowledging he had been once in the wrong. Melissa, who soon after returned from the country with her father, received information of what had happened, and was greatly rejoiced at it, as her heart was pre-engaged, when her father would have had her give her hand to Pamphilus. Thus was a double tyranny avoided, and all parties made happy by an unexpected event."

Appendix C: Richard Corbould's Illustrations to the Novelist's Magazine Edition (1785)

[The *Novelist's Magazine*, edited by James Harrison, was founded in 1779 and appeared weekly in sixpenny instalments until its demise in 1789. It reprinted prose fiction, making popular English novels and novels in English translation widely available in cheap but attractive form. Among over sixty works that it reprinted (almost all from before the 1770s because of copyright restrictions) were two novels by Sarah Fielding: *The Adventures of David Simple* in volume nine (1782) and *The History of Ophelia* in volume nineteen (1785).[1]

Each novel published in the *Novelist's Magazine* was embellished with original engravings by prominent illustrators, a feature that helped to increase the magazine's sales. Among the most prolific of these book illustrators was Richard Corbould (1757-1831), who designed the engravings for *Ophelia*.[2] Other novels that Corbould illustrated for the *Novelist's Magazine* include Francis Coventry's *Pompey the Little* and Smollett's *History and Adventures of an Atom*. Later, for *Cooke's Pocket Edition of Select Novels* (1797-99), he contributed illustrations for novels by Defoe, Henry Fielding, Charlotte Lennox, Smollett, Sterne, and Goldsmith, and, in subsequent series by Cooke, Swift's *Gulliver's Travels* and Richardson's *Pamela*.

Corbould's designs for *Ophelia*, each executed by a different engraver, illustrate three of the novel's four books (all except book two). Each plate consists of an illustration framed by an ornamental border, with dates ranging from 20 August to 3 September 1785. As

---

1   For accounts of the complex history of the *Novelist's Magazine*, see Robert D. Mayo, *The English Novel in the Magazines, 1740-1815* (Evanston, Ill.: Northwestern UP, 1962) 363-7; G.E. Bentley, Jr., *Blake Books* (Oxford: Clarendon, 1977) 597-602; and Carol de Saint Victor, "The *Novelist's Magazine*," *British Literary Magazines: The Augustan Age and the Age of Johnson*, ed. Alvin Sullivan (Westport, Conn.: Greenwood P, 1983) 261-3.

2   For Corbould and his engravers in the *Novelist's Magazine*, see Hans Hammelmann, *Book Illustrators in Eighteenth-Century England*, ed. T.S.R. Boase (New Haven: Yale UP, 1975) 27.

was standard in the *Novelist's Magazine*, no titles or captions were provided.

The first of Corbould's designs, engraved by James Heath, is a frontispiece. It illustrates the scene in which Ophelia is seated "at the Bottom of an old Yew Tree," while Mrs. Herner and the clergyman Mr. South are seated on "a Bench full in my View" (187). The figure of Mrs. Herner, who "had pulled up her Head till she was as upright as a May-pole," is suitably stiff, but the building portrayed in the background seems in much better repair than the "Castle ... tottering with Age" (170) depicted in the novel. Corbould's second design, engraved by Anthony Walker, illustrates the moment when Lord Dorchester meets Ophelia, together with her aunt, for the first time (46). Corbould follows Fielding's text in depicting a full moon shining on the brook, as well as on Lord Dorchester, illuminating his face. The words spoken by Lord Dorchester at this critical moment, "stay! beauteous Angel, stay," can also be readily envisaged. Corbould's final design, engraved by Angus, shows Ophelia emerging from a faint. She is in Lord Dorchester's arms, "while he was holding a Bottle for me to smell to," with her maid also coming to her aid (239). The characters here are somewhat wooden: Lord Dorchester, in particular, seems too composed, and insufficiently affected by Ophelia's plight.

The *Novelist's Magazine* was immensely successful, selling 12,000 copies of each weekly number at the height of its popularity. Volume nineteen, in which *Ophelia* was published, also contains Smollett's *Humphry Clinker*, with illustrations by Edward Francesco Burney, and Coventry's *Pompey the Little*, with illustrations by Corbould. Two recent Fielding critics have reproduced Corbould's *Ophelia* illustrations: Linda Bree uses his frontispiece design of the heroine and the ruined castle as the frontispiece to her monograph, while Moira Dearnley illustrates her chapter on the novel with Corbould's design of the initial meeting between Lord Dorchester, Ophelia and her aunt.[1] That Dearnley also cites the text of the *Novelist's Magazine* edition points to the need for a modern edition of *Ophelia*.]

---

1 Linda Bree, *Sarah Fielding* (New York: Macmillan, 1996) frontispiece; Moira Dearnley, *Distant Fields: Eighteenth-Century Fictions of Wales* (Cardiff: U of Wales P, 2001) 73.

Figure 1. Ophelia observing Mrs. Herner and Mr. South, in front of the ruined castle (page 187); engraving by James Heath. Courtesy of McMaster University Library.

Figure 2. Lord Dorchester, accompanied by his servant, encountering Ophelia and her aunt, in the grounds of their cottage in Wales (page 46); engraving by Anthony Walker. Courtesy of McMaster University Library.

Figure 3. Lord Dorchester supporting Ophelia, who has fainted, while her maid assists (page 239); engraving by Angus. Courtesy of McMaster University Library.

Appendix D: A Victorian Critic of Ophelia: Clementina Black's Essay of 1888

[In 1888, Clementina Black published an essay entitled "Sarah Fielding" in the *Gentleman's Magazine* 265, 485-92. In addition to *The Adventures of David Simple* (1744), which had always been Fielding's best-known novel, she discusses *Familiar Letters Between the Characters of David Simple* (1747) and *Ophelia*: her analysis of *Ophelia* was the first to appear after the magazine reviews of 1760. As Linda Bree remarks, Black's revisionist essay "begins to establish Fielding's place in a specifically feminine tradition of writing by pointing out the influence of *Ophelia* on *Evelina*."[1]]

Oblivion has odd caprices, and in literature, as in the world at large, we are sometimes at a loss when we try to discern the definite unfitness which has interfered with survival. Sarah Fielding, praised—and justly praised—in her lifetime by Richardson on the one hand, and by her brother, Henry Fielding, on the other, is probably not known at this moment to a dozen readers. She has become one of those writers whose good things any man may steal without fear of detection. Yet the good things are plentiful, and any leisurely reader may find it very much worth his while to bestow a few hours upon "David Simple" or "Ophelia," or even the "Familiar Letters." Leisurely, however, he must be; and he will do well to bear in mind the observation made by Dr. Johnson upon a greater than Sarah Fielding. "Why sir," said the Doctor, "if you were to read Richardson for the story your impatience would be so much fretted that you would hang yourself."[2] Miss Fielding is not, indeed, as long-winded as her admired friend Richardson (it is only the immortals who can be that, and survive), but she has the comfortable prolixity of her day, and is by no means in a hurry to get on to the next incident. It is for the sprightly narrative, the happy phrase, the ironical turn of mind, that these volumes are worth reading.

[*A paragraph on Fielding's life and two pages on* David Simple *follow.*]

---

1   Linda Bree, *Sarah Fielding* (New York: Macmillan, 1996) 147.
2   See James Boswell, *Life of Johnson*, ed. George Birkbeck Hill, rev. L.F. Powell (Oxford: Clarendon, 1934-50) II. 175.

The "History of Ophelia" lacks the sprightly charm, the cheerful optimism of "David Simple." The scenes are darker; the central interest more serious and more painful, and the close by no means so unhesitatingly joyful. Yet, in some points the second novel is at least the equal of the first. The sketches of character are as lively as ever, the epigrams are perhaps even more numerous, and the narrative is comparatively free from intrusive Cervantic episodes. It is the heroine this time whose innocence and sincerity are contrasted with the falsehoods of a corrupt society. The story is that of Lovelace and Clarissa over again; but, with a heroine unsuspicious of her danger, and with a hero less practised in wickedness, and capable of being turned from his design. Ophelia has been brought up by an aunt in absolute seclusion, and has lived without any other companion in simplicity and complete ignorance of evil. A young nobleman, Lord Dorchester, accidentally discovers their cottage, and shortly afterwards carries off Ophelia. He takes her to London, where she passes for his ward, and introduces her to a certain Lady Palestine, a relation of his, at whose house she begins to see "the polite world." Her determined sincerity exposes her to a good deal of misconstruction, but she perseveres. "I have learnt," she says, for the story is written in the first person, "that nothing is a crime in polite circles but poverty and prudence. A person who cannot contribute to the follies of others may perhaps be pardoned if she only complies with them; but if she attempts to be rational she must not hope for forgiveness."[1] Her open friendliness towards one Sir Charles Goodall[2] excites Lord Dorchester's jealousy; and, after writing her an angry letter in which he renounces her for ever, he goes away. Ophelia, amazed and distressed beyond measure, falls ill, and only recovers her health on his return. But jealousy still appears to her an inexplicable sentiment, the rather that: "By what I could learn, the general practice of deceit makes people appear so much better at first than on a long acquaintance they prove to be, that to continue to love them rather than to cease to do so should be termed inconstancy."

The ill-starred Ophelia is presently abducted a second time—on this occasion by a jealous rival—and imprisoned in an old castle in the country where she sees only a few rustic squires and their wives. The brief sketch of "country society" is of a kind to make the gloomiest pessimist rejoice in having at least been born out of reach of the eighteenth-century squirearchy. It represents a group among whom Squire Western[3]

---

1 See above, 109.
2 I.e., Sir Charles Lisdale; Black's error.
3 The notably boorish and uncouth father of Sophia, the heroine of Henry Fielding's *Tom Jones* (1749).

would have been quite in keeping. Ophelia escapes by the assistance of a clergyman and soon afterwards is taken by Lady Palestine to Tunbridge Wells. Her ignorance of etiquette permitting her to dance with Lord Dorchester after refusing another partner, leads to impertinent speeches and a duel. Readers of "Evelina" will remember in that novel a precisely similar incident.[1] There is indeed a curious parallelism throughout the two stories; a likeness in unlikeness, which deserves a moment's consideration. In each case a simple-minded heroine is brought suddenly from a country seclusion into "society;" in each she passes from place to place, and from one set of company to another; and in each she is the recorder and censurer. Sentences might sometimes be transferred from one novel to the other without any perceptible jar. The description, for instance, of a lady who "lived in a perfect convulsion of civility" would come as naturally from Evelina as from Ophelia. Yet the essential spirit of each author differs completely from that of the other. Miss Fielding is a moralist, while Miss Burney is content to be a satirist. "Evelina" is a comedy throughout; even the heroine excites our sympathy chiefly by her discomfiture in laughable situations. But "Ophelia" is nearer to being a tragedy; the distress of virtue and sincerity at the contact of vice and falsehood is not a comic theme; and it is only in accessory details that the ridiculous can find a place.

I have used the word "tragedy," but I do not mean that there is anything dramatic about the talent which "Ophelia" exhibits. On the contrary, it shows a lack of nearly all the specifically dramatic gifts. Feelings and motives are understood; Miss Fielding's admirers are not far wrong in praising her knowledge of the human heart; but there is little real display of character. Lord Dorchester, with his vacillations, his jealousy, his remorse, and his eventual reform, is the nearest of all her persons to living humanity; perhaps, indeed, we do at the end know him as well as Ophelia herself does. There is, however, one passage in which wounded affection and righteous indignation strike out a dramatic spark. It is the speech of Ophelia when he appeals to her afresh after she has found him out and left him. "That I love you," I replied, "I am much too well convinced by painful experience, but you have so forfeited my esteem that I cannot comply with your proposal. I could not be happy if I was married to you, consequently should not make you so. Your passion for me is the same as it was; all the difference is in the companions of it. While accompanied by hope, you know how little I was obliged

---

1 See Appendix G below.

to you for it; now despair has taken its place; it has blinded you, and I believe you think your affection all you say it is.... I have lost all my confidence in you, and detest the rest of your nation. I will go where I shall be excluded from mankind, where virtue makes every action open and intelligible; there I am capable of living happily without learning the arts that here hide every real thought. If this resolution is painful to you, make it likewise beneficial; trust me, so corrupt a people cannot be taught virtue but by suffering. Affliction will purify a heart perverted by education and custom; it takes off the varnish from glaring vices, and shows them in their own dark colours. If you really suffer, consider to what it is owing; learn to hate vice, which as certainly carries its punishment as virtue does its reward along with it. But why should I think you can suffer long enough to do good? Your heart is not made like mine, therefore I cannot judge of it."[1] That last outcry following upon the suppressed bitterness of the would-be unimpassioned moralising, strikes suddenly home with the quick stroke of genius. If Sarah Fielding had written many such pages as these her works would surely not have lain to-day labelled by every compiler of handbooks with the epitaph "forgotten."

At last, even Ophelia's aunt pleads the lover's cause, and to her Ophelia listens. "I arraigned his principles and conduct with more severity, I believe, for finding he had an advocate, for I felt a satisfaction in hearing him a little excused ... Her opinion gave a sanction to my yielding; I could call my weakness obedient." So she yields, and "Lord Dorchester's excessive joy made me feel that pleasure in my consent which reason had denied me." He on his part gave her aunt "every assurance that could make her easy, and, what is more extraordinary, he fulfilled them all, and rendered the rest of our lives a scene of bliss.... Mine was a dangerous trial, and I think my imprudence in making it deserved a punishment rather than a reward; which has increased my gratitude to Heaven for a state of happiness by no means merited."[2]

[*Two pages on* Familiar Letters Between the Characters of David Simple *conclude the essay.*]

---

1 See above, 257.
2 See above, 274, 275, 276.

Appendix E: Sarah Fielding's Remarks on Clarissa (1749)

[Samuel Richardson's great tragic novel, *Clarissa,* was first published in three instalments between December 1747 and December 1748. One month after the appearance of the final, three-volume instalment, in January 1749, Sarah Fielding published her *Remarks on Clarissa,* an imaginative fifty-page pamphlet written in the form of an epistolary exchange between two characters, Miss Gibson and Bellario. The concluding letter from Miss Gibson to Bellario is of particular relevance to *Ophelia.* Miss Gibson envisages an alternative to Lovelace: a reformed rake who could have won Clarissa's heart and secured her hand in marriage, just as Dorchester finally wins the heroine's consent in *Ophelia.* The text is taken from the Augustan Reprint Society facsimile edition, nos. 231-32, intro. Peter Sabor (Los Angeles: William Andrews Clark Memorial Library, 1985) 50-56.]

Miss GIBSON *to* BELLARIO.

SIR,

Your Good-nature in sending me your Thoughts on *Clarissa,* with a Design to give me Pleasure, I assure you is not thrown away; may you have equal Success in every generous Purpose that fills your Heart, and greater Happiness in this World, I am sure I cannot wish you.

Most truly, Sir, do you remark, that a Story told in this Manner can move but slowly, that the Characters can be seen only by such as attend strictly to the Whole; yet this Advantage the Author gains by writing in the present Tense, as he himself calls it, and in the first Person, that his Strokes penetrate immediately to the Heart, and we feel all the Distresses he paints; we not only weep for, but with *Clarissa,* and accompany her, step by step, through all her Distresses.

I see her from the Beginning, in her happy State, beloved by all around her, studying to deserve that Love; obedient to her Parents, dependant on their Will by her own voluntary Act, when her Grandfather had put it in her Power to be otherwise; respectful and tender to her Brother and Sister; firm in her Friendship to Miss *Howe*; grateful to good Mrs. *Norton,* who had carefully watched over her Infant Years, and delighted to form and instruct her Mind; kind to her Inferiors; beneficent to all the Poor, Miserable, and Indigent;

and above all, cultivating and cherishing in her Heart the true Spirit of Christianity, Meekness, and Resignation; watchful over her own Conduct, and charitable to the Failings of others; unwilling to condemn, and rejoicing in every Opportunity to praise. But as the Laws of God and Man have placed a Woman totally in the Power of her Husband, I believe it is utterly impossible for any young Woman, who has any Reflection, not to form in her Mind some kind of Picture of the Sort of Man in whose Power she would chuse to place herself. That *Clarissa* did so, I think, plainly appears, from her steady Resolution to refuse any Man she could not obey with the utmost Chearfulness; and to whose Will she could not submit without Reluctance. She would have had her Husband a Man on whose Principles she could entirely depend; one in whom she might have placed such a Confidence, that she might have spoke her very Thoughts aloud; one from whom she might have gained Instruction, and from whose Superiority of Understanding she would have been pleased to have taken the Rules of her own Actions. She desired no Reserves, no separate Interest from her Husband; had no Plots, no Machinations to succeed in, and therefore wanted not a Man who by artful Flattery she could have cajoled madly to have worship'd her; a kind Indulgence, in what was reasonable, was all her Desire, and that Indulgence to arise from her own Endeavour to deserve it, and not from any Blindness cast before her Husband's Eyes by dazzling Beauty, or cunning Dissimulation; but, from her Infancy, having the Example daily before her of her Mother's being tyrannized over, notwithstanding her great Humility and Meekness, perhaps tyrannized over for that very Humility and Meekness. She thought a single Life, in all Probability, would be for her the happiest; cherishing in her Heart that Characteristic of a noble Mind, especially in a Woman, of wishing, as Miss *Howe* says she did, to pass through Life unnoted.

In this state of mind did *Lovelace* first find *Clarissa*. She liked him; his Person and Conversation were agreeable, but the Libertinism of his Character terrified her; and her Disapprobation of him restrained her from throwing the Reins over the Neck of a Passion she thought might have hurried her into Ruin. But when by his Artifices, and the Cruelty of her Friends, she was driven into his Power, had he not, to use her own Words, treated her with an Insolence unbecoming a Man, and kept her very Soul in suspense; fawning at her Feet to marry him, whilst, in the same Instant, he tried to confuse her by a Behaviour that put it out of her Power to comply with him; there was nothing that she would not have done to oblige him. Then indeed she plainly saw that her Principles and his Profligacy, her Simplicity and his Cunning, were not made to be joined; and when she found such was the Man she liked best, no Wonder her Desire of a single Life should return. She saw, indeed, her own Superiority over *Lovelace*, but it was his Baseness that made her behold it. And here I must observe, that in the very same Breath in which she tells him, *Her Soul's above him*, she bids him *leave her*, that Thought more than any other makes her resolve, at all Events, to abandon him. Was this like exulting in her own Understanding, and proudly (as I have heard it said) wanting to dictate to the Man she intended for a Husband? Such a Woman, if I am not greatly mistaken, would not desire the Man to leave her because she saw her Soul was above him; but on the contrary, concealing from him, and disguising her Thoughts, would have set Art against Art, and been the more delighted to have drawn him in to have married her, that she might have deceived him, and enjoyed the Thoughts of her own Superiority for Life. As I remember, he never asks her fairly to marry him but once, and then she consents: But how different in every Action is she from the sly and artful Woman, who would have snatched at this Opportunity, and not have trusted him with a Moment's Delay, whilst *Clarissa*, being then ill, consents, with a Confidence that nothing but her Goodness and Simplicity could have had in such a Man.

Tho' *Clarissa* unfortunately met with *Lovelace*, yet I can imagine her with a Lover whose honest Heart, assimilating with hers, would have given her leave, as she herself wishes, to have shewn the Frankness of her Disposition, and to have openly avowed her Love. But *Lovelace*, by his own intriguing Spirit, made her Reserves, and then complained of them; and as she was engaged with such a Man, I think the Catastrophe's being what is called *Unhappy*, is but the natural Consequence of such an Engagement; tho', I confess, I was not displeased that the Report of this Catastrophe met with so many Objections, as it proved what an Impression the Author's favourite Character had made on those Minds which could not bear she should fall a Sacrifice to the Barbarity of her Persecutors. And I hope that now all the Readers of *Clarissa* are convinced how rightly the Author has judged in this Point. If the Story was not to have ended tragically, the grand Moral would have been lost, as well as that grand Picture, if I may call it so, of human Life, of a Man's giving up every thing that is valuable, only because every thing that is valuable is in his Power. *Lovelace* thought of the Substance, whilst that was yet to be persued; but once within reach of it, his plotting Head and roving Imagination would let him see only the Shadow; and once enter'd into the Pursuit, his Pride, the predominant Passion of his Soul, engaged him to fly after a visionary Gratification which his own wild Fancy had painted, till, like one following an *Ignis fatuus*[1] through By-Paths and crooked Roads, he lost himself in the Eagerness of his own Pursuit, and involved with him the innocent *Clarissa*, who, persecuted, misunderstood, envied, and evil-treated as she had been, by those from whom she had most Reason to hope Protection, I think could not find a better Close to her Misfortunes than a triumphant Death. Triumphant it may very well be called, when her Soul, fortified by a truly Christian Philosophy, melted and softened in the School of Affliction, had conquered every earthly Desire, baffled every uneasy Passion, lost every disturbing Fear, while nothing remained in her tender Bosom but a lively Hope of future Happiness. When her very Griefs were in a manner forgot, the Impression of them as faint and languid as a feverish Dream to one restored to Health, all calm and serene her Mind, forgiving and praying for her worst Enemies, she retired from all her Afflictions, to meet the Reward of her Christian Piety.

The Death of *Clarissa* is, I believe, the only Death of the Kind in any Story; and in her Character, the Author has thrown into Action (if I may be allowed the Expression) the true Christian Philosophy, shewn its Force to ennoble the human Mind, till it can look with Serenity on all human Misfortunes, and take from Death itself its gloomy Horrors. Never was any thing more judicious than the Author's bringing *Lovelace* as near as *Knight's-Bridge* at the Time of *Clarissa's* Death; for by that means he has in a manner contrived to place in one View before our Eyes the guilty Ravager of unprotected Innocence, the boasting Vaunter of his own useless Parts, in all the Horrors of mad Despair, whilst the injured Innocent, in a pious, in a divine Frame of Mind is peaceably breathing her Last. "Such a Smile! Such a charming Serenity" (says Mr *Belford*) "overspreading her sweet Face at the Instant, as seemed to manifest her eternal Happiness already begun."

Surely the Tears we shed for *Clarissa* in her last Hours, must be Tears of tender Joy! Whilst we seem to live, and daily converse with her through her last Stage, our Hearts are at once rejoiced and amended, are both soften'd and elevated, till our Sensations grow too strong for any Vent, but that of Tears; nor am I ashamed to confess,

---

1 A light flitting from place to place; figuratively, a delusive guiding principle or hope.

that Tears without Number have I shed, whilst Mr. *Belford* by his Relation has kept me (as I may say) with fixed Attention in her Apartment, and made me perfectly present at her noble exalted Behaviour; nor can I hardly refrain from crying out, "Farewell, my dear *Clarissa*! may every Friend I love in this World imitate you in their Lives, and thus joyfully quit all the Cares and Troubles that disturb this mortal Being!"

May *Clarissa*'s Memory be as triumphant as was her Death! May all the World, like *Lovelace*, bear Testimony to her Virtues, and acknowledge her Triumph!

I am, with many Thanks, Sir, for your most obliging Letter,

Your *most obedient*, &c.

HARRIOTE GIBSON.

Appendix F: From Françoise de Graffigny's Letters Written by a Peruvian Princess *(1748)*

[Françoise de Graffigny's only novel, *Lettres d'une Péruvienne*, was first published in Paris in 1747. An English translation of 1748, *Letters Written by a Peruvian Princess*, proved to be very popular: it was reprinted in Dublin in the same year, and further English editions appeared in 1749, 1753, and 1759.[1] Before writing *Ophelia,* Sarah Fielding could have read either the French original or any of these English editions. Of particular relevance to her novel are the central chapters in which the heroine, Zilia, who has been abducted from her Peruvian home, is brought by her admirer, Déterville, to Paris. In the three chapters (XIII, XVI-XVII) printed here, from the 1748 London edition, Zilia recounts to her beloved intended husband, Aza, her initial impressions of Paris, including visits to the theatre and the opera.]

LETTER XIII.

At last, my dear *Aza,* I am got into a city called *Paris:* Our journey is at an end, but, according to all appearances, so are not my troubles.

More attentive than ever, since my arrival here, to all that passes, my discoveries produce only torment, and presage nothing but misfortunes. I find thy idea in the least of my curious desires, but cannot meet with it in any of the objects that I see.

As well as I can judge by the time we spent in passing thro' this city, and by the great number of inhabitants with whom the streets are filled, it contains more people than could be got together in two or three of our countries.

I reflect on the wonders that have been told me of *Quito,*[2] and endeavour to find here some strokes of the picture which I conceive of that great city: But alas! what a difference?

---

1   See David Smith, "The Popularity of Mme de Graffigny's *Lettres d'une Péruvienne:* The Bibliographical Evidence," *Eighteenth-Century Fiction* 3 (1990): 1-20.

2   Formerly part of Peru, now the capital city of Ecuador.

This place contains bridges, rivers, trees, fields: it seems to be an universe, rather than a particular seat of habitation. I should endeavour in vain to give thee a just idea of the height of the houses. They are so prodigiously elevated, that it is more easy to believe nature produced them as they are, than to comprehend how men could build them.

Here it is that the family of the *Cacique*[1] resides. Their house is almost as magnificent as that of the Sun: the furniture and some parts of the walls are of gold, and the rest is adorned with a various mixture of the finest colours, which prettily enough represent the beauties of nature.

At my arrival, *Deterville* made me understand that he was conducting me to his mother's apartment. We found her reclined upon a bed of almost the same form with that of the *Incas*, and of the same metal.* After having held out her hand to the *Cacique*, who kissed it bowing almost to the ground, she embraced him; but with a kindness so cold, a joy so constrain'd, that, if previous information had not been given me, I should not have known the sentiments of nature in the caresses of this mother.

After a moment's conversation, the *Cacique* made me draw near. She cast on me a disdainful look, and, without answering what her son said to her, continued gravely to turn round her finger a thread, which hung to a small piece of gold.

Deterville left us to go and meet a stately bulky man, who had advanced some steps towards him. He embraced both him, and another woman who was employ'd in the same manner as the *Pallas*.[2]

As soon as the *Cacique* had appeared in the chamber, a young maiden, of about my age, ran to us, and followed him with a timid eagerness that seem'd remarkable. Joy shone upon her countenance, yet she did not banish the marks of a sorrow that seem'd to affect her. *Deterville* embraced her last, but with a tenderness so natural that my heart was moved at it. Alas! my dear *Aza*, what would our transports be, if, after so many misfortunes, fate should reunite us?

---

* The beds, chairs, and tables of the *Incas* were of massy gold [de Graffigny's note].

---

1 A Peruvian provincial magistrate; the Princess is referring to Déterville.
2 A generic term for princesses.

During this time I kept near the *Pallas*, whom I durst not quit, nor look up at,[*] out of respect. Some severe glances, which she threw from time to time upon me, compleated my confusion, and put me under a constraint that affected my very thoughts.

At last, the young damsel, as if she had guess'd at my disorder, as soon as she had quitted *Deterville*, came and took me by the hand, and led me to a window where we both sat down. Tho' I did not understand any thing she said to me, her eyes full of goodness spoke to me the universal language of beneficent hearts; they inspired me with a confidence and friendship which I would willingly have express'd to her; but, not being able to utter the sentiments of my mind, I pronounced all that I knew of her language.

She smiled more than once, looking on *Deterville* with the most tender sweetness. I was pleasing myself with this conversation, when the *Pallas* spoke some words aloud, looking sternly on my new friend; whose countenance immediately falling, she thrust away my hand which she before held in hers, and took no farther notice of me.

Some time after that, an old woman, of gloomy appearance, entered the room, went up towards the *Pallas*, then came and took me by the arm, led me to a chamber at the top of the house, and left me there alone,

Tho' this moment could not be esteemed the most unfortunate of my life, yet, my dear *Aza*, I could not pass it without much concern. I expected, at the end of my journey, some relief to my fatigues, and that in the *Cacique's* family I should at least meet with the same kindness as from him. The cold reception of the *Pallas*, the sudden change of behaviour in the damsel, the rudeness of this woman in forcing me from a place where I had rather have staid, the inattention of *Deterville*, who did not oppose the violence shewn me; in a word, all circumstances, that might augment the pains of an unhappy soul, presented themselves at once with their most rueful aspects! I thought myself abandon'd by all the world, and was bitterly deploring my dismal destiny, when I beheld my *China*[1] coming in. Her presence, in my situation, seemed to me an essential good: I ran to her, embraced her with tears, and was more melted when I

---

[*] Young damsels, tho' of the blood royal, show a profound respect to married women [de Graffigny's note].

---

1 A maidservant or chambermaid.

saw her touch'd with my affliction. When a mind is reduced to pity itself, the compassion of another is very valuable. The marks of this young woman's affection softened my anguish: I related to her my griefs, as if she could understand me: I asked her a thousand questions, as if it had been in her power to answer them. Her tears spoke to my heart, and mine continued to flow, but with less bitterness than before.

I thought, at least, that I should see *Deterville* at the hour of refreshment; but they brought me up victuals, and I saw him not. Since I have lost thee, dear idol of my heart, this *Cacique* is the only human creature that has shewn me an uninterrupted course of goodness; so that the custom of seeing him became a kind of necessity. His absence redoubled my sorrow. After expecting him long in vain, I laid me down; but sleep had not yet sealed my eyes before I saw him enter my chamber, followed by the young woman whose brisk disdain had so sensibly afflicted me.

She threw herself upon my bed, and by a thousand caresses seemed desirous to repair the ill-treatment she had given me.

The *Cacique* sat down by my bed-side, and seemed to receive as much pleasure in seeing me again, as I enjoy'd in perceiving I was not abandon'd. They talked together with their eyes fixed on me, and heap'd on me the most tender marks of affection.

Insensibly their conversation became more serious. Tho' I did not understand their discourse, it was easy for me to judge that it was founded on confidence and friendship. I took care not to interrupt them: but, as soon as they returned to my bed-side, I endeavoured to obtain from the *Cacique* some light with regard to those particulars which had appeared to me the most extraordinary since my arrival.

All that I could understand from his answers was, that the name of the young woman before me was *Celina*; that she was his sister; that the great man, whom I had seen in the chamber of the *Pallas*, was his elder brother, and the other young woman, that brother's wife.

Celina became more dear to me, when I understood she was the *Cacique's* sister, and the company of both was so agreeable, that I did not perceive it was day-light before they left me.

After their departure, I spent the rest of the time, destin'd to repose, in conversing with thee. This is my happiness, my only joy: It is to thee alone, dear soul of my thoughts, that I unbosom my heart; thou shalt ever be the sole depositary of my secrets, my tenderness, and my sentiments.

LETTER XVI.

I have so few *Quipos*[1] left, my dear *Aza*, that I scarce dare use them. When I would go to knotting them, the dread of seeing an end of them stops me; as if I could multiply by sparing them. I am going to lose the pleasure of my soul, the support of my life: nothing can relieve the weight of thy absence, which must now weigh me down.

I tasted a delicate pleasure in preserving the remembrance of the most secret moments of my heart to offer thee its homage. My design was to preserve the memory of the principal customs of this singular nation, to amuse thy leisure with in more happy times. Alas! I have little hopes now left of executing my project.

If I find at present so much difficulty in putting my ideas into order, how shall I hereafter recall them without any foreign assistance? 'Tis true they offer me one; but the execution of it is so difficult, that I think it impossible.

The *Cacique* has brought me one of this country savages, who comes daily to give me lessons in his tongue, and to shew me the method of giving a sort of existence to thoughts. This is done by drawing small figures, which they call *Letters*, with a feather, upon a thin matter called *Paper*. These figures have names, and those names put together represent the sound of words. But these names and sounds seem to me so little distinct from one another, that, if I do in time succeed in learning them, I am sure it will not be without a great deal of pains. This poor savage takes an incredible deal to teach me, and I give myself more to learn: yet I make so little progress, that I would renounce the enterprize, if I knew any other way to inform myself of thy fate and mine.

There is no other way, my dear *Aza*; therefore my whole delight is now in this new and singular study. I would live alone: all that I see displeases me, and the necessity imposed on me of being always in *Madame*'s apartment gives me torment.

At first, by exciting the curiosity of others, I amused my own: but, where the eyes only are to be used, they are soon to be satisfied. All the women are alike, have still the same manners, and I think they always speak the same words. The appearances are more varied among the men; some of them look as if they thought: but, in general, I suspect this nation not to be what it appears; for affectation seems to be its ruling character.

If the demonstrations of zeal and earnestness, with which the

1 A Peruvian record-keeping device, made of knotted cords.

most trifling duties of society are here graced, were natural, these people, my dear *Aza*, must certainly have in their hearts more goodness and humanity than ours: and who can think this possible?

If they had as much serenity in the soul as upon the countenance, if the propensity to joy which I remark in all their actions, was sincere, would they chuse for their amusement such spectacles as they have carried me to see?

They conducted me into a place, where was represented, almost as in thy palace, the actions of men who are no[*] more. But as we revive only the memory of the most wise and virtuous, I believe only madmen and villains are represented here. Those who personated them rav'd and storm'd as if they were wild, and I saw one of them carry his fury so high as to kill himself. The fine women, who seemingly they persecuted, wept incessantly, and shew'd such tokens of despair, that the words they made use of were not necessary to shew the excess of their anguish.

Could one think, my dear *Aza*, that a whole people, whose outside is so humane, should be pleased at the representation of those misfortunes or crimes, which either overwhelmed or degraded creatures like themselves?

But perhaps they have occasion here for the horror of vice to conduct them to virtue. This thought starts upon me unsought, and if it were true, how should I pity such a nation? Ours, more favour'd by nature, cherishes goodness for its own charms: we want only models of virtue to make us virtuous; as nothing is requisite but to love thee in order to become amiable.

LETTER XVII.

I know not what farther to think of the genius of this nation, my dear *Aza*. It runs thro' the extremes with such rapidity, that it requires more ability than I possess to sit in judgement upon its character.

They have shewn me a spectacle intirely opposite to the former. That, cruel and frightful, made reason revolt, and humbled humanity: This, amusing and agreeable, imitates nature, and does honour to good sense. It was composed of a great many more men and women than the former: they represented also some actions of human life; but whether they expressed pain or pleasure, joy or sorrow, the whole was done by songs and dances.

---

[*] The *Incas* caused a kind of comedies to be represented, the subjects of which were taken from the brightest actions of their predecessors [de Graffigny's note].

The intelligence of sounds, my dear *Aza*, must be universal: for I found it no more difficult to be affected with the different passions that were represented, than if they had been express'd in our language. This seems to me very natural.

Human speech is doubtless of man's invention, because it differs according to the difference of nations. Nature, more powerful, and more attentive to the necessities and pleasures of her creatures, has given them general means of expressing them, which are well imitated by the songs I have heard.

If it be true that sharp sounds express better the need of help in violent fear, or acute pain, than words understood in one part of the world, and which have no signification in another; it is not less certain that tender sights strike our hearts with a more efficacious compassion than words, the odd arrangement of which sometimes produces just a contrary effect.

Do not lively and light sounds inevitably excite in our soul that gay pleasure, which the recital of a diverting story, or a joke properly introduced, can but imperfectly raise?

Are there expressions in any language that can communicate genuine pleasure with so much success as the natural sports of animals? Dancing seems an humble imitation of them, and inspires much the same sentiment.

In short, my dear *Aza*, every thing in this last show was conformable to nature and humanity. Can any benefit be conferred on man, equal to that of inspiring him with joy?

I felt it myself, and was transported by it in spite of me, when I was interrupted by an accident that happened to *Celina*.

As we came out, we step'd a little aside from the croud, and lean'd on one another for fear of falling. *Deterville* was some paces before us leading his sister-in-law; when a young savage, of an amiable figure, came up to *Celina*, whisper'd a few words to her very low, gave her a bit of paper which she scarce had strength to take, and retired.

Celina, who was so frighten'd at his approach as to make me partake of her trembling, turned her head languishingly towards him when he quitted us. She seemed so weak, that, fearing she was attack'd by some sudden illness, I was going to call *Deterville* to her assistance: but she stop'd me, and by putting her finger on her mouth, required me to be silent. I chose rather to be uneasy, than to disobey her.

The same evening, when the brother and sister came into my chamber, *Celina* shew'd the *Cacique* the paper she had received. By the little I could guess in their conversation, I should have thought she loved the young man who gave it her, if it had been possible for one to be frighten'd at the presence of what one loves.

I have made other remarks, my dear *Aza*, which I would have imported to thee: but alas! my *Quipos* are all used; the last threads are in my hands, and I am knotting the last knots. The knots, which seemed to me a chain of communication betwixt my heart and thine, are now only the sorrowful objects of my regret. Illusion quits me, frightful truth takes her place; my wandering thoughts, bewilder'd in the immense void of absence, will hereafter be annihilated with the same rapidity as time. Dear *Aza*, they seem to separate us once again, and snatch me afresh from thy love. I lose thee! I quit thee! I shall see thee no more! *Aza*, dear hope of my heart, how distant indeed are we now to be removed from each other!

Appendix G: From Frances Burney's *Evelina* (1778)

[Frances Burney's highly successful epistolary novel, *Evelina* (1778), is indebted to *Ophelia* in various ways. Two scenes discussed in the Introduction (28-29 above) are reprinted here. In the first, Evelina writes to her guardian, the Reverend Arthur Villars, about her misadventures at a ball. Her ignorance of dancing etiquette, which causes her considerable distress, has its counterpart in *Ophelia*, in which the heroine's similar ignorance leads to a duel (220-25). In the second, Evelina writes to Villars about Captain Mirvan's malicious application of smelling salts to the nostrils of her grandmother Madame Duval, taking up the scene in *Ophelia* (117) in which the heroine uses smelling-salts to comic effect. These excerpts, from Volume I, are printed from the Broadview edition of *Evelina* (2000), ed. Susan Kubica Howard, pp. 120-27 and 177-78.]

LETTER XI.
Evelina in continuation
Queen-Ann-Street, April 5, Tuesday morning.

I have a vast deal to say, and shall give all this morning to my pen. As to my plan of writing every evening the adventures of the day, I find it impracticable; for the diversions here are so very late, that if I begin my letters after them, I could not go to bed at all.

We past a most extraordinary evening. A *private* ball this was called, so I expected to have seen about four or five couple; but Lord! my dear Sir, I believe I saw half the world! Two very large rooms were full of company; in one, were cards for the elderly ladies, and in the other, were the dancers. My mamma Mirvan, for she always calls me her child, said she would sit with Maria and me till we were provided with partners, and then join the card-players.

The gentlemen, as they passed and repassed, looked as if they thought we were quite at their disposal, and only waiting for the honour of their commands; and they sauntered about, in a careless indolent manner, as if with a view to keep us in suspense. I don't speak of this in regard to Miss Mirvan and myself only, but to the ladies in general; and I thought it so provoking, that I determined, in my own mind, that, far from humouring such airs, I would rather not dance at all, than with any one who should seem to think me ready to accept the first partner who would condescend to take me.

Not long after, a young man, who had for some time looked at us with a kind of negligent impertinence, advanced, on tip-toe, towards me; he had a set smile on his face, and his dress was so foppish, that I really believe he even wished to be stared at; and yet he was very ugly.

Bowing almost to the ground, with a sort of swing, and waving his hand with the greatest conceit, after a short and silly pause, he said, "Madam—may I presume?"—and stopt, offering to take my hand. I drew it back, but could scarce forbear laughing. "Allow me, Madam," (continued he, affectedly breaking off every half moment) "the honour and happiness—if I am not so unhappy as to address you too late—to have the happiness and honour—"

Again he would have taken my hand, but, bowing my head, I begged to be excused, and turned to Miss Mirvan to conceal my laughter. He then desired to know if I had already engaged myself to some more fortunate man? I said No, and that I believed I should not dance at all. He would keep himself, he told me, disengaged, in hopes I should relent; and then, uttering some ridiculous speeches of sorrow and disappointment, though his face still wore the same invariable smile, he retreated.

It so happened, as we have since recollected, that during this little dialogue, Mrs. Mirvan was conversing with the lady of the house. And very soon after another gentleman, who seemed about six-and-twenty years old, gayly, but not foppishly, dressed, and indeed extremely handsome, with an air of mixed politeness and gallantry, desired to know if I was engaged, or would honour him with my hand. So he was pleased to say, though I am sure I know not what honour he could receive from me; but these sort of expressions, I find, are used as words of course, without any distinction of persons, or study of propriety.

Well, I bowed, and I am sure I coloured; for indeed I was frightened at the thoughts of dancing before so many people, all strangers, and which was worse, *with* a stranger; however, that was unavoidable, for though I looked round the room several times, I could not see one person that I knew. And so, he took my hand, and led me to join in the dance.

The minuets were over before we arrived, for we were kept late by the milliner's making us wait for our things.

He seemed very desirous of entering into conversation with me; but I was seized with such a panic, that I could hardly speak a word, and nothing but the shame of so soon changing my mind, prevented my returning to my seat, and declining to dance at all.

He appeared to be surprised at my terror, which I believe was but too apparent: however, he asked no questions, though I fear he must think it very strange; for I did not choose to tell him it was owing to my never before dancing but with a school-girl.

His conversation was sensible and spirited; his air and address were open and noble; his manners gentle, attentive, and infinitely engaging; his person is all elegance, and his countenance, the most animated and expressive I have ever seen.

In a short time we were joined by Miss Mirvan, who stood next couple to us. But how was I startled, when she whispered me that my partner was a nobleman! This gave me a new alarm; how will he be provoked, thought I, when he finds what a simple rustic he has honoured with his choice! one whose ignorance of the world makes her perpetually fear doing something wrong!

That he should be so much my superior every way, quite disconcerted me; and you will suppose my spirits were not much raised, when I heard a lady, in passing us, say, "This is the most difficult dance I ever saw."

"O dear, then," cried Maria to her partner, "with your leave, I'll sit down till the next."

"So will I too, then," cried I, "for I am sure I can hardly stand."

"But you must speak to your partner first," answered she; for he had turned aside to talk with some gentlemen. However, I had not sufficient courage to address him, and so away we all three tript, and seated ourselves at another end of the room.

But, unfortunately for me, Miss Mirvan soon after suffered herself to be prevailed upon to attempt the dance; and just as she rose to go, she cried, "My dear, yonder is your partner, Lord Orville, walking about the room in search of you."

"Don't leave me, then, dear girl!" cried I; but she was obliged to go. And now I was more uneasy than ever; I would have given the world to have seen Mrs. Mirvan, and begged of her to make my apologies; for what, thought I, can I possibly say to him in excuse for running away? he must either conclude me a fool, or half-mad; for any one brought up in the great world, and accustomed to its ways, can have no idea of such sort of fears as mine.

My confusion increased when I observed that he was every where seeking me, with apparent perplexity and surprise; but when, at last, I saw him move towards the place where I sat, I was ready to sink with shame and distress. I found it absolutely impossible to keep my seat, because I could not think of a word to say for myself, and so I rose, and walked hastily towards the card-room, resolving to stay with Mrs. Mirvan the rest of the evening, and not to dance at all. But before I could find her, Lord Orville saw and approached me.

He begged to know if I was not well? You may easily imagine how much I was embarrassed. I made no answer, but hung my head, like a fool, and looked on my fan.

He then, with an air the most respectfully serious, asked if he had been so unhappy as to offend me?

"No, indeed!" cried I: and, in hopes of changing the discourse, and preventing his further inquiries, I desired to know if he had seen the young lady who had been conversing with me?

No;—but would I honour him with any commands to her?

"O by no means!"

Was there any other person with whom I wished to speak?

I said *no*, before I knew I had answered at all.

Should he have the pleasure of bringing me any refreshment?

I bowed, almost involuntarily. And away he flew.

I was quite ashamed of being so troublesome, and so much *above* myself as these seeming airs made me appear; but indeed I was too much confused to think or act with any consistency.

If he had not been swift as lightning, I don't know whether I should not have stolen away again; but he returned in a moment. When I had drunk a glass of lemonade, he hoped, he said, that I would again honour him with my hand, as a new dance was just begun. I had not the presence of mind to say a single word, and so I let him once more lead me to the place I had left.

Shocked to find how silly, how childish a part I had acted, my former fears of dancing before such a company, and with such a partner, returned more forcibly than ever. I suppose he perceived my uneasiness, for he intreated me to sit down again, if dancing was disagreeable to me. But I was quite satisfied with the folly I had already shewn, and therefore declined his offer, tho' I was really scarce able to stand.

Under such conscious disadvantages, you may easily imagine, my dear Sir, how ill I acquitted myself. But, though I both expected and deserved to find him very much mortified and displeased at his ill fortune in the choice he had made, yet, to my very great relief, he appeared to be even contented, and very much assisted and encouraged me. These people in high life have too much presence of mind, I believe, to *seem* disconcerted, or out of humour, however they may feel: for had I been the person of the most consequence in the room, I could not have met with more attention and respect.

When the dance was over, seeing me still very much flurried, he led me to a seat, saying that he would not suffer me to fatigue myself from politeness.

And then, if my capacity, or even if my spirits had been better, in how animated a conversation might I have been engaged! It was then I saw that the rank of Lord Orville was his least recommendation, his understanding and his manners being far more distinguished. His remarks upon the company in general were so apt, so just, so lively, I am almost surprised myself that they did not re-animate me; but indeed I was too well convinced of the ridiculous part I had played before so nice an observer, to be able to enjoy his pleasantry: so self-compassion gave me feelings for others. Yet I had not the courage to attempt either to defend them or to rally in my turn, but listened to him in silent embarrassment.

When he found this, he changed the subject, and talked of public places, and public performers; but he soon discovered that I was totally ignorant of them.

He then, very ingeniously, turned the discourse to the amusements and occupations of the country.

It now struck me, that he was resolved to try whether or not I was capable of talking upon *any* subject. This put so great a constraint upon my thoughts, that I was unable to go further than a monosyllable, and not even so far, when I could possibly avoid it.

We were sitting in this manner, he conversing with all gaiety, I looking down with all foolishness, when that fop who had first asked me to dance, with a most ridiculous solemnity, approached, and after a profound bow or two, said, "I humbly beg pardon, Madam,—and of you too, my Lord,—for breaking in upon such agreeable conversation—which must, doubtless, be much more delectable—than what I have the honour to offer—but—"

I interrupted him—I blush for my folly,—with laughing; yet I could not help it, for, added to the man's stately foppishness, (and he actually took snuff between every three words) when I looked round at Lord Orville, I saw such extreme surprise in his face,—the cause of which appeared so absurd, that I could not for my life preserve my gravity.

I had not laughed before from the time I had left Miss Mirvan, and I had much better have cried then; Lord Orville actually stared at me; the beau, I know not his name, looked quite enraged. "Refrain—Madam," (said he, with an important air,) "a few moments refrain!—I have but a sentence to trouble you with.—May I know to what accident I must attribute not having the honour of your hand?"

"Accident, Sir!" repeated I, much astonished.

"Yes, accident, Madam—for surely,—I must take the liberty to observe—pardon me, Madam,—it ought to be no common one—that should tempt a lady—so young a one too,—to be guilty of ill manners."

A confused idea now for the first time entered my head, of something I had heard of the rules of an assembly; but I was never at one before,—I have only danced at school,—and so giddy and heedless I was, that I had not once considered the impropriety of refusing one partner, and afterwards accepting another. I was thunderstruck at the recollection: but, while these thoughts were rushing into my head, Lord Orville, with some warmth, said, "This lady, Sir, is incapable of meriting such an accusation!"

The creature—for I am very angry with him,—made a low bow, and with a grin the most malicious I ever saw, "My Lord," said he, "far be it from me to *accuse* the lady, for having the discernment to distinguish and prefer—the superior attractions of your Lordship."

Again he bowed, and walked off.

Was ever any thing so provoking? I was ready to die with shame. "What a coxcomb!" exclaimed Lord Orville; while I, without knowing what I did, rose hastily, and moving off, "I can't imagine," cried I, "where Mrs. Mirvan has hid herself!"

"Give me leave to see," answered he. I bowed and sat down again, not daring to meet his eyes; for what must he think of me, between my blunder, and the supposed preference?

He returned in a moment, and told me that Mrs. Mirvan was at cards, but would be glad to see me; and I went immediately. There was but one chair vacant, so, to my great relief, Lord Orville presently left us. I then told Mrs. Mirvan my disasters, and she good-naturedly blamed herself for not having better instructed me, but said she had taken it for granted that I must know such common customs. However, the man may, I think, be satisfied with his pretty speech, and carry his resentment no farther.

In a short time, Lord Orville returned. I consented, with the best grace I could, to go down another dance, for I had had time to recollect myself, and therefore resolved to use some exertion, and, if possible, appear less a fool than I had hitherto done; for it occurred to me that, insignificant as I was, compared to a man of his rank and figure, yet, since he had been so unfortunate as to make choice of me for a partner, why I should endeavour to make the best of it.

The dance, however, was short, and he spoke very little; so I had no opportunity of putting my resolution into practice. He was satisfied, I suppose, with his former successless efforts to draw me out: or, rather, I fancied, he had been inquiring *who I was*. This again disconcerted me, and the spirits I had determined to exert, again failed me. Tired, ashamed, and mortified, I begged to sit down till we returned home, which we did soon after. Lord Orville did me the honour to hand me to the coach, talking all the way of the honour *I* had done *him*! O these fashionable people!

Well, my dear Sir, was it not a strange evening? I could not help being thus particular, because, to me, every thing is so new. But it is now time to conclude. I am, with all love and duty,

Your
EVELINA.

From LETTER XIX.

This entertainment[1] concluded with a concert of mechanical music: I cannot explain how it was produced, but the effect was pleasing. Madame Duval was in extacies; and the Captain flung himself into so many ridiculous distortions, by way of mimicking her, that he engaged the attention of all the company; and in the midst of the performance of the Coronation Anthem,[2] while Madame Duval was affecting to beat time, and uttering many expressions of delight, he called suddenly for salts, which a lady, apprehending some distress, politely handed to him, and which, instantly applying to the nostrils of poor Madame Duval, she involuntarily snuffed up such a quantity, that the pain and surprise made her scream aloud. When she recovered, she reproached him, with her usual vehemence; but he protested he had taken that measure out of pure friendship, as he concluded, from her raptures, that she was going into hysterics. This excuse by no means appeased her, and they had a violent quarrel; but the only effect her anger had on the Captain, was to encrease his diversion. Indeed, he laughs and talks so terribly loud in public, that he frequently makes us ashamed of belonging to him.

---

1   At Cox's Museum: a museum assembled by the jeweller and silversmith James Cox, featuring valuable, intricate jewel-studded mechanisms.
2   "Zadock the Priest," an anthem by Handel composed for the coronation of George II in 1727 and also used for the coronation of George III in 1760.

Select Bibliography

Primary Works

The Adventures of David Simple. Intro. Ernest A. Baker. 1744. London: Routledge, 1904.

The Adventures of David Simple. Ed. Malcolm Kelsall. London: Oxford UP, 1969; reprinted and revised, 1987 and 1994.

The Adventures of David Simple and Volume the Last. Ed. Peter Sabor. Lexington: UP of Kentucky, 1998.

The Adventures of David Simple. Ed. Linda Bree. Harmondsworth: Penguin, 2002.

The Correspondence of Henry and Sarah Fielding. Eds. Martin C. Battestin and Clive T. Probyn. Oxford: Clarendon, 1993.

The Cry. Intro. Mary Anne Schofield. 1754. NY: Scholars' Facsimiles and Reprints, 1986.

The Governess, or Little Female Academy. Intro. Jill E. Grey. 1749. London: Oxford UP, 1968.

The Governess, or Little Female Academy. Intro. Mary Cadogan. London: Pandora, 1987.

The Lives of Cleopatra and Octavia. Ed. R. Brimley Johnson. 1757. London: Scholartis, 1928.

The Lives of Cleopatra and Octavia. Ed. Christopher D. Johnson. Lewisburg: Bucknell UP, 1994.

Remarks on Clarissa. Ed. Peter Sabor. 1749. Augustan Reprint Society, nos. 231-2. Los Angeles: William Andrews Clark Memorial Library, 1985.

Secondary Works

Battestin, Martin C., with Ruthe R. Battestin. *Henry Fielding: A Life.* London: Routledge, 1989.

Bree, Linda. *Sarah Fielding.* New York: Macmillan, 1996.

Burrows, J.F., and A.J. Hassall. "Anna Boleyn and the Authenticity of Fielding's Feminine Narratives." *Eighteenth-Century Studies* 21 (1988): 427-53.

——. "Henry and Sarah Fielding: The Authorship of *The History of Ophelia* (1760)." In preparation.

Dearnley, Moira. "'Ye chaste Abodes of happiest Mortals': *The Histo-*

ry of Ophelia." *Distant Fields: Eighteenth-Century Fictions of Wales.* Cardiff: U of Wales P, 2001. 68-79.

Downs-Miers, Deborah. "Springing the Trap: Subtexts and Subversions." *Fetter'd or Free? British Women Novelists, 1670-1815.* Ed. Mary Anne Schofield and Cecilia Macheski. Athens: Ohio UP, 1986. 308-23.

Grossman, Joyce. "'Sympathetic Visibility', Social Reform and the English Woman Writer: *The Histories of Some of the Penitents in the Magdalen-House.*" *Women's Writing* 7 (2000): 247-66.

London, April. "Sarah Fielding." *Dictionary of Literary Biography, vol. 39, British Novelists, 1660-1800.* Ed. Martin C. Battestin. Detroit: Gale, 1985. 195-204.

Paul, Nancy. "Is Sex Necessary? Criminal Conversation and Complicity in Sarah Fielding's *Ophelia.*" *Lumen* 16 (1997): 113-29.

Probyn, Clive T. *The Sociable Humanist: The Life and Works of James Harris 1709-1780.* Oxford: Clarendon, 1991.

Paulson, Ronald. *The Life of Henry Fielding: A Critical Biography.* Oxford: Blackwell, 2000.

Poupard, Dennis, and Mark W. Scott, eds. "Sarah Fielding, 1710-1768." *Literature Criticism from 1400 to 1800*, vol. I. Detroit: Gale, 1984. 267-80.

Rizzo, Betty. *Companions without Vows: Relationships among Eighteenth-Century British Women.* Athens: U of Georgia P, 1994.

Sabor, Peter. "Richardson, Henry Fielding and Sarah Fielding." *The Cambridge Companion to English Literature 1740-1830.* Ed. Thomas Keymer and Jon Mee. Cambridge: Cambridge UP, 2004. 139-56.

Schofield, Mary Anne. "Sarah Fielding." *Masking and Unmasking the Female Mind: Disguising Romances in Feminine Fiction, 1713-1799.* Newark: U of Delaware P, 1990. 108-27.

Skinner, Gillian. "Sexual Innocence and Economic Experience: The Problems of *Amelia* and *Ophelia.*" *Sensibility and Economics in the Novel, 1740-1800: The Price of a Tear.* London: Macmillan, 1999. 37-58.

Spencer, Jane. *The Rise of the Woman Novelist: From Aphra Behn to Jane Austen.* Oxford: Blackwell, 1986.

Starr, G.A. "From Socrates to Sarah Fielding: Benevolence, Irony, and Conversation." *Passionate Encounters in a Time of Sensibility.* Ed. Maximillian E. Novak and Anne E. Mellor. Newark: U of Delaware P, 2000. 106-26.

Thomas, Donald. *Henry Fielding.* London: Weidenfeld and Nicolson, 1990.